A Presumption in Perthshire

An Elspeth Duff Mystery

Ann Crew

Front and back cover photographs of a view of Loch Tay and the Courtroom at the Sheriff's Court, Perth by Ann Crew ©2007

Cover designed and publishing format by Nancy Largent ©2020

Author photograph by Ian Crew

ACE/AC Editions
All rights reserved.
ISBN-13: 9798685942883

Library of Congress Control Number: 2020918060

Individually published through Kindle Direct Publishing Company, a division of amazon.com

anncrew.com

elspethduffmysteries.com

Also by Ann Crew

[In Order of Publication}

A Murder in Malta

A Scandal in Stresa

A Secret in Singapore

A Crisis in Cyprus

A Gamble in Gozo

A Deception in Denmark

A Blackmailer in Bermuda

Praise for *A Murder in Malta:*

To all my friends in Pitlochry

A Note on Scottish Law

Presumption: the <u>act</u> of <u>believing</u> something is <u>true</u> without having any <u>proof</u>, as in 'presumed innocent'.

A Presumption in Perthshire involves the Scottish criminal justice system, which is unique and quite different from those in England, America, and Canada. Scottish law derives from the early days of Scotland jurisprudence and remains the law of the kingdom today.

In Scotland a *procurator fiscal* is somewhat equivalent to a public prosecutor in England or a district attorney in the States. A *solicitor* is a lawyer who represents a client and an *advocate*, similar to an English barrister, pleads a case in court. In this novel, Maxwell Douglas-Forbes is a *solicitor advocate*, who both represents his client and pleads his case in court. This position is fairly new in Scotland. The *advocate depute,* representing the *Crown*, prosecutes the case in court.

The jury in a case consists of fifteen men and women, and the final verdict only requires a majority vote by them. They are allowed to take notes during a trial and are provided with a pen, paper, and a clipboard. There are three verdicts allowed: *guilty, not guilty,* and *not proven.* As of 2007, the date of the story in this book, if a case is found to be not proven, the accused goes free, but there will always be a lingering doubt in the public's eye as to the defendant's innocence. The judge for the trial confers the sentence. A capital crime such as murder is tried in the High Court, as is depicted in this book. In the Perth Sheriff Court courtroom, the defendant sits facing the judge and people who testify stand to the side on a raised dais.

List of Characters

Elspeth Duff, special security advisor to Eric, Lord Kennington, owner of the Kennington hotel chain. She is called 'Peth by her two cousins.

Sir Richard Munro, British High Commissioner to Malta, Elspeth's husband and Johnnie, the Earl of Tay's old friend. He is called Dickie only by Elspeth, Johnnie and Biddy.

Lady Marjorie Munro, Richard's first wife, now deceased

Alistair Craig, Elspeth's first husband, famous fight and weapons choreographer in Hollywood, and father of her son and daughter.

John (Johnnie) Robertson, ninth Earl of Tay, Elspeth's first cousin

Lady Elisabeth (Biddy) Baillie Shaw, née Robertson, Elspeth's first cousin and Johnnie's sister, widow of **Ivor Baillie Shaw**

Louisa, Countess of Tay, née Boyd, Johnnie's current and third wife

(Lady) Fiona Duff, née Robertson, Elspeth's mother, who has relinquished her title

James Duff, Elspeth's father, a solicitor in Pitlochry, Perthshire

Peter Craig, Elspeth's son, a lawyer in San Francisco

Lucy Lee, his fiancée, neurological surgical resident at a famous university hospital in the San Francisco Bay area

Her parents, residents of the Berkeley hills near San Francisco

Elizabeth (Lizzie) Foxworthy, née Craig, Elspeth's daughter and mother of twins, Thomas and Timothy

Denis Foxworthy, her husband

Eric, Lord Kennington, Elspeth's employer and owner of the Kennington hotel chain

Pamela Crumm, his business partner and Elspeth's close friend

Kathleen, Countess of Tay, Johnnie's first wife who died in childbirth

Helen, Countess of Tay, née Trenton, Johnnie's second wife who left Johnnie for another man called **Ross MacCombe**

Madeline MacNaughton, née Fergusson, Johnnie's *inamorata*

Detective Inspector Simon Kennedy, from the Police Tayside Police in Perth

Paul Hodges, a shady lawyer hired by Louisa

Maxwell Douglas-Forbes, QC, a well-known solicitor advocate in Perth

Various members of the media

Marly Beaufort, Johnnie's landlady

Roger Beaufort, her husband and Johnnie's friend

Charles (Charlie) Baillie Shaw, Biddy's son and heir to the Tay earldom

Adair Gordon, procurator fiscal in Perth

Robbie MacPherson, Biddy's farm manager

The eighth Countess of Tay, Johnnie and Biddy's mother and Elspeth's aunt

Tobias, Tay Farm's black and white border collie who lives in the barn

Jean MacPherson, Robbie's wife and housekeeper at

Tay Farm

Alice MacNaughton, Madeline's mother and Biddy and Elspeth's school friend

Her husband

Alex and Mary Baillie Shaw, Biddy's second son and her daughter

Bounce, the Duffs' golden retriever

Various hospital staff

Kaitlin Logan, private detective

Miles Markham and **George Hiller**, members of the Perth Land Development Consortium

Billy Bong, so-called 'Australian chap, the biggest crook in Edinburgh'

Ron Dawes, an eyewitness to the murder

Jake Jones, another eyewitness

Hamish MacDonnell, advocate depute, prosecuting for the Crown

A pathologist

Rosa Browne, charwoman who discovered the body

Joshua MacCallum, the Tay's neighbour in Perth

Norman Smith, forensic technician

Dr Joan Nicholson, director of a hospital clinic at the Edinburgh Royal Infirmary

Cecilia Clark, clerk at New Register House in Edinburgh

Rodney Turnbull, another neighbour

Thomas Lawton, of the Perthshire Land Development Consortium

Gloria MacNeil, an accountant

Part 1

Tay Farm

Preface

San Francisco, Friday/Saturday, July 13th-14th, 2007

Alistair Craig, Elspeth Duff's ex-husband, walked into the room of the Kennington San Francisco hotel where she had arranged for the family dinner to be held the night before their son Peter's wedding. A curvaceous actress, younger than Peter and definitely recognisable to anyone who even skimmed the tabloid press in a supermarket queue, draped herself on Alistair's arm. Richard Munro wondered why Alistair had brought her, almost as if he wished to upstage his own son's wedding. Elspeth was standing with Richard and her family, greeting the guests as they came in. Alistair caught Elspeth's eye and smiled at her in a challenging manner. Elspeth looked back without blinking. Once their coats had been taken, Alistair and the actress came over to Elspeth. Before they had crossed the room, however, Elspeth turned to her cousin, Johnnie Tay, who was standing next to her, and their eyes met in mischief. Her husband saw their glances cross, and he spoke quietly to his wife with trepidation.

"I saw that look, Elspeth, and suspect you and Johnnie are up to no good," he said.

Elspeth smiled her broadest and most innocent smile, in the same way she had when she was a teenage tomboy and about to join her cousin in hijinks that often made them both burst out in guffaws of laughter. Usually they were able to drag a reluctant Richard along with them.

Alistair and his companion were fast approaching

Elspeth's family. He did not give her name, as he must have presumed they all knew her.

"How do you do?" said Elspeth in her most haughty voice, which mimicked the voices of the very members of the Scottish aristocracy she so often disdained. Richard, standing beside her, gagged.

"And you are?" she asked.

The actress looked uncomprehending that there might be people in the world who did not recognise her and gave her name.

Elspeth continued. "Let me introduce you to my family, then. This is my cousin, the Earl of Tay, and his sister, Lady Elisabeth Baillie Shaw, my mother Lady Fiona Duff, my father James Duff, Esquire, and my husband, Sir Richard Munro, Her Majesty Queen Elizabeth's High Commissioner to the Republic of Malta. I'm Lady Munro."

Richard knew that Elspeth loathed titles and seldom used hers, to which she was entitled by her marriage to him, and that she had constantly begged her cousin Johnnie to give up his. Richard had never heard Elspeth's mother called by her title before. As the daughter of an earl, her title was legitimate, although like her daughter Fiona Duff, she eschewed it. He saw the actress blanch. Elspeth had pulled a trump card few Americans knew how to handle—the British use of titles. Johnnie Tay was grinning as he watched the actress's ego deflate. As she and Alistair moved on, Johnnie whispered in his cousin's ear. Richard could just hear.

"Elspeth, you were splendid! Even I quaked at our seeming grandeur!"

Richard was of another opinion. He turned to them and said, "Elspeth, I'm not sure if your joke was wicked or cruel, or both."

Elspeth scowled. "Serves him right. How dare he bring such a person to a family affair, and particularly when I'm paying for it!"

"I thought you and Alistair parted on amicable terms," Richard said.

"Civil ones. Then he pulls a stunt like this." Her eyes blazed.

When Peter's fiancée's family arrived, Elspeth was kinder. "I'm Elspeth Duff, Peter's mother. Let me introduce you to my family, my mother and father, James and Fiona Duff, my cousins, Johnnie Tay and Elisabeth Baillie Shaw, and my husband, Richard Munro."

Later, when the actress had gone off to refresh herself before dinner, Alistair Craig took Elspeth aside, although within Richard's hearing.

"Elspeth, I thought you might remarry but not to stuffy old Richard Munro. Never in my wildest dreams would I have imagined it. What in the world do you see in him? He was always so pompous and too, too correct. You were never that way. You used to be rather fun, but I see you've changed."

Elspeth did not take the bait. She looked at Alistair and said sweetly, "I married Richard because I love him." With that she turned and joined the other guests.

Richard knew Elspeth did love him. Their separate careers kept them apart much of the time, but their times together were filled with love, laughter and passion, in ways that Alistair Craig could not have imagined, and that were neither stuffy nor too, too correct. Elspeth later conceded to Richard that she felt rather sorry for Alistair, who had to make do with actresses over half his age, but she was convinced he was more in love with himself than anyone else and that all the starlets were only a bauble in the showcase of his Hollywood life.

1

The following morning as they woke, Elspeth spoke to Richard with great concern in her voice. "Dickie, after the party last evening, Johnnie came up to me and asked if he could come see us this morning before the wedding breakfast. He said it's about his divorce from Louisa, and he sounded bitter. I told him eight o'clock. I hope it's all right with you."

Richard rolled over in bed and looked at the digital clock on the bedside table. "In half an hour? Can you get ready in that time?"

"Absolutely. I had the hotel see to our clothes after we arrived, but we'd better be quick about it."

"Mmm," he assented pleasurably and kissed her. She replied in kind and then rose from their bed. "What do you suppose could be so bad that Johnnie would want to see us this morning and not postpone it until after the wedding?"

"I've no idea but knowing Johnnie he wouldn't ask unless it's important. I'll ring down to the front desk and get coffee and tea sent up."

Johnnie Tay arrived at the designated moment, looking haggard.

Elspeth poured coffee for herself and tea for her cousin and husband. "Now, Johnnie, why the urgency?"

He looked at his cousin and his old friend. "Louisa wants to take the farm." Louisa was Johnnie Tay's third wife and their marriage had lasted only three years. It had been a

5

mistake from the first.

"I don't understand. What do you mean take the farm?" Elspeth asked.

"She wants ownership of the farm as part of the divorce settlement."

"Tay Farm? It's Biddy's! Yours, of course Johnnie, by right, but really Biddy's. Is Louisa that vindictive? I wasn't aware that she had even visited the farm since the first days of your marriage."

"She hasn't, but she wants to do anything to destroy me, including hurting Biddy," Johnnie said and put his head in his hands. "Elspeth, you're the only one I can think of who could help."

"Help? I'd hardly recognise Louisa if she walked in. Our family has not exactly been enamoured with her. How do you expect me to help?"

"By finding something on her?"

"You mean some scandal in her background that might help your cause?"

"Exactly. You're the sleuth."

"But, Johnnie, I have my job. I can hardly ask the Lord Kennington to release me from my employment while I go dig up dirt on a nasty divorce case in my family. I've taken far too much time off in the last two years with my head injury and then marrying Dickie."

Richard sat listening without speaking. He watched the two cousins who had been in his life since he had come to stay with them between his terms at Oxford. Johnnie still remained his friend. He had loved Elspeth since that time, but she had only recently become his wife.

Richard asked, "Does Biddy know?"

Johnnie shook his head. "I just learned about it myself before leaving Scotland to come here. Biddy flew with your parents from Edinburgh on an earlier flight. I haven't seen her alone since we arrived in San Francisco. I'm not too sure how she will react. The farm means everything to her."

"Johnnie," Elspeth said, "do you have any idea if there is any impropriety in Louisa's background that could be used against her?"

"I'm not sure. I was such a fool to marry her, but she insisted," Johnnie said.

"I see," said Elspeth. Johnnie by nature could be impetuous. Since it was a trait of which she had also been accused, particularly by her husband, she empathised with Johnnie's current plight. She glanced across at Richard.

Richard held her eyes and seemed to read her thoughts. "I think I know where you are going, Elspeth. No West Marin for the immediate future."

Elspeth owned a small retreat in western Marin County where she and Richard had spent much of their wedding trip the year before, and they had hoped to recreate some of the magic of that time after Peter and Lucy's wedding.

"No, I think not," she said.

Johnnie Tay looked puzzled by this exchange.

Elspeth asked her husband, "Are you all right with that?" He nodded.

"Johnnie, we can fly back to the UK tomorrow, and I can give you until Thursday, July 26th. Then I need to be back in London, and Dickie is returning to Malta soon afterwards. You know we'll have to tell Biddy immediately. Dickie and I will want to stay at the farm with her. Can telling her wait until after the wedding? Let's not spoil it for Peter and Lucy."

Relief spread over Johnnie Tay's face. He rose, kissed his cousin's cheek enthusiastically and shook Richard's hand. "Too bad Elspeth's my first cousin," he said in parting. "You're a lucky devil, Dickie."

As they were making final preparations for their departure to the wedding, Elspeth turned to Richard. "You know you'll have to sit with what's-her-name, the actress, at the ceremony, don't you? Alistair and I will be in the first pew together."

"The thought had crossed my mind," he said, grinning.

"Dickie! What thought?"

He turned to his wife and, careful not to disturb her lightly and deftly applied makeup, brushed her lips with his. "That Alistair is a fool to have given you up. No, my dearest one, I don't need to look at another woman, especially one as young and self-centred as Alistair's starlet. You are all I've ever wanted."

She had no cause to doubt him.

On arrival at the church, he and Elspeth were led to the front pews where she was seated in the first row and he in the second. From where he sat, he was able take notice of his surroundings and Peter and Lucy's many friends being ushered into in the church. Lucy's mother, wearing a brocade cheongsam with an elegant silk jacket decorated with fine embroidery, had been seated when Elspeth and Richard entered. She sat erect, her eyes glowing. She smiled warmly at Elspeth and Richard, but her face became stoically polite when Alistair and the actress came down the aisle at the last moment.

Alistair hustled in just as the first music was being played.

He looked about to see if he were being noticed, nodding his head to one side and then the other. Richard doubted Alistair knew many of the guests, but he suspected the point was to be seen and recognised. The actress looked withdrawn beside him and did not meet Richard's eyes or speak when he moved over, letting her enter his pew. Looking totally out of place, she remained silent and shifted uneasily throughout the ceremony. Her bright red dress was inappropriately low cut, and Richard could see the eyes of the male congregation peering at her deep cleavage. Her acting skills did not seem to help her in her current awkward situation. The space between Elspeth and Alistair felt like the positive ends of two magnets, their body language repelling each other, and they hardly exchanged a word. Richard had often wondered about Elspeth's current relationship with her ex-husband. She had said it was civil, but he suspected there was more quiet hostility than she let on.

One could see the joy in Lucy's father's face as he escorted his beautiful daughter, simply clad in white, to meet Peter at the altar. One would hardly know that she was a top neurological surgical resident at a famous Bay Area university's teaching hospital, because her face beamed with such uncomplicated happiness. As Peter turned towards Lucy, the love in his face mirrored hers.

Immediately after the bride and groom's departure from the wedding lunch, Alistair and his actress friend hurried from their table and disappeared, never reappearing again. Elspeth linked arms with Richard and together they joined Lucy's parents, chatting warmly and promising future meetings.

In the end Richard wondered how he would relate to his

new stepson. Would Peter warm to him after the cold reception he and Marjorie had always received when they visited Elspeth and Alistair in Hollywood years before? Richard somehow felt that they would be on polite terms but never intimate ones. He knew Elspeth would fight this vigorously, but he was not one to open his heart easily.

When they returned to the Kennington San Francisco after lunch, Elspeth threw off her shoes, which were new, fashionable, and which she proclaimed were slightly uncomfortable. She put her arms around Richard and rested her cheek on his shoulder. He kissed the top of her head tenderly.

They had invited Elspeth's family to their suite and had ordered tea, although they had all eaten richly at the wedding luncheon and probably did not need any further food or drink. Elspeth's daughter Lizzie and her husband Denis declined to join them as they were staying at the reception to dance with Peter and Lucy's friends, and Fiona and James Duff cited their age and withdrew to their rooms at the hotel. Biddy and Johnnie, however, had accepted the invitation, meaning that they could no longer prolong the bad news.

"Unfortunately, especially at the end of such a joyous occasion, Dickie, we must face Biddy and tell her about the farm," Elspeth said. "I think we'd better be straightforward because Biddy wouldn't like it if we didn't tell her."

Her hands found his and clung tightly to them, and he could feel she was dreading the interview ahead. Richard had been acquainted with the Tay/Robertson/Duff family for over forty years and had learned that the bonds of kinship and love that bound them together were unbreakable, and he knew now was the time to call in those bonds. After marrying Elspeth, he felt he had become irrevocably tied to the family.

When the knock came at the door, Richard opened it and saw Biddy and Johnnie were standing together. Biddy was looking a bit giddy, not from drink but from happiness, but Johnnie seemed dour. Richard invited them in.

"Peter and Lucy looked so besotted," Biddy gushed. "You must be ecstatic, 'Peth, with your brood now married and to such wonderful people. Let's hope mine do as well."

Richard looked into Biddy's face, so like Elspeth's but without the overlay of sophistication that Elspeth had gained from her work and life experiences, both happy and otherwise. Biddy led a country life in the Highlands of Scotland and, having once envied her cousin's life of travel and glamour, had retreated gratefully to Tay Farm after Elspeth had involved her in a murder investigation at one of the Kennington hotels two years before. Richard remembered it far too well, as he too had been involved.

Richard went up to Biddy and led her to the sofa. Elspeth sat next to her and put her arms around her.

"What's this about?" Biddy asked. "None of you looks as delighted as I am."

Johnnie took a seat opposite her and with a deep frown regarded his sister and said, "Biddy, we may lose the farm." He paled as he said it.

"Lose the farm?" she said. "How possibly? The mortgages are paid, and we are turning a profit."

Johnnie's face writhed with pain. "Louisa means to get it in the divorce settlement."

Confused, Biddy turned to Elspeth, "Does he mean it, 'Peth?"

Elspeth clenched her jaw. "Yes, I'm afraid so."

"No," Biddy cried. "No, she can't. The farm is mine, ours! Why would she want it? She hates the country."

"She means to spite me," Johnnie said.

"By taking my home away from me? What kind of creature is she, Johnnie? Ivor and I brought the farm back from disaster to profitability." Biddy was referring to her late husband, Ivor Baillie Shaw, who had died four years before.

Elspeth drew her cousin to her. "Biddy, Dickie and I are coming to Scotland to fight this. We have rebooked our flight so that we can be there by Tuesday. Is it all right if we stay with you at the farm? We can stay at my parents' home if it's inconvenient."

"Oh, please 'Peth, stay with me. I'll need you to help us out of this. And you, Johnnie, can you come as well?"

"I'll be there too, Biddy, and stay as long as I can," he said.

Johnnie squeezed his eyes in pain and then opened them with gratitude. His voice was hoarse as he said to Richard, "I think the two of them are tougher than Louisa, don't you?"

"I'd bet my life on it," Richard said.

2

Richard stood looking out over Loch Tay and remembered a young girl who was dressed in a kilt that was slightly too large for her, a man's pullover that had moth holes in it, mismatched socks below bright red knees, and mud-covered brogues, come rambling through the lower meadows and up the path to the farmhouse. She held a book in her hand and kept referring to it, first talking to the air, and then referring to the book again. Two Labrador retrievers gambolled happily at her side. Her light brown hair was tousled by the wind and kept getting in her eyes. She pushed the unruly tendrils away with an expression of annoyance. Forty-one years later he stood in the same spot and wrapped his arms around the woman who was once that girl and who was now his wife. She leaned back into his chest and put her hands over his.

"Do you remember the day we met?" he asked, nuzzling her hair.

"Yes," she said with a laugh. "My father was on his way to Aberfeldy on business and had dropped me at the road at the top of the loch. I had trekked the last few miles to the farm, and I think I was practicing my lines from *Much Ado About Nothing*. Mother had me cast as Benedick and Biddy as Beatrice. It's a wonder I didn't trip all over myself, but I always learned my lines more easily if I was tramping along in

13

the fresh air rather than sitting inside. I remember not paying attention to where I was going and almost running smack into you."

"Do you remember your first words to me?" Richard asked.

Elspeth frowned. "Probably one of the lines from the play," she said.

"Yes. From Act Four. I can still recall them, even to this day."

She turned and smiled up at her husband. "Tell me, Dickie. I've forgotten."

"You said '*I do love nothing so much in the world so well as you. Is that not strange?*' Then you nearly bumped into me. I think only my shadow warned you I was there. You looked up startled and said, 'Oh, hello, who are you?' I fell in love with you instantly since you had just expressed your love for me, although we had not yet been introduced."

"Are you certain you are not making this up?"

"Absolutely certain."

She turned in his arms and kissed him softly on the cheek. "Dear Dickie, I think you are a hopeless romantic," she said.

"In your case, completely hopeless," he responded and again quoted Benedick's first line, leaving off the second, because he did not find loving Elspeth strange at all.

They stood together watching heavy clouds from over the loch, slowly obscuring the highland peaks beyond, and finally the rains came, forcing them to retreat into the farmhouse.

*

Elspeth had not expected Biddy to be in the kitchen at this time of day as she generally was in the barns attending to the animals, but she was sitting alone at the kitchen table and it was clear that her mood was dark. She had set out teacups, a box of tea bags and a tin of biscuits, but they were placed haphazardly, which was uncharacteristic of her usual attention to detail. The kettle boiled violently on the Aga without Biddy seeming to notice its whistle. Her head was resting on her arms which were crossed on the long wooden table that for many years had served as workspace, dining table, and frequent gathering place of the family.

Biddy glanced up as they came in. Elspeth could not tell if she wanted them there or not, but the pleading look in Biddy's eyes could not be ignored.

"Do you really think you can make it right, 'Peth?" she said. "Can you save the farm?"

"I don't know," Elspeth said honestly, "but I'll try. You know that." Elspeth thought of the numerous times she and her cousin had sat at this same table. More often it had been Elspeth, not Biddy, who had come to seek comfort and advice. Now their roles were oddly reversed. Elspeth trusted Biddy's wisdom, but now Biddy was pleading for Elspeth's assistance in a matter that was deeply personal.

"Shall I leave you alone?" Richard asked. Elspeth looked up at him and nodded.

"Biddy, I promised Elspeth I would go round to Loch Rannoch and fetch some warmer and more suitable clothing for us. We always leave some there. I should be back in two hours or so."

Elspeth nodded to him. "Thank you, Dickie. Mother always puts them in the cedar cupboard upstairs after we leave. You have a key. Take your time."

"Let me bring some supper back. I'll stop by the Co-op in Aberfeldy and see what they have to offer," he said and was gone.

Elspeth took the kettle off the burner and poured hot water into a teapot she found on the shelf, warming it and emptying it, and then pouring water over tea leaves she found in a canister by the cooker because she preferred fresh tea to the teabags on the table.

Biddy looked gratefully at her cousin, who handed her a hot cup of properly brewed tea. Then she began to cry. Elspeth came over to her and put her arms lovingly around her and said nothing until the sobs that racked Biddy's body finally stopped.

How different their two lives had been, Elspeth thought, as she held her cousin. Biddy had married her first love when she was a student at St. Andrew's and had lived happily with him in the Scottish Highlands, never needing to go beyond Tay Farm for fulfilment. Her husband's death four years ago had left Biddy in charge of the farm, and quite unexpectedly she had taken over the management of it and been successful beyond her family's expectations. Biddy's three children being adults, her life now centred around the running of the farm and the families whose livelihood depended on its prosperity. In contrast, Elspeth from the very first had pushed acceptable boundaries. Her appetite for the life of intellect had taken her to Cambridge in pursuit of a law tripos, and there she had become engaged to a mercurial person whose murder had haunted her for much of her life. After leaving Cambridge she joined Scotland Yard, eloped to America with another unsuitable man and spent twenty years in Hollywood with him.

Unlike Biddy, Elspeth had not found contentment. Her keen but restless mind was always unable to grasp any real

16

happiness, the kind that seemed to fall so naturally to Biddy. Then eight years ago Elspeth had taken her life in hand, divorced her husband, joined the Kennington Organisation, and found a real sense of security in her own independence, but just over a year ago she sat at this same table, crying into a mug of tea, as she was torn by her love for Richard Munro and her need not to be subsumed in a subordinate position as an uxorial adjunct to his job as high commissioner. Biddy's advice had made Elspeth see she could find a way that would work for her, so that she could keep her job and marry Richard too. Dear Biddy. She had become the stable one, the person to rely on, as close to a sister as Elspeth would ever have. Biddy had wrapped Elspeth in the protective coat of her wisdom and simple warmth and helped Elspeth more than once in the helter-skelter continuum of her life. Now Elspeth hoped she could return Biddy's gifts in kind, using skills that were inherent to her job to solve the surreal dilemma of Louisa's wanting to take possession of the farm.

Finally Biddy drew herself from Elspeth's arms, sat back, looking at the old and familiar kitchen, and said, "Our tea is getting cold."

"No matter," Elspeth said. "Biddy, you know we are going to fight this, Johnnie, Dickie, you and I, but I fear it may not be pleasant. I'm going to need to ask questions, particularly of Johnnie, that will probably require uncomfortable answers. I'm afraid in all the changes in my own life over the last eight years, I haven't paid much attention to his life. It sounds as if it's been rather disastrous."

"Awful," said Biddy as she rose, emptying their cups and brewing another pot of tea. The homely activity seemed to settle her. She brought the pot to the table, blew her nose and poured out the fresh tea.

Elspeth knew that Johnnie's relationship to the women in his life had been as rocky as hers with the men in hers. Had Biddy's marriage not been so successful, Elspeth might have thought it was a curse laid on their generation of their family, but Biddy's happiness convinced Elspeth that Johnnie and her troubles must have been of their own making.

Elspeth tried to remember all she could of Johnnie's life after Oxford. When she was still at Cambridge, Johnnie had married a woman he had met at university, and they had four happy years together. The families approved and the succession seemed assured until his wife's child was stillborn. The young countess committed suicide a week later. Her death was explained away as complications due to childbirth, but Johnnie had revealed the truth of her suicide to Elspeth. Johnnie's second wife did not have the fineness or intelligence of his first one, but she was, as the family said, 'terribly good for Johnnie'. No heir appeared after fifteen years, at which time the second countess disappeared in the company of another man. Their divorce was not contested as far as Elspeth knew. Louisa was another matter altogether. She was neither approved of by the family nor terribly good for Johnnie. He ran off one weekend and married her in a ceremony conducted by a questionable minister and told the family only after the fact. As far as Elspeth remembered, Louisa had only come to the farm on one occasion, at which time she had seemed disappointed at the smallness of Johnnie's family estate and repelled by her unexpected confrontation with the farm animals and exuberant house pets that Biddy and her husband kept. No one could understand why Johnnie had chosen Louisa, but for Johnnie's sake the family hoped they were happy together. Now this.

By the time Johnnie Tay arrived at the farm later that evening after spending the day in his office in Perth, Richard had not yet returned from Loch Rannoch. Having regained her sense of composure after talking to Elspeth, Biddy was busy finishing the farm chores for the day, having left the main house to allow Johnnie and Elspeth to speak in private. They withdrew to the sitting room, which was inappropriately called the 'morning room' as it faced west and never got any morning sunlight. It did, however, afford a long view of Loch Tay and the highland peaks and had been Elspeth, Biddy and Johnnie's grandmother's favourite spot in the house once she had resigned herself to the depleted fortunes of the Tay earldom in the troubled years of the early nineteen thirties and to the loss of the larger house in Perth.

Johnnie lit the fire in the stone-faced fireplace, which had been laid with logs and kindling earlier. Still in the clothing she had taken to California, but which was not suited to the harshness of the Highlands even in early summer, Elspeth found an old woollen plaid of Biddy's lying on the sofa and threw it over her shoulders. It contrasted sharply with the fine cut of her wardrobe she had put on in San Francisco the morning before.

John, the ninth earl of Tay, looked older and more haggard than he had at the wedding. He leaned against the mantelpiece and looked down at Elspeth, who had seated herself on the sofa. His face was joyless.

Elspeth dreaded what she had to say. "Johnnie, this isn't going to be easy. I'm going to have to ask questions which you won't want to answer, not to me or anyone else in the

19

family, including Dickie. I may bring up matters in your personal life that are intimate, but I don't know any other way to get to the bottom of your problem. You probably won't disclose anything I haven't heard before."

Elspeth held her cousin's eyes, which were as intensely blue as hers. "I thought you only dealt with the misdeeds of the well-to-do at the Kennington hotels. Surely you couldn't have heard the many sordid things of lesser beings?" Johnnie said wryly, but his bonhomie failed.

"The transgressions of those in high-priced places are no different from any others. The surroundings may be different, but the crimes are no prettier. If you want me to help you, you'll need to answer my questions as truthfully as you can. You mustn't lie to me or even gloss over the truth," Elspeth said. "That will get us nowhere."

Johnnie looked at her a long time, pain slowly spreading over his face. "Promise me that you won't tell Dickie or Biddy," Johnnie said, "They don't need to know all of the scruffy specifics."

"I'll promise you this, Johnnie, I won't tell them unless it becomes absolutely necessary to save the farm or to save you. Now tell me the truth."

Johnnie said through his teeth, "Louisa is going to have a baby. My solicitor told me just before I left for San Francisco. That's why she wants the farm. She says it's for the child. I don't understand as we have a perfectly fine home in Perth." He turned his eyes away from Elspeth as he said so.

Elspeth neither lowered her gaze from him nor showed any reaction to his statement.

"How far along is she?" she asked.

"Two or three months, I think."

"Is the child yours?"

Johnnie turned his eyes away and cleared his throat before speaking. "It's a possibility."

"Has she been with other men, as well?"

"At least one I know about. There may be others. Louisa was never particularly monogamous."

"I thought you said you had been separated for over a year. Did you have sex with her two or three months ago?" Elspeth did not mince her words.

"Yes," Johnnie said barely audibly.

"I see. Did she consent?"

"Is that important?"

Elspeth kept her gaze steady and her voice professional. In retrospect she knew she sounded harsh. "Yes, very. If she didn't, you could be in serious trouble."

"I'd hardly force myself on her, 'Peth. I went to see her to ask her to reconsider some of the terms of the divorce. She mocked me and lured me into bed. I have never hated her, or myself for that matter, as much as I did in that one act."

"Do you think she might have done so to cover the possibility that the child was someone else's?"

"That would be like her. This is ugly, isn't it? God, if I could just go back and undo it."

"Yes, Johnnie, it is ugly, but I admire you for owning up to what you did. This secret can stay between the two of us right now, at least until the child begins to show. If she does have the child, there are enough tests these days to prove its paternity."

"I think she's using the baby to get more from me, but I still don't know why she wants the farm," Johnnie said. "She hates country life."

"With land prices being what they are today, the farm and its land must be worth a great deal of money, several million anyway."

"You're right."

"Doesn't the farm pass from you to the next earl?"

"Yes."

"What if the child is yours and it's a girl? Won't the title and farm go to Charlie in the event of your death?" Charlie was Biddy's oldest son and the current heir to the earldom of Tay.

"A woman can inherit and assume the title 'Countess of Tay', if there is no close male in the line of succession. Charlie, however, is considered close enough to me to be next in line."

"Are you sure? Have you asked your solicitor?"

"She's looking into it but suspects it's true," Johnnie admitted. "Louisa thinks so anyway."

Elspeth blew out her breath. "I have always hated this title rubbish. Why don't you denounce the whole thing? Dissolve the earldom. The whole thing is so archaic."

"You've always wanted me to dissolve it, haven't you?"

"You know I have."

"You found it useful at Peter's wedding."

Elspeth reddened. "I used them in spite. That wasn't very admirable of me, was it?"

"You did it magnificently. Where did you learn those haughty tones?"

"From Lady Marjorie's sister-in-law, but that is a story for another time." Lady Marjorie was Richard's first wife and daughter of the Earl of Glenborough. Marjorie's family's aristocratic roots and upper-class accent were unquestionable

22

and long established, and Elspeth, whose acquaintance with Lady Marjorie's family had been painful, had shamelessly used their disdainful tones to put down her ex-husband at the wedding. Despite her protest to Johnnie, she did not feel any great regret in doing so.

Johnnie's face broke into a smile, mercifully breaking the tension between them.

"Do you have any ideas, 'Peth, about Louisa, I mean?"

"I may have. Do you think Louisa would recognise me? I only met her briefly that one time after your wedding when you brought her here to meet us."

"She probably would know you. You look too much like Biddy, despite the difference in your clothes and hair. Louisa isn't particularly bright, but she is sly."

A plan was forming in Elspeth's mind. "I want to see her if I can."

"You won't be able to change her mind. She can be extraordinarily stubborn once she gets an idea in her head."

Elspeth considered this. "I may not be able to, but I may be able to convince her to come to the farm. She might like to see what farm life is really like."

"Do I detect skulduggery?"

"From me?" Elspeth said smiling with mock innocence, but then she became serious. "If you are to keep the farm, we have to convince her she doesn't want to take possession of it. I also want to discover if she really is pregnant and, if so, how far along."

"Would you know?"

"Yes, and so would Biddy."

"You aren't going to involve Biddy in this, are you?"

"She doesn't need to be told about the baby, but she may

have guessed. She and I have had five children between us, and we are well aware of the early signs even before the baby shows."

"And Dickie? Are you going to involve him in your plan?" asked Johnnie.

Elspeth warmed inwardly at the thought of her husband. "Dear Dickie," she said. "He hasn't changed much, you know, Johnnie, since our summers together in the nineteen sixties. He will be doubtful at first but will eventually come round. Where is Louisa now?"

"In Perth. She is staying at our house, but I'm staying in a flat attached to a house owned by a friend. It's a damnable life."

Elspeth felt a sudden empathy for her cousin. "You and I haven't always been very good at choosing members of the opposite sex, have we?"

Johnnie shook his head. "No, not very. You should have married Dickie years ago rather than running off with Alistair."

"It wouldn't have worked. Can you image me in Lady Marjorie's place?"

Johnnie laughed. "Frankly, no, but you seem happy with him now. One has only to look at the two of you to know that."

Elspeth lowered her eyes and flushed. "I hope someday you will be as happy."

"I do too," he said. "Where there's life, there's always hope, I suppose." Bitterness filled his voice.

Elspeth rose and touched her cousin affectionately on the arm. "Now let's get down to our plotting," she said. "Dickie will be back soon, and Biddy will be in from her chores."

When Elspeth and Johnnie proposed their scheme over dinner, both Biddy and Richard had the same reaction.

"Invite Louisa here? Why on earth?" Biddy said.

"Elspeth and Johnnie, I don't trust you two," Richard added.

"Don't you see, we have a very simple plan," Elspeth said. "Louisa has no real idea of all that happens on a farm. Granted she may just want to get back at Johnnie by demanding the farm, but perhaps if she sees how much work is involved, she might prefer a different settlement." Elspeth did not mention the baby.

"How exactly do you think you can get her to come out here?" Richard asked.

"I thought, acting as a third party, I'd get in touch with her and tell her Johnnie was considering giving in to her wishes and that we would like to show her how the farm was managed. It doesn't need to run as smoothly as it usually does while she is here. We can make sure of that."

"Elspeth, I'm not certain that's honest," Richard said. "I fear you and Johnnie are reverting to your old ways. They have not always served you well."

"I think they may this time. After all what harm is there in it?"

3

Louisa, Countess of Tay, was not what Elspeth had expected. She had rung Louisa from the farm, and almost immediately and with alacrity she had accepted Elspeth's invitation to lunch at the Kennington Edinburgh. Elspeth borrowed Johnnie's saloon car to make the journey there. Richard offered to drive her, but she declined, saying she needed to face Louisa alone.

Elspeth had rung ahead to the hotel to make sure they were given a private corner in the dining room where they could talk undisturbed. The manager remembered her from an earlier case and assured her request would be honoured.

Elspeth knew Kennington hotels were designed to impress. Obviously Louisa's reaction was not an exception to the rule. She blathered on about the elegance of the dining room as they were led to their table.

"Elspeth, cousin," the countess breathed. She was severely overdressed and, being overweight, fit too snugly in her clothes. She had applied too much makeup, and Elspeth detected something not quite true in her accent. She must ask Johnnie how they met and what his initial attraction to her was. Considering Louisa's present manner Elspeth could not fathom why he was drawn to her. In an older era Louisa would have been considered 'common', an adjective that had never been used for any other member of the Tay family despite

26

their many faults.

After they were settled at their table, Elspeth said, "Louisa, I want to thank you for coming. I know we met when you first married Johnnie, but it was a large gathering and I feel I hardly said a word to you. You don't mind our getting together like this, do you?"

Elspeth suggested a particularly sumptuous lunch, which, if Louisa were indeed two or three months pregnant, most probably would have disgusted her. Elspeth chose simpler fare for herself. When the order was served, Elspeth sat back, ready to initiate the next stage in her plan.

"I'm sorry that you and Johnnie are having hard times. I understand because I had the same experience with my first husband. Men are quite awful." Elspeth prevaricated without the least compunction. She was glad Richard was not with her, as he often chastised her for using falsehoods as a means to an end without the least sense of guilt. "I fully understand your wanting the farm. For the child," Elspeth said charmingly. "I have two children, as you know, and they are such a comfort. I grew up in the Highlands, and there's no better place for a child to roam and experience all the delights of the country without the dreariness of town."

The highly spiced and garlicky fish dish, the thought of which would have turned most woman in early pregnancy nauseous, arrived and was served with the usual Kennington attention to detail.

"One of my favourites," said Elspeth, "from a Kennington recipe that has never been revealed, even to me. Lord Kennington likes to keep all his ingredients and cooking methods secret." At this point Elspeth knew Johnnie would have laughed and Richard would have looked disapprovingly because she was not known for her culinary skills. Louisa looked puzzled when Elspeth's meal was served and at the simple salad and roasted chicken the waiter put in front of her. She wondered if Louisa was intelligent enough to see the trap. Elspeth almost, but not quite, felt sorry for her.

Elspeth ordered a bottle of wine for them and poured out a large glass for Louisa and a small one for herself. "I find wine a great solace during hard times, don't you?" she said and offered a toast to womanhood. "Now Louisa, I've convinced Biddy that you should come down and stay at the farm, since it might soon be yours. I promised her to be there too, but I have to leave for London on Thursday next. Can you come for the weekend?"

Louisa took a long drink from her wineglass and seemed to relax.

"You must love your job with the Kennington hotels with all this luxury every day."

"Oh, yes, it's quite definitely bearable. I'm lucky to be a part of the Kennington Organisation." Elspeth laughed but did not mention the crimes, the murders, the attempted murders, or the usual stressful conditions that made up her job.

Louisa ate her meal with relish and drank most of the bottle of wine. Elspeth ordered another. She sensed that this indulgence was one that a woman two or three months into a pregnancy could not have tolerated. The bait had been taken. Afterwards Elspeth had enough decency to offer Louisa a ride back to Perth, knowing the countess was in no condition either to drive or negotiate public transport. Elspeth made arrangements with the hotel for Louisa's car to be brought to Perth that afternoon.

When Elspeth left the countess at her doorstep, she had

the forethought to say that she would confirm Louisa's arrival time at Tay Farm late the next day. She wondered if Louisa would indeed remember that they had made the appointment. As Elspeth steered Johnnie's car back towards Loch Tay, she smiled at the ease with which her scheme had worked.

Johnnie was waiting alone at the turnoff to Tay Farm. He opened the passenger door and said to her, "Let's drive down to the road a bit before going back. Tell me what happened."

"She may be pregnant, Johnnie. Her colour was high, but, if she is, she is well beyond the first trimester. At two or three months I would have thrown up the entire meal I gave her."

"Graphically but not elegantly put, 'Peth. Are you certain?" Johnnie said with a grin.

"No, not certain. Women react differently to pregnancy, but if she could tolerate her meal, she would be in a small minority. If she is indeed pregnant, she is well beyond morning sickness."

"Is she coming to the farm?"

"Yes, tomorrow. I think you should stay away, and Dickie as well. He won't like it, but I'm sure my parents won't mind if you bunk at Loch Rannoch, if you don't want to go back to your friend's flat. Mother and Daddy aren't due home until next week. I called Lizzie to ask how long they were planning to be in East Sussex, and she said they are quite happy being grandparents for a while longer, or at least Mother is."

"Even I, 'Peth, fear your wily ways."

"So I won't trouble you with them, and most certainly not with Dickie. Just trust me, Johnnie. Louisa is no match for me and Biddy. I feel sorry for her."

"How are you going to explain this to Dickie?"

29

"I'm not sure. I'll think of something."

*

Richard watched Elspeth and her cousin disembark from the saloon car. It concerned him that Johnnie looked worried but Elspeth looked smug. He hated that conspiratorial look in his wife because it reflected her impetuous streak that often precluded any reasonable discourse with her.

Elspeth and Johnnie burst into the kitchen. "She's coming tomorrow, at least if she remembers," Elspeth said triumphantly. "I think it best if you men aren't here. What a piece of work our Louisa is. She'll never guess what I have in store for her."

That night he lay next to her, smelling the sweetness of her body close to him and wondering how such a soft creature could have such devious ways. He had been annoyed with her many times before, but now the irritation was fuelled by love rather than frustration. Her deep breathing told him she was asleep, but he silently pledged his love to her once again. But, he thought, Elspeth, you are like a witch from *Macbeth*. *Double, double, toil and trouble*, and *I do love no one so much in the world so well as I love you*. Elspeth turned in her sleep and put her head against his shoulder. Unhearing, she grunted contentedly.

*

"Why are you once again involving me in something I'm not too sure I want to be a part of?" Biddy asked her cousin as they walked out towards the sheep shearing pen. The morning was cool, and Elspeth was glad for the country woollens and stout shoes that Richard had brought her from her parents' home on Loch Rannoch.

30

"You want to keep the farm, don't you? Just don't be surprised when Louisa is here that things don't run as smoothly as they usually do. Have you ever kept a rooster in the room adjoining your bedroom and had it crow at dawn?"

"You wouldn't, would you?" Biddy looked horrified.

Elspeth grinned. "For starters," she said. "Now let's think up some other foul deeds, no pun intended of course. The sooner Louisa finds that life on the farm is not as idyllic as she thinks, the better. I promise no bodily harm, only emotional discomfort."

Biddy could not help laughing.

"Do you use these techniques at the hotels?" Biddy asked, laughing

"If I did, Eric Kennington would fire me immediately and with just cause," Elspeth responded.

When Biddy finished managing the morning chores around the farm and instructing the farm hands on their duties for the day, and Elspeth returned from her walk, they found Richard and Johnnie in the kitchen. The Aga was fired up and bacon was frying. The two men were in deep conversation, which they broke off when the two women entered.

"Is it too early to ring Louisa and remind her of her visit here?" Elspeth asked Johnnie.

"A bit. I won't try until after ten."

Elspeth looked at her watch and saw it was just past eight. Biddy busied herself with preparing the rest of the breakfast, and Richard volunteered to set out the tea and coffee.

Elspeth said to Johnnie, "Shall we have a brief chat outside and leave these two to minister to our needs?"

As they walked out to the courtyard, which was sheltered

31

from the wind, Elspeth's face had lost its merriment.

"Johnnie, how did you meet Louisa? She doesn't seem. . ."

"Quite our sort?" Johnnie posited.

"I try to be more egalitarian than that," Elspeth said, "No, I was thinking of the words 'even marginally intelligent'."

"You have always been the brainy one in the family, 'Peth. Not all of us put so much worth on intellect."

"You haven't answered my question. Why the attraction? There must have been something, in the beginning anyway."

"She seemed quite fun, at first, and she was still young enough to have children. I do so want to have children. I often think of you and Biddy, and your broods, and see how much happiness you get from them. Wasn't I supposed to be the one to produce the heir to the title? But it wasn't just that. Louisa in her way is all right, or was until about a year ago."

"Why is she divorcing you?"

"Rather the other way round," Johnnie said. "I'm divorcing her."

This surprised Elspeth. "You didn't tell me that. Why?"

"The other men. And besides," he said shyly, "I've found someone else."

Elspeth turned to her cousin. "You should have told me this."

"I didn't want to complicate things for you."

"Now I understand why Louisa might want the farm and wants to bear your child. She doesn't want to lose her status or title. Who is this someone else?"

"I don't want her involved. I'll tell you after all this is over."

"No, Johnnie, you must tell me now. Do I know her?"

"You know her family. She is younger and so you probably don't know her."

"Who and how much younger?"

"She is Alice Fergusson's daughter. Her name is Madeline MacNaughton and she is thirty-three."

"Alice Fergusson was at school with me and Biddy. Really, Johnnie. But I suppose there is still the question of the heir. Does Louisa know about Madeline?"

"No, I don't think so. I'm sure her lawyer would have brought it up if she did. I'm citing adultery. Louisa has been quite open about her extra-marital affairs."

"Could Louisa accuse you of the same?"

"This is the twenty-first century, 'Peth. Besides we have been discreet."

"Let's hope so. Things are complicated enough."

"Help me, 'Peth. I love Madeline. I never thought I'd find anyone like her. Yes, I know once it's out there will be all the old jokes about May and December, but that doesn't change how I feel about her. You must understand. About loving, I mean."

Elspeth thought of Richard and smiled. "Yes, of course. Sometimes it takes a long time to find someone whom you can trust enough to love completely. But, Johnnie, you are in a dangerous position. You must know that. Does your lawyer know about Madeline?"

"No. As I said we've been discreet. You're the only other person beyond Madeline herself who knows."

Elspeth looked at Johnnie and could see he was struggling with his feelings. "I'll keep your secret, but what if Louisa is pregnant with your child?" she asked.

"You said you thought she was further along than two or

three months."

"Possibly, but I have no absolute proof. It's hard to tell because of her weight."

They walked out beyond the farmyard and into the pastures. Clouds covered the sky and the wind had come up. Elspeth drew her jacket around her and shivered.

"I heard you go out last night. Was it to see Madeline?"

"Yes. Her family has a remote cottage above Strathtummel, which is where we meet."

"Before we go in," she said, "promise me something."

"If you wish."

"Don't involve Madeline in the divorce. In fact, if I were you, I would stop seeing her until everything is settled between you and Louisa."

"That could be months. I can't do that."

"Johnnie, real love can last months or even years without continual nurturing. That happened between me and Dickie. If Madeline loves you, she will wait. Promise me you won't see her until everything is finalised."

"I had planned to see her again on Saturday. I'll talk to her. I'll let you know then."

They heard Biddy calling them to tell them breakfast was ready, and they retreated out of the wind.

At ten o'clock Elspeth rang Louisa but got no reply. She rang again at eleven and then at noon, each time without success. Louisa apparently did not want to be contacted.

4

Elspeth was the first to see the police car coming down the drive. Richard and Johnnie had gone off together, scrambling down the banks of the burn that skirted the farm, and had disappeared into the trees. Both looked boyish. Elspeth had become accustomed to thinking of her relationship with Richard as his primary link to her family, but she reminded herself that Richard and Johnnie had been friends at Oxford before she had met Richard. Their manner suggested they had gone back to the camaraderie they had at university, so were happy to leave Elspeth tucked away in the library with her book and had quite forgotten the present situation in their lives.

The room had changed little since Elspeth's childhood, except in one corner, where Ivor Baillie Shaw had set up a computer on a long library table and where Biddy still did the farm books, now on a flat-screened computer that took up minimal space. Vintage leather-bound bankers' boxes filled with printed versions of the computer files were aligned neatly along the wall and a low wooden file cabinet had been pushed under a window. A fire was burning in the grate, and Elspeth had curled up in one of the oversized chairs. On one of the bookshelves that surrounded the room Elspeth had found a large, leather-bound picture book that now must be almost a century old. Her grandfather used to read to her when she

35

visited the farm as a child; the heavily illustrated stories took place in Singapore and Sydney and Shanghai, all of which then seemed completely imaginary to the young Elspeth, but now were places that were almost as familiar to her as Edinburgh or London. The book, however, lay unread on her lap, as she puzzled over Louisa's lack of response to her phone calls that morning.

The library was on the drive side of the house, away from the loch, and the French windows allowed Elspeth to see the blue and lime green chequered police estate car drive through the farm's main gates. Biddy customarily left the gate open during the day to accommodate the various comings and goings of the postman, farmhands, delivery people, and occasional visitors, and closed it only when darkness came. Only recently had she begun to lock it at night, but the key was readily available on the key rack by the kitchen door for anyone who needed it. The gaudy police car came down the hill and pulled up in front of the main door of the house, which now was seldom used. A plainclothes policeman stepped from the car and knocked authoritatively.

Elspeth watched all this from her perch in the library, and then finding her jacket, which she had thrown on one of the chairs, put it around her shoulders. By this time, the policeman was banging harder, trying to rouse someone from within and suggesting to his uniformed partner that they use a battering ram. Elspeth undid the bolts and opened the door.

"May I help you?" she asked, thinking he was lost.

"I'm looking for Tay Farm," he growled.

"Then come around to the side door. I don't think this door has been opened for years. We all use the kitchen door." She led him round the house.

"I'm Detective Inspector Simon Kennedy from the Criminal Investigation Department of the Tayside Police in Perth, and I'm here to see Lord Tay. I understand he owns the farm." He pulled out his warrant card.

After leading the inspector to the kitchen, Elspeth said, "My husband and Lord Tay have gone on a walk down towards the loch. Is there anything I can do for you? I'm Elspeth Duff, John Tay's cousin."

Elspeth had dealt with the police enough in her career to know from the inspector's stiffened face that he had come to the farm bearing distressing news.

"What is it, Inspector?"

"I'm here to inform Lord Tay that his wife is dead," he said stolidly.

Elspeth's thoughts raced to Louisa the day before, a woman filled with an inherent need for self-gratification and a lusty enjoyment of things overdone. To imagine her dead was unbelievable. No one had been more alive than the slightly tipsy Louisa that Elspeth had deposited at her home in Perth the day before. Elspeth did not share these thoughts with the inspector but instead reverted to the cool manner she used to detach her feelings when difficulties arose in her professional or personal life. She hoped the inspector would not interpret this as indifference, but she did not feel any grief at his news, nor did she choose to express any. Her silent but immediate reaction was one of relief, that Johnnie and Biddy now would be spared Louisa's demands for the farm, but she did not impart these thoughts to the inspector.

"Can you tell me when she died?" Elspeth asked without mentioning her meeting with Louisa the day before.

"She was found by her housekeeper this morning," the

37

inspector said so tonelessly that Elspeth's suspected that Louisa's death had not been a natural one.

"Has a cause of death been determined?" Elspeth asked.

The inspector did not answer immediately, eyeing Elspeth up and down and frowning. Finally he said, "I think that should wait until I can speak to Lord Tay."

Elspeth smiled her most persuasive smile, one that had cracked harder nuts than the inspector, but he did not bend.

"Our family is very close, inspector. We don't hide secrets from one another." Elspeth wished her words were truer. "Louisa's death will affect all of us." She did not say how, but relief flooded her when, through the window, she saw Richard and Johnnie approaching on the path up from the loch. Johnnie had his arm casually round Richard's shoulder, apparently making light of some comment Richard had just made. Richard threw back his head and laughed.

"Here they are now, Inspector, so you can tell us all, now that we are together."

When the two men arrived and had shed their coats, Elspeth made the introductions, and the inspector once again drew out his warrant card.

*

Detective Inspector Simon Kennedy was not in a good mood when he was asked to go to Tay Farm because he did not like dealing with the nabobs, as he called the gentry, and was resentful that he had been sent to find the husband of Lady Tay to give him the news of her untimely death. His reception at Tay Farm, which looked more like a grand hall than a farmhouse to him, had not alleviated his mood nor his resentment over his task. His politics were republican and nationalist, and he had little liking for the aristocracy, as he had been born in a downtrodden part of Edinburgh and had risen through the ranks of the police force by sheer natural ability in dealing with the more destitute and hardcore elements of the Scottish population, to which he could relate. Yet when he had been offered the post in Perth, which carried with it the promotion from detective sergeant to detective inspector, he had accepted it quickly but missed the roughness of the streets of his native city. Now he had to deal with situations like this. He had only handled a case with the privileged classes once before, and the experience had been unpleasant.

The woman who had appeared as he had knocked at the main door to the house seemed amused by his error, and he felt distinctly uncomfortable in her presence. She's a cool one, he thought. All dressed up to look as if she were on a film set at a Scottish castle and, her haughty head raised high, looking at him with a smirking smile that he was sure was filled with her contempt of him. She sounded like those posh people on the telly, English, not Scots, although her surname sounded Scottish. What was it? Elspeth Duff? None of her type belonged in the new Scotland, free of the long arm of London and its highfaluting ways, once the Scots had gained its independence from England. But DI Kennedy knew that, if he were to impress his new superintendent, he would have to cope with the task he had been given, unpleasant though it might be, and not let his personal politics intervene.

The woman in the modish clothing led him into the kitchen not a sitting room, as he would have expected, probably contemptuous of his accent and social standing. Then she had started asking questions, as if she had the right. She seemed to want to charm him, but she did not.

39

Then, blessedly, the two men arrived. He took the tall, thin one to be Lord Tay because he looked stiff and disdainful enough to be a lord, but Elspeth Duff had introduced the other as Lord Tay, a man who looked like he had more of the common touch. At least he would be easier to speak to.

"Johnnie," Elspeth Duff said, "I'm afraid DI Kennedy has unsettling news." The inspector was confused by her words. Unsettling, not bad, nor sad, nor distressing. He thought he saw some sort of signal go between Lord Tay and Elspeth Duff, but he could not be sure of its meaning. He allowed her to tell his news to the earl.

"Louisa was found dead this morning," she said. DI Kennedy almost thought her tone was such that the news was not regretted by her or his lordship and somehow was a relief to them.

The tall, thin man whom Elspeth Duff had identified as her husband, but who had a different name from hers, was the only one who seemed startled by the news.

"Good God," he said. "Louisa? But how possibly? Please explain, Inspector."

Despite this man's aristocratic looks, DI Kennedy felt he was the only one who had any comprehension of the difficulty of his mission or who was upset with his news.

"I regret to say," Simon Kennedy said looking at Richard and not the others, "that she has been murdered."

5

"Murdered?" Johnnie said, his tone a half octave above its usual baritone.

Richard watched his friend, trying to judge Johnnie's feelings, but neither his expression nor voice registered anything but his desire for clarification.

The detective inspector repeated himself, "Murdered."

No one spoke and the silence lingered uncomfortably. The inspector looked down at the slate floor and ran his foot across it, making a small rasping sound. He cleared his throat.

"I hope, Inspector," Richard said, abhorring a verbal vacuum when an explanation was warranted, "you will tell us how."

"She was strangled with a curtain cord."

"I see," said Johnnie, tonelessly.

"When?" Elspeth asked. "Last evening or this morning?"

"The pathologist hasn't said. The initial postmortem is being performed today."

"Oh," Johnnie and Elspeth said almost simultaneously.

Richard, who in the daily routine of his diplomatic work dealt with the tense situations, could sense an impasse and consequently intervened.

"Inspector, this news comes as a great shock to us all." He was not sure he spoke accurately, but it seemed the right thing to say. "As painful as it may be to Lord Tay, perhaps you can

41

be more specific."

"She was found in her sitting room with the curtain cord tied tightly round her neck. I don't think she suffered for very long."

"We are thankful for that," Richard replied. He glanced over at Johnnie and Elspeth, but they were both staring at the floor. The silence grew again, but neither Elspeth nor Johnnie seemed willing to break it.

The inspector grazed the floor again with his heavy shoe. "I need to know where all of you were last evening and earlier this morning," he said.

Neither Elspeth nor Johnnie responded, which forced Richard to reply. "We all were here, Elspeth, Johnnie, his sister, and I. We had dinner together and retired at about ten o'clock."

"And none of you went out after that?" the inspector asked.

"No, I think not," Richard said. "We all had just come from a wedding in San Francisco, and we all were anxious to go to bed early. Surely, you can appreciate that, Inspector."

After speaking, Richard realised the comment seemed condescending because he suspected the inspector had never left Scotland, but it served as a credible alibi, as it seemed they needed one.

The inspector seemed to gather himself together. "Lord Tay," he said, addressing Johnnie directly. "When did you last see your wife?"

Johnnie shifted his weight from one foot to the other before speaking. His answer was strained. "You'll undoubtedly learn, if you do not already know, that my wife and I are estranged. I've not seen her since early May. We are

42

divorcing."

"Is there anyone who can confirm that was the last time?"

"I'm not too sure how," said Elspeth under her breath, "anyone can confirm the absence of an act."

Watching the inspector's reaction to Elspeth's words, Richard regretted her challenge, as pertinent as it may have been. Richard suspected that the inspector was not used to dealing with the likes of his wife. The inspector grimaced, confirming Richard's assumptions that Elspeth had not made a good impression on the policeman. He wondered how to diffuse the tension in the room, which could not serve the family's best interests, and tried to think how best to lessen the hostility that now surrounded them. Richard dealt with controversy at the highest levels in the international community, and the discomfort of a local Scottish policeman would have seemed child's play had it not been for the seriousness of the situation.

"Inspector," he said, "your news has been a shock to all of us. Perhaps you can give us time to take in what happened."

The inspector looked at Richard as if he were the only sane person in the room.

"Of course," he said, "but I want to question Lord Tay further. I advise you, your lord," he said, stumbling on the correct way to address Johnnie, "that as the husband of the deceased you automatically fall under suspicion. I would prefer to speak to you at the station in Perth. I recommend that you do not leave Perthshire and that you might want a solicitor to be with you when you come in for questioning. Please present yourself at the Tayside Police Station on Barrack Road in Perth tomorrow afternoon at three o'clock. I'll inform the front desk that you will be coming."

43

With those words, the inspector turned on his heel and left the three of them.

*

Biddy Baillie Shaw had not been privy to this conversation and was surprised when she returned from the upper garden to see a police car in the drive. She thought perhaps the police were lost and hurried down the drive to see if she could be of assistance. The young police constable, who was standing by the car parked next to the barbed wire fence by the animal enclosure, turned towards her as she approached.

"May I help you in some way?" Biddy asked.

"No, madam. The inspector's down at the house."

"The inspector? But why?"

"He's down at the house," the constable said, again, this time his face reddening.

"Very well then," she said, and made her way down the drive to the kitchen door. As she opened it, she nearly bumped into the inspector, who was making an awkward exit and nearly upended Biddy's basket full of vegetables from the garden. Biddy apologized for her near collision with him. He mumbled something that she did not understand and made a hasty retreat.

Biddy entered the kitchen and saw Johnnie, Richard and Elspeth all in different positions of distress. Elspeth was leaning against a doorframe, her head thrown back against it, her eyes closed and teeth clenched, Richard was gripping the back of one of the high-backed chairs that surrounded the table, and Johnnie was at the sideboard pouring himself a whisky.

"Well?" she said, which seemed to bring them all back to

reality, "What's all this about?"

Johnnie spoke first. "Damn, Biddy, Louisa's been murdered." He swallowed the entire glass of whisky he had just poured.

Biddy took a moment before she totally understood. "Murdered? But 'Peth just saw her yesterday. How can she have been murdered?"

Johnnie answered. "She was strangled with a curtain cord. She was found this morning by the char, who informed the police."

Biddy put down her basket on the drain board of the large sink. "Why did the inspector come here? Surely a phone call would have sufficed?"

No one responded.

Finally Richard answered. "He said Johnnie, as Louisa's husband, was the most likely person to kill her and that he was to present himself at the police station in Perth tomorrow afternoon, solicitor in tow."

Biddy looked round at her brother. "Johnnie, how absurd!"

He evaded her glance. "It is absurd, isn't it?" he said.

He turned to her, his eyes pleading. "It seems that wretched policeman finds me the most likely suspect, the estranged husband, prime candidate to be the murderer."

Biddy turned around to where Elspeth was standing. She had not changed her pose although she had opened her eyes. "You're the investigator, 'Peth; are there any grounds for this?"

Biddy watched Elspeth nod her head. "It's not unusual for this to happen, especially when a divorce is in process."

Elspeth's answer was so neutral that Biddy suspected

45

Elspeth was dealing with more emotions than her outward demeanour showed. Biddy knew her cousin well enough to see the consternation behind her expressionless face.

"Then how would you advise Johnnie?" Biddy asked Elspeth.

"I think we need to find him the best solicitor in Perth," she said. "Perhaps Daddy can help. I'll call him directly." Then Elspeth smiled. "I expect he's finding the role of loving grandfather in East Sussex with Lizzie's twins a bit tiring, particularly after the flight back from San Francisco. Mother enjoys the fuss, but I doubt he does."

*

Her father, being well into his eighties, was not comfortable with the world of mobile phones, instant messaging, or even e-mail, so Elspeth had to resort to her daughter's home landline. After making appropriate conversation with her daughter who was still treating her coolly after the resolution of the problem in Bermuda, Elspeth asked to speak to her father. When he came on the line, Elspeth hurriedly explained the situation in Perth. Elspeth trusted her father implicitly and gave heartfelt thanks as he offered advice.

"I'll be back in Scotland tomorrow morning. I feel quite extraneous here, and I'm sure Lizzie and your mother won't miss me," he said. "I've already have a booking on the sleeper train to Pitlochry, arriving early tomorrow morning. Can you come to my office first thing? I'll find the name of a good solicitor for you. I have one in mind. In fact, he's a solicitor advocate, a QC, and one of the best lawyers in Perth. Shall we set our meeting for nine o'clock? If I'm not there, my clerk will let you in."

With the immediate need to finding a solicitor dispensed with, discomfort once again settled on the kitchen. Johnnie finally banged down his glass and said, "This really is the last straw from Louisa," as if she had arranged her own murder. Biddy stopped scrubbing the new potatoes she had liberated from her garden basket.

"Johnnie, you and I need to talk," Biddy said.

Sensing that neither their presence was particularly welcome in the kitchen at the moment, Elspeth suggested to Richard that they retire to the library. Relief flooded Biddy's face, and Johnnie slumped in his chair without acknowledging their departure.

Elspeth's childhood storybook lay open on the sofa where she had left it a short while but what seemed an eternity ago. The fire was still burning but needed a stir, which Richard attended to, putting another log on the grate, for although the afternoon was mild, the rooms in the old house tended to keep in dampness. He then took his place beside his wife on the sofa, and she reached out and took his hand.

"Dickie," she said, looking up at him, "there's something I need to tell you. It's quite serious. Somebody left the farm last night in one of the cars. It must have been about eleven." She held tightly to his fingers. "Johnnie said he did."

"I see," Richard said. "Then what I told the inspector was not exactly accurate."

"It was up to a point, I suppose. We all did go up at about ten o'clock. I think you were the only one the inspector believed, and you stated what you thought to be true."

"But Johnnie was here this morning," Richard said. "He and I shared tea before you and Biddy came into the kitchen."

"How did he seem then?"

47

"He said he still was feeling terribly jet lagged and was looking forward to getting back to his usual routine."

"Which might explain his being up well into the night," Elspeth speculated. "His absence doesn't help his case with the police."

"Do you honestly believe Johnnie could have killed Louisa?"

"It's one of many possibilities. I wish I knew what time he got back to the farm."

"Are you worried, Elspeth?" he said.

"Yes, terribly."

"May I ask why?"

Elspeth considered relating Johnnie's confidences earlier that day with Richard, although she had promised not to do so. What had she said to Johnnie? She would only share his secrets to save the farm or to save him. Perhaps now was the time to save him from being accused of Louisa's murder. She decided to tell Richard most of what she knew, but leave out Madeline, at least for the time being. She wanted to see if she could meet Madeline first and talk to her privately.

"Johnnie thinks Louisa was pregnant and the child might be his."

"Oh," said Richard with a swallow. Elspeth wasn't sure if he was shocked or not. "I thought they've been separated for a long time."

"Yes, they have."

"Then how could she . . .?"

That's why I'm worried. Johnnie did have sex with her after their separation, just once, but, of course, that's all it takes."

"Is that why you went to Edinburgh, to see if she was

pregnant?"

"That was part of it. I also wanted to get her to the farm to see how difficult it was to manage."

"Was she?"

"Was she what?"

"Pregnant?"

"I'm not sure. She could have been. She was overweight so she might not have been showing yet. When the police finish the postmortem, we'll know."

"If she was, can't they determine the father of the child?"

"Yes, but it may take a bit of time. Certainly longer than it will take *The Scottish Sun* to make a story of it. ***Scottish Earl Accused of Killing Estranged Wife! She Was Preggers! Whose Child Was It?***

Richard winced. "Is there any way we can stop it?"

"Eric Kennington or Pamela Crumm could have, but I don't think we can. We just must hope that she wasn't pregnant, and we can prove Johnnie innocent."

"Do you know where he went last night?"

"I know where he said he went, but as yet I have no proof."

"Will you tell me?"

"Dickie, you must trust my instincts right now. I may be able to locate the person he was with, but I may not."

"A woman?"

"He said so."

"Do you know who she is?"

"I know who Johnnie said she was, but I want to corroborate it with her before I say any more. She doesn't need to be dragged into this if we can avoid it. I don't think the solution lies in his friendship with her."

"It lies with whom or what then?"

"Louisa, and by association Johnnie. As I sat here earlier, I realised that I haven't really known Johnnie as an adult. I still think of him the way he was during those wonderful summers we were together, carefree, unattached, unworried, with everything before us. Now here we are four decades later, each with our own past and personal baggage. You have told me yours, and I've not hidden mine from you, but Johnnie is different. What has Johnnie become? I meet him at christenings and weddings and occasionally at the farm when I came for a visit, but I don't know what's inside him that makes him who he is now. How did he feel when Kathleen died? Did you know she committed suicide rather than face Johnnie with her failure to bear an heir?"

Richard drew back and blew out his breath. "No, I didn't," he said. "I knew her only slightly at Oxford, but I was already working at the FCO and had been posted to Burma when she died."

"And Helen? How did Johnnie feel when she ran off with another man? You and I have had our disappointments in love over our lifetimes, but neither one of us was ever thrown over by our spouses. How did Johnnie feel when Helen left? What about Louisa? Was she just someone he married on the rebound, or did Johnnie at one time have feelings for her other than just sexual ones? I've no idea, but I'm positive that all this has bearing on Louisa's murder. The woman he saw last night may be his alibi for the night of the murder, and she also may be the first real happiness he has been able to find since Helen left." She found his eyes again. "I don't want to deny that to Johnnie. You and I more than most know what a gift that sort of happiness is, particularly when you aren't young.

That's why I want to protect the woman. For Johnnie's future, if he has one."

*

The conversation which took place between Biddy and Johnnie was equally speculative. Johnnie owned the farm as it was so-called 'immovable property', the indentured portion of his earldom, but he had had no wish to remain there after his boyhood and preferred living in Perth. He had turned it over to Biddy and her late husband. Biddy had spent her entire life on the farm, raising her three children there as well. Her grandparents had lost what remained of the other 'moveable property' of the earldom, but they could not sell the farm and were reduced to living there. Biddy had greater interest in retaining the farm, and she knew Johnnie would do everything in his power to keep it for her.

"Johnnie, you don't suppose Louisa's death had anything to do with the earlier business, do you?" Biddy turned from where she was standing at the sink, but she did not meet his eyes and focused her attention on the half-washed leek in her hand.

"About our agreement, you mean? I don't see the connection."

"There was a reason Louisa wanted the farm, not just the money but something else."

"Which brought to mind our earlier business?"

"Louisa's new lawyer. He was involved in the other matter too."

"Perhaps he approached her when her first lawyer seemed too ready to settle. Mr Paul Hodges, I sense, is of a less savoury type and would appeal to Louisa's ilk."

"You did nothing wrong, Johnnie. You just got caught in

51

a trap. I blame both Louisa and Paul Hodges for that."

"And you single-handedly got me out of the mess."

"Did I? Didn't I merely do what any other family member would do?"

"You saved me and the farm. I've a feeling you would do it again without blinking an eye."

Biddy turned back to the sink, took up another leek, and began scrubbing it. "Yes, of course I would," she said. "Then, the same lawyer shows up like a bad penny, and suddenly we became in danger of losing the farm once again."

"I can't see how this has anything to do with Louisa's death," Johnnie said. "Besides there's no chance of losing the farm now."

"Perhaps not. I just don't like the connection, that's all."

"Johnnie rose, extracted the leek from Biddy's hand and took her by the shoulders. "We'll be all right now. You'll see."

"What if they arrest you, Johnnie?"

"They have no evidence."

"I wonder," Biddy said. "Why didn't the police just ring us to let you know about Louisa?"

Neither one had an answer.

"Johnnie, you know that you, my family, and the farm are the very core of my existence. There's little else that matters to me. I would lie and cheat and steal for all of you, and I won't allow you to be convicted of this crime." Biddy flared her nostrils and drew in her breath.

"Do you think I'm guilty?"

"I have no idea whether you are or not, but it doesn't matter" she said. "I know you left the farm last night."

Johnnie gave a skewed smile. "It seems like everyone

except Dickie knows that secret, but I didn't go to Perth and kill Louisa."

Biddy looked at her brother for a long time, not knowing whether to believe him or not. Finally she turned back to her vegetables and said, "I pray to God that that's the truth."

6

Maxwell Douglas-Forbes was just entering his office on Charlotte Street in Perth when his law clerk came up to him. "Max, there's a James Duff on the line. He says he knew your father and that they had worked on several cases together. He asked if you could speak to him privately."

"Did he say what it was about?"

"He said it had to do with the Tay murder."

"Ah," Max said. "The case seems quite open and shut. It's undoubtedly the husband. I wonder what James Duff wants. I don't recall the name."

"He also said he was Lord Tay's uncle."

Max had been keen to dismiss James Duff until he heard this piece of news. "Is he still on the line?"

"Yes, I believe so. I told him you were coming in, and he said he would wait."

Max shed his mackintosh and went into his office, shutting the door.

"Douglas-Forbes here," he said. "Is that you, Mr Duff?"

Max listened to James Duff's request. Max was well enough known in the legal profession and sufficiently well off financially that he now only accepted cases that interested him. The Earl of Tay's case seemed ordinary enough, husband kills estranged wife, probably in a fit of anger. Max was not impressed by titles; he had seen the underside of too many

54

members of the gentry and aristocracy, and he had never heard of the Earl of Tay or the Duffs before. But, unbeknownst to Max, James Duff knew how to be persuasive, a trait he had passed on to his daughter, and finally Max agreed to see him.

"I'm going to plead age," James Duff said in response, "and send another member of the family, my daughter, who is John Tay's cousin and a trained investigator. I think she will be more eloquent than me in winning you over."

Max did not know what to expect from James Duff's daughter. An hour after he hung up the phone, his clerk announced that there was a Ms Elspeth Duff to see him. Before Elspeth walked into his chambers, he envisioned her as being a typical Scotswoman of middle age and good breeding, who perhaps dabbled a bit in village crime. He did not expect the urbane and handsome woman who walked in.

Crossing the room, Elspeth walked, as she always did, with grace and confidence, and put out her hand. Her expression radiated assurance, and her clothes and jewellery showed excellent but restrained taste.

"Mrs Duff, is it?" Max asked, noting her rings.

"If we must be formal, then I prefer Ms, without acknowledgment of any marital status." Max could hardly resist her provoking smile.

After they were seated, he said, "I take few new clients these days, but your father said you would convince me to take on Lord Tay."

"I hope you will," she said. "Johnnie will need a well-respected lawyer in Perth. I understand you are such a person."

"Is he guilty of killing his wife?"

"I don't know. I hope not. Either way, we want the best legal counsel for him."

"You are blunt, Ms Duff."

"Do I have any other choice?" she said.

"My fees are high," he said, but seeing her wardrobe, he thought this might not make a difference.

"I suspected they might be," she said. "Will twenty thousand pounds do as a start? I have just transferred that amount into my account at the Royal Bank of Scotland, and I can write out a cheque for you if you wish."

"Are you convinced I'll take the case?"

"No," she said, "but if you do, there's a great deal more to it than simple strangulation."

"You intrigue me," he said.

"I'm trying to," Elspeth countered.

Max laughed. He thought Elspeth was outspoken but found her determination compelling. He also liked her for the intelligence he saw in her eyes, something he could say of very few of his clients. He made an instant decision, one he would never regret, as it would change his life. "All right, then, I'll take Lord Tay on as my client because you have persuaded me I should."

"Then let me tell you who I am," Elspeth said, "because you will find that I poke my nose into your case far more often than most clients probably do." She told him of her law tripos at Cambridge, her former association with Scotland Yard, and her current position with the Kennington hotel chain. She did not mention her husband or his rank, but Max suspected he must be a man of some distinction. Elspeth wrote out the cheque and put in on his desk.

"Now can we begin?" she asked.

As Max had not expected to accept Johnnie Tay's case, he had not cleared his calendar but decided he would do so after completing some pressing business at hand.

"Will you come back at half past four and bring Lord Tay with you?" he asked. "We can discuss the details then."

*

Elspeth had several hours to fill before her forthcoming appointment with Max, and she decided in the interim to visit the scene of the crime. She probably would not be able to cross the police barrier, but she expected the press had set up some sort of reconnaissance, and they might prove to be useful.

Johnnie Tay had done well in business, despite his lack of success with women. He had entered the computer age when it was still young and had a core of young, loyal technical staff who relished working from their own homes, thus saving Johnnie a large degree of overhead. He had not been lured by the dot-com boom or not been caught in its bust, because he had concentrated on developing useful software in a niche market. On the proceeds of his business, he had been able to buy a home in a fashionable cul-de-sac east of the Tay River in Perth several years after he was married to his second wife, Helen, and he had continued to live there until filing papers for divorce against Louisa the year before.

Elspeth had only once visited Johnnie's home and then briefly, as she had lived in London or abroad much of her life since the purchase of the house. Rather than losing the parking spot where she had left Biddy's Land Rover near Maxwell Douglas-Forbes office, she found a taxi and gave the address. She asked to be set down several streets away from the crime scene, asked the taxi to wait and walked the rest of the way.

As she expected, the police had set up a press area and several reporters and cameramen were sitting languidly on camp chairs. In her job at the Kennington hotels, Elspeth was used to dealing with the media and approached a woman who was dressed in a business suit. Elspeth gleaned correctly that she was a television reporter.

"Is this where the murder took place?" Elspeth asked as if she did not know.

"Yes, worse luck," the woman said. "She was strangled by all accounts by her husband. Poor thing. Husbands can be brutal. Haven't you heard about it?"

"Vaguely," Elspeth lied. "I don't know the details of the murder."

"They're not very pretty. Yesterday the police were called in and discovered the countess strangled with the curtain cord twisted around her neck. I understand from interviewing the domestic who found her that the place was roughed up a bit. Furniture had been knocked over, as if there'd been a struggle before he strangled her, but there was no sign of forced entry."

"Quite dreadful," Elspeth said. "I met her once or twice, but I didn't know her well enough to call her a friend."

"It shows that the aristocracy are no different from the rest of us, I suppose. Title and money are no good to you after you're murdered," the photographer beside the woman said.

"Do you really think her husband guilty?" Elspeth asked. "He hasn't been arrested, has he?" Elspeth knew the answer to her question but did not let the reporter know this.

"I don't think so but almost assuredly he's guilty. An open and shut case," the photographer said.

"Who else could it be?" another reporter said.

Who else, indeed? Whoever it is, I will find him, Elspeth

thought. The murder was not the sort of crime a woman would have committed. Yet Elspeth was concerned at the media's certainty that Johnnie was at fault. His innocence would make the murder seem sordid rather than sensational, and the press, after all, had to do their jobs.

Having surveyed the site of the murder scene, next Elspeth went round to the guest quarters where Johnnie had been living. She gave the taxi the address but, as she paid the fare, she realised Johnnie's temporary flat was close to his erstwhile home. Fortunately the media did not yet seem to have found their way to the flat. She did not know the owners of the main house but decided she would knock anyway. A woman about Elspeth's age answered the door and looked enquiringly at Elspeth, seeming to recognise her, but then not.

"I'm Elspeth Duff," she said to the woman, "Johnnie's cousin."

"I thought you looked familiar, but, of course, you look like Biddy. So far, we have been spared the press, although every time I open the door, I expect them. Do come in. May I offer you a cup of tea? I was just sitting down to one. My name is Marly Beaufort."

"Mrs Beaufort . . ." Elspeth began.

"Marly, please."

"Then call me Elspeth. I can't stay but a moment as I have an appointment with Johnnie's lawyer, but I did want to see where he has been living."

"You're Johnnie's cousin who is the detective, aren't you?" Marly asked.

"Not exactly a detective. I work in security for the Kennington hotels."

"Very posh," Marly said, raising her eyebrows. "Didn't

Johnnie go out to Malta about a year ago to your wedding?"

Elspeth smiled. "It seems my past is known. He did."

"And to your son's wedding in San Francisco last week. My goodness, you do seem to have a lot of weddings in your family."

"Only two," Elspeth said, grinning now. Marly, since I have been accused of being a detective, may I ask you several questions?"

"Certainly."

"Was Johnnie here the night before last?"

"The night of the murder, you mean?"

Elspeth nodded.

"It is quite impossible to say. Roger, my husband, and I had gone out to dinner. The lights were on in his flat when we returned, but the curtains were drawn. It must have been close to midnight as it was just getting dark."

"Was his car here?"

"Yes, but that was not unusual. Parking has become so dreadful in Perth that we all have begun to use taxis, or we walk if it is close enough."

Elspeth calculated the distance from the Beaufort's home to the spot where Louisa had been murdered and thought it an easy walk. It had only been a three-minute taxi ride and perhaps would be a fifteen-minute walk at most.

"Did the police come looking for Johnnie yesterday?"

"No. That's odd, isn't it? You would have thought they would have come here first."

"It would have been unless they didn't know Johnnie was living here. May I ask a favour?"

"Of course."

"Will you not tell anyone about Johnnie's car unless, of

60

course, it's the police. Rumours are already abounding that Johnnie murdered Louisa, and I'm sure you don't want to add fuel to the fire."

"Certainly not. Where is Johnnie now?"

"He's at Tay Farm with Biddy, but the police want to question him tomorrow."

"Do you think he's innocent? Things weren't particularly cordial between Louisa and Johnnie in the end."

"I'm going to do everything I can to prove him innocent. May I come back to you at some point and talk to you further, when I have more time?"

"Certainly. Johnnie has spoken of you and your husband so often. I feel as if we know you. Will your husband be with you? I'd like to meet him."

"Richard? I'll have to ask him."

*

Elspeth reached Max's office just before their appointment because she had decided to walk from the Beaumont's to his office and had stopped for lunch. Max was waiting for her, but Johnnie had not yet arrived.

"I checked on you, you know," he said.

"I would've been disappointed if you hadn't," she acknowledged.

"Ms Duff . . ."

"If we are to work together, you must call me Elspeth."

"Max," he replied. "I also contacted the police and asked that they delay questioning Johnnie until Monday, because I'm representing him and needed time to review the case."

"Am I to assume that you don't work at the weekend?"

"I work when I like," Max said. "My wife died two years ago, and I often find working weekends fills the void. You seem anxious to be involved as well."

"Absolutely."

"I spoke with a Ms Pamela Crumm at the Kennington Organisation in London. She verified your employment, spoke highly of your capabilities and told me you were not expected back at work in London until the twenty-sixth of this month. She also said that if she could be of any help, I should call her. She obviously had read the morning press and knew some of the reported details of the case."

Elspeth laughed. "Pamela has a strange fascination with the tabloid press."

Max turned to his desk and picked up a copy of *The Times*. "Unfortunately the news made it into the more serious press, although it appeared at the bottom of page twelve and didn't speculate who murdered the countess."

Elspeth opened *The Times* and read the brief report. "I think we need to get to work," she said.

*

After receiving a phone call from Elspeth who briefed him on her talk with Maxwell Douglas-Forbes, QC, Johnnie walked across Charlotte Street with some trepidation. He was grateful that Elspeth had been able to persuade the lawyer to represent him. Johnnie knew Max Douglas-Forbes by reputation and had heard he had saved many clients from prison, but Johnnie saw no way out of his current predicament even with a clever lawyer. If he were indeed tried for the crime, the police would have gathered enough evidence to point towards his guilt. How like Louisa to get herself murdered just when he was about to get rid of her and marry Madeline. Madeline! He did not want her involved.

Perhaps Elspeth could find a way out of all this mess. He

had heard so much of her exploits over the last nine years with the Kennington Organisation, particularly about the case in Stresa, where his sister had aided Elspeth, and he admired Elspeth for her wit and intelligence. Could she use these talents to help him now?

He arrived late at Maxwell Douglas-Forbes's office, pleading that he could not find a place to park his car. When he entered the inner chambers, Max was talking to Elspeth, and she seemed relaxed and to be almost enjoying herself. Johnnie shook his head.

Max Douglas-Forbes was not what he expected. He was a tall man with a burly chest, penetrating eyes, a full head of greying hair, and a firm handshake. He looked Johnnie in the eye but revealed no hint of his feelings about the reason Johnnie was there, or his guilt or innocence.

Elspeth explained that she had convinced Max to take the case and to begin immediately. He had also agreed that she could work in tandem with him. Max's influence with the police had convinced them that Johnnie's questioning could be put off until the beginning of the week.

"Lord Tay," Max said, "I'm pleased to meet you. My wife knew your wife, Helen." Having made a personal connection, Max continued. "Your cousin has given me some of the details of the case, but I'll need to speak to you at length. I hope you're willing to answer some hard questions, because without them I can't credibly defend you. My aim will be to have you found innocent if and when the case comes to trial. Are you willing to co-operate with me?"

Johnnie cleared his throat and looked at Elspeth. She nodded as if asking him not to hold back. "I'll do everything needed to beat the police accusations, if I can," he said

"I want you here in the morning after I go to fetch the police report, so that you can answer my questions. I want to be thoroughly briefed before the police see you next."

"Max will go with you to the police station on Monday," Elspeth added. "He has been able to delay your questioning until then."

So it is 'Max' already, Johnnie thought.

"Good," Max said. "At first I told Elspeth I won't be available this weekend, but I've decided your case supersedes a round of golf."

*

Elspeth did not return to the farm until well after six, but she had called ahead to say she was driving over to Loch Rannoch to her parents' home to tell her father the news about Max and about the delay in Johnnie's interview with the police. Before her return Richard and Biddy sat in the morning room, lingering over a single malt together.

"Dickie," Biddy said, "do you think 'Peth can clear Johnnie of suspicion?"

He savoured the peaty taste of his drink, always finding it purer in Scotland than other parts of the world, and looked at Biddy over the rim of his glass. He had spent little time alone with her over his long acquaintance with Elspeth's family, but as he sat there with her, he marvelled at how closely she resembled Elspeth, at least physically, but how much softer she was both in personality and appearance. He looked at her and knew that this softness made her the prettier of the two cousins, despite her lack of attention to her clothes or her hair, but Richard loved Elspeth's edginess and fierceness and never regretted his choice between the two cousins. He also knew that Biddy was Elspeth's closest confidant in matters involving the heart.

"Biddy, we know Elspeth fights her own demons that have nothing to do with anything but her own doubts about herself. Perhaps we are the only two people in the world who are aware of that. I fear this matter with Johnnie will take her back to her own earlier mistakes, which I had hoped she had put aside with our marriage. She will act intrepidly to clear Johnnie, but she'll take much of the pain of it silently into herself. We must help her with this because she won't speak of it, even to me. Right now, I suspect, when she was in Perth she was in full professional mode, but when she comes back here, she could realise how vulnerable Johnnie is."

They heard the Land Rover come into the drive, and they both rose and went outside.

Elspeth emerged from the car and said, "This is a wretched vehicle to drive, Biddy. Have you ever considered a new one?"

Richard and Biddy laughed. Elspeth was hardly the suffering heroine.

The three of them settled in by the fire, and Elspeth told them about what she had learned, including her recruitment of Max Douglas-Forbes, her conversations with the reporters at Johnnie's home, and her talk with Marly Beaufort.

Richard looked at his wife and could sense her tenseness. "Elspeth," he asked, "what are you trying to discover?"

"Hopefully Johnnie's innocence, but beyond that, the truth."

"Do you think them mutually exclusive?" Biddy asked.

"I wish I could be sure," Elspeth said, "but I like Maxwell Douglas-Forbes, and I think he'll be our best ally. He seems to have some sway with the police, as he spoke directly to the chief superintendent about Johnnie. I'm going back to Perth in the morning to work with Max. He said he might have a copy of the latest police reports by then. He wants to question Johnnie after he reads them. I suggest he could come out to the farm this weekend for a meal, so that he could meet us all and speak with Johnnie on his own turf. I'll ask him when I see him tomorrow."

"I could have one of the lambs slaughtered for Sunday lunch," she said with the nonchalance of a farmer.

*

Dinner that evening was a strained affair. With Elspeth's help, Biddy had made a leek and cheese flan using the vegetables from her garden. They left it in the oven too long and the cheese top was scorched because they forgot their dinner preparations as they spoke to each other about Johnnie and Louisa.

"Maybe you can give me some information, Biddy. Do you know why Johnnie married Louisa? I would have thought he had better judgment," Elspeth said.

Biddy shook her head. "After Helen left, he drank too much, and a year later started associating with a rather swinging crowd. Odd for a man in his late fifties, don't you think, or is it? I expect Louisa made him feel younger and probably in her common way made him feel attractive. She had a great deal to gain by marrying him, and I expect he still was thinking about producing an heir. Her young age may have appealed to him."

"What I don't understand," Elspeth said, "is Johnnie saying, not once but several times, that Louisa wasn't 'quite monogamous'. Do you know if she really cheated on him? It sounded as if he tolerated it. Was it something the crowd he

66

got into did as a matter of course? Such things weren't unusual in Hollywood and, of course in the hotel industry we turn a blind eye when it's tactful. Am I too naïve in thinking Scotland might be a bit more conservative?"

Biddy laughed. "You should come home more often, 'Peth. Although I hardly condone these things myself, things have changed since we were young, and many people are more open about their affairs."

"But if Johnnie really did want an heir, don't you think he would prefer one whose upbringing was better?" Elspeth asked. "I think that would matter. Besides, how long were Johnnie and Louisa married before they split up? Three years? And no child?"

"Perhaps she was too selfish to want one," Biddy suggested. "Her current pregnancy can't have been unplanned."

"You know about the pregnancy?"

"Everyone in Britain will soon, won't they?" Biddy said, pain crossing her face. "I'm certain the gutter press will make much of it."

"As yet I can't figure out why would she get pregnant after their separation? Do you think she did it purposely to make it appear that Johnnie was the father? For a hold on him? To fend off the divorce?"

"Probably so he won't marry Madeline," Biddy said. "I suppose Johnnie has told you about her?"

Elspeth was surprised. "I thought he hadn't said anything to you about her."

"He didn't need to. It was apparent something had changed in Johnnie's life about a year ago, and I know him well enough that I only needed to poke round to know what had caused it. I think his love for her is genuine, more so than any of the others. She is divorcing her husband, I think because of Johnnie."

Elspeth considered Johnnie's relationship with Madeline MacNaughton and their discretion when meeting. Discreet enough? Certainly not enough to hide it from Biddy. Lovers have a way of thinking they are being circumspect when in actual fact they are being blatantly obvious. She knew that from her work at the Kennington hotels, but the Scottish Highlands certainly offered more places to hide an affair than at a hotel. Still Richard had almost immediately supposed that Johnnie was involved with another woman, and Biddy knew it for a fact. For Johnnie's sake, Elspeth knew she would try to protect Madeline, but wondered if she would be able to.

The acrid smells of burning cheese from the oven broke through their conversation.

No one commented on the burnt flan at dinner, and they all discreetly scraped the char from their portions of the pie. Conversation was desultory, and no one addressed the topic of the murder or Maxwell Douglas-Forbes.

Elspeth could bear it no longer. "We need to prepare for the press," she finally said. "They will come, you know, once the first reporter reads the police reports."

"Why would they come here?" Biddy asked.

"In search of the Earl of Tay, estranged from his murdered wife," she said gravely. *"The Scottish Sun* and the *News of the World* can hardly ignore such a banner event when Scottish nobility are involved. Otherwise it might have gone unnoticed as just another sordid crime in a small city in Scotland." Elspeth hoped she had kept the exasperation out of her voice, but she feared she had not been successful, as all the people in the room were well aware of her thoughts on the nobility. "They may come as early as tonight, as the sun won't set for another several hours, and they won't have any trouble navigating the roads, narrow as they are."

"How could they find me?" Johnnie asked.

"After you moved out of the house in Perth, where did you list your permanent address?" Elspeth asked.

Johnnie swallowed a piece of the burnt flan with a gulp.

"Here?" Elspeth guessed.

He nodded.

"Then they won't be long."

Later, when Elspeth and Richard had retreated to their bedroom, she said, "Dickie, I don't think this is going to be easy, and despite Biddy's hopes, I'm not sure Johnnie can be proved innocent."

"Why is that?" he asked.

"There are too many factors working against him. Louisa's pregnancy, particularly if it is real, poses two problems. If the child was Johnnie's, he could be accused of spousal rape as well as double murder. If the child wasn't, this would give Johnnie every reason to murder Louisa in pique."

Richard took Elspeth into his arms. "Will you tell me who the other woman is?"

Elspeth leaned her head against Richard's chest. "I think I must. Johnnie told me and Biddy confirmed it as we were making dinner. Johnnie wants to protect her. Her name is Madeline MacNaughton."

"Is he really serious about this Madeline?"

"Biddy says so, more so than any of the others. Her

existence, if known, can only further damage Johnnie's case. Biddy says Madeline is in the middle of a divorce as well. Being the other woman in a murder trial could hardly help her there."

"What a tangle," he said.

"It is," Elspeth said. "For all of us."

7

Max was waiting for Elspeth when she arrived at the appointed hour with Richard in tow. Having risen early and getting to his chambers by seven, Max was able to review the morning press. That Friday afternoon he had put in a call to police headquarters to see if he could obtain a copy of the police reports on Louisa's murder. The police honoured his request and would have them ready for him at nine in the morning. He said he would collect them personally.

"May I present my husband?" Elspeth said as she entered. "Richard Munro, Maxwell Douglas-Forbes. Richard is acting as my chauffeur, and I also wanted Richard to meet you, as he is one of Johnnie's oldest friends."

Max took Richard's hand firmly. They were of equal height, but Max was hefty where Richard was slender. Max worked out vigorously to keep his weight in check, but he was heavy-boned, and had large hands which although carefully manicured gave the impression of physical strength.

Richard returned the handshake. "I hear you have been brave enough not only to take on Johnnie's case but my wife as well," he said with a grin. "You'll find her an indefatigable ally. Both of us want to see Johnnie cleared of any wrongdoing."

Max, whose ability to quickly assess people seldom proved wrong, was surprised by Richard Munro. He had not

71

envisioned Elspeth's husband, but, if he had any mental picture, it would not have been of Richard, but rather someone of less imposing stature and a more compliant nature. Richard was undoubtedly a man accustomed to his own authority, aristocratic, correct, and conveying the confidence of those who were accustomed to being in command. On first acquaintance he liked Richard but tacitly wondered about his relationship with Elspeth. They both appeared to have strong minds.

"I'll do my best to defend Lord Tay," Max assured him. "Will you be staying on with Elspeth at Tay Farm after the weekend?"

"Until Thursday when I need to return to Malta. Elspeth and I had originally planned a holiday together in California after her son's wedding in San Francisco recently. We hadn't expected to be in Scotland."

"Malta?" Max asked.

"I'm in the diplomatic service there," Richard said, not elaborating.

Max appealed to Elspeth. "Explain something to me. If you had not planned to be in Scotland, what brought you here?"

"Johnnie asked me to come because he was concerned that his wife was demanding possession of Tay Farm in the divorce settlement."

"Is that important enough for you to change your plans?" This seemed odd to Max.

"Max, please understand that I come from a small and close-knit family. Johnnie and his sister, Biddy, are like a brother and a sister to me, although they are my first cousins. Biddy, Lady Elisabeth Baillie Shaw, Johnnie's sister, lives at

Tay Farm and runs it on a day-to-day basis. It's the centre of her life now that her husband is dead. I'd always thought the land was somehow entailed to the Tay earldom although Lady Elisabeth manages the farm. I need to find out more of the details, but my father, with whom you have spoken, has already offered his assistance. He has served as solicitor to the Tay family ever since he married my mother sixty years ago."

"Do you know who Louisa's solicitor was in the divorce?"

"No, you will have to ask Johnnie."

"And his?"

"I also have no idea. We hadn't got that far in our discussions."

"What have the two of you discussed?" Max asked, remembering Elspeth's initial statement that the case involved more that an estranged husband killing his wife. "If I'm to represent Lord Tay satisfactorily, I'll need to know as much as possible about him, whether it is pretty or not."

"I suspect I'll have to admit all I know," Elspeth said with a smile, "ugly though it may be. His wife, Louisa, told him she was pregnant. Johnnie asked me to find out if she was. I felt it would put a different disposition on the divorce and on the nature of the farm's ownership."

Now Max was intrigued, not only by the new information but also by Elspeth's involvement in it. "Was she pregnant?"

"I think the postmortem will tell us for certain."

"Could Lord Tay have been the father?"

"There is a chance he might have been, but I don't think so."

"What makes you think not?" Elspeth glanced over at Richard, and Max noted that he scrupulously looked away. "If

73

we are to be true allies, you must tell me why you think not," Max added.

Elspeth took in her breath. "I took Louisa to lunch at the Kennington hotel in Edinburgh and gave her food and wine that no woman in her first trimester could have tolerated," Elspeth confessed.

"I see," he said, trying to suppress a grin at Elspeth's tactics. "Your method seems a trifle unconventional. You said in the first trimester. Why?" Max could see he had hit a nerve in Elspeth. "It won't do any good you not telling me."

He watched Elspeth consider her response, which seemed to disquiet her. "Johnnie slept with Louisa about two or three months ago. Just once. He said she provoked him into it."

"So you gave her food which would sicken a woman two or three months into her pregnancy," Max suggested. He remembered his wife's reactions during the first three months of her pregnancies with their two sons.

"It seemed a good idea at the time," Elspeth admitted. "I didn't know what would happen later."

"Did you tell Lord Tay about the lunch?"

"Yes, he was at the farm when I returned from Edinburgh. We talked immediately after I returned."

"Who was staying at the farm?"

"Me, Johnnie, his sister, and Richard."

"Were you all there the night Louisa was killed?" Max asked, watching Elspeth carefully. If he was going to trust her, he wanted her to tell the truth. He sensed she was debating whether or not she should.

"On the night of the murder we all went to bed about ten o'clock, I think," Elspeth said, and then paused, "but Johnnie went out later. I don't know at what time he returned, but he had breakfast with us the next morning."

"Did he give any explanation as to his whereabouts?"

"At the time no one thought to ask, as there seemed nothing significant about it."

Max heard hesitation in Elspeth's reply but let it pass, although he suspected she had told only part of the truth, and her answer was evasive.

"Yes, of course," he said. "Can you corroborate this, Mr Munro?" Because of Richard's silence throughout Max's questioning of Elspeth, he seemed startled when Max directed his questioning away from his wife.

"All except for Johnnie's leaving. I slept quite soundly through the night."

"Did you see Lord Tay the next morning?"

"Yes, he and I came down to the kitchen before Biddy and Elspeth, and we were hunting for the ingredients for breakfast. We'd even started cooking the bacon."

"When you were doing so, what sort of things were you discussing?"

"Other than the breakfast preparations, his business mainly. He keeps me current of the world of computer software, but half the time I haven't a clue what he's talking about. We also talked about my new boat."

"Did you talk about anything personal, his wife, his divorce, or anything related to them?" Max asked.

"No, I don't remember that we did. I leave that sort of thing to Elspeth. She's quite good at finding solutions to sticky problems," he replied. Max believed him.

"You said that you and Lord Tay are old friends. How long have you known each other?"

"Forty some years. We were at Oxford together and I

spent two summers at Tay Farm then. We've been friends ever since."

"Did you meet your wife during those summers?"

"Yes."

"Then you have been married a very long time."

"No," Richard said with a shy grin. "We were married only a year ago."

Max was puzzled but since Elspeth and Richard's marriage were of no importance at the moment, Max went back to the subject of Johnnie.

"Was Louisa his second wife?" he asked Richard. Max knew Johnnie had been married before.

"No, his third. His first wife died in childbirth; his second divorced him."

"Do you know how long Lord Tay and Louisa were married?"

"About three years," Richard said. "They didn't have a family wedding, and we weren't invited."

"Did you attend the others?"

"Yes, both. I was his best man at the first and was on home leave when my first wife and I attended the second."

Max wanted to pursue this topic but decided to let it wait. He turned back to Elspeth. "Does Lord Tay have any living children?"

Elspeth shook her head.

"Who is heir to the title then?"

"Biddy's, Lady Elisabeth's, older son, Charles Baillie Shaw through the female line."

"Does he live here in Scotland?"

"No, he currently lives in New York. He is a correspondent for *The Financial Times* and is assigned all over the world. Right now he is covering the United Nations."

"Would he have any interest in unseating his uncle for the title?"

"Charlie? None at all. Like many of us in the family, he deplores the use of titles, and he's liberal in his thinking despite his employer. I think he would be delighted if Johnnie had an heir and took the onus of the inheritance off him. He simply likes being 'Mr Baillie Shaw 'or 'Charlie', not even 'Charles'."

Max looked at his wristwatch. "I told them we would be at the police station at nine to pick up the police reports. Richard, may I call you Richard, do you mind waiting here? I'd like to take Elspeth with me."

Richard nodded his consent and was obviously glad to turn the proceedings over to his wife.

As they walked to the police station, Max said, "Sorry to have grilled the two of you so much in there. It's a litmus test I use with new clients, to test their honesty. This isn't easy for you, is it?"

"No," she admitted, "but I did tell you the truth."

"Most of it, except where Lord Tay went the night of the murder. That, Elspeth, is the first dishonest thing you have said to me, or rather it wasn't dishonest as much as evasive."

"I think you should ask Johnnie, not me. It must be his decision to tell you," she said, her head held high.

"It's important so it could give Lord Tay an alibi, should the police decide to arrest him."

"If they do arrest Johnnie," she asked, "how long will it take before he comes to trial?" Max suspected she was avoiding his line of questioning.

"It depends how quickly the Crown can make their case

or how quickly we can irrefutably prove his innocence to such a degree that the Crown will drop the case altogether."

"I prefer the second route," she said.

"We all do. But from what you and Richard have just told me, Lord Tay's innocence will be hard to establish. The procurator fiscal is less tractable than a jury. Do you have any ideas as to how we might proceed?"

"I'll bow to your expertise, but also ask that you give me some leeway to conduct my own investigation."

"Is this why Richard said I was brave to take you on?"

Elspeth laughed. "Unfortunately I have dragged him into several incidents at the Kennington hotels where he was sometimes endangered or I was, and put him in situations where he had to rescue me. Once he did save my life when I was coshed over the head and another time when I was almost strangled. I suspect he would prefer me to find a more sedate profession."

"Such as being his wife? I assume that you don't live together all the time."

"We make up for the lack of it when we are together," Elspeth said with a laugh. "When I lived in America, they called it 'quality time'."

Max hid his secret admiration of a woman of such spirit and a man who was willing to put up with it. He personally preferred a gentler type.

Maxwell Douglas-Forbes's reception at the police station was cordial. The constable on duty at the desk greeted him by name, and an inspector came out from his office, a folder in hand, explaining that DI Kennedy was away for the day but had left the report for Max.

"Can you tell me the gist of the report?" Max asked.

The inspector complied. "Lady Tay's housekeeper found her body on Friday morning and called 9-9-9. When we arrived at her home, we found that the countess had been strangled by one of the cords that held back a curtain in the drawing room. We still don't have the results of the postmortem, which I expect this afternoon, but DI Kennedy talked to the pathologist, who speculated that the death took place between midnight and two o'clock in the morning."

"Are there photographs of the crime scene?" Max asked.

"Yes, but you'll have to ask the procurator fiscal for them," the inspector replied.

"Who has been assigned?" Max asked.

"Adair Gordon."

"Good. I've worked with him before." Max did not add that only once had Adair bettered him in court, a fact he would tell Elspeth later.

"Will I be able to see the crime scene?" Max asked.

"Again, ask Mr Gordon,"

"I will," Max said. "Thank you for the report."

As they walked back to Max's offices, Max turned to Elspeth.

"Gordon's a conscientious chap but not a brilliant one. We're lucky in that. He'll investigate the obvious, probably finding Lord Tay the most likely suspect, but he is also honest and cooperative, and I think won't withhold evidence which could help our case. We need to strategise as to what we want from him."

"Why did you take me to the police station with you, Max?" Elspeth asked.

He was not surprised by her question. "I want them to

know that we are working together. I think in the coming days I am definitely going to need your help."

He watched her raise a carefully shaped eyebrow at him and knew then that he not only liked but also trusted her.

When Max and Elspeth arrived back at Charlotte Street, Johnnie was waiting in Max's chambers. He looked strained and as if he had not slept well. Max shook Johnnie's hand. "Lord Tay, I have assured your cousin that I'll do all I can for you, but you must answer my questions truthfully. Our conversation here is privileged. I've asked Elspeth to be present, but of course you can talk to me alone if you wish."

Johnnie looked at Elspeth and a flicker of a smile appeared. "He wants me to trust you, 'Peth. Can I?"

Elspeth was glad to see some life come into in Johnnie's eyes, and said, "Of course you can, but trust him too, Johnnie—completely. It's the only way we'll be able to beat this."

He threw a brief look of defiance at her. Elspeth could not tell if Max had seen it, but she was beginning to understand that he did not miss much.

"Lord Tay, are you aware fully of the crime with which you may be charged?"

"That I murdered Louisa. I owe someone a great favour for doing so, but I didn't kill her."

"Quite so," Max said. "Will you tell me why someone did you such a great favour?"

"Louisa was a very selfish woman. When I asked for the divorce, at first she was amenable but then hired one of the most disreputable solicitors in Perth to represent her. Together they planned to take everything they could get, including Tay

Farm, which is mine by grant. Truthfully it really is my sister Biddy's. Without the intervention of her and her late husband we would have gone into bankruptcy years ago."

"Who is Louisa's lawyer?"

"A sleazy character called Paul Hodges."

Max raised his eyebrows and nodded. "I grant you his practices have been questioned in the legal community before, but I didn't realise he took divorce cases. Usually he is involved in property development. By the way, what was the basis of your divorce?"

"Louisa slept around with just about any presentable man who would have her."

"Adultery?"

"Yes."

"When did you become aware of this behaviour?"

Johnnie pressed his lips together and said nothing.

Max repeated his question.

"I knew she had had multiple partners before I married her, but I thought our marriage would change that," Johnnie finally admitted.

"It didn't?"

"I thought so at first, but, frankly, no, our marriage seemed to have no effect. She was quite open about it and ridiculed me for suddenly becoming prudish."

"Lord Tay, if you knew this about the countess, why did you wait so long before filing for divorce?"

Elspeth sat as still as she could and waited for Johnnie's reply. She hoped he would be honest, but he was not.

"I'd become rather a laughingstock around Perth," he said.

"Enough to want to murder her?" Max asked. "If you

knew about her indiscretions before you married her, why the change?"

Elspeth discerned the sharpness of Max's questioning. She saw Johnnie floundering, but she did not come to his rescue.

Elspeth watched Max bait the trap. "Did you meet someone else, Lord Tay?"

Johnnie blanched. "No!" His protest was too emphatic.

"What's her name?"

"I won't have her dragged into this."

"You can tell me now or tell me later, but your denial just now was too thinly veiled for any jury member to feel sympathy for you. If I can get you to confess to another liaison on your part to me in less than a few seconds, the advocate depute at your trial will be able to do just as quickly. You make me certain that the charges of adultery could go both ways."

Johnnie put his head in his hands and sought advice from his cousin. "What am I to do, 'Peth?"

"Max is on our side, Johnnie. Tell him the truth."

"I won't have her harmed! I don't care if I hang."

Max said, "We haven't had hanging people in Britain for over forty years, but a life sentence is not a desirable alternative. Please be truthful with me. It's the only way I can help you."

"Have you told him, 'Peth?"

Elspeth shook her head. "I promised you I wouldn't tell anyone."

"Did you tell Dickie?"

"No, but he guessed. Biddy knows as well, but I don't know how."

"God! Are there no secrets anymore?" Johnnie cried. "Mr Douglas . . .?"

"Maxwell Douglas-Forbes. Call me Max. We'll be spending a great deal of time together until this problem gets resolved."

"May I see Elspeth alone?" Johnnie pleaded.

"If you wish. Elspeth, I'll wait outside. Take your time."

*

Max left Johnnie and Elspeth in each other's company. When he was gone, Elspeth said, "How can I reach Madeline? She must be sick with worry, as she undoubtedly has seen the press and knows that you have become fodder for the tabloids."

"God!" Johnnie said again.

"The Almighty probably won't help, Johnnie, but maybe I can. You'll have to tell Max about Madeline eventually. Were you with her the night of the murder?"

Johnnie nodded. "Yes. I went to her flat outside Dundee. I left her before four, well in time to be back at the farm for breakfast. How did you know?"

"I couldn't sleep after we went upstairs. Dickie went out like a light, but I lay awake long afterwards. That's why I heard you leave."

Johnnie smiled for the first time. "You've never been an easy person, 'Peth, and I feared Dickie might not always find you as pliable as he once thought."

"Fortunately so far he has been completely loving," Elspeth said, raising her head in defiance. "but now we have to get you out of this mess."

"Do you think you can?"

"I'm not certain, but I'll do everything I possibly can.

Have you talked to her since last night?"

"We are seeing each other this afternoon."

"In Dundee or Perth?"

"Neither. It's too risky. She's in the midst of divorce proceedings, and her husband may have detectives following her. We usually meet in a deserted cottage once occupied by shepherds on Madeline's family land up above Strathtummel. It's near the public footpath from Loch Tummel to Blair Atholl, but out of view to walkers. You may remember it. Her family lives nearby, so she stays with them and can walk to the cottage easily. I can park in any number of places near there and join her. We have repaired the building just enough so it's dry and vaguely comfortable."

"Johnnie, is it wise to see Madeline now?"

"I must," he said. "I can't leave her with doubts about what is happening."

"Be careful."

"Believe me, I will be. Madeline is too precious to lose."

You are too, Elspeth thought, but did not say so.

8

Elspeth and Richard left Max's chambers at the same time as Johnnie, but they decided to have lunch before returning to the farm. Johnnie, anxious about his forthcoming tryst with Madeline, declined their invitation and drove back to Tay Farm alone. As he made his way down the drive, he realised he had not spent time alone at the farm for many years; in fact he had no memory of a time when he last had. When Biddy's husband, Ivor, had been alive, the farmhouse was always a hive of activity, Ivor being a passionate gentleman farmer and a community advocate for the farmers and farmland preservation around Loch Tay. Since his death, Biddy had led a quieter life, but her devotion to the farm and its stewardship kept her active most of the day and often into the evenings when an animal was ill, injured or giving birth, or when a neighbouring farmer's family needed help. Despite the well-bred and quiet upbringing that the eighth Countess of Tay had given her daughter, Biddy had a way of rattling around and making the farm seem a place alive to the world and exciting, even in its everyday activities and mundane chores.

Biddy was nowhere to be found, so he went in the kitchen to see about getting some lunch. He sat staring at the Aga, which offered him neither warmth nor a hot lunch, and finally rose in frustration, hoping to find some food in the refrigerator. He was interrupted in his search by the entrance of Robbie MacPherson, Biddy's farm manager. He was looking for Biddy.

Apprising him of her absence, Johnnie followed Robbie into the barn, where Tobias, the black and white collie who guarded the barn by night and took proprietary control of the sheep and farm animals by day, greeted the two men with enthusiasm. Robbie commented that Tobias probably could run most of the day-to-day activity on the farm by himself and found Lady Biddy a pleasant diversion who offered a hand to nuzzle or a pat on the head.

Robbie suddenly became shy, as if not wanting to ask him a question but needing to do so nonetheless.

"I'm sorry about Lady Tay," he said awkwardly. "Will you be all right?"

Robbie was younger than Johnnie, but the years of sun, wind, rain, and outdoor living made him seem ageless and gave Johnnie the sense that Robbie was somehow his keeper and protector, in the same way he cared for Biddy, deferentially but with a hidden sense of earthy superiority. Johnnie had been only semi-conscious of this before, but the bond that existed between their two families, centuries old, suddenly overwhelmed Johnnie. He suspected Biddy was well aware of the interrelationship and nurtured it. Despite what could happen in the investigation of Louisa's murder, Johnnie resolved to become more aware of his inheritance, with its interweaving of tradition, dependence, and loyalty.

Accustomed to a bachelor's life since leaving Louisa, Johnnie declined Robbie's offer of lunch with the MacPherson family, saying he would fend for himself. He returned to the farm's kitchen, which had suddenly taken on new and unexplored dimensions, human ones filled with history, life, and future promise. In the past, had he let down the Tay/Robertson family by being so disinterested in the farm? He had seldom reflected on his nobility before. At fourteen he had inherited the earldom from his father, who had died leaving his son nothing but a title and a rundown farm. The eighth countess had languished after that and only survived to see her daughter married to Ivor Baillie Shaw, which was a disappointment considering his family were untitled industrialists, and her son, childless and was attempting to make a life for himself in business without any early success. The distance of his parents had not bothered Johnnie, as it was all he had ever known, and he had kept his title, more for its social and commercial advantage than as the responsibility he owed it. How could he now take back his lack of caring for the farm? Trust Max, Elspeth had said. Yes, he would now, for his own sake as well as for Biddy's—and for Madeline's. Johnnie had no conception until now of the closeness of the families around Loch Tay, but he knew Biddy must, but it was his responsibility by right, a factor which had never occurred to him before.

Thoughts of Madeline washed over him, and he let out a sharp breath. In that instant he was flooded by his fear that he might be arrested for committing Louisa's murder, and his foolish presumption that what had existed between him and Madeline before the murder would not change. Even if Madeline did still love him, and she might not after reading the news of Louisa's murder, and even if she did agree to marry him in the end, nothing could ever be the same. There would no longer be the sublime stolen moments when they talked about their coming freedom, there would no longer be the untainted hope of life together, and there always would be the lingering echo of uncertainty, ever so faint, that Johnnie, if tried and the majority of the fifteen jurors considered the case 'not proven', rather than 'innocent' was somehow dangerous. Johnnie went towards Biddy's cupboard where she kept her best malt whisky and then turned away from it, as he knew it contained escape and not resolution. In the refrigerator he found some cheese, an apple, and some cider, which he took out and looked at wistfully, remembering the lavish meals at Peter's wedding in San Francisco.

As he was about to prepare this meagre fare, he was relieved when Jean MacPherson bustled in with freshly baked meat pies, a bottle of fresh milk, and assurances that it was no trouble to prepare lunch.

"May I say," said Jean," that it's sad news about Lady Tay, Lord Johnnie, although I never knew her."

Johnnie was not quite sure how to reply. He had no idea if the MacPhersons knew of his plans to divorce Louisa, but he suspected they might.

"It's difficult for all of us, I think, particularly my sister," he said, "since the farm means so much to her." He did not elaborate beyond that, but he knew that the MacPhersons had been loyal to the Earls of Tay since Culloden. In all that time they had respected their social boundaries, keeping to what they considered their place, even in the equalitarian society of modern times. He knew Biddy had often tried to break down this distinction, but the MacPhersons would not allow it. The Tay/Robertsons were aristocracy, and the MacPhersons were not despite their co-existence over the centuries. Johnnie also knew they would defend him to the death.

"There never was a better woman than Lady Biddy," Jean said, "and I'm not the only one around here to say that. You should come home more often, Lord Johnnie, and see what she means to us all."

Everything in Johnnie now wanted to, and he also wanted Jean and Robbie MacPherson to say the same about him in future.

Jean was more direct than her husband. "We're all behind you, you know."

"I'm beginning to understand that, Jean."

"Have you a good lawyer who can help you so they don't arrest you, like the papers say they might? Mr Duff must have found you one."

"My uncle and Elspeth assure me he is the best."

"Well, Miss Elspeth does seem to have come up right, although we all have worried about her. She became so glamorous after she went to England, but her life wasn't always what one might call usual. Imagine her marrying your friend Sir Richard after all that time. A true Scots gentleman. She should have done it forty years ago. Still I do like her children despite their Lowland father, who never wanted to come here and be with us. It must have saddened Miss Elspeth during all those years she was in America. I consider Miss Lizzie and Mr Peter are true Highlanders, even if they choose to live abroad."

Johnnie inwardly laughed that Jean considered Lizzie's English residence as being 'abroad', although Peter's home San Francisco undeniably was. He wondered what Jean would make of Lucy, Peter's new wife, whose family were probably distinguishing themselves as mandarins in the imperial courts of China when the Scots still wore poorly dyed saffron-coloured kilts, painted their face blue, and covertly worshipped the spirits of the hills and glens.

Jean set a place for Johnnie at the large table and busied herself about the kitchen. He offered Jean a place next to him, but she made excuses, which he expected were false. Johnnie realised that the MacPhersons were more a part of the farm than he was, and regret filled him. He had wasted so much time while he was away; how could he now make up for it?

9

The police arrested Johnnie Tay as he drove out from the farm on his way to see Madeline MacNaughton. They allowed him to return his car to the barn, but then handcuffed him, read him his rights, and bundled him into the backseat of the police car. Seeing the police action, Elspeth rushed from the house. She wondered how best to be discreet in her words to Johnnie but could only say quickly, "What time was your appointment today?" She tried to keep her voice neutral.

"Three-thirty," he said. "Can you go in my place?" Then he was thrust into the back seat of the police car.

Elspeth took out her mobile and rang Max. He promised to be at the police station when Johnnie arrived.

Elspeth then made an instant decision. She ran into the house, found Richard in the library and begged him to take her to Strathtummel. Explaining why, she found a pair of stout shoes under the coat rack and took a mackintosh that had been left there. They ran out to Johnnie's car, which still had its keys in the ignition, and soon were speeding along the narrow roads towards Loch Tummel.

It was drizzling when Elspeth finally made her way up to the cottage where Madeline and Johnnie held their trysts. Richard parked at the inn below the footpath, and Elspeth had scrambled her way up the slippery path, losing it briefly and then finding it again. She remembered the cottage from her childhood ramblings around the loch and was grateful her memory served her well. She saw the cottage over a crest of a hill and hidden from the path, as invisible as Johnnie had said.

Madeline was standing at the door of the cottage and looked up with obvious concern as Elspeth made her way down the slope.

As she approached the cottage, Elspeth was surprised by Madeline's appearance. She was slender, close to six feet tall, and had naturally black hair and deep green eyes that set off her fair skin. Her eyes stared warily at Elspeth under her dark lashes.

Elspeth considered the best way to approach her. Finally, she called out, "Madeline, I'm Elspeth Duff, Johnnie's cousin. He asked me to come."

Madeline tensed at Elspeth's approach. "Johnnie's spoken of you many times," Madeline said. "Why have you come here? Have they arrested him?"

Elspeth nodded. "Yes, they did, just as he was leaving Tay Farm to come here. He asked me to take his place. Please believe me, Madeline. I'm here for you both."

Tears filled Madeline's eyes, and she did not bother to wipe them as they slid down her cheeks.

"Johnnie said I should trust you. Isn't it strange? He said that long before this happened. I don't even remember in what context. He said you were the brains of the family."

"Harsh criticism in my day when I was at the Blair School for Girls," Elspeth countered. "We haven't much time, so I need to be direct with you. Madeline, Johnnie is in serious trouble. All the members of his family, myself included, are doing what we can to save him. As careful as you both thought you were being in not showing your closeness or revealing your relationship, your affair has come to the attention of a number of people. When I talked to Johnnie this morning, he asked me to keep you out of his current troubles, but I'm not certain I can do so even if you co-operate with me. I understand your own personal circumstances are complicated. Johnnie wants you to stay away so you don't get hurt, but, if I'm not mistaken, that's not in your nature."

"How can you know me so well in a few minute's acquaintance?" Madeline asked.

"It's part of my responsibility of my job to assess people quickly, and if that makes me too direct, please forgive me. You must not be offended by what I have to say, as there is little time, so I don't have the luxury of politeness. On my journey over from Loch Tay, I tried to consider what best to say to you, but I've come to the conclusion that there's only one question that is vital for you to answer. Do you really love Johnnie, or is this just a passing fling? I hope your answer will be honest. Nothing will help you and Johnnie but the truth." Elspeth hoped the straightforward approach would work with Madeline.

"Have you ever been certain you were in love?" Madeline asked.

Elspeth flushed. "Three times," she said, "and the first and second time I was wrong. The third time was with Richard, and that happened rather late in life."

"Richard?" Madeline seemed confused. "Oh, you mean Dickie Munro."

"Yes," Elspeth said, "with Dickie. Did Johnnie tell you this too?"

"He said he envied Dickie because he was so happy. He wanted us to be as happy as you two."

"I understand you are currently married."

"Yes, but in the process of divorce."

"Did you love your husband when you married him?"

"I thought so at the time. My mother expected me to marry in my early twenties, and I obliged her without considering an alternative. Darryl, my husband, isn't a bad person, but then Johnnie came into my life and that was it. I didn't know what real love was until I met him."

"Tell me how you met," Elspeth said.

"He hired our firm, Smith and Glass in Dundee. He wanted us to design a new advertising campaign for his software, and they assigned his account to me. He walked into the room, and I fell in love with him."

"On the spot?"

"Funny isn't it? Madeline MacNaughton, business professional, distinctly married, had an older man walk into her office and the earth shook. Did it happen that way with you and Dickie?"

"It took a bit longer," Elspeth said. She did not mention forty years.

"So the honest answer to your question is that this is not a passing affair; I hope it will be something permanent when we are both free."

"Good," Elspeth said. "If that's so, it makes it easier. How much are you willing to risk for Johnnie? Again, I need an honest reply."

"I expect you don't want me to say 'everything'."

Elspeth nodded. "Every person has ultimate limits. You're right, 'everything' isn't ever an option unless you are willing to die for a cause and sacrifice all those you love in the process. I hope we don't reach that point."

The rain had started in earnest, and they took refuge

inside the cottage, where there were a large bed with two pillows and a duvet thrown over it, a rough table, two chairs and a paraffin heater. Madeline found a match and lit the heater.

"It's not a very inviting place," Madeline said. "That's why Johnnie and I come here. No one else would want to. When we were together it doesn't matter where we are. I can make you a cup of tea if you like."

Elspeth accepted, and Madeline opened a tin box, took out two mugs and a packet of tea bags. She let the water run from the tap of an old sink, filled the kettle and put it on the top of the heater. Elspeth watched Madeline as she went about her preparations. She was so different from any of Johnnie's three wives. Kathleen was fair, witty, and fragile; Helen also fair but healthier and hardy; and one couldn't really tell about Louisa because all of her natural features had either been altered or embellished. Madeline appeared self-possessed, well spoken, and comfortable with herself. Elspeth felt instinctively that Madeline would say what she believed, but did she really know what that was? A less observant person than Elspeth might not have seen Madeline's face struggle with her replies.

Elspeth sat in one of the two chairs, and Madeline took the one opposite her. Both were silent for a moment while sipping their tea.

Elspeth said, "I wasn't sure exactly what I would say to you if I did find you, so forgive me if my thoughts develop as we speak. First of all, I need to know where you were the night Louisa was killed."

"At my flat outside Dundee."

"Yes, Johnnie said that. Can anyone corroborate that? Did

anyone see Johnnie there?"

"The housekeeper at the main house may have, but she's rather deaf and goes to bed early."

"What time did Johnnie arrive?

Madeline took a deep breath. Elspeth knew that Madeline was grappling with her answer.

"If it were at the time of the murder, it would give him an alibi, wouldn't it?"

"It might. Johnnie left Tay Farm before midnight. It was finally getting dark and I heard him go, but he was back for breakfast. If he was with you, he would have to pass through Perth to get there if he took the main roads, and he could have stopped to see Louisa either coming or going. It would have been different if Perth were not on the way, but of course it is, and you haven't answered my question yet."

"Johnnie was with me from about two in the morning until the first light came up in the sky, perhaps at half past three. We seldom met at my flat because we feared either Louisa or Darryl, my husband, would have a detective watching, but, because I hadn't seen Johnnie since before he went to San Francisco and I had to be late at a dinner with clients, we decided to risk it so that we could be together longer and in a more comfortable space."

Elspeth wasn't sure from Madeline's tone if she was telling the whole truth or not.

"No one saw you together?" she asked.

"Not that I know of."

"Please don't take offense at my next question. I have a reason for asking it. Have there been other men at your flat at night?"

"No! I love Johnnie. Why would there be other men?"

Elspeth wanted to find certainty in Madeline's answer but was not sure it was there. Elspeth knew the answer to her next question, but she purposely asked it. "How long does it take to drive from your flat to Loch Tay?"

"About an hour and a half, probably less. At this time of year, Johnnie would have made his return trip in the light, which would have made it faster. He drives like a maniac sometimes. I caution him all the time, but it doesn't do much good."

Elspeth wished she knew the exact time Louisa had been murdered and if it had been closer to summer's dusk or dawn.

"Madeline, you must think very carefully about this. If your involvement with Johnnie becomes known, you may have to testify if he is brought to trial. The media will not be gentle on you as the case has become sensationalised because of Johnnie's title, that cursed thing. You can come forward, or you can wait to see if the police or procurator fiscal discovers your affair with Johnnie. There's the slim possibility that your relationship with him will remain hidden, but I doubt it. You can admit your connection with him but you will have to come to your own judgement on that. I don't want to influence you in any way. I'm just sorry all this has happened. You don't have to tell me now what you decide to do. But I have another question. How do you and Johnnie normally communicate?"

"I use my office phone during the day to ring his office, so that it will appear like a business call."

"When did you and Johnnie set up your meeting the night of Louisa's death?"

"He rang me at the office just after he returned from San Francisco. I don't know from where, probably the airport in Edinburgh. He could have used his mobile."

"Which will be on his mobile bill and easily traceable, but it could have been business as you say."

Madeline looked down at her tea, which she had hardly touched. "How is he?"

"Johnnie? He looked scared when they arrested him. At this point there's so little we can do for him. We know so few of the facts of what happened the night Louisa was killed, and we need to know much more to clear Johnnie of the crime."

Madeline paled and fear filled her eyes. "Is there any chance he's guilty?"

"Unfortunately, a chance exists. There's also the possibility that he will be found guilty by the jury even if he is innocent. Even if under Scottish law his case is 'not proven', his life will never be the same again because he will always be suspected of the crime. Our family has hired one of the best solicitor advocates we can find, and I'm working with him. According to Max, Maxwell Douglas-Forbes, Johnnie's lawyer, I can meet Johnnie directly, as he is currently being held at the jail at the Perth police station until he is formally charged, which will probably be on Monday. Max said there is a chance he will be granted bail."

Madeline's grief shook her body. "What does one do in a murder case?" she asked. "Have you ever been involved in one before?"

"Unfortunately in several, and each one was different. Our best hope is that Johnnie is innocent and that the real murderer is found."

"You aren't convinced he is, are you, innocent I mean?" Madeline said.

Elspeth considered her answer carefully. "Johnnie has several compelling reasons to kill Louisa, and now that I have met you, there seems to be one more." Elspeth wondered if Johnnie had told Madeline about Louisa's threat that she was pregnant but chose to say nothing about it. "He may have been with you early Friday morning, but he still would have had time to kill Louisa."

"Does he say he's innocent?"

"He hasn't entered a plea as yet. Max will undoubtedly persuade him to plead innocent."

Madeline looked miserable. "Can you find out what really happened?" she begged.

"I'm going to try. I can't do any more than that. But right now the media are blowing any information they have out of proportion, as they so often seem to do. It sells papers and boosts ratings. I need hard facts, and we don't have them all. Max has a copy of the police reports and hopefully soon of the postmortem."

Elspeth realised how dispassionate she must sound. It was an old habit, making her mind dominate her heart when she could not deal with her own emotions. Richard had taken her to task for this often enough. Elspeth also knew that in Madeline's presence she could not emotionally succumb to her own fears for Johnnie's well-being and his possible guilt. She saw the distress in Madeline's eyes, and did what any mother instinctively would do. She rose, came to Madeline and drew her from her chair. Although Madeline stood a half a head taller than Elspeth, she took the younger woman in her arms and held her, as she would have done with own children. Elspeth could feel the tightness in Madeline's body and then slowly it relaxed into a bout of flowing tears.

"This can't be happening to us," Madeline finally said, fumbling in her pocket for a handkerchief. "What am I to do?"

"For the moment, stay away from Johnnie, which is what he asked, but let me keep in touch with you. Do you have a mobile?"

"Yes, but Johnnie always said the calls can be tracked."

"Usually, but not always. I may have access to a secure line we can use, but I'll have to get authorisation to use it. Give me your number, and I'll call you as soon as I know. Let's have a code. If you are unavailable when I call you, call me back and say something like, 'The courier should be there at . . .', and give me a time when we can talk. If you need to reach me and get my voicemail, leave me a message, saying you 'will be at the church at. . .' Courier and church are the key words. Can you remember that?"

Madeline had regained her composure and nodded. Elspeth made her repeat the directions.

Elspeth looked at her watch and it was now well past four. She felt Madeline was now feeling calmer than when they first met, and Elspeth said she must leave.

"You will let me know about Johnnie and how he is?"

"Of course," Elspeth said with a smile filled with tenderness. "We're all in this together, and we all want the same results."

"Tell him I love him and I'm putting my faith in you."

"I'll do all I can, but I think you already know that."

Madeline chose to stay at the cottage as Elspeth made her way up over the crest of the hill and back to the road below. It was still raining when Elspeth arrived at the bottom of the path. Her mackintosh was damp all the way through and the hat she had pulled from the pocket offered little respite. Relief flooded her as she saw Johnnie's large saloon car in the lay-by where he was parked. The motor was running, hopefully producing heat, and Richard sat at the steering wheel and appeared to have fallen asleep over a newspaper.

She slipped into the warm car and leaned over to kiss him in thanks.

"You are wet and clammy, Lady MacDuff," he said using his pet name for her. He touched his cheek where her icy lips had rested, "and definitely not looking up to your usual standards. I think it's time I took you back home to the farm."

She was shivering, not only from cold but from fear for Madeline and Johnnie. Richard must have felt that as he leaned over, took off her wet hat and kissed her properly, probably scandalising any passers-by. Elspeth did not care.

"Now tell me about Madeline," he said at last.

*

After Elspeth left, Madeline sat a long time staring at her half empty mug. What Elspeth had said had shaken her, not in the way Elspeth said it, which was direct and unemotional, but in her admission that she did not know if Johnnie was guilty or not. Madeline had met Johnnie only a year before but thought because of their intimacy she understood him completely. Elspeth had known Johnnie all her life, and, although she did not say so, she was not convinced of his innocence. What did Madeline really know about Johnnie? The rapture of their lovemaking, certainly, his humour and carefree spirit, the details of his business that he told her, and his closeness to his family particularly his sister, but had she really grasped all the workings of his mind? The one thing he seldom mentioned was his marriage to Louisa. He had told her his marriage had never been successful and that it was over, but little more. Until now Madeline had not needed more assurance than that. She was sure she knew Johnnie well enough to love him for the rest of her life, but before her conversation with Elspeth, she did not feel the need to understand all the complexities of Johnnie's past life.

Johnnie had spoken of Elspeth many times, but she was different from what Madeline had expected. She had expected Elspeth's intelligence and directness as Johnnie had warned her of that but had not expected Elspeth's grace, handsomeness, or final gesture of caring. She had supposed that Elspeth would take on the murder case, as she was a trained investigator, but had not considered that Elspeth might feel some personal vulnerability in doing so. Johnnie's vision of Elspeth must have come from a different time, probably from their childhood together. Johnnie had described the abandoned summers he had spent between terms at Oxford with his sombre friend Dickie Munroe and his tomboy cousin, Elspeth Duff. After the last half hour with Elspeth, Madeline could not imagine Elspeth other than the sophisticated, serious woman that she had become and wondered if Elspeth still had any of the fun in her that Johnnie had described.

More worrisome was Elspeth's warning that if Madeline's affair with Johnnie were discovered that she would become fodder for the press. A good portion of Madeline's initial fascination for Johnnie had been his joyous disregard for formality, despite his title. He had told her that he kept using it, over protestations from his cousin, because he thought it helped in business. Now the media's fascination with the nobility was blowing a sordid crime into a national scandal. She wanted to save Johnnie, but if she came forward, the cost to her family as well as to herself would be catastrophic. She would probably lose everything in her divorce, and, if Johnnie were convicted of the crime, she could lose him too. Madeline, despite her grief, was thankful that Elspeth had not advised her what to do. The decision needed to be hers alone. She did not know if the press or the police would find her, but she felt she could rely on Elspeth and Johnnie's other family members. For this she was grateful.

The rain had abated outside the window. Madeline turned off the paraffin heater, washed out the mugs under the cold-water tap, rinsed them with what was left of the hot water in the kettle, and slowly made her way back to her parents' home. When she arrived there, she controlled her tears, but she had not yet made up her mind as to what her best course of action would be, both for herself and for Johnnie.

*

The news of Johnnie's arrest for the murder of his wife was first made public over the late news on ITV. Madeline had gone to bed, but her mother and father always stayed up for the ten o'clock news.

"How ghastly," Alice MacNaughton said. "His sister and I were at school together. Do you think it is true?"

"I would trust the police, my dear," her husband said. "Even in these modern times they are careful with the nobility and wouldn't arrest one of its members without just cause. I always thought there was something a bit off with his family. Biddy Baillie Shaw seems quite stable, but don't I remember that her cousin got involved in a murder when she was at Cambridge and then eloped to Hollywood? Not quite acceptable behaviour."

"Yes, Elspeth Duff. Always the brainy one but often off in the clouds somewhere. I read recently in *The Times* she has married Richard Munroe, who used to spend summers here with Johnnie Tay when they were at Oxford. He's ambassador in some extraordinary place like the Crimea and has been knighted. They were married out there."

Malta and Yalta are often confused in the minds of the non-travelling public.

10

Johnnie Tay sat on the blue plastic mattress spread on the low concrete bench in his cell and stared at the steel toilet. The view didn't offer him either pleasure or diversion. They had given him a rough blanket and a pillow in exchange for his watch, signet ring, wallet, belt, shoes and the contents of his pockets. They had allowed him to keep his reading glasses but had not given him anything to read. He stared at his hands and abstractly wondered why they looked so much more veined than they had the day before. Would they hang him? No, Max said they didn't do that anymore. Johnnie had no way to prove his innocence without involving Madeline, which he would not do. He could imagine what the consequences would be if their affair was discovered. It would mean scandal for her family as well as his, but most of all it would give the police and courts an indisputable reason for his wanting to kill Louisa. He lay back against the concrete wall of his cell and let out a long, silent wail. He could think of no way out.

His pessimistic thoughts were interrupted by a police constable, who put handcuffs on him and told him to come along; there was someone to see him. He was shown into a bare room with a table, four chairs, blue-grey walls, a video camera and audio equipment—and Maxwell Douglas-Forbes. If there could be any relief at all to the churning of Johnnie's stomach, just seeing Max helped.

Earlier when Johnnie had arrived at the rear entrance

police station in Perth, he was brought into the back of the building, and the gates to the police yard were closed definitively behind him. He had been taken to the charge desk, where two police officers admitted him. They made him place his hands on the counter, he had been given his rights once again and then put him in the barren cell. They had not told him the reason for his arrest, but he did not have any doubts. Now Max told him why.

"It's a damn lie!" Johnnie said. "No one could have seen me. I wasn't there."

DI Kennedy came into the room and turned on the DVD camera and audio. A police constable was with him.

"Please state your name, address, date and place of birth and your nationality," the inspector said.

"John Edward Charles Robertson, ninth Earl of Tay, Tay Farm, near Kenmore, Perthshire, born November 6th, 1948 in Perth. I am a British citizen."

"Are your currently living at that address?"

"No, I am staying with friends here in the city, Marly and Roger Beaufort." He gave the address.

"I see," the Inspector said. "That's quite close to the house where the murder took place. Wasn't that also your home until recently?"

"On the night of the murder I was staying at my ancestral home on Loch Tay," Johnnie said, defiantly avoiding the inspector's question.

"You have the right to know why you are charged," the inspector said. "At the scene of your wife's murder, your previous home, we found numerous fingerprints. We need to take yours to compare them with those we found, and we need a DNA sample as well. These will be taken after we finish here. We understand you are in the process of divorcing your wife and therefore you must not have been on good terms. Since the house where we found the body belongs to you, we assume you have a key. Where were you on the night of Louisa Tay's murder?"

"At home on Loch Tay, as I said."

"Did you see your wife on the night she was murdered?" DI Kennedy continued.

"No."

"You seem very confident."

"I was divorcing Louisa, yes, but I preferred that the legal system make our separation final, not murder. I deny emphatically that I killed Louisa. I have nothing more to say."

Johnnie could see Max out of the corner of his eye. Max was nodding his head slightly.

Max stepped in. "Make no comment, Lord Tay. I feel it's too early in the investigation of the murder for the police to begin to cross examine you. We will leave that until you are brought to trial."

On the next few of the inspector's queries, Johnnie took Max's advice.

"We are charging you with the murder of your wife, Louisa, Countess of Tay," DI Kennedy said in exasperation. "We believe there was enough evidence at the crime scene to suggest you visited her home on the night of the murder, and you had both opportunity and motive to kill your wife. In our report to the procurator fiscal we will note that you deny being there. Do you wish to add anything else?"

"No comment," said Johnnie.

"Then we will return you to your cell now. Since it is Saturday, your formal hearing will be on Monday morning.

We will send your comments on to the procurator fiscal who will write up a report and present it to the court. Mr Douglas-Forbes, we assume you will be in attendance."

*

Max Douglas-Forbes rang the number for Tay Farm which Elspeth had given him to make sure he was welcome there. Biddy Baillie Shaw answered the call, and on hearing it was Max, she expressed her anxiety about Johnnie and wanted to know how he was coping and all the details of the arrest, but Max pleaded the need to speak to Elspeth in person to relay what had happened in Perth.

Distress filling her voice, she gave him instructions to the farm, including a special way to sound his horn when he arrived so that someone could come and open the gate, which she had kept locked ever since hearing of Louisa's death.

On arrival, Max was surprised when he saw a woman come up the drive. She was dressed in baggy corduroy trousers, a fleece, Wellington boots, and a floppy rain hat, but as she approached, Max noted how much she resembled Elspeth, or more truthfully Elspeth unadorned.

"Are you Lady Elisabeth by any chance?" he asked.

"Yes, and you are Mr Douglas-Forbes. Elspeth has told me you had agreed to represent my brother. We're all grateful."

Considering her title, Max was surprised by Biddy's appearance.

"May I come in?" he asked.

"Yes, of course. Elspeth and Richard are not here, but please do. I'm not too certain I can help in any way, but I can offer you a cup of tea or perhaps something stronger. I expect them back at any time. They, as much as I, will want to hear what's happening with Johnnie."

Max parked his car by the barn and followed Biddy into the kitchen. The room radiated the warmth. The ceilings were low, the floor uneven from centuries of traffic and cleaning, and the atmosphere radiated familial closeness. None of this escaped Max. Biddy was at home here and made him feel much more welcome than he had in many of baronial establishments of past clients. Yet what struck Max most of all was how comfortable Lady Elisabeth was with herself. Elspeth had been daunting when she came to his office, but Lady Elisabeth seemed unpretentious and settled in her home. She took his coat and hat and hung them on a peg by the door. He saw a kettle was already boiling on the Aga. Judging from the contents of the bowl on the large table in the middle of the room, she had been peeling potatoes.

"Perhaps we should wait until Elspeth and Richard return," he said. "I've been able to obtain the unofficial results of the postmortem and have talked to the procurator fiscal about the charges being brought against Lord Tay. This being the weekend, he will be charged with Louisa's murder on Monday, although normally it is done within twenty-four hours of an arrest. Perhaps during that time Elspeth and I can think of something to keep him from being tried, but you must be prepared for that eventuality."

Her face contorted, and she turned towards the cooker and fumbled with the kettle. "Thank you for including Elspeth," she said hoarsely.

Her distress hit him in a strange way. This lovely woman, however ill-dressed, did not deserve to hear what he had to tell her. He felt she would be more sensitive to it than Elspeth.

"By the way, Elspeth didn't tell me how distinguished her

husband was. I checked him on the Internet," Max said, searching for a way to extricate himself from Biddy's obvious pain.

At his words Biddy seemed to regain a modicum of composure. "Dickie? Johnnie, Elspeth and I call him that. It was his sobriquet at Oxford because he looked like Earl Mountbatten. I suppose Dickie is quite distinguished now, but we all have known him for decades, long before any of his honours. He was almost a member of the family even before he married Elspeth, and now he really is family. Can you imagine that she put him off for forty years before saying yes? They were only married last year—in Malta. As you might well imagine now that you have met Elspeth, she can be a bit headstrong at times and their courtship was not an easy one. Thankfully they seem to be quite happy now."

Max laughed. He had discovered Elspeth's strong will, admiring it from afar, but liked Lady Elisabeth's easier manner and openness more.

He declined tea and something stronger as he did not intend to stay for long. Had he not been lonely on Saturday afternoon, he would not have come at all. The postmortem results, and his interview with Johnnie and the procurator fiscal would have waited until Monday, but sitting in the inviting kitchen of Tay Farm, he was glad he had acted on the spur of the moment, rung and asked to come. Besides it would do well to know something about Lord Tay's roots and family background.

"Would you tell me a bit about your brother?" he asked. "Not anything specific about his arrest or charge, but what sort of person he is?"

"What sort of things?" She seemed puzzled.

"Did he confide his feelings to you?"

"How can I answer that? Sometimes, but at times he would withdraw into himself."

"And his relationship with the countess?"

"With . . .? Oh, you mean Louisa. She didn't seem much of a countess, not like my mother and grandmother, who took being the wife of the lord, as poor as they were, seriously. Johnnie was never very good at choosing women. His first wife, Kathleen, was ethereal, quite beautiful, but unstable. The family said she died in childbirth, but actually she committed suicide after miscarrying Johnnie's son. His second wife, Helen, had all the potential for being a good wife for him, but she suddenly after fifteen years of marriage ran off with another man. It quite shattered Johnnie. He sat here for hours in the chair you are sitting in now, asking me and my late husband, Ivor, how he had failed Helen. He was obsessed by it."

"What became of Helen?" Max asked.

"I have no idea. She simply disappeared. Johnnie instigated divorce proceedings against her for desertion. It was all very murky because she was off in Italy or somewhere."

"And then?"

"One day Johnnie produced Louisa and said he had married her."

"Did that surprise you?"

"Surprise me? I wasn't at all surprised. No, but it did surprise my husband."

"Why?"

"My brother, like all of us, needs to be loved. He had chosen two women who by rights should have loved him, but, if you look at it realistically, they were more absorbed in their own needs than Johnnie's. They didn't love Johnnie in the way I loved Ivor, or the way Elspeth loves Dickie . . . Richard."

"But why Louisa? I can understand that Lord Tay would be a catch for her, but what did he see in her?"

"Shall I be blunt?"

"Yes, please do. I'm your brother's lawyer and what you tell me will stay with me."

"Sex," she said. "On his part anyway. I don't know about hers."

"Just sex? That seems harsh."

"What other redeeming quality did Louisa have? I didn't know her well but could see nothing admirable in her."

"You didn't like her?"

"Not at all, that is, from what little I knew of her. Mr Douglas-Forbes, I care for most people and things, but for Louisa I make, made, an exception."

Max saw for the first time the same intensity in Lady Elisabeth's piercing dark blue eyes that he had seen in her cousin's.

Biddy suddenly took up a potato and began peeling it, severely paring off more than the outer skin and then she chopped it more finely than its companions in the bowl.

"You love Lord Tay, don't you?" Max said.

"Other than my children, my brother is my only immediate family since my husband died. There's Elspeth too, of course, but she has gone on to lead her own life far from Perthshire and the everyday bits of our lives.

"She would defend you with her life, I think."

"Oh yes. 'Peth has her fearless side. It's part of her passionate nature that she so carefully hides behind her cool mind. Ask Richard if you don't believe me."

"I think I do believe you. You know the case against your brother is extremely serious. The results of the postmortem and the contents of the latest police report do not help. If we are going to work on Lord Tay's case together, call me Max."

"Biddy," she said, putting down her peeler and extending her hand.

*

When Richard and Elspeth arrived back at the farm, they saw a fashionable and new SUV, untainted by the mud of the countryside. Elspeth was still jangled from her meeting with Madeline, and Richard suggested that they delay their return to the farmhouse despite Elspeth's wet condition.

"I suppose we can't hide from the world forever, Dickie," she said, "and I'm cold and would like dry clothes. Biddy wouldn't have let anyone who she doesn't know through the gate. I'm curious who the owner of that car might be."

They entered the kitchen to find Max Douglas-Forbes in close conversation with Biddy. Neither one looked up when Richard and Elspeth came in.

"So you see, Biddy, how critical this is," he was saying.

"Poor Johnnie. This will go against him, won't it?" she replied.

Richard cleared his throat. Both Biddy and Max seemed startled.

"Oh, dear," said Biddy, "I didn't hear you come in. 'Peth, you look like a drowned rat. What in the world happened to you? You both know Mr Douglas-Forbes, of course. He has come to tell us about Johnnie's arrest and the charges against him. I asked him to wait until you returned."

Max nodded at them both. Richard went forward and

shook Max's hand. Elspeth smiled in acknowledgement, but immediately pleaded the need to change out of her wet clothing. "Can whatever is so critical bear waiting another ten minutes while I get dry?"

"Let me prepare drinks for us something in the meantime. "Tea, sherry, whisky?" Biddy suggested.

Elspeth did not wait to see how the men would reply but retreated to the room she and Richard were sharing. She returned promptly as promised, with dry clothes and hair.

Tea had been settled on, and Elspeth accepted a cup because she wanted its warmth more than its contents. Biddy had laid out a cake, but it had not yet been sliced.

Max took out a large envelope and drew out a document. "I exerted some pressure on the police pathologist, whom I have known for years, and he gave me an advance copy of the preliminary results of the postmortem on Louisa. It isn't official yet, and the procurator fiscal doesn't need to know I have a copy. I'll request an official one on Monday when Johnnie's charged."

Biddy looked round at Elspeth. "Max was just about to tell me the contents when you and Dickie returned, although I expect, 'Peth, you'll be more familiar with the technical language than either me or Dickie."

"Have you read it, Max?" Elspeth asked.

"Yes, most of it. Not the medical references, which I'll have my clerk check, but all the salient points. They're not pretty, but postmortems never are."

"How did she die?" Richard reached across the table and took Elspeth's hand, which was still cold. His concern warmed her.

"Strangulation, with the cord from one of the curtains.

Technically it was asphyxiation. Unconsciousness probably occurred within a minute or two from the time the cord was pulled around her neck, and death shortly after that."

"Were there any other marks on the body to indicate that she could have been struggling with her attacker?" Elspeth asked.

"No, which is strange unless she knew who he was and was not afraid of him. If that was the case, she could have been caught by surprise. Although there are reports that some of the furniture was overturned."

"How was she dressed?" Elspeth asked.

"From the photographs the pathologist gave me, casually. Red tee shirt with sequins, dark leggings, and a tight yellow cardigan." He handed a photograph to Elspeth.

"Make up," Elspeth said, "and it was quite heavy. Max, that could indicate she hadn't gone to bed for the night. What time did she die?"

"The body temperature and the state of rigor mortis point to somewhere between eleven Thursday evening and two Friday morning."

"I see," Elspeth said and felt the warmth in her body drain away. Madeline could not offer Johnnie an alibi, if she chose to do so, because the hours he was with her meant he could have been in Perth before he went to see her. Besides, the Beauforts had confirmed his car was at the flat at their home. "I suppose I have to ask. Was she pregnant?"

Max nodded at Elspeth. "Actually she was. About four and a half months along."

"Are they going to do DNA testing to see who the father was?"

"We can request it. They took Lord Tay's DNA when he

was charged, so we can only hope he will be cleared."

"Boy or girl?" Elspeth asked.

"A boy."

"Then if we are to believe Johnnie, and the baby was over four months along, it can't have been his, but I'm not sure that will help Johnnie. She could have taunted him about the child and said he would have to accept it as his heir. From what Johnnie has said, that was the kind of thing Louisa would do."

"Enough to provoke him to murder her?" Max asked.

Elspeth wondered. The Johnnie she remembered had always been even tempered and merry, but that was a childhood memory. She had met Louisa and could understand that she might incite murderous passions in the man who was divorcing her, particularly because he had met a more suitable woman and wanted to marry her. Elspeth could not imagine Johnnie grabbing a curtain cord in a rage, but he had admitted to her that Louisa had seduced him into her bed two months before. Elspeth had no idea how deeply Johnnie's resentment lay or what might make him snap. Hadn't she just told Madeline that every person has an ultimate limit?

Biddy unexpectedly broke in. "No," she said. "Johnnie wouldn't kill her even for that."

The three of them all turned to her.

"Why?" Max asked.

"Johnnie has never been able to kill anything, except perhaps a midge or a mosquito," Biddy said. "That's one reason he never wanted to stay on the farm. We don't kill things here for pleasure, but farming does involve slaughtering animals. He turns green when I talk about killing a chicken or sending the lambs to the abattoir. I never tell him how we dispose of some of the animals that became the food I was serving when he came here. I used to tease him that he should become a vegan. I always was the bloodless one, not Johnnie."

"I'll remember that," Richard said dryly, "in case your cousin becomes more than I can cope with."

Elspeth threw a look at him and said, "Fiend! Biddy, don't listen to him."

This bit of repartee broke the tension in the room. Biddy laughed. "Now Max, you can see how irreverent my family is even in times of crisis. Will you stay for dinner?"

"I suppose it depends on what you are serving," he said.

"I have a roast hen, which I bought from a local farmer, and it was already plucked. The potatoes and vegetables were grown here on the farm. The only thing I need to attack with a knife is the packet of so-called fresh mushrooms I bought at the Co-op."

Max took a deep breath and said, "There is one other thing. The police say they have two eyewitnesses who saw Johnnie at Louisa's house at the time of the murder. That's why they arrested him."

Silence engulfed the room and shock crossed Biddy, Elspeth, and Richard's faces.

"But that's impossible!" Biddy said.

"Damn! Poor Johnnie." Richard said.

"Are they reliable witnesses?" Elspeth asked.

Max swallowed, his task obviously a painful one. "Reliable enough for the police to accept their evidence. Had it been only one witness . . ." he began and then let the thought die. "They came forward this morning after we collected the original police report, Elspeth. Certainly I'll check their veracity, but for now the police believe them. I'll get to the bottom of this." Something in Max's tone was reassuring. "I hope my news doesn't mean you'll be rescinding my dinner invitation. I'd like to stay."

*

After the chicken and potatoes were roasting in the Aga's oven, Biddy invited Max to see the farm, leaving Richard and Elspeth alone in the kitchen. Elspeth set about laying the table for dinner, and Richard poured her a sherry and a single malt whisky for himself. They went into the morning room and lit the fire, which had been laid earlier.

Elspeth drew Richard down to the sofa, and he put his arm around her.

"The witnesses may damn Johnnie, despite Biddy's protestations," Elspeth said. "I also fear we'll have difficulty paying for his defence. Max will need to get detectives now, and there'll be the preparation for the trial. I gave him twenty thousand pounds, but I expect that will hardly do in the long run."

Richard drew his wife gently to him. He could smell the scent of her newly washed hair. "Do you think Johnnie did it? Louisa's actions would try any man with the news of her pregnancy and wanting to use it to get possession of the farm."

Elspeth sat up and said, "I have no idea if he did it or not. That's a real problem. Everything we have learned points to his guilt. Madeline's alibi no longer has any staying power, as Johnnie easily could have stopped in Perth to see Louisa on the way to Dundee. If asked, the Beauforts will have to testify they saw his car. Confirmation of the pregnancy makes things worse, giving him a strong motive."

"Yes, that and Louisa wanting to take the farm. Wouldn't that be more provoking to Biddy, who has just so freely admitted her bloodlessness?" Richard spoke in jest, but the words came too close to the truth.

"Oh, please, Dickie, let's not even entertain such a thought." Elspeth put her forehead on her husband's chest and shook her head back and forth slowly. "What a tangle," she said, "and I've no idea how to unravel it. In any case, I need to be in British Columbia next Saturday morning and cannot say to Eric, 'Sorry, scandal is ruining my family and I must stay in Perthshire'. Not when the Governor General of Canada is staying at the Kennington Victoria, and I'm in charge of hotel security the week she's there. What am I to do?"

"Trust Max."

"Trust Max? He's not a member of the family."

"No, but didn't you tell Johnnie to have faith in him? Max seems to be taking special pains with the case. I've never known a lawyer before who spent Saturday afternoon and evening with clients he hardly knows. My sense of Max is that this case has struck a personal chord in him."

"What sort of chord?"

"It's only a feeling I have. Like the ones you sometimes have. Perhaps I have a bit of Scottish sensibility too."

Elspeth cuffed him lovingly. It was an old joke between them.

"Nothing concrete," Richard continued, "but when Max and I were waiting for you when you were seeing Johnnie alone this morning in his chambers, I found something profoundly dependable in Max."

"Was it only this morning we were in Max's office? So much has happened since then. Dickie, I trust your judgment and therefore will do the same with Max, but I can't just let go. I'll call Pamela to see if I can't set up a secure link on my satellite mobile to stay in touch with Max and Madeline when

I'm away. I can't think of any other way."

*

Elspeth rang Pamela Crumm's private number in London. Elspeth expected her friend and employer would be at home, probably working. She also knew that her ring would be unique on Pamela's phone. Pamela answered immediately.

"I wondered, Elspeth ducks, when you would call. Even the press in London cannot pass up the arrest of a Scottish peer for the murder of his estranged wife. In any case, I like Johnnie Tay. I found him a perfectly charming dinner partner the night before you were married, but I thought he had a rakish side to him. I suppose you are not going to tell me everything but instead ask for some big favour. Not more time off, I hope. Eric wants you in Canada on Friday evening. He's determined only you can handle the situation with the Governor General at the Victoria hotel."

Elspeth had been given the assignment a month ago, and before leaving for Peter's wedding, she had put all the pieces in place for her arrival in Victoria as scheduled. Pamela had anticipated Elspeth's return from California would find her rested after a holiday at her retreat in Marin County and fully recovered from the unpleasantness at the Kennington Gibraltar just weeks before.

Pamela had a fascination with the lurid press that transcended her responsibilities of tracking the lives of notables who stayed or might stay at the Kennington hotels. The pictures of Lord Tay's arrival at the Tayside Police Office in Perth, his hands linked together by handcuffs, had not escaped a photographer who was lingering at the station, and he had sold his prize picture to his voracious pals at *The Scottish Sun* and the *News of the World*. Pamela had picked up the London addition of *The Sun* when she saw the headlines on her way home from her office and remembered the call from Maxwell Douglas-Forbes asking her to verify Elspeth's position with the Kennington Organisation. Before answering his request, Pamela had done an Internet search and discovered who Max really was. She was impressed that the Tay family had found such a prominent lawyer so quickly and supposed correctly that Elspeth had some involvement in this.

"No, as much as I wish I could delay here, Eric insists there's no one else he can trust to send to Canada. He has already told me that," said Elspeth with a half-smile.

"Here, I suppose, is Perthshire, not California," Pamela said archly.

"Didn't I say that? Oh, I'm sorry, Pamela. I thought that would be apparent."

"It is. Now what is the favour?"

"Can you give me another secure line on my mobile, one which is untraceable and which I can use to keep in touch with Perthshire when I'm in Canada?"

"M'friend, leave it to me. Is dear Richard there with you?"

"Yes, we all came back from San Francisco immediately after the wedding."

Pamela chuckled as she knew Elspeth so well. "You may be privy to the details of all the events there, ducks, but your shorthand eludes me. The countess wasn't murdered until Thursday night. Why were all of you in Perthshire directly after Peter's wedding? Was it lovely?"

From long habit Elspeth followed Pamela's non sequiturs. "It seems a long time ago, but, yes, the wedding was completely lovely. I like Lucy enormously and also her family, but of course Alistair was thoroughly inappropriate, arriving with a buxom starlet on his arm." Elspeth mentioned the name and Pamela guffawed. "I promise a full report when I return to London on Thursday," Elspeth said.

"I'll make the arrangements on Monday morning. Keep me posted on what's happening there. You can always count on my help."

"Oh, Pamela, I only hope we can afford Max Douglas-Forbes. Do you think I can ask Eric for a raise?"

"He already thinks he pays you far too much. But don't worry; I'll see what I can do. Do count on me to help. I'll see about getting that private line for you."

When she rang off, Elspeth could not have imagined how much help Pamela would actually give her and her family during the coming weeks.

*

Max followed Biddy out of the kitchen and into the farmyard. He remembered the feelings that had surrounded him when Elspeth walked into his office and asked him to represent John Tay, a victim of his wife's infidelity whether he had killed her or not. Max was feeling alone and betrayed by his wife's death. She had not died lovingly in his arms of some rare disease but rather in a fiery car crash from which they extracted her and the corpse of one of the clerks in his law practice. He had known they were lovers, but he had assured the police that his wife was simply giving his clerk a lift. This had happened three years ago, but the wound had never healed. Therefore even without Elspeth's persuasiveness, he would have accepted the case for the defence in John Tay's arrest for the murder of his perfidious wife once Elspeth had explained the circumstances.

11

The eighth Countess of Tay would have been mortified had she known that her daughter would serve someone as notable as Maxwell Douglas-Forbes, QC, in the farm's kitchen, but the events of the day seemed to dwarf formality, and consequently the few remaining pieces of antique furniture belonging to the Tay estate were left unoccupied in the formal dining room. They all had more to drink that night than a temperance society might condone, but the circumstances seemed to warrant it. Biddy offered Max a bed in one of the spare rooms, which he accepted wisely, and she found him a pair of her son's pyjamas, which were short for him but roomier than a pair of Richard's.

Max tossed in the unfamiliar bed and finally fell to sleep just hours before dawn. He had pulled the curtains upon retiring and slept until almost eight. Biddy lay silently in the night and did not sleep. Elspeth and Richard retired to their room, but an uncomfortable silence lay between them. None of them could find a way to save Johnnie Tay.

Richard watched Elspeth undress, but she did so without seeming to care. She normally favoured silk pyjamas, but tonight she donned a shapeless flannel nightgown, which he knew was Biddy's. She drew a heavy and unattractive wool dressing gown around herself and went to the window. She

123

stood for a long time looking out the window towards the loch without moving or coming to him, as was her habit when they were together.

Finally she said, "Not tonight, Dickie. I think I'll sleep in one of the other bedrooms."

Richard's heart froze. He had heard those words so many times from his first wife, who at first forborne his needs, and then barely tolerated them. In the end they had reverted to companionship without conjugal closeness. Elspeth had never been like this before. Since first making love with him in Cyprus, she never had asked that they sleep apart. Why now, my precious one, he thought? Why now? Has this whole thing with Johnnie affected you so profoundly? He came near her at the window but did not touch her. She did not move towards him, but he could feel her across the space between them.

"Tell me why?" His voice cracked.

"How could you want me near you?"

"I love you."

"Still? After today? How can you even tolerate any member of our family?"

"Your family is my family now."

"Are we? No, Dickie, we aren't. You are so wonderfully fine, and we are so. . ." she paused as if to find the words, ". . . so incredibly fouled up. Look at the trouble Johnnie is in. Look at the mess of my life. Look at Biddy, the most stable of us three. She goes to bed every night with a double whisky, when she's attractive enough to marry again if she gave herself half a chance. What can you find in our family that attracts you enough to claim membership?" Elspeth's voice was constricted.

He came towards her, but she moved away from him.

"Love," he said simply.

"Love? How can we be in the least bit loveable?" Elspeth put her arms around her body and lowered her head to her chest.

"How long have we known each other?" he asked.

She did not need to answer.

"For all that time I have loved you. I knew Johnnie before I met you and he has remained one of my closest friends. I know Biddy less well, but she is so much like you, that I care for her too."

"I never before thought you a fool, Dickie."

"Elspeth, I have known you all for a very long time. When Johnnie and I were at Oxford, we shared as brothers. Your life in Perthshire was so different from mine. My parents were cold, correct and cared for me and my brother as if we were a responsibility, not children to be loved. No one could fault their tending to our upbringing and education, but I never remember either one touching me, kissing me or even saying a light word to me. When I met Johnnie at Oxford, I couldn't believe that a person could be so free in accepting his family, their nurturing, and their love. When I came here during the summers between my years at Oxford, I was overwhelmed by you all. Love, laughter, irreverence, intellectual banter, camaraderie, and even warm acceptance of each other's faults were a part of you all. These qualities were not affected; they just were. You have no idea how strange and wonderful that was to me."

Elspeth did not move.

Richard continued. "Do you think I love you now because when we walk into a room every person stops, the women jealous of your fine demeanour and the men envious you are my wife and not theirs? Do you think I love you because we spend grand times together in the luxury of the Kennington hotels? Do you think I love you because you enhance my career when you grudgingly attend diplomatic receptions, and everyone wants to know who you are? Do you think I love you only because we share so much exhilaratingly physical passion together? I love you for everything you are, your family, your past, our future, who you are, and who I am. Elspeth, I have loved you since I met a rather badly dressed, passionate tomboy who nearly ran into me telling me that she loved no one else in the world more than me and then apologizing for her ineptness. You've been doing the same thing ever since, even tonight. You do not need to apologize for who you are or for your family. They are a deep and old part of who I am. Until I came here to Tay Farm when I was at Oxford, I didn't know what love was."

She said, "But Johnnie."

Richard drew nearer to her but did not touch her. "Johnnie was my closest friend at Oxford. We were such mismatched friends. I knew I loved only one girl in the world, you, Elspeth, but Johnnie was different. He liked girls, not just from the women's colleges, but all sorts of girls, town and gown alike. I spend a great deal of time bailing him out of difficulties. I feel a grave sense of déjà vu this week. I've helped him many times before, and I don't plan to desert him now. Now will you come to bed with me, you silly goose? You haven't the good sense of Biddy's barnyard animals despite your fine education and undeniable elegance, and where did you get that horrid nightgown?"

She turned, drew her arms around him and did not answer.

Elspeth tossed uneasily all night, and Richard lay close to her, sleeping on and off and caressing her gently to calm her, but to no avail. But some time during the night she shed the nightgown and, when he awoke in the morning, his hand reached for her and found the softness of her body under fine silk pyjamas.

*

The brightness of the early hours of morning brought no relief to them. A ragged foursome finally emerged into the kitchen well past eight o'clock, and Biddy began preparing a semblance of breakfast. Max had dressed himself in his clothes from the previous day. Biddy had paid little attention to her appearance and was dressed in clothes fit for the morning chores on the farm. She was turning bacon languidly in the frying pan. A wire basket of eggs, probably fresh from the hencoop, sat next to the Aga. Elspeth and Richard arrived in the kitchen in fashionably cut dressing gowns but neither one radiated modishness. Richard poured out the juice and Elspeth tended to the toast. All looked tired.

Max watched this family with pain in his heart. Their tragedy was deep, but he saw them all as a single loving unit. His family had been that way when he was young. Biddy reminded him of his mother, who ran a grand house not a farm and dressed in tweeds not corduroys and fleece, but he saw in Biddy the same care for her family, which only intensified in times of trouble. He looked at Elspeth, and Richard too. Knowing now who Richard was and assuming Elspeth ranked high in the Kennington Organisation, Max was admiring of how the two of them, in their rich clothing, worked beside Biddy without consideration of their far more luminous lives.

127

Max suddenly loved this family and wanted more than was professionally acceptable to save Johnnie, Lord Tay, from life in prison.

Max took his leave after breakfast but could not simply return to his house in Perth and forget the Tay case. Instead he went to Charlotte Street and unlocked his silent chambers. The light on his answer phone was blinking madly. It had been quiet when he left on Saturday afternoon to see Johnnie at the jail. He pressed the relevant buttons and listened to two messages that had to do with another case. Then he saw the two heavy beige envelopes engraved with a seal he did not recognise propped against his desk lamp. One was addressed to him and the other simply read 'For Elspeth Duff'. Max had no idea how they had been placed there. He must ask his clerk.

After reading the contents of his letter, Max retreated to his home, showered, shaved and changed his clothes. Then he got back in his SUV and turned back to Tay Farm.

*

"Here's Max again," Elspeth said as she looked out the window of the kitchen.

Max burst into the room. "This came for you," he cried.

All three people in the kitchen stopped what they were doing. Elspeth and Richard were now dressed, and Biddy had shed her fleece, indicating the morning chores had been completed.

Max handed Elspeth the envelope, which she tore open when she saw the engraved Kennington coat of arms.

The handwritten message was simple.

> *Dear Elspeth,*
> I *have far too much money for an old*

woman with no family. No, you may not object.
I have promised Max to pay for all Johnnie
Tay's expenses, including those of the best
detectives he can find to catch the real killer.
The money is mine to do with as I please, and I
will not demand all the details, unless of
course you consider telling them to me.

Pamela.

Elspeth's eye filled with tears both of gratitude and exasperation. "Oh, Pamela, you idiot," she said to no one in particular. She handed the note to Richard.

Biddy and Max looked puzzled.

"Pamela Crumm insists that she will pay for all of Johnnie's legal expenses. That is so like Pamela," Elspeth explained.

She smiled, wiping away a tear that had fallen across her cheek, and shook her head. "Pamela found Johnnie rakish at our wedding. That would be enough for her. She is an incurable romantic. Besides, she must expect Johnnie will be cleared."

Max looked askance at Elspeth, who asked Richard to pass round the note.

Biddy looked in wonderment at her cousin. "Why would Pamela do this?"

"I think the significance of the note is self-evident. Biddy and Dickie, you know Pamela. She has the most generous heart I ever have known, but it is captured in a body bent by a childhood disease and with too big a brain. She has lived through all the problems of my life since we met nine years ago. She defends me against Eric Kennington, when he becomes his most imperious. No person who was not a member of my family could have been a better friend to me. She knows that."

Biddy turned to Max. "What now?"

"Now we begin our fight," Max said.

*

The fight for Johnnie Tay's innocence would consume them.

Biddy begged Max to take her to the jail to see Johnnie, but he seemed reluctant.

"The conditions in the jail are very unsavoury," he said. "You must prepare yourself, not only for the dreadful conditions there, but also for how they have upset your brother, particularly after being accused of Louisa's murder."

"Those conditions would be worse for Johnnie than for me," Biddy protested. "Mr Douglas-Forbes, I do not shrink from adversity."

Max smiled. "What happened to 'Max'?" he asked.

"All right, Max," she said, a smile breaking through her protest. "Then you'll agree to take me?"

"Yes, but I would like to come with you. I've been there many times. The first time was the worst."

"After Johnnie is arraigned—is that the right word—will he remain there?" Biddy asked.

"Unfortunately not," Max admitted. "If the court will not grant bail, they will take him to the prison, where conditions are worse."

"Then I must get used to them, mustn't I?" said Biddy, her head held high.

Max looked at the magnificent woman who had just challenged him and knew he could never go back from that moment. He thought he might be falling in love with her and was not too sure what he was going to do about it.

*

After Max and Biddy had left the farm, Elspeth rang Pamela, who cackled gleefully. "Now, ducks," she said, "I want you to let Maxwell Douglas-Forbes solve the case, and you can get on with your job." Elspeth knew her friend well enough to know Pamela was hiding her real feelings about her generous gift.

Next Elspeth rang her father and asked if she and Richard could come round to the Duff home beside Loch Rannoch. She wanted to talk to him about the next steps they should take to find Louisa's murderer. She went into the kitchen where Richard was happily preparing some sandwiches and humming a tune under his breath. He turned to her as she came in.

"You never cease to amaze me, my dearest" he said.

"Amaze you. Whatever for?"

"For your friends in high places and their willingness to help you."

"Pamela is a real jewel, Dickie, as you know. I can't imagine what her life must be like. Our society puts so much emphasis on physical beauty, that to be struck down so early in life with a disease which so diminishes one's body must make demands on one that none of the rest of us can possibly understand. And, to think what a success she has made of her life despite the disease. My life would be so much less without her, and some days I think that without her I would have quit my job ages ago."

"Is she that rich that she can afford an open purse as far as Max is concerned?"

"I have no idea, but I suspect she's very rich indeed. Did

you know she owns forty-five percent of the Kennington Organisation shares?"

Richard let out a whistle.

"She keeps Eric in line by threatening to resign and sell her shares. Of course, she never would and they both know that. It's a dance they do."

"Elspeth, when you asked to keep working after we were married, I was wrong to hope you might come to Malta and live there with me full time. I can't imagine you there now. You, like Pamela, are so much a part of the Kennington Organisation, and your work is so much a part of you."

"Except I don't own forty-five per cent of the Organisation's shares."

"I'm not too sure I could manage a wife with that much money. You are already hard enough to handle," he teased.

"Am I?" she said half mocking and then she said almost sadly, "I don't give you a peaceful life, do I?"

"No, but I find our marriage perfectly splendid, as I had hoped it would be, and in any case you have given me both your love and a family to care for."

"Thank you, Dickie," she said kissing him boldly. "Do you miss me in Malta?"

"Sometimes, usually at night. Since we have never lived in Valletta together, I have not become accustomed to your being there. Do you miss me?"

"Only in London," she said, "since we have shared so much together at the flat. I consider London our home. When I'm working, I only let myself think of you after I have gone to bed. I put myself to sleep with these thoughts and let them glide into erotic dreams of you." She grinned. "Now let's wrap those sandwiches and take them over to share with Daddy.

Isn't there some cake left from tea yesterday, and Biddy won't mind if we take this fruit? Daddy never eats properly when Mother is away."

*

"Max," Biddy said as they left the farm, "how long will it be before they try Johnnie?"

She had changed into tweeds and a fashionable silk scarf that Max suspected might have once belonged to Elspeth. He noticed Biddy was wearing lightly applied makeup and had combed out her hair, which suited her natural beauty. Although unlike Elspeth, who walked with the grace of well-bred European women, Biddy's bearing could not be mistaken for other than what it was, the natural assurance of the British aristocracy, no matter how much Elspeth disparaged that heritage. Both Biddy's mother and grandmother were ladies in their own right and would not let Biddy develop the undignified manner of so many of her friends when she was growing up. Somehow the tweeds accentuated this.

Max knew that in Scotland cases were heard as swiftly as possible and that charges were brought against the accused quickly, usually within twenty-four hours. The weekend had delayed things but, as hard as that might be on Johnnie, it gave Max time to prepare Johnnie's family.

"I hope to know on Monday," Max said. "Unless we can find a good reason for a delay, it might be a matter of weeks or several months, depending on many cases the High Court has before it."

"That doesn't give us much time to prove his innocence," Biddy said, "but you must try."

"I'll put every resource I have into it," he assured her. "The police will be gathering further evidence; their purpose is to establish who committed the murder and how."

"Max, I want you to use Elspeth's expertise. She sometimes makes light of the seriousness of her job, but she has unravelled several murders when the police failed."

"I find your cousin very disconcerting," he said. "From her outward manner one would never suspect she was so . . ." Max tried to find a neutral word.

"Fierce? She is. She worries about it often. It almost kept her from marrying Richard. She always said she would make an unsuitable wife for him."

"What is Richard's response to that?"

Biddy laughed, remembering their childhood. "He never had a chance with Elspeth. He fell in love with her the moment they met. She was only fifteen at the time. When they were young, she and Johnnie would do the most preposterous things, and they would drag Dickie, Richard, along like a sheepdog who didn't want to be left out of the fun, although he saw the trouble ahead. Elspeth has always been mischievous. I know because I was often lured into trouble by her when we were children. Her saving grace, however, was that she took full responsibility if something went wrong, which it often did."

"I'm not certain that's a recommendation. We have no room for error here if we are to save your brother."

"There are moments when she reverts to her old mischievous ways, but she is a brilliant investigator. You only need to ask Pamela Crumm, or Lord Kennington, who expects her to set things straight when they go horribly wrong at his hotels. She feels acutely the need to clear Johnnie, although she may not admit it. She has to leave Scotland on Thursday and that has put a great burden on her. She told me her next assignment involves one of the highest officials in the Canadian government, someone who cannot be put off. She travels in high circles and I used to envy her. She once got me involved in a case at the Kennington Stresa hotel on Lago Maggiore, and I learned from that experience I much prefer the simplicity of farm to all the luxuries of the Kennington hotels if one had Elspeth's job."

Max drove on, wanting to know more about Lady Elisabeth Baillie Shaw, not her cousin. Max considered asking Elspeth about Biddy's husband. Would Biddy allow another man in her life? He felt the strongest urge to know and then checked himself. He was Lord Tay's lawyer, and as such, must put that relationship first. On the narrow roads that led out of the farm towards the A9 and Perth, he negotiated his SUV around a large lorry, barely avoiding scraping his side mirror and resolved to concentrate on his driving, not the woman beside him. It was a hard task.

*

At police headquarters in Perth, Max duly registered both himself and Biddy with the sergeant at the charge desk and obtained permission for the two of them to see Johnnie. A police constable led them to Johnnie's cell. Biddy held her head high and tried to shut out the string of drug-induced curses she heard from one of the prisoner's cells. The smell of disinfectant, barely covering the odours of urine and vomit, filled her nose, and she tried not to think that Johnnie had endured this for almost a day. She had never known Johnnie to have any sympathy for the plight of the less fortunate or that he had ever really considered it. The last night in jail must have been agony for him.

When she was led into the cell, Johnnie's eyes, sunken in

their sockets, were filled with pleading.

"Biddy, get me out of here. It's more than I can bear." He looked around at Max. "May I speak to my sister alone?" he asked. Max nodded and left the two sitting together on the concrete bench that was the only furniture in the cell.

Biddy rose and came over to Max as he left. Without words, she put her hand to his cheek, an oddly familiar gesture, but that did not bother her. They all owed so much to him, even in these early days, but it also was more, an inner faith in and an immediate attraction to Max, not as Johnnie's lawyer but as a man. Max acknowledged her touch with a sad smile and then was gone.

"Johnnie, I . . ." she started, but could not find the right words. "We want you out of here, all of us. You should be back at the farm, where you belong."

"The farm is yours," he said. "Not mine. You belong there, not me."

"No," she said, "I'm only its steward."

"But you love it, don't you?"

"Yes," she said simply, "it's my whole life now that Ivor is dead. I'll go to great lengths to make sure it is preserved for our family."

"Charlie doesn't want it, though."

"No. He takes after 'Peth and enjoys his jaunts round the world."

"Or Alex or Mary?"

"No, I'm afraid not. I only hope your children will."

"Bah!" was all Johnnie said, and squeezed his eyes hard shut to hide the tears.

"I'm sorry. Perhaps I shouldn't have brought that up, but Madeline is still young enough to have children."

"If they don't hang me," he said.

"They don't hang people anymore. Good heavens," his sister said.

"Perhaps not with a rope, but they do in the public eye."

"Would that matter to Madeline?"

"How should I know? I never thought to ask her if she would marry a man accused of murdering his wife." His cynicism bit. "Did 'Peth speak to her?"

"Yes, yesterday afternoon."

"Did Madeline agree to stay away?"

"I'm not sure. You must ask 'Peth. She said she wanted to come to see you later, perhaps tomorrow morning before the hearing. She and Dickie have gone over to consult Uncle James. I'm sure she'll tell you what happened with Madeline when she comes."

"Damn it, Biddy, how much more of this can I take?"

"We have to see it through to the end," she said. She held his eyes, but he soon turned his face away.

"I suppose we have no other choice."

"'Peth promised to tell you about Madeline tomorrow. Have you told her everything, Johnnie—about the agreement?"

"Some of it."

"But not all."

"No, not all. No one needs to know everything except the two of us."

"If you go to trial, it may come out. I think you should be straightforward with 'Peth."

"Why? You won't break our confidence, will you? I don't want her to know."

"No, I won't break it. You know that. But now?" She left

her thought in the air.

"Damn Louisa! One would hardly have thought she had the intelligence to ask for the farm."

"She couldn't have. There must have been someone else behind her demands. Do you have any idea who?"

"By the time I left her, she was moving in a very nasty crowd."

"Would she have told them about the farm?"

"Perhaps."

"Did she know everything?"

"I haven't a clue. There is no reason she should have. Who would have told her?"

"You?"

"Me?"

"When you were not quite sober?"

"That's hardly fair, Biddy," he said, grinding his teeth.

"I don't plead to be a member of a temperance society, God knows, but the nights you have a glass too many have been a problem with you ever since Helen left."

Apparently not wanting to admit to his weakness, Johnnie turned from his sister. "Why do you bring Helen up?"

"Because that's when it started," Biddy said without mincing her words.

"You couldn't possibly understand."

"Perhaps not personally, but I have held the hands of many people in the same situation and heard their tears and their excuses. Your situation was not unique, Johnnie."

"Helen abandoned me. I never could find a reason. What had changed between us?"

Biddy walked to the bars of the cell and wrapped her arms around herself. "You have to accept that she did, although we may never know why. Helen wasn't a fool like Louisa. Do you know if she is still alive, Helen I mean?"

"I've no idea."

"I think 'Peth might be able to find her."

"Biddy, don't tell her about our arrangement. She has moved on from Perthshire, chosen to marry Dickie and spend her time elsewhere. The farm can no longer be of any concern to her." Johnnie walked over and stood next to his sister. "Whoever would have thought she would marry him? Somehow it amuses me."

"She genuinely adores him."

"Yes, that's obvious. Well, I wish them both a long happy life together, as mismatched though they be."

They stood quietly for a while without speaking. Biddy watched the contortions of his face and could not make out what he was thinking. He met his sister's cobalt blue eyes which were similar to his own. "Thank you all for loving me," he said. And then he let the tears flow, chocking on great sobs.

"Help me, Biddy," he cried out. "Help me."

*

James Duff, Richard, and Elspeth sat in the drawing room of the Duff household, preparing to eat Richard's sandwiches, the cake, and the fruit because it was raining intermittently, and did not allow them to picnic outside. Elspeth had found a teapot in her mother's kitchen and made tea for them. James had set out small folding tables for each of them and lit the fire.

"Unless there's compelling evidence for the court to delay the trial," Elspeth's father said, "Johnnie's case will probably be heard in about two months." Elspeth had seldom seen her father so dispirited.

"Daddy, I want to talk to Johnnie's solicitor at your firm, the one who was handling the divorce, but I also have something else to ask of you."

"Which is?"

"I want to see all the files on the Robertson/Tay family. Deeds, wills, marriages, deaths, everything and anything."

"Elspeth, there are boxes and boxes, going back to the time I married your mother, sixty years ago."

Elspeth remembered the boxes sitting in the storage room of her father's offices in Pitlochry. "Well, perhaps not all, but everything to do with Johnnie, the earldom, his personal files, Biddy and Ivor as his long-time tenants, and the grant of the farm itself. Can you give me access to these?"

"Yes, tomorrow if you wish. I'll speak to Portia MacRoberts, who was handling Johnnie's divorce. Is it important, now that Louisa is dead?"

Elspeth glanced around at her husband, who had cocked an eyebrow. "I know, Dickie. I'll be covered in dust, which always makes me sneeze. Will you come tomorrow and help?" Elspeth knew he could not refuse, although he had not been trained in the law. Certainly his diplomatic career had taught him how to read the fine print.

12

On a road somewhere in Scotland, Saturday afternoon, July 21st

Misery fled down Madeline MacNaughton's body as she turned the two-seater north along the coast and pressed down on the accelerator once more, but she could not drive away from her pain or her indecision. Previously in her life, she had always taken the expected way, been the obedient child and followed a path into matrimony considered safe and proper. At thirty-three she was empty, career-focused and childless by choice, and in a marriage that no longer gave her any fulfilment. Then came her affair with Johnnie Tay.

Elspeth Duff's question to Madeline had rattled her. The echoes of Elspeth's voice came back to her. "Do you really love Johnnie, or is this just a passing affair?" Elspeth had asked for honesty, but until the day before Madeline thought she could answer without equivocation. She pushed her car on as if she had somewhere to go and was late, but she had no plan. The road was crippled by weekend drivers and summer tourists, and she accelerated around them angrily, throwing water from the puddles at them. Madeline knew how much she wanted her love for Johnnie to be real and everlasting, but she was angry that when Elspeth challenged her for an immediate answer because not so much her words but rather her thoughts had been confused. Her speed and recklessness were not

141

helping her grasp why she had evaded Elspeth's question, so she pulled over into a scenic turnout and disentangled herself from her car. A mild wind came off the loch, whose name she had forgotten, catching the bottom of her mackintosh and long hair. She walked to the sign describing some historic moment at this spot, clutched on to its sides, and hoped the stout steel posts would steady her.

She thought of Johnnie, not the one languishing in his cell in Perth, but as the man with whom she had wanted to spend the rest of her life. Elspeth had neither prettified the consequences of Madeline's commitment to Johnnie now nor had she offered Madeline any facile or safe way to respond, and, as searching as Elspeth's demands had been, Madeline respected their brutal directness. Anything less would have been condescending.

She let the wind blow leaves and heavy air at her and wanted to shout at God, but she knew it would do no more good than the excessive speed of her car to help her to quell her fear, both for herself and Johnnie. Turning on her heel, she folded herself back into her car and proceeded more sedately back towards Dundee to the empty flat where Johnnie had come to her four nights and a lifetime ago.

13

The media's arrival was hastier than anyone could have prophesised. They appeared at the gate of Tay Farm soon after Elspeth and Richard had locked it behind them on their return from Loch Rannoch. Soon a helicopter was hovering above. As she was emerging from the barn, Biddy saw Johnnie's saloon car make its way down the drive. She ran to it, grabbing both Richard and Elspeth's arms as they came towards her. She pulled them back into the barn.

"We're going to have to get rid of them," Biddy said, pointing to the press vans and the helicopter. "I have a plan."

Elspeth looked at her questioningly.

"How good are you at herding sheep?" she asked Richard.

Richard looked askance. "Herding sheep?"

"Here," said Biddy, "take Robbie's hat." Then she whistled shrilly, and a black and white collie came to her, its tail wagging.

"Dickie, this is Tobias, the farm's sheep dog. He's going to teach you how obstructive sheep can be. Come, Toby, the sheep need their evening exercise. Luckily, we have them penned for shearing as normally they roam free. In the meantime, 'Peth, could you go inside and call Robbie MacPherson? I'm going to need his assistance, if we are to carry out my plan successfully."

She explained her idea, which made Elspeth grin. Biddy

143

had, after all, inherited a bit of the family mischief.

Biddy found another hat, more disreputable than the one she had given Richard, and put it on. She led him out of the barn up to the sheep shearing pen. She took a key, undid the padlock, and opened the gate and using a series of whistles prompted Toby.

"Come, Toby, let's run the sheep."

The sheep began to bleat, but Toby, with a series of short barks and nips, herded the sheep up the drive. A reporter, who was attempting to climb over the gate, retreated hastily, a cameraman catching him as he fell.

Biddy whistled again. Toby made for the reporter's heels.

"Ye'll have to clear the way," Biddy said attempting a Scottish burr. "Sheep arnna afraid of the likes of ye."

Toby growled.

"Is she here?" a reporter asked.

"Who're ye referrin' to?"

"The sister of the murdering lord."

"Whoever ye are, move on. This is a peaceful farm. We tend to our sheep, right, Dick? We have no ken of ye and why ye're here. Now if ye'll get back, we need the road for the sheep."

"Is the lady, his sister, at the house?"

"Ye have no right information. Now I see there's the rainstorm a'comin'. They are verrry heavy here. Please clear the way for yon sheep." She whistled for Toby. He growled again.

The rain did come, violently, causing the media to retreat to their vans, but they did not move on.

One persistent one said, "Will you give us an interview, luv?"

"I dinna ken what ye're after with all your Londun ways. Now move ye on."

"Then she's not here?"

"If ye mean the earl's sister, no, she's no aboot. Now let the sheep pass."

The rain came long and hard, and Biddy, Dickie, and their flock of sheep were thoroughly drenched by the time they reached the MacPherson farm down the road. They found Robbie by the hearth.

"Lady Biddy and Sir Richard," he said with concern. "You're soaked through."

"Worse," said Biddy, "we have the whole flock from my pen, and Toby as well. He's eager to settle them for the night. It was the best I could do to drive off the press, but they only retreated to a short distance. Can you help, Robbie?"

"First come in and get warm. I'll put the sheep in my own pen and bring them back tomorrow for the shearing." He went outside and from the series of whistles that followed, Biddy knew her sheep were safe for the night. Robbie returned fifteen minutes later.

"Lady Biddy, Miss Elspeth called and said the poachers might be out tonight hunting a wild boar, a very big one. She said she wanted me and some of the hands to come up to the farm, get the shotguns and go after them." Robbie obviously knew the absurdity of this but was not sure he should have taken Elspeth's call as a joke.

Biddy and Richard began to laugh, and Robbie's face broke into a broad grin.

"Elspeth must have thought," Biddy said chuckling, "a wild boar with poachers tracking them might set terror in the veins of our city press corps, but I don't want to physically harm the people in the vans, just to scare them. Can you find a way for me and Richard to get back to the farm without their knowing?"

"Wouldn't you like to be part of the fireworks?"

"No, Robbie," she said. "I'll leave that to you and anyone you can scare up to help you. But come, you will need the shotguns from the case."

Before dispatching the more adventurous farm hands in their 'search for the wild boar and poachers', Robbie led Richard and Biddy back to the farm by a back track down along the loch. Biddy's father had kept his guns in a locked cabinet in the barn's gunroom, and Biddy and Ivor had never bothered to move them, since guns no longer had any use round the farm other than the odd shooting at a fox who became interested in the hens or a hawk who found a wounded lamb. Biddy dispensed the six shotguns that were on a rack and sent Robbie off to find 'the poachers and the wild boar'.

As Biddy and Richard walked back from the barn, Biddy looked puzzled. "That's very odd. One of Daddy's rifles is missing from the gun cabinet, where the shot gun shells where kept. I must ask Robbie about it in the morning."

The farmhands started letting off shotgun blasts soon afterwards, and the vans slowly withdrew. But they were back in the morning.

*

Dinner was a quiet affair. Elspeth cooked some scrambled eggs, and Biddy found some cold ham, tomatoes and cheese in the refrigerator, and she laid out some oatcakes. They all picked at their food, but their minds focused on the shots outside.

"Despite the ruse of the wild boar," Elspeth finally said,

"we still have the problem of the aggressiveness of the press. I have to deal with this all the time at the hotels and find that some directness helps. I suggest, Biddy, that if you are up to it, in the morning you go to the gate, and explain to the media that the working of the farm must continue. Take them some coffee every so often, make it weak and bad, with milk that is about to turn and no sugar, and then let them moulder. After several days without any activity, I think they will clear off to find the nearest coffee house and not return. But, Biddy, for heaven's sake, speak normally. Dickie tells me even he could see through your attempts to imitate a Scottish burr."

Biddy laughed. "I never had your talent at mimicry, 'Peth, although you would think I could do better at a burr, having lived here all my life. All right, I'll take your suggestion, and be at my most uppity tomorrow morning. How long do you think they will last?"

"I think the weather may be a factor, but unfortunately the forecast is for fair skies tomorrow," Elspeth said. "But now we have another problem. Since I need to be in Pitlochry in the morning, I think Dickie and I should go stay with Daddy tonight and hopefully not be followed by the press. Still, I fear there may be stragglers who are not afraid of wild boar, poachers, or random gunshots and who could see our car leave. When it's finally dark, perhaps we can slink out some back way. Is the track through the lower meadow still passable?"

Biddy nodded. "Yes, if you take the Land Rover. I won't be using it as tomorrow is sheep shearing, and I'll be here all day. The shearers will be here right after breakfast. I can always use Johnnie's car, if I need one."

"We can wait until just as it's getting dark or if there's

147

another rainstorm. That way the helicopter won't find us," Richard suggested. He knew the track Elspeth had mentioned, as he had driven the tractor along it many times with Johnnie in happier days.

This plan agreed on, they turned on the late television news. Elspeth recognised the television correspondent from her visit to Johnnie's house in Perth, but now she was standing on the road above the farm. "With the Earl of Tay in jail now, where is his family? Are they supporting him?" The woman looked cold, not being dressed for the wind off the loch or the coming storm, but she went on undauntedly with her report. "A local farmwoman who was interviewed by this reporter said earlier that the earl's sister, Lady Elisabeth Baillie Shaw, is not at the Tay family farm here on Loch Tay. We are following leads as to her whereabouts." The camera had caught Biddy and Richard, luckily both unrecognizable under their battered hats, driving the sheep to the gate and Biddy answering to the reporter's questions earlier.

"If ye mean the earl's sister, no, she's no aboot. Now let the sheep pass."

"Dickie was right," Elspeth said laughing. "As someone born and bred in the Highlands, Biddy, you might learn, when necessity requires it, to sound like a Scot, not a bad Hollywood version of one."

The television report was blessedly short, and the reporter did not mention the wild boar or the poachers.

14

With the diversion of several more shotgun blasts, Richard and Elspeth made their escape from the farm along the track though the lower meadow, Biddy's cantankerous Land Rover lumbering down it. One reporter saw the car from a distance but was tired enough not to realise that as it emerged from the farm garages it carried occupants from the farm who did not belong to the shooting party. Richard and Elspeth circled around to the south, avoiding the media vans, and were half-way to Loch Rannoch before they felt assured that they had not been followed and could therefore relax. They drove up over the moor and down to Kinloch Rannoch. The narrow, tree-lined road on the north side of Loch Rannoch was deserted at this time of day, and they made good progress without having to pull into a layby and let others through.

They approached the Duffs' large stone house, which stood in silhouette against the last stage of twilight. Every time Elspeth saw the building, she felt the warmth of being at home, although she had not lived there since she entered Girton College, Cambridge. She had grown up at the house, and her parents were still a mainstay in her life.

The iron gate at the bottom of the drive was shut, and Elspeth fumbled for her Blackberry to get the code for the electronic lock. Her mother was getting forgetful, so her father had set the combination to be the six figures of Elspeth's birthday, 310750. Richard got out of the car and opened the gate. They proceeded up the drive, which was surrounded by sycamore trees, now in full leaf. Elspeth could see a light in the drawing room window, and suspected that her father was waiting by the window to see the headlamps of their car.

Instead, they found James Duff asleep by the fire. Bounce, the Duffs' golden retriever, woke the household, including the cat who was sleeping on James's lap. It ran its nails into his leg thus provoking a yowl from Elspeth's father. The dog greeted Elspeth and Dickie with her tail furiously wagging in welcome.

Elspeth had told Dickie that she now considered London their home, but deeply inside the old stone house above Loch Rannoch would always be her real home. What would happen to it when her parents died? She would not keep the house but would grieve its loss. Perhaps some other member of the family would want it, Lizzie and Denis perhaps, but to her it would not be the same without her parents living there.

Monday morning she lay in the early light and let her eyes roam around the room that had been hers since she was a small child. This had been her sanctuary, even during her university years, until she married Alistair Craig and moved to California when she was twenty-six. It was here where as a teenager she had studied seriously enough to be accepted into Girton College to read law, here where she had slept after rapturous days at Tay Farm when she, Johnnie, and Richard were young, and here where she grieved Malcolm Buchanan, her fiancé at Cambridge, when he had been murdered. Alistair had never been here as he loathed the Scottish Highlands, which she supposed was a blessing, but Richard had come often over the years, as he had formed a bond with her parents when he was young.

There was little change in the bedroom even after she left for America. She had replaced Malcolm's photograph on one of the bookcases with a black and white one taken forty years before. It showed her and Johnnie extending their arms up to the forces in heaven and Dickie between them looking supercilious but apparently holding them both up. Alongside it was a brightly coloured canvas, painted by one of Alistair's Hollywood friends, of her two children making a sandcastle on Malibu beach when they were young. On her old desk by the south window was a copy of a large photograph in a silver frame of Richard in his full regalia as a Knight Commander of the Order of Saint Michael and Saint George. She had smiled lovingly when he had given it to her on their marriage, and she knew he gave it to her with great pride. The original of the photograph in her office was in their flat in London and stood next to a photograph taken the year before of him looking blissfully happy standing on the deck of the retreat in Marin County with oak trees and the Pacific Ocean behind him. The latter image was how she always remembered him when they were apart. The only other new addition to the room was a bed wide enough for them both to sleep in, which after their marriage Fiona Duff had adorned with travel blankets from the Munro and MacDuff clans, both cheerfully red and green. Fiona had mistakenly crossed them so that the MacDuff rug was on Richard's side of the bed and Munro on Elspeth's. Neither one told Fiona of her error and left them where they had so caringly been placed.

Richard slept soundly beside her, and she listened to the

rhythm of his deep breathing that was now so familiar. When she was growing up, she had lain in this same room imagining what life would bring her and what the man would be like whom she would marry. She never imagined it would be Johnnie's sombre friend from Oxford, Dickie Munro, but now as she had reached middle age her heart was sure she had made the right choice, after all her earlier failed attempts at happiness. She rolled over towards him and put her arms about him. He did not wake but grunted contentedly. She lay her cheek on his back and slowly fell back to sleep. She woke again well after the sun was stabbing its bright rays through the east windows. Richard was gone, but his love lingered about her.

She smelled coffee brewing, which she knew was meant for her, and she called downstairs to see how long she had to dress. Richard assured her that he and her father were happily preparing breakfast from the ingredients of the basket Biddy had given them before they left the farm, and Elspeth could take her time.

As she chose her clothes from the wardrobe, the day ahead took on a less happy aspect. It was Monday, and she and Richard were booked to return to London on a late Thursday afternoon flight from Edinburgh. That gave her just three full days. What was it she hoped to discover? Louisa's sudden demand for the farm seemed paramount, but how was Elspeth to gain access to the mind of someone who was now dead? Would Portia MacRoberts, Johnnie's solicitor in the divorce, have any idea? Elspeth also wanted to know about the ownership of the farm. During the early nineteen thirties her grandparents, the seventh earl and his wife, had lost almost everything in the stock market crash, but he could not sell the farm because it was not allowed by the grant of the earldom. Her uncle, the eighth earl, kept his family there without any mention that he might like to rid himself of it. Elspeth was not clear why, since neither her grandparents nor aunt and uncle showed any interest in farm life. The farm was a special place for Elspeth, as she remembered happily the many years she had romped there with her two cousins. It was there, too, that she had first met Richard, which at the time had little significance for her but now had transformed her life. The farm was worth saving, not only for Biddy's sake, and for all theirs. Would today's revelations in James Duff's law firm of Duff, MacBean and MacRoberts turn up anything that would help?

Elspeth's breakfast was waiting for her. Richard had even decorated their plates with some fresh strawberries that Biddy had grown in her kitchen garden and put in the basket, those which had not been squashed in their evening ride over the lumpy track and the narrow roads over the moor. James Duff was reading *The Times*, which thankfully had not deigned to follow the ins and outs of the Tay arrest in Perth and had relegated the story of Johnnie's arrest to the bottom of page twelve, although Elspeth expected they would see the screaming headlines in the Scottish newspapers. This morning the Duff house seemed quite normal except for the incredible anxiety she was feeling inside.

"Will you come with me today, Dickie?" she asked her husband, who was removing her mother's frilly apron after turning off the cooker. She suppressed an internal giggle and wondered what his distinguished colleagues at the Foreign and Commonwealth Office and the European Commission would think if they saw him in his present guise. "I'm afraid some of the work will be very dusty."

"Lady MacDuff," he said, "since when is a knight of the realm put off by a little dust when in pursuit of the truth? Lead on." His voice was light but the serious look in his eyes belied his humour. Elspeth felt that he too was worried about the press of time and his own commitment to return to the British High Commission in Malta on Friday.

*

James Duff pleaded the necessity of leaving for his office in Pitlochry in order to get the appropriate papers together for Elspeth to read. He asked Elspeth and Richard to walk the dog before they came to the office later. Bounce bounded happily beyond them and was content with the occasional stick Richard threw for her.

Richard took his wife's arm as they walked on the narrow road beside the loch. This gentle act woke in him the reality of his marriage. He had not expected his marriage to Elspeth to change him although he had watched her change. She had softened, at least when alone with him. She still had moments of great vulnerability, such as the one at the farm two nights before, but he sensed her growing trust in the sustainability of their marriage. He had never dreamed that a relationship like theirs could exist. His first visions of her when he had been a teenager had been of passion, ones in which she now reciprocated freely, but these dreams had not included his own personal growth and deeper emotional fulfilment. Sometimes when she was busy with some task, she would look up at him and smile. Then she would lower her eyes and go back to what she was doing. His heart would always bang against his chest when she did this because the look was not calculated, but rather a simple statement of what their relationship had become. He had never supposed that he could love someone as much as he loved her now, everything about her, her 'lumps and bumps' as she called them. She had taught him to laugh freely, to observe the minutiae of the world, which was so important to her profession, and to enjoy the vagaries of human existence, whether it met with the highest standards of social interaction or not. Elspeth seldom condemned people's life experiences, other than her own perhaps, and she had taught him to do the same. Where he once had been censorious, he now was simply amused; she had offered him that gift. She had also given him a real family, people for whom he deeply cared, and most of all she had given him herself. He closed his eyes and held on to her arm without voicing his thoughts.

To the unwitting eye they would have appeared to be a normal Scottish couple, perhaps a bit more finely dressed than most, walking their dog and enjoying the morning sun, although they were deeply engrossed in what appeared to be serious conversation. It might have been about a household concern rather than a murder.

A car passed and hurriedly drove on, without stopping. Richard recognised the couple in the car as belonging to one of the Duffs' neighbours to whom he had been introduced on several occasions. Their rudeness in not stopping or waving was perhaps explained by their reluctance to greet the family of a possible murderer.

Elspeth looked at them go. "The MacLeods seem no longer to recognise us. How terribly sad. Please don't tell Mother; she is rather fond of them, but our presence has been noticed and soon will be known all round the loch. Things seldom go unnoticed here."

Then she returned to the topic at hand. "Dickie, I'm worried. Everything seems to be going against Johnnie. Like Biddy, I can't see him murdering anyone, even if provoked."

He covered her hand with his, which she gently squeezed, although he sensed her thoughts were elsewhere, but she seemed grateful at the touch.

"From all you know of Johnnie," she asked, "do you think he could have murdered Louisa?"

Richard thought before answering. Finally he said, "No, but my opinion alone won't stand up in a court of law. What do you hope to find out today?"

She stopped and leaned her head against his shoulder. "I lay in bed this morning, looking at that silly photograph taken of us when we were young. I tried to remember our adventures together. We never hurt anyone with our pranks, you know. Biddy was a bit ruffled when we found her and Ivor kissing in the hayloft in the barn, and, as you know, I still bear the scar on my back where I fell off the ladder afterwards, perhaps in just retribution for being so bratty. But it all was in fun. We never intentionally harmed a thing. But I haven't really known Johnnie since then. Do you have any idea who he has become?"

At that moment Bounce demanded another stick and Richard obliged. He paused. "I don't think he has changed. He never had good judgement about women, and I only hope Madeline is different. He was always lured by a pretty face or a flirtatious eye."

Richard remembered the numerous times at Oxford when Johnnie would get into a scrape with a woman. Sometimes she was from the town and had enjoyed a pint too many with Johnnie in a pub. Sometimes she was of the gown and was attracted more to Johnnie's title and good looks. Richard had often intervened in both cases and kept his friend from committing his affections where he should have not.

Richard shared these thoughts with Elspeth. She listened carefully as he recounted several instances.

"You knew Kathleen at Oxford. What was she really like?" Elspeth asked. "I suppose she had your approval?"

Richard stopped and turned to Elspeth. When they had been young, she had often accused him of being too avuncular. "Do you think I needed to give it?" he asked.

"Probably," she said looking at him with a small smile. "You always wanted to direct my affairs of the heart when I was younger; I can't imagine it was different with Johnnie."

Although she spoke flippantly, he knew there was great sorrow beneath her words, particularly considering his harsh criticism of her affair with Malcolm Buchanan and her marriage to Alistair Craig, but in retrospect how correct his criticism had been. Richard loved Elspeth so much that he could almost read her thoughts.

He thought about Johnnie's first wife. "Kathleen was the first woman Johnnie seemed attracted to who had any dignity. She was at one of the women's colleges, I don't remember which, and seemed very bright and merry. She was also fragile, both physically and mentally, and I think that appealed to his caring nature. He always was that way, which may explain Biddy's contention that he would hurt nothing more than an insect. When I first met Kathleen, I applauded Johnnie's choice and urged him to settle his heart. He was always off helping her during their last term at Oxford, and they married soon after they both came down from university. I was happy to be his best man and hoped she would ground him. None of us could have guessed she was so unstable and would take her life when she did not produce the desired heir."

He did not recall if Elspeth was at the wedding or not, but suspected not, as it occurred shortly after Malcolm Buchanan's murder. He knew Elspeth had retreated to Loch Rannoch to grieve the loss of her fiancé weeks before Kathleen and Johnnie were married and that she could not have coped with Johnnie's marriage at that time in her life.

"And Helen?" she asked about Johnnie's second wife.

"Helen was different. She resembled Kathleen, being fair, but did not have Kathleen's intelligence or dependence. Her robustness must have appealed to Johnnie after Kathleen died. That became the most important thing to Johnnie. The loss of both Kathleen and their stillborn son had shaken him. Some nights when he had had a dram or two too many, he would confide in me that he felt responsible for Kathleen's death. What a burden that must have been. But when he met Helen in Edinburgh about a year after Kathleen died, he seemed to pick up. She seemed fun and healthy, and I thought she suited Johnnie. Shortly after their marriage, Marjorie and I went out to Burma, so I lost touch with Johnnie for a long while.

"We, of course, saw them when we returned to Scotland to see both our families," Richard continued, "but the visits were brief. Marjorie looked down on Helen a bit, but that was not unusual as Helen was not as Marjorie said 'a member of our set'. At times I would see Johnnie alone, and he would always mention that he hoped for an heir. But after fifteen years it never happened. Then one night Helen simply disappeared."

"Disappeared?" Elspeth asked. "I knew she had left Johnnie, but I never asked for the details. Did she simply vanish from the face of the earth? Or did she run off with someone?"

"The latter, I fear. She left a note for Johnnie saying she was going abroad with someone else and would not contest a divorce."

"Poor Johnnie," Elspeth said. "I had no idea. I should've asked."

"I didn't see Johnnie for several years after that. Marjorie and I were abroad most of the time and then she got ill. You had best ask Biddy about that time. She would know."

"I shall. When did you first learn about Louisa?"

"Just after Marjorie's death. I should have been more attentive, but my concerns were elsewhere. In fact I only met Johnnie once after he married Louisa, in Edinburgh, when I was settling Marjorie's affairs. We met on the street, and he told me about your leaving Alistair and going to work for the Kennington Organisation. Your news rattled me more than I can say, but I had my own personal problems with Marjorie's death. I knew Johnnie had remarried but forgot to ask much about it, because my mind was so filled otherwise."

"Did you ever meet Louisa?"

Richard shook his head. "Normally Johnnie is the demanding one in our relationship and would have poured everything out to me, but my own emotions were so entangled at the time with Marjorie's illness and death that I had fallen into my own personal abyss and didn't honour Johnnie's needs for my friendship, which I had been doing most of my life." His regret was deeper than he could convey, even to Elspeth. Would she understand?

"Louisa doesn't fit in with my perception of Johnnie," Elspeth said. "Yes, she was of child-bearing age, but why would Johnnie want someone like that for the heir's mother? I hate all this, Dickie, the heir, entitlements, the beastly title. Look where it has led him."

Richard stopped and looked down at Elspeth. "You became egalitarian over all those years in California, didn't you?"

"No, I always felt that way, probably because my mother did too. Did you see her blanch at Peter's wedding when I used her title? I've never heard her use it. She has always been perfectly happy to be Daddy's wife, plain Mrs James Duff. She hasn't needed to establish her quality or worth by using a title.

Richard had heard this diatribe from Elspeth many times before, and he simply leaned over and touched her hair with his lips.

"It isn't your title that I dispute," she continued. "You earned it, but how did Johnnie earn his? Or Louisa hers? Countess, indeed. What a load of total rubbish. If Johnnie were simply John Robertson of Perth, would the national media be lingering outside the farm forced to drink Biddy's purposely badly brewed coffee and trying to get photographs of the murdering earl's sister? The incident would hardly bear notice even in the local press after a day or two."

15

Richard drove Biddy's Land Rover along the banks of Loch Rannoch, through Kinloch Rannoch, and then on past Loch Tummel towards Pitlochry. By his side, Elspeth's thoughts turned inwards, and self-doubt twisted inside her. Had she been sure of Johnnie's innocence her task would have been easier. She wanted to be certain of it, but she could not be. She had tried to expunge the thought that the only other person who would benefit substantially from Louisa's death was Biddy. Despite the mirth at dinner the other night with Max, Biddy did have a quality of steeliness and did not share Johnnie's dislike of killing. Even as a child, Biddy would not leave the barnyard when a chicken was killed, or the lambs taken for slaughtering. Elspeth did not know the depths of Biddy's feelings about the loss of the farm. Elspeth was suddenly flooded with dismay because she was unaware of where Biddy had been the night of the murder. Elspeth had heard Johnnie leave the farm but where was Biddy? They had all climbed the main stairs of the farmhouse to their respective bedrooms that night, but later Biddy, whose bedroom was at the far end of the hallway, could have slipped down the back stairs and gone out. Elspeth tried to remember where the Land Rover was when they had gone to bed on Thursday night. Most likely it had been in one of the garages by the barn, but it also could have been in the lower field that she and Richard

161

had surreptitiously crossed the night before. She turned to Richard, who was concentrating on keeping the Land Rover straight on the road, his chin set and his knuckles white from struggling with the wheel. She did not want to disturb his concentration, as Biddy's Land Rover was hard to control and too wide for the road. Elspeth knew that Biddy, so soft and pretty, would kill with just cause, but would that include murdering her brother's troublesome wife? Elspeth realised she would have to confront Biddy and felt nauseous at the prospect.

Elspeth also was grappling with her own feelings. Having confronted Richard with the shortcomings of her family, she could not ignore them herself. At what point did family loyalty block the need for the truth? If she did discover that Johnnie or Biddy had murdered Louisa, what would she do? Hide it from Max? What then? The pounding repetition of these last two words would not leave her mind.

As they passed alongside Loch Tummel, Elspeth's thoughts turned to Madeline. Had she calmly returned to her work in Dundee and pretended that nothing had happened that could tear her life apart forever? At the cottage Elspeth had seen Madeline's grit but how far could it be tested? Madeline was still young and at that age steadfastness often faded when difficulty presented itself. What could Elspeth tell Johnnie about Madeline's resolve when she saw him at the jail in Perth later?

She was so far immersed in her thoughts that she was startled when Dickie spoke, echoing her thoughts.

"Will Madeline defend Johnnie publicly?" he asked.

"I have no idea. The decision is hers. She knows the risks."

"How fearless do you think she is?"

Elspeth was not certain and said as much to Richard. "There's so much for them both to lose. The easy way would be for Madeline to walk away. She's young and attractive. There could easily be someone else later on."

"Do you think she'll abandon Johnnie?"

"It will be the test of their love if she doesn't. When I left her at the cottage, I sensed she was struggling not only with the actuality of Johnnie's arrest but also lost hope."

They drove on, silent above the grumble of the engine. "Elspeth, where are you going with this?"

Richard glanced over at her, and in that short moment she saw his own anxiety and his fear for his friend. His question flooded her once again with misgivings about her own ability to help her cousin in a tangle he had created for himself.

"I wish I knew," she said, rubbing her forehead with her fingertips, hoping it would relieve her tension. "It's so much easier to investigate a crime when it isn't your kith and kin who are involved. I want Johnnie to be innocent, but is he? What do you think?" she said quietly. "There's no one else with such good motive or opportunity." She did not mention Biddy.

*

Fearing that either she or Biddy's Land Rover would be recognised, Elspeth directed Richard through the back streets of Pitlochry and into the private car park behind her father's offices on Bonnethill Road. James Duff was waiting for them at the back door of the turreted stone building and whisked them inside.

"I've laid out the boxes you wanted to see," he said, "I don't know what you will learn, but if there's anything there that will help Johnnie, please find it. Portia has a court appearance today and asked if she can talk to you tomorrow morning."

"Let me slink into the streets and buy the wicked papers," Richard suggested, "No one will recognise me, and we should know the worst that the British public is being told about Johnnie." He left Elspeth and her father alone.

When he returned, Richard found Elspeth in her father's conference room and spread the lurid national press out on the table. *EARL DRAGGED INTO JAIL Could be remanded to prison today* one headline read and underneath it was a recycled photograph of Johnnie in handcuffs being taken into the Perth police station. Another read *IS LORD TAY GUILTY?* Underneath was a line reading *Family has no comment. The Courier*, a local Perth paper, was kinder. *LORD TAY ARRESTED*, it headlined matter-of-factly, *Formal charges to be filed today*.

"My father has left for lunch," Elspeth said, "but has entrusted me with the family boxes. He has already ordered something to be sent in for us. Shall we eat first or get down to work?"

"It depends on how messy the meal. One would not like to see tomato sauce adorning your family archives in perpetuity."

When the local delicatessen delivered lunch, he opened the box. "Sandwiches, rather delicious looking ones at that. Definitely no tomato sauce."

The brie and cranberry sandwiches, without tomato sauce but with some excellent relish, were accompanied by some organic fruit juice. Elspeth suspected the deli had added these without confirming with James Duff what type of cold drink would be required. Fish paste and cucumber sandwiches and strong tea would have been more like his idea of a perfect picnic lunch.

"Let's get to work before we eat," Elspeth said.

The heavy file boxes sat in soldier like rows and differed only in their apparent age. The oldest ones bore carefully handwritten labels, the ones in the middle had typewritten ones, and the latest were computer generated. Elspeth found the section for the Robertson/Tay/Duff families and saw the first box read "Seventh Lord Tay and family". Since the earl, her grandfather, had become bankrupt, he must have been pleased that his daughter's husband was a lawyer and would handle his affairs without fee. The eighth earl's box was ascribed in the same hand. Johnnie's box was the first to have a typed label. Elspeth drew it from the shelf, noticing its neighbours reading Lady Fiona Mary Elisabeth Duff née Robertson, Frederick Keith Duff, both handwritten, Lady Elisabeth Constance Mary Baillie Shaw, née Robertson and family, typed, and Elspeth Fiona Duff and family, the last label computer generated. Knowing the outcry it would have provoked from his daughter, her father had not added the names of her two husbands, but the boxes must have copies of all the important papers relating to her relationship with them and to her two children. Despite his advancing years, her father still kept his family carefully documented and in legal order.

Elspeth opened the ninth earl's box to find neatly tied bundles of documents tied with archival ribbon. The first packet comprised of Johnnie's certificate of birth and the record of his christening. The next contained items pertaining to his education. She untied the third, which related to his marriage to Kathleen. The marriage certificate was there along with her certificate of death. The suicide had not been recorded as such, the cause of death being 'died in childbirth'. In between the pages was a certificate of the stillborn birth, a male child without a name. Elspeth brushed her fingers across this in a silent tribute, while trying to block out how much pain the events recorded on the thin pieces of paper must have caused Johnnie. Elspeth found papers that stated Johnnie had received a settlement of ten thousand pounds from his joint life assurance policy with Kathleen that probably had given him enough to start his first business, which had sadly also died in its infancy. Next came his and Helen's marriage certificate and a life assurance policy benefiting Johnnie if she died. Elspeth noticed the policy was current, which surprised her, but then again Helen was not dead, and Johnnie still could have renewed the policy on her. Also there was a copy of the last will and testament for them both, but Elspeth knew it would have become void on Johnnie's remarriage. Underneath everything was an unsigned copy of Johnnie's divorce petition citing Helen's desertion. Elspeth presumed the signed copy would be in Edinburgh.

Elspeth then took up the documents relating to Johnnie's marriage to Louisa. The marriage appeared to have been a civil one, not a church one, and the signatures on it wavered above and below the lines provided for the bride and groom and two witnesses, whose names Elspeth could not decipher. She hoped Johnnie had been more sober than his scrawled signature would indicate. Copies of Johnnie and Louisa's wills, both dated three years before, followed and life assurance policies in the amount of a million pounds each, which Elspeth found startling. This gave Johnnie one more motive to kill Louisa. Elspeth found a separate box for Tay Farm that held photocopies of the original grant of the earldom from the Duke of Cumberland as King George II's agent in Scotland, dated May 1746, and original grant deeds to the farm. She touched the copies of royal documents with loathing, for although her family had been on both sides of the Jacobite rebellion, Elspeth could never forgive what 'Butcher Cumberland', in the name of his father George II, had done to the Highlanders. Nothing in the box related to any entailment of the land, but the grant deed stated, in words abounding with f's in place of s's, that the deeds to the lands and farm would belong to the current holder of the earldom, whether male or female, and could not be revoked.

Elspeth carefully retied and replaced the packets in Johnnie's box and rose from the table. She filled Richard in on what she had learned.

"Do you think any of that will help Johnnie?" he asked.

"I have no idea, but I hope so. Let's have lunch and then go into Perth. I need to talk to Max and then see Johnnie at the jail. I hope Biddy is managing without her Land Rover. Do you mind, Dickie?" She sighed. "This is hardly the holiday after Peter's wedding that we imagined."

His caring eyes reassured her worried ones. He did not need to answer with words.

Before they left Bonnethill Road, Elspeth tried to ring Madeline, but only got her voice mail. The message said Madeline would not be returning to her office until Wednesday and gave the name of an associate who would be handling any questions.

Where was Madeline?

16

On Sunday evening, drained from her attempts to run away from herself, Madeline had gone to her office, changed the message on her answerphone, and left an e-mail for her employers that she needed to take a few days off and she planned to return on Wednesday. She also e-mailed two important clients, who were expecting presentations by the end of the week, informing them that she was not well but would make sure their projects were not neglected in the meantime. She undocked her laptop and took it with her. Where could she go? She considered her flat, but its yawning emptiness the night before had spooked her. She needed a place devoid of Johnnie.

She turned her two-seater north, following the road that bordered the coast along the North Sea. As a child, her parents had taken her to a small, cranky cottage near a village by the coast that had been let to summer holidaymakers by farmers in an effort to make ends meet. Madeline tried to remember exactly where it was. No one would think of looking for her there, she thought. She took out her road atlas and found a likely spot. After a long time searching, she found the place, which seemed deserted. She went on along the road and found the farm she recalled from her childhood. A ruddy-faced woman about her own age answered her knock. The cottage

168

was free until Wednesday, the woman said, and Madeline could have it for twenty-five pounds a night. No credit cards were accepted. Madeline fumbled in her bag, found forty pounds and promised the rest the next day after she could find a cash point. The woman said the closest one was in Montrose.

She had brought an overnight bag with the bare necessities, but not enough for four days. In the morning she would venture into Montrose, but for now the loneliness of the cottage, the fact that she probably was out of mobile phone range, and the discomfort of the accommodations calmed her. She threw her case on the lopsided bed, went to the ancient cooker, and put on the kettle. Then she laughed. She had neither tea nor food for dinner or breakfast, and the villages she had passed through appeared to have shut down for the weekend, but dealing with these necessities of life was far easier than dealing with her feelings about Johnnie. Where had she last seen a town larger than the village? Perhaps fifteen miles away? She got in her car, reversed and went to fetch the few things required for her existence that night. In a small, beleaguered shop still open on Sunday evening, she found pork pies that were of dubious freshness, a tin of baked beans, a half dozen eggs, a small loaf of questionable white bread, some butter, some beyond the best before date tea bags, and some powdered coffee creamer, all of which sent up flags considering her normally healthy regimen. But circumstance overcame philosophical nutritional principles. She paid the man in the shop and was grateful for the sustenance.

She finally returned to the cottage where she could no longer avoid confronting her feelings. She had no Internet connection, and her mobile phone signal came and went erratically. Because of the lateness of the summer nights, she did not need to use the lights in the cottage, but its interior felt eerie despite the light in the sky. She walked outside with her cup of tea into the poorly tended garden and wished she had never met Johnnie Tay.

She went to bed but could not sleep. Madeline was not naturally inclined to morbidity, but it overcame her. Finally she rose and took a sleeping pill.

Waking early and refreshed by the dull flavour of the tea she had bought the night before, she donned the running clothes and trainers she had put in her overnight bag and tied back her black hair. Five kilometres, no better ten, would do more good than mouldering in her own sorrow. Tucking her mobile in her pocket in case of emergency and pulling a bottle of water from her car, she headed towards the sea. At first, she thought only of her stride and soon set a pace that was familiar. Only then did her thoughts return to Johnnie.

Why had she considered life with a man twenty-eight years her senior? Words like early widowhood, left to raise the children alone, and being burdened with his failing health all flickered through her mind. Was that really the life she wanted? She shook herself. She had gone into her affair with Johnnie without hesitation. He gave her something other men in her life had not: gentleness, humour, kindness, and most of all a real sense of deep love for her, not only as a woman but as a person. She found no artifice in him, and she had opened up to him as she had to no other person in her life. Elspeth Duff had challenged her to consider the truth of her feelings, and Madeline knew she would have to answer Elspeth's ultimatum, come what may.

She ran on, watching one foot and then the other pounding the ground. Her breath and pulse regularised, and her adrenalin kicked in as it always did on her long runs. Finally she slowed her pace and found a rock where she could rest, stretch and drink some water. As she took the water bottle from her pocket, her mobile fell to the ground. Madeline saw she now had a steady signal. Had Elspeth tried to call her at her office? If so, she would have only reached the message on the answerphone. Madeline rang through to her office and checked her messages remotely. Elspeth had left a number. Madeline checked her watch and saw it was well after ten. Would Elspeth be reachable? Madeline tapped Elspeth's number.

*

Richard and Elspeth were approaching Kinloch Rannoch when Elspeth's mobile rang. Madeline did not identify herself, but Elspeth recognised her voice. Madeline was panting as if she had run out of breath. Elspeth wondered why.

"I need to I see you," Madeline said. "Please. Tomorrow and alone if possible."

"Where are you?" Elspeth asked.

Madeline chuckled. "Sitting on a rock near the sea trying to reconcile the fact that I'm about to take the biggest risk of my life with a problematic likelihood of success."

"Then you want to help him?"

"I'll do anything I can."

"Good," Elspeth said. "Can you be in Perth tomorrow afternoon?"

"When and where?"

Elspeth gave the address of Max's chambers.

When Elspeth had rung off, she looked over at her husband.

"Madeline?" he asked without needing an answer. "Brave

171

woman."

"Yes, very brave. Now I have just acquired one more person to save."

17

Max watched Elspeth, who frowned as he told her the formal charge given by the court against John Robertson, Earl of Tay, for the murder in the first degree of Louisa Robertson, Countess of Tay.

"First degree, not second? That's not good, but how can they bring these charges so quickly?" Elspeth asked Max.

"The police report is quite clear. They found several items of Lord Tay's clothing in Louisa's sitting room, but most condemning of all was a mackintosh with a note in it addressed to him and dated the July 5th, which would imply that he left it in the house sometime after that. Johnnie's fingerprints were everywhere. Another reason they arrested him was that two eyewitnesses came forward, who said they had seen Lord Tay running from Louisa's house shortly after midnight. The witnesses identified him in a police line-up after he was brought to the police station on Saturday."

Elspeth listened in horror. "But most of those things seem hardly possible. Fingerprints last a long time, so Johnnie's fingerprints do not surprise me, but the other things?"

Max considered how best to tell Elspeth the worst piece of news. "There's one other thing, which damns him more than anything else. Louisa's baby was his. They took his DNA when he was booked. The police requested a priority check on Johnnie's sample considering the severity of the crime, and

173

this morning the pathologist suggested that there are enough matches to the foetus's DNA that there can be a match for the paternity. A further test will need to be done to verify this. The pregnancy was over four months along."

Elspeth let out a short cry. "But Johnnie said," and then she stopped.

"What did he say?"

"That he had had sex with her about two months ago, only once, and the only time since the time they had separated. It doesn't match up, if the baby was more than four months along."

"We only have his word," Max said. "Adair Gordon, the procurator fiscal, seems to be building a case that will be hard to refute. I've always considered him a fair man, and we can't discount solid evidence. What else did Johnnie tell you? I need him to be forthcoming as I need to know everything I can to fight the fiscal's presumptions."

"Max, Johnnie was in Perth at the time of Louisa's murder. Unfortunately there's a witness who saw his car there."

Max grimaced. "I thought you might have good news for me."

"Even worse, Johnnie has a life insurance policy in case of Louisa's death for a million pounds."

Max put his hand to his forehead. "Now we have a real challenge on our hands. Are you up to it, Elspeth?"

"Do I have any choice?" she said.

"Then let's sit down and get to work," Max replied. "Here is where you can help. I need you to talk to Biddy and find out everything you can about Louisa. I'll take on Johnnie now that the formal charges have been made."

"Max, he may not trust you yet."

"Does he trust you?"

"He came to me in San Francisco before my son's wedding just over a week ago and asked for help, not about the murder because of course it hadn't yet been committed, but about saving the farm from Louisa's clutches. The farm has been the core of Biddy's life since her husband Ivor died. When we told her the news about Louisa wanting to take the farm, she seemed totally shattered. Yet with Louisa's death the whole issue seems to have gone away. I read both Johnnie and Louisa's wills this morning in my father's office. She left everything to Johnnie. Johnnie's was more circumspect. He left her life tenancy for the house in Perth and a living, similar to what I understand was in the original divorce settlement. The farm, which is 'immoveable property'—is that the correct term? — must be left to any direct heir of his, male or female. If there is none, Biddy's son Charles through the female line, would be the next in line to inherit the title if Johnnie has no heir. I read the original grant of peerage, and under the grant the farm does go to the legitimately born heir to the title and oddly stipulates 'male, or female if there is no close male heir'. I find that incredibly enlightened for the eighteenth century, although to my knowledge there has always been a male heir to step in. Oddly Johnnie left his business to Biddy in trust for his children, if any, and to her children if he died without issue. Other than running the farm, Biddy has no business experience, so I can't quite fathom his reasoning."

"Perhaps you should ask Biddy why. I presume he discussed the provisions of the will with her," Max said. "You ask Biddy and I'll ask him as well."

"Let me warn you, you'll find Biddy and Johnnie have

very strong bond between them. As often as we were thrown together as children, they shared secret parts of their lives only with each other and not with their bratty first cousin called Elspeth. When I was a child, and an only one at that, I was jealous of their closeness and often wished I had a brother like Johnnie and a sister like Biddy."

Max smiled at her candour. He could see the worry on her face.

Elspeth continued, "Louisa wanted Johnnie to think that the child she was carrying was his, which now it seems is true. That would make the child his legitimate heir under the law, and would give the child the title and the farm if anything happened to Johnnie, wouldn't it?"

"Yes, it seems so," Max agreed. "Can you make arrangements for me to review the grant of peerage?"

"Yes, of course. My father has a copy in his office, but how would Louisa have known?"

"Grants of peerage are in the public records."

"Louisa didn't strike me as the sort to go poking around in the dusty records of the past. My image of Louisa, overdressed and overweight, delighting in the spicy fish dish at the Kennington Edinburgh, keeps jumping into my head. Greed filled her eyes as she dug into it, but I can't remember any glimpse of intelligence in them when I met her."

Elspeth explained the details to her lunch in Edinburgh with Louisa. "It always comes back to the farm and Louisa's wanting it, doesn't it?" Elspeth added. "That seems to hold some significant clues we don't yet understand. Max, we have a great deal of work to do!"

"Do you think Johnnie and Biddy are holding something back?"

Max watched Elspeth set her jaw. "It wouldn't surprise me, but I intend to find out," she said. "Come to the farm when you can. There's much we still need to learn, and Biddy may be the key."

*

Elspeth did not relish going to see Johnnie at the Tayside Police Station jail, particularly in light of Max's information. She left Max's office and found Richard waiting for her in the reception area. Imploring him to bear with her and promising to tell all that she had learned after she had seen Johnnie, she made her way on foot to the police station. She registered in and was led to the visitors' room near the cells. The smell of fear filled her nostrils and dominated above the other more olfactory odours of antiseptic and human bodily functions.

"They haven't decided what to do with me yet. I'm hoping for bail rather than prison, although I may not be able to pay for them to post it. The procurator fiscal said he would be back to Max shortly, but I'm still waiting," he said. "Biddy said you saw Madeline."

"Saturday afternoon, at the cottage above the loch. We talked a long time. She said I was to tell you that she loved you."

"Even after all this?"

"Yes."

"Does she know about Louisa and the baby? Max told me the results of the postmortem."

"No. Max didn't know the results at the time I saw Madeline, but I think it won't matter."

"Would it to you if Dickie had the same complication?"

"I'd hope not."

"But you're not certain."

177

"If you love Madeline as much as I love Dickie, you will find a way to trust her instincts but be sensitive to how she must be feeling right now. My sense is that the love she feels for you can be tried, and she won't come up short."

"Will she stay away from me, as I asked?"

"I left the decision to her. She knows the consequences if she doesn't. But, Johnnie, there's one thing I must ask you and please answer truthfully. Where were you when you first left the farm on Thursday night? Madeline said you did not arrive at her flat until two on Friday morning, and I heard you leave before it was completely dark. Max told me that the murder was probably committed just after midnight."

Johnnie moved uncomfortably in his chair.

"As I remember, I drove to the end of the Loch Tay at Kenmore and sat there to watch the light go out of the sky. I was feeling euphoric about seeing Madeline, since we had been apart for ten days. She agreed that I could come to her flat near Dundee but only when it was dark enough to hide my arrival. That doesn't give one much of a window at this time of year. We agreed on two o'clock."

"Did anyone see you in Kenmore before you left for Dundee?"

"I doubt it. Who would be about? I left the loch a bit before midnight."

"Did you go through Perth?"

Johnnie set his jaw and averted his eyes from Elspeth. "I went by my flat to get some things, since I didn't have any fresh clothes since the trip to San Francisco. I was in Perth but only briefly."

"Marly Beaufort said she had seen a light in the flat. I wasn't certain if you had your lights on a timer the way Dickie and I do in London."

"You saw Marly?"

"I went round to your flat on Friday after first meeting Max."

"And Marly saw the light?"

"Yes, she and Roger were coming home from a late dinner party. Marly said it was already dark."

"Did they see me?"

"No, not you, only the light and your car."

"That puts me in Perth at the time of the murder without any witness to dispute it. How could everything go so wrong?"

"It gives the Crown a good deal of circumstantial evidence, but if you are innocent, we will have to find out what the truth is. When did you last see Louisa?"

"I haven't seen her since that dreadful night two months ago. I wish I could remember the exact date."

"How did you know she wanted to take the farm?"

"Through her solicitor, and mine."

"Was the farm part of the original terms of the proposed divorce settlement?"

"No. Nothing was ever said about the farm until the day before we left for San Francisco when my lawyer called me."

"Do you have any idea why the change?"

"The baby?" he speculated.

"No, I don't think so. Louisa could have known about the baby before she seduced you, probably to trap you into admitting paternity. There must be something else. I promise you I'll find it if I can."

"Are you confident you can?"

"Honestly, no, but I won't see you convicted of this crime. Max and I will have to find reasons for all the damning evidence. I have an appointment to see Portia MacRoberts in the morning. I hope that's OK."

"What do you hope to accomplish by doing that?"

"My instincts keep bringing me back to Louisa and the fact that she suddenly developed an interest in the farm. There's a link missing, and I thought if I talked to Portia, she could help me find it."

"Is there any way I can see Madeline in person?" he asked. "Did Max tell you they could send me to prison this afternoon if I can't meet the conditions of bail?"

Elspeth blew out her breath. "The decision has to be hers. I told her that."

"What would she want with an old person like me?"

"Don't sink into self-pity, Johnnie. There's no place for that now. We are all with you. You must keep your spirits up."

"You are beginning to sound avuncular like Dickie used to be," he said. "Has marriage done that to you? You used to be fun."

Elspeth winced at the mimicking of her first husband's words at the pre-wedding dinner. "I still can be fun but not when your future is on the line, but it is, and we all need to be as resourceful and clearheaded as possible. You can't drown yourself in self-doubt, Johnnie. I won't let you. Too much is at stake."

"Have you ever been in jail? Have you any idea what it is like?"

"Yes, I have been, twice, but only for a few hours."

"As a suspect?"

"Yes."

"For what?"

Elspeth's eyes glared. "Murder the first time. Murder of

not of one person but two the second time."

"You 're lying."

"No, I'm not, and the first was in a place that has a lot less friendly jail than Perth. Ask Dickie, but I did something about it other than wallowing in my sorrow."

Johnnie Tay looked askance. "Are you serious, 'Peth?"

"Absolutely. Did I mention that the second time the real murderer tried to blackmail me as well? And that someone tried to murder me twice?"

Suddenly Johnnie put back his head and laughed uproariously. "You've always needed to best me, haven't you? Did someone really try to murder you twice?"

Elspeth cocked an eyebrow and said, "Not twice, three times, in two different places on two different continents. The first time I was injured rather badly. You may remember when I was in hospital in London, or maybe Biddy didn't tell you. Dickie did rescue me all three times, and I'd have married him for that alone."

Elspeth watched Johnnie slowly recover.

"You'll never change, will you? Always up to a challenge. Well, 'Peth, you've made your point."

"Johnnie, I'm guilty of reverting to the bantering we did in childhood, when I feel such deep, searing pain about your case. Our family doesn't say that very much about our feelings to each other, but Dickie has taught me how sustaining the repeated use of the words 'I love you' are. I love you, Johnnie, and I'll do everything I can to get you out of this mess."

When Richard and Elspeth returned to the farm from Perth, Elspeth suggested to Biddy that the two of them walk out to the barn. Richard, discreetly, said he would go find

Robbie and see if the media hounds had taken their final departure.

Biddy and Elspeth stood in the doorway of the barn. The pungency of the hay filled their noses. Biddy insisted on a clean barn and did not tolerate the smell of animal waste to linger. She led Elspeth to a stall, where an unshorn ewe lay in a bed of straw. The sheep's head was wrapped in gauze.

"Poor thing," Biddy said, leaning to touch the ewe's face. "She got caught in a fence. I discovered her yesterday when we were rounding up the sheep for the shearing, I fear she could lose an eye." Elspeth watched her cousin's tenderness towards the animal.

"They all are important to you, aren't they, the animals, I mean?" Elspeth said.

"Both the animals and the people. They're our roots, 'Peth, although both you and Johnnie have decided to ignore them and live elsewhere." The intensity of Biddy's response startled Elspeth. "I raised this ewe," Biddy continued, "and her mother. I helped when she had a difficult delivery. Look at her. She may not be a hugely intelligent creature, but one can tell she has feelings, and she's a part of my stewardship of the farm. I've also sent her lambs to be slaughtered. What does that make me, heroine or villain? Life on a farm may seem simple to the uninitiated, but it's a daily affirmation of life—and death. Running a farm is not for the faint of heart. I can see why Johnnie left the farm to Ivor's and my management. Ivor taught me to appreciate its complexities, which I found odd at times as he had been raised in Edinburgh. Having the whole responsibility thrust on me also helped after Ivor died. We had worked so hard to make a success of the farm that I needed to carry on, and I feel often as if Ivor is still here with me."

"Have you ever wanted to remarry, Biddy?"

Elspeth's cousin shot a glance at her. "Following your example?"

"Not precisely," Elspeth said. "My example wasn't exactly smooth as you know all too well."

"Do you have a candidate in mind?" Biddy asked. Elspeth heard a touch of bitterness in her voice. "Loch Tay is not brimming with unattached men of a certain age who might consider an eligible widow of the same age who is more often found in Wellington boots than designer clothes and who has a brother accused of murder. My credentials are somewhat lacking."

Elspeth considered Max but did not share this thought with Biddy. Instead she said, "Things aren't looking good for Johnnie."

"Have you found anything to help?"

Elspeth leaned against a post at the edge of the stall and shook her head. "Nothing I can put my hands on. I just keep going back to Louisa. If Johnnie didn't kill her, who did, and most of all why? Even in the short time I was with her, I felt she really was a simple soul."

"Simple and not very appealing, I'm afraid," Biddy said. "I couldn't like her even for Johnnie's sake. He knew that, and after a while stopped asking me to be friends with her."

Elspeth walked beyond the stall to the ladder to the hayloft where she had played so many times as a child. She turned back to Biddy and said, "Murder takes a great deal of passion. You must remember that from the affair in Stresa. Who in Louisa's life could have felt that strongly about her? What kind of compulsion did he feel that made Louisa's murder a necessity?"

"Do you think it was a man?"

"Undoubtedly. I suspect Louisa had few women acquaintances. Most women would react to her the way you did. I felt the same way as well, but she did have a certain sexual appeal that would attract men and perhaps excite their passions."

"Do you think the crime was a sexual one?"

"No. Max told me the official postmortem showed Louisa was not sexually assaulted nor had she had sex recently. It might have been because of her condition."

"What possible reason could there be then?" Biddy came round to where her cousin was standing and hugged her. Elspeth returned the gesture.

The question, however, had bothered Elspeth from the onset. "Something important enough to the murderer for him to want to silence Louisa permanently."

"You don't think it was a crime of the moment?"

"No. Max said Johnnie will be tried for premeditated murder. I need to find out why. A crime of the moment would carry the charge of murder in the second degree or involuntary homicide."

Elspeth watched Biddy's face fill with bleakness. "It all sounds very frightening," she said.

"Yes, it is very frightening. Biddy, can you tell me anything else about Louisa, even things you heard from Johnnie, that would suggest why she was murdered?"

"Will you give me time to think, 'Peth? Because I disliked Louisa, I spent little time considering what her life might have been like."

Elspeth sensed evasion in Biddy's response.

"Of course. When you saw Johnnie at the jail, what were his reactions?" Elspeth asked.

"His emotions ran the whole gamut. He wants to see Madeline, but he knows the foolishness of it. He hates being cooped in, but also knows he could be taken to prison which undoubtedly more unpleasant than jail, if he can't meet any bail conditions."

Elspeth grimaced. "Yes, I know. He told me this morning, but I don't remember Johnnie ever being so pessimistic. When did this start?"

"Since Helen left. There were several years when I feared he would lose his business because he started drinking heavily. He seemed to slacken off after he married Louisa, and since Madeline he has seemed to have recovered. Now this. Is there any way, 'Peth, that Johnnie could see Madeline?"

"I don't know if she has the courage to see Johnnie or not, and I don't know where she is. When I rang this morning her using a code we set up, I got a new message on her office answerphone, which probably means she was in her office at some point after Saturday when I saw her. I hope for Johnnie's sake she hasn't bolted, but she has every good reason to do so. I'll keep trying though."

"Seeing her would help him enormously."

"It's a lot to ask a young woman who could lose everything including Johnnie if she comes forward. I don't have any sense of how much resilience she actually has."

"Try to reach her. Even a message would mean a great deal to him."

They walked to the door of the barn and saw Richard coming towards them. Elspeth waved at him in an invitation to join them.

18

Biddy Baillie Shaw watched the shearers' rhythmic motions in a ritual as ancient as the days when shepherds had first inhabited the highlands. The puzzled but accepting faces of the sheep, even when faced with the razors, remained the same year after year, as if they did not know why they were to be shorn. As the shearing went on it became a palliative to her fears for Johnnie's future, and she found comfort in the familiar routine. In retrospect, she and Johnnie had made the right decision about the way to keep the farm, but it had not come easily.

After satisfying herself that she was free of her obligation to the men working outside, Biddy returned to the farmhouse. Robbie MacPherson would be able to handle the rest. The kitchen phone was ringing when she came in, and Max was on the other end of the line. He asked to see her to tell her in person about Johnnie's arraignment.

Unexpected pleasure filled her when Max identified himself, an emotion that took her by surprise, as her main contact with him had been regarding her brother. He asked to come to the farm.

When preparing for Max's visit, Biddy looked at herself in the mirror and saw only the fine lines at the sides of her eyes and the corners of her mouth. At least they were

186

testament to a happy life, but not for the first time in the last several days she wished she had Elspeth's skill with makeup and dress. She found a heavy silk scarf that Pamela Crumm had provided when she had gone to Italy to help with the situation at the Kennington Stresa and chose some gold earrings Elspeth had given her for Christmas the year before. Biddy had been delighted with the gift, as she loved pretty things, but until now had no reason to wear them. Max arrived just as Biddy was smoothing her hair. Hoping she would pass muster, she checked herself in the mirror by the door before opening it to his knock. His smile told her that she had succeeded.

Before asking about Johnnie she led him into the morning room and invited him to sit down. Max looked around the room pensively.

"This is place where my family has gathered many times, both in happiness and despair," she said. "Now tell me about Johnnie and what happened in court."

"Lord Tay didn't take the charge of first degree murder well," Max said. "I'd warned him of the consequences, but when the procurator fiscal told him that he would grant bail at a cost of a half a million pounds, Johnnie blanched. I'm trying to see if I can get the bail reduced and ask Johnnie if he would be willing to accept an 'undertaking', which means he could come home before the court date is set. He will be restricted to the farm and not be allowed to contact anyone associated with the crime. He will also have to surrender his passport."

"Restricted to the farm?" Biddy said, her voice flat.

"Yes."

"Can anyone visit him here?"

"Yes, of course, if they are not connected directly with the

187

case."

Biddy looked up at him with an incredulous look. "My family is everything to me. I'll do anything to get Johnnie off."

"Can you find his passport for me? I need to give it to the procurator fiscal."

"Will you explain the charges against him to me?" Biddy asked. She listened calmly, swallowing hard several times.

"I can't believe all these things are true," she finally said. "Have you talked to Elspeth?"

"Yes."

"Tell me, what does she feel?"

"That everything comes back to Louisa and the farm."

"And the farm?" The pitch of Biddy's voice changed slightly. "Why the farm?"

"I don't know yet, but Elspeth and I intend to find out."

Biddy put her hands over her face and began to cry. Max leaned over and touched her arm tenderly.

"Biddy, please trust me. I've worked with cases in the past that were more desperate than Lord Tay's. There's always hope. The court date should be set soon."

"When?"

'Usually a matter of a few months, when the high court, before which he will be tried, comes to Perth."

"That long? Why?" Biddy sobbed.

"It allows the police to gather all the evidence, but it helps us too. We have to discover enough information that we can clear Johnnie of this charge."

"Elspeth leaves on Thursday. I don't know how much she can do by then to help you."

"We'll see," Max said tenderly.

When Biddy gained control of her emotions, she suggested they walk down to the loch. He took her arm on the steep places in the path, and she refrained from mentioning that she came this way almost every day, knew the roots and rocks well enough not to have to watch for them and had never fallen. She led them to a stone bench that her grandmother had had built seventy years before, when she first had to reconcile living at the farm rather than at the large house in Perth. The bench afforded the best view of the loch and the highland peaks beyond, which today stood beautiful and stern in the distance.

They stood looking at the view without speaking. Max finally broke the silence. "This place is very special for you, isn't it? I can see the way you move through its space, intimately but respectfully. Have you lived here all your life?"

"Homebody Biddy," she said. "I have. I was the only one of the three of us, me, Elspeth, and Johnnie, who wanted to stay. The farm goes with the peerage, you know. It is mine by tenancy not by right."

"Then Lord Tay *is* the rightful owner," he said in affirmation.

"Not that the current owner of the title, Johnnie, cares, or my son Charlie, who is next in line. I feel such a responsibility towards the farm. The Robertsons have been here since time began, but in the twenty-first century, none of them but me seems to want to carry on. It makes my responsibility greater."

"Do you know why Louisa suddenly wanted the farm for herself?" he asked.

"It most assuredly was not her idea. You never met Louisa, but the thought of sheep manure and perpetual mud

189

certainly would have made her sick. Frankly, I don't know whose idea it was for her to take the farm. I have a feeling that her lawyer must have thought she could sell it after she took possession, but of course she couldn't."

"No, but she could possibly have leased it," Max said.

Biddy could feel her insides churn and to hide her discomfort, she looked upwards and pointed out a raven. "They come when something dies," she said. She hoped Max would turn his attention to the bird and away from her, because she was aware of his closeness, which unsettled her. He was only momentarily diverted.

Suddenly Max swung around and looked at her. "Biddy, what is Lord Tay hiding?"

The abruptness of the question took Biddy off guard. She reddened. "I don't know what you mean," she said. Could Max guess she was not telling the whole truth?

"There is something, isn't there? I haven't been in the legal profession for as long as I have without having a sense of these things. Will you tell me?"

She turned away from him and felt coldness grow between them. "If there is anything," she said, her voice cracking, "Johnnie will have to tell you."

"You can't?"

"I won't," she said, setting her jaw. "It has nothing to do with Louisa's murder."

"At this point everything is relevant," he said. "Let me decide its importance."

"Shall we go back to the house?" she said with a dignity that mimicked her Edwardian grandmother, the seventh countess.

Max stiffened. "Yes, of course," he said. He did not take

her arm on the ascent up the path and departed soon afterwards.

Biddy slammed the kitchen door after he was out of earshot and put her face in her hands, choking back tears. Damn, damn, damn, she thought. How far can this go?

*

Max drove up the drive to the farm with mixed feelings. Up to this point he had admired Biddy for her softness but with her last words by the loch he saw that Elspeth's assertion of Biddy's steeliness was well-founded. He felt depleted. Not only had he not been able to ask Biddy the questions he had planned, but he also felt he had alienated her to the point beyond which there was no return. Elspeth had warned him about the bond between Johnnie and Biddy, and now he had seen it first-hand. What recourse did he have?

On the spur of the moment, he decided to ring Elspeth, as she had given him her mobile number and urged him to call her at any time. When she answered he could hear the engine of a car in the background.

"Elspeth, is it possible for us to meet later this afternoon? I know we set a time for tomorrow, but there are several things I would like to ask you about Biddy and Johnnie that may have a bearing on the case."

"Richard and I are just leaving Perth and on our way to Loch Rannoch now," she said. "Would you mind going there rather than my coming to Perth?"

"Fine. I'm just coming from Loch Tay, where I saw Biddy and told her the news. Give me directions."

Elspeth recited directions along the roads where she had grown up and which had changed little in fifty years.

"We should be there in about an hour," Elspeth said. "My

father is at home if you get there first. I'll ring him and tell him you're coming. I'm sure he'll welcome someone who can tell him about Johnnie's case."

Max found James Duff in his garden, tending roses which were in full bloom. Max introduced himself and found the same intelligence in James's eyes that he had seen in his daughter's, although the father's eyes were brown and the daughter's the same disturbing deep cobalt blue as her cousin's.

"Come and sit in the garden. Richard and Elspeth aren't here, and I don't know when to expect them. Have you come from the farm?"

"Yes," Max admitted.

"Tell me about Johnnie. Has he been granted bail?

"He has and it was set at a half a million pounds. I'm trying to reduce that. He will be allowed to stay at Tay Farm but can't leave it."

"Tell me the exact charges," James Duff requested.

Max did so.

"It seems Adair Gordon does have a case. He never was terribly brilliant, but he is dogged. You must know that."

"I do. Mr Duff, this case has crept under my skin, and because at this stage in my career I can do much of what I like, I presumed on your niece's hospitality and invited myself to Tay Farm where I told her the news. It was a difficult encounter."

"You will find Biddy the most stable of the lot," James said without preamble. "Much as I love my daughter, she has made some bad mistakes in her life. Johnnie, of course, now seems to have found himself in a terrible mess, and I hope you can extricate him from it. Biddy took her life in hand when she married and always came out on top. It's a pity about Ivor, her husband, though. He was only fifty-five when he died. He seemed in the peak of health and then ten days later was dead."

"That must have been difficult for her."

"At first of course, but she rallied almost immediately. It amazed us all. Biddy was always the pretty and soft one, Johnnie always followed the beat of his own drum and it led him in the right direction only part of the time, and Elspeth was the quick and irreverent one. Elspeth's mother and I often despaired. As much as she loves her daughter, I think Elspeth's mother would have preferred a daughter like Biddy, but I wouldn't have changed Elspeth a bit. You may find her handsome but do not be distracted by that. She has a clever but sometimes artful mind, despite her fine clothes and elegant deportment. She will surprise you."

Max laughed. "Are you warning me against her?"

"Quite the contrary. Be glad she's on your side."

"Mr Duff, your family puzzles me. Can you tell me where the loyalties are?"

James sat back on the garden bench and looked Max in the eye. "That's a very good question. The three of them, Johnnie, Biddy and Elspeth, will stick together, they always have, but there is a special bond between Biddy and Johnnie that is their own, and Elspeth isn't a part of it."

"Yes, Elspeth told me."

"Don't discount it."

"It sounds like you are advising me to tread carefully."

"I am."

"Do you know if they're hiding anything?"

"I really don't, but they may be. They never have shared

their secrets with me."

"I asked, but Biddy shut me down so quickly that I can't help thinking there is something."

"I can tell you're astute, Mr Douglas-Forbes. It's a pity we have not worked on a case together before. Do not let the pair of them hinder your investigation. Take some advice from an old man and have faith in Elspeth. She has the keenest mind of the lot of them. She has both the fault and the blessing of being able to subdue her feelings to her intellect and always has done."

"You seem to know your daughter very well."

James Duff did not respond other than with a loving smile.

"Can you tell me more about Lord Tay?"

"Johnnie? What exactly?"

"Could he have murdered Louisa?"

"Could he, or did he?"

"I asked if he could. None of us know if he did, except Johnnie himself."

"And possibly Biddy. She wouldn't betray him. Could he have murdered Louisa? Any person who is provoked far enough could kill another. Certainly war affirms that. But, is killing in his nature? No."

Max took a deep breath and said what he did not want to be true. "Could Biddy?"

James Duff sat silently for a long moment before he answered. "I want to say no again."

"Want to?"

"Of the three of them, Biddy feels the most deeply. Perhaps that is why she was so happy in her marriage and why she is so successful at running the farm. She cares for the animals, the men who help her about the farm, and the people who live around Loch Tay. She tends to the ill among them all and celebrates their joys as if it were her own. Most of all she cares for Johnnie and her children. Could she kill to protect those she loved? I wouldn't want to put her to the test. I hope Louisa didn't do so. You don't suspect Biddy, I hope?"

Max tried to digest what James had just told him, but he found his own feelings getting in the way. He did not want Biddy Baillie Shaw to be implicated, but as her brother's lawyer, he could not dismiss the possibility.

Their conversation was interrupted by the arrival of Elspeth and Richard. Bounce, who had been asleep at James's feet, bounded to the car in greeting. Max drew back as they approached. His mind was in turmoil. He had a petulant client, whose sister had entered his heart, and whose cousin disconcerted him. He wished momentarily he had not agreed to see Elspeth, but he knew she was a strong ally and the one hope for him to find out more of the truth. His question about family loyalty to James Duff had been carefully chosen but the old man's answer had not been reassuring. As Elspeth and Richard approached, he decided he needed to talk to Elspeth alone.

The two of them walked along the road that bordered Loch Rannoch. There was no traffic, and they were not disturbed by curious or evasive neighbours.

He felt a strange companionship with her, although a long time passed before either one spoke.

"Things didn't go well at the farm, did they?" she said finally. "Biddy shut down, I expect, when you wanted to know something that involved Johnnie. They have always stuck together."

"You cut to the chase, Elspeth. How did you know?" Max asked.

She bit her lower lip. They have always done so, but you shouldn't allow that to hinder you. Tell me what you want to know. I'll work on them."

He chuckled. "Are you so confident?"

"I've known them all their lives and mine. Given time I can wheedle things out of Biddy."

"Do you have the time?"

She shook her head regretfully. "Unfortunately, I have only two more full days here before I must return to work in London, but I can try. Max, there's something else I need to discuss with you. I've been in touch with the woman in Johnnie's life, the one he was divorcing Louisa for in order to marry. I've talked to her about coming forward and warned her how devastating the consequences will be for her, but she has agreed to talk to you. I've asked her to come to your office tomorrow at half past three. I hope that wasn't too presumptuous of me."

"Not at all, but what do you think that will accomplish?"

"Johnnie was with her the night of the murder."

"At the time Lady Tay was murdered?"

"Not according to the police's eyewitnesses, but from two until half past three in the morning in her flat near Dundee, about a half hour away from Perth."

"What is her name?"

"I'll let her tell you tomorrow."

"You seem secretive."

"I have reason to be," Elspeth said, raising her eyebrows.

Max laughed, knowing he was enjoying Elspeth's provocative approach to things, despite the seriousness of the affair. He wondered how much of this the Kennington Organisation tolerated, but he knew they would not keep her in her position if she offended either the hotel guests or Lord Kennington himself.

They turned back to the house and walked on in silence.

Finally Max said, "Elspeth, I'm going to need your help, even from afar. Do you have a way I can contact you securely when you go back to work?"

Not knowing how important it would be in the weeks to come, Elspeth provided the number of the secure line, although she asked him to use it as infrequently as possible.

*

During the night, Richard Munro woke and saw Elspeth standing silently by the window, her strong features silhouetted against the last stages of twilight.

"What are you thinking?" he asked.

She came round and sat beside him on the bed. "I'm not certain I can save them both," she said.

"Both? Johnnie and Madeline?"

"No, Johnnie and Biddy. What worries me is that they are hiding something, just as Max suggested."

"You aren't thinking that . . ." Richard let his thought hang. ". . . that they are in it together? Unfortunately, Dickie, I can't dismiss the possibility."

"Where are you going with that thought?"

"I have absolutely no idea."

19

The next morning Elspeth walked out along the loch, Bounce the retriever loping happily along at her side. Her mind was filled with the futility of having only two and a half days left before she and Richard needed to return to London. What could she do in that short of a time to find out the truth, even if it implicated her cousins' involvement in Louisa's murder? She had risen early, as she could not sleep, and left Richard tangled in their covers and unaware of her departure. Despite her marriage to him and all the joy it brought her, she still often needed time to be alone. She walked out on a promontory at the edge of the loch near her parents' home, and without thought started skimming stones across the surface of the water. She had done the same thing as a child when trying to work out a perplexing problem. Bounce had gone off chasing a red squirrel and left Elspeth to ponder the ability of a stone to skip numerous times across water without sinking. Was there a metaphor in it? How often did people's personal relationships skim the surface of reality? She did not know Johnnie anymore, nor had she for a long time. She knew about Kathleen's suicide, of course, because Johnnie had told her, but she hardly knew Helen and had only met Louisa twice. Elspeth could not understand Johnnie's relationship with any of his wives. She and Johnnie had simply skimmed along the surface together for the last forty years.

Elspeth felt she knew Biddy better, but did she really? When she lived in California, Elspeth seldom visited Perthshire. Since joining the Kennington Organisation, most of her life had been spent at the Kennington hotels around the world, and she had made her home base in London, close to the corporate offices of the hotel chain. She had visited her parents when she had been able to do so, but after marrying Richard, she usually spent her free time in Malta with him or he in London with her, and she had come less often to Perthshire. Elspeth had shared her anxiety over marrying Richard with Biddy, but what had Biddy told her about her own personal feelings at that time? Elspeth had not been in Perthshire for Biddy when Ivor died and did not know how Biddy had grieved. Elspeth felt she had become a skimming stone across the surface of Biddy and Johnnie's lives and she regretted it.

"Eleven," a deep baritone voice behind her said.

"Twelve," she protested, finding Richard beside her. She had not heard him approach. She put her arms around him and gave him a perfunctory good morning kiss.

"What were you thinking about?" he asked.

"About how little I know about Biddy and Johnnie, what passions they have, and what dark places."

"Or what might drive them to commit murder?"

"Yes, that too, but I don't want it to be so. Dickie, will you come with me to the farm and Perth later today after I talk to Portia MacRoberts?"

"It will be my pleasure, as being with you is always my life's greatest joy, but particularly if I can be of help."

"I want us to visit the scene of the crime, but first there are some things I need to ask Biddy."

"Carry on Lady MacDuff," he said. "I'm at your disposal."

She grinned at the pet name he used for her since they first met and which he used when he suspected her of mischief.

Elspeth left Richard in deep conversation over toast and marmalade with her father on the situation in Iraq and the political repercussions in the prime minister's resignation, and made her way into Pitlochry alone. Portia MacRoberts, Johnnie's divorce lawyer, had agreed to meet her at nine.

Portia MacRoberts was the granddaughter of one of James Duff's early partners at Duff, MacBean and MacRoberts, and she had followed her own grandfather and father into the firm. It was a familial role that Elspeth had once envisioned for herself, and therefore she entered Portia's office with some curiosity to see if Portia would mirror what she might have become had she returned to Pitlochry after Girton, but Portia surprised her. She was small and feminine, was wearing a becoming floral pattern dress overlaid with a smartly tailored jacket that would be as smart in London as it was here, and her eyes greeted Elspeth's with intelligence and warmth. Portia's curly red hair was cut expertly to convey professionalism but loosely enough to flatter her delicately featured face, which Elspeth suspected Portia used to its full advantage on the unsuspecting. Portia rose from her neatly ordered desk and came across the room as Elspeth entered. She was surprised at the firmness of Portia's handshake.

"I won't equivocate," Portia said to Elspeth as she motioned her to a chair in front of her desk. "I'm a bit in awe of you. Your father does tend to rave about your exploits, and, even if his words are only half true, you certainly lead an interesting life."

Unsure as to what her father might have said, Elspeth simply smiled and said, "There are interesting moments, but like every job mine is mainly routine. I want to thank you for taking the time to see me. I promised the family I would try to help with Johnnie's problem and therefore want to know as much as I can about the circumstances that led up to Louisa's death. Although the divorce is now a moot issue, it seems to present complications that may be relevant to Johnnie's current dilemma. I hope you don't mind the directness of my questions."

"Of course not. I'll answer as best I can although criminal law is not my speciality."

"Johnnie was filing for divorce from Louisa, I understand, and not the other way around. When did he first come to you?"

Portia rose, went to the line of wood-faced files behind her, and drew out a diary. "On Thursday, the twentieth of September last year." Then Portia grinned. "Do you want the exact time?"

Elspeth shook her head and immediately liked Portia's ability to laugh at her lawyerly ways, but also knew how important precision might be in helping to save Johnnie.

"Johnnie and I discussed the best way he could file for a divorce. Scotland is rather antiquated in what constitutes grounds for divorce. Grounds include if your spouse has committed adultery, if your spouse has behaved unreasonably, if you and your spouse have lived apart for more than one year and both of you consent to the divorce, or if you and your spouse have lived apart for two years or more and one does not consent."

"Why did you decide on adultery as a reason as opposed to any of the other grounds?"

"Lord Tay had, of course, secured his business so that Lady Tay could not touch it, but he also had sufficient personal assets to want to protect them. If she appeared to be the offending party, he had a better chance."

"May I ask what terms you were negotiating? I know this may be privileged information."

"It is, but because Louisa is dead and also because of your relationship to Johnnie, I'll tell you. Louisa would keep the house in Perth and be given a decent but not extravagant income until she remarried, if she ever did. The money would be in a trust so that she could not touch the capital. Johnnie was concerned that Louisa had friends who might take advantage of her if they knew she had access to a large amount of money."

"Could he prove adultery on her part?"

"We hired a detective. It only took a week to get definitive evidence. Johnnie said she never kept her affairs secret."

"Johnnie seems to have been more generous that I would have been, but, then again, men can be more forgiving than women in my experience. Did you advise Johnnie against such generosity?"

"I thought he offered more than he needed to, but he seemed to want to be rid of her."

"Did he give you a reason?"

"No, but one didn't have to look far to see that Louisa could be burdensome to someone like Johnnie."

"You didn't probe into his affairs further?"

"I chose not to, unless or until I had to. I always find it best to keep things clean until they want to become dirty."

"Did Louisa acquiesce to the terms immediately?"

"They had lived apart, I gather, for several months, when Lord Tay came to me. He had told her he would be filing for divorce, but her response was desultory. That seemed to fit what Lord Tay told me about her. Her solicitor didn't return my calls until January although he had been sent the decree in November. Do you want the day, date, and time?"

Elspeth saw a twinkle in Portia's eyes, despite the seriousness of their topic.

"No," Elspeth said, "but I'm curious as to why it took Louisa and her solicitor so long. Did he counter with more demands?"

"Only perfunctory ones. He wanted the allowance for Lady Tay's expenses to go up by twenty per cent and a maintenance fund set up for the house, but he told me Louisa would not contest the divorce."

"Making Johnnie free and clear as soon as all the papers had been finalised. Do you have any idea why Louisa suddenly came and demanded the farm?"

"She changed solicitors."

"Did that surprise you?"

"Yes, it did rather. Her original solicitor is someone I deal with all the time. We work well together and can usually agree on terms without rancour, but suddenly I had a call from a solicitor in Perth whom I normally don't associate with family law. His name is Paul Hodges, and he has a poor reputation in the Perthshire legal establishment. He normally deals in business property transactions, often skirting but not violating the law.

"Do you have any idea why the change?"

"None, but I suspect the demand for the farm was Mr Hodges's idea and a way for him to leverage more out of Johnnie. If his reputation bears any credence, this would not be unusual."

"Did you meet Mr Hodges?"

"Only once, shortly before Johnnie went to San Francisco. I'll be frank with you. I found him distasteful, which is not particularly professional on my part. I've not seen him since he conveyed his demands to me. Now, of course, there's no longer any need for the divorce. I hope I don't have to deal with him again."

"Did you explain to him that the farm was linked to the peerage?"

"Yes, but he said he had ways around that."

"Did he say how?"

"No, but, if we had been in a melodrama, he would have rubbed his oily hands together and sneered."

"That bad?"

"Perhaps it just was his musky scent," Portia said wryly, "although he could have done with a better tailor and barber. It's strange that I should be affected by that, as it should make no difference these days, but I was. Your father and my grandfather always insist we dress presentably as a visual way to represent the firm."

"May we talk again?" Elspeth asked. "I need to leave Scotland on Thursday but have arranged for a secure line on my mobile on which we can talk freely."

"Certainly, if there is anything more I can add, let me know. Until Mr Hodges came along, everything was very straightforward. I thought it would be over by now," she said in parting.

Later when Elspeth and Richard arrived at the farm, Biddy was sitting alone in the kitchen preparing a sandwich. She rose to greet them and asked them to join her. Once they were seated, the conversation turned to the thing uppermost in their minds.

"Have you heard from Max? When will they release Johnnie?" she asked.

"I think that may be predicated on when Max can arrange for the bail." Elspeth answered. "Are you planning to see Johnnie today?"

"Yes, later this afternoon I'll be driving into Perth and thought if he were released, I could bring him back to the farm. Have you found anything to help, so that I might give him some good news?"

"I spoke with Portia MacRoberts this morning. She felt that Louisa's demands changed when she hired a new lawyer. Portia had little time for the man, and I trust her judgment. I must let Max know and may come to Perth with you. I need to talk to Johnnie again about Louisa and the divorce, and why he thinks Louisa changed lawyers." "I have absolutely no idea."

20

Elspeth took Richard's arm companionably as they approached the house where Louisa had been killed. Police tape still surrounded the gate and garden and a constable stood on guard, but there were no longer any signs of the media. They crossed the quiet street.

"Biddy told me that Johnnie bought this house when he first made a success of his business. He and Helen had been married for about five years I think, but in all those years, I was only inside once. Did you ever visit?"

"Like you, only once. Marjorie and I detoured through Perth on our way from Edinburgh to Glenborough Castle. It was during Helen's time and she was a wonderful hostess."

Elspeth wrinkled her nose in dislike. Her own disastrous visit to Glenborough Castle had ended in dreadful rudeness on her part towards her hosts and had almost ended her decision to marry Richard, an incident she preferred not to remember.

"Let's stand here for a moment and see who comes and goes in the neighbourhood," Elspeth said. She dived into her shoulder bag and brought out a street map of Perth.

"Now let me see," she continued, a bit too loudly as a man with a small dog let himself out of a house next door to Louisa's. Elspeth commented *sotto voce* to her husband that one's respectable appearance carried weight with the casual passer-by.

The man approached; his eyes lowered.

"I say," Richard said, "would you help us?"

The man hearing Richard looked up.

"We are looking for, what is the address, my dear?" Richard asked Elspeth.

Elspeth thought rapidly and gave the address of a childhood friend from the Blair School for Girls. She knew it was nearby. Then she fumbled with the map.

The man bade his dog sit, took the map from Elspeth's hands, unfolded it and pointed the way.

"Has there been a fire across the street?" Elspeth asked innocently as the man handed the map back to her.

The man looked incredulous. "No, that's where the murder took place," he said.

"Murder?" Richard said. "The one in all the papers? My wife and I have just come from Malta, and I'm afraid we know nothing about it. It must have been dreadful for you."

The man seemed to warm to the topic. "The worst part was the press. They were here for three or four days, but have now mercifully departed. The murder itself was quiet in comparison. Just a bit of shouting, but the countess, the one who was murdered, did occasionally have loud parties. At times we had to call the police."

"Was she having a party the night she was murdered?" Elspeth asked, knowing better. "That must have been very disturbing for you."

"Not at all. In fact it was exceptionally quiet that night. I brought the dog out about the time the newspaper said the murder was committed, and no one was about. But that's usual for a Thursday night. He must have gone in the back door. It was her husband who did it, you know. I hadn't seen him

207

around for quite some time before then."

"Oh, did you see him?" Richard asked. Elspeth shot an approving glance at him because his voice sounded so convincingly unknowing.

"Heavens, no, thank goodness. I like to stay out of that sort of thing. None of business. Now let's see, if you go left round the corner . . ." The man reiterated his directions and was gone.

Elspeth led Richard out of hearing of the police constable and said, "Dickie, you are becoming quite as devious as I am."

His eyes twinkled briefly. "We didn't get anything useful from the man," he said. "I don't think the policeman at the gate will allow us another chance at asking for directions. So where do we go next?"

"To the Beauforts. I want to talk to Marly again and introduce you to them, and I know she wants to meet you."

They heard Marly undo the locks on the door after an eye examined them through the peephole in the door. She expressed delight over seeing Elspeth again, smiled warmly at Richard and invited them in.

"The press were here," she said, "but thankfully they have gone. I thought they might be returning. You must be Richard." She extended her hand. "Come in for a coffee. I can easily prepare lattes for you on my new espresso machine."

They found Roger Beaufort at the kitchen table telecommuting, with the local newspaper spread out in front of him. The headlines could not be missed.

They made cursory conversation as Marly prepared their coffee, but once settled, Elspeth came straight to the point.

"How well do you two know Johnnie?" she asked.

"We have been friends since he was married to Helen," Roger said. "Johnnie and I have shared some business dealings as well. We must have known each other for the last ten years."

"How well did you know Louisa?"

Marly handed round the sugar, which both Elspeth and Richard declined. "When Johnnie first married her," she explained, "we invited her to our parties, but she was quite different from us. I think she was as uncomfortable as we were, and soon, even if we invited her, she would find some reason not to come."

"Can you tell me how she was different?"

"Common," Roger said with a sniff. The fact had not escaped Elspeth.

"Do you know what sort of people Louisa did see socially?"

"Rather a faster crowd than we are," Marly said. "What do they call them in crime fiction? The high rollers?"

"Meaning?"

"The people in the business community who are out to make a quick profit and don't really care about Perth and its history." Roger answered. "You know the sort: developers from Manchester and Birmingham who think of Scotland as a place for their picking, bankers who are willing to lend money for questionable projects, lawyers who are willing to find the loopholes in the law. We fought several of them on their plans to develop the area around one of our historic parks, and finally took the whole thing to court. We finally won but it cost us all a great deal of money. No matter where we stamp them down, however, they seem to pop up again, like moles in the garden." Disgust filled his voice.

"The problem is worldwide, I'm afraid," Richard said. Elspeth and I saw the same thing when we were in Cyprus together, and it is happening in Malta as well."

"Damn shame," Roger said. "It's not as if they mean to put down roots here. Those of us whose families had lived here for generations are beginning to band together to see how much of Scotland's heritage we can protect."

"Where did Johnnie stand in all this?" Elspeth asked.

"You would think as a Scottish lord he would have more concern, but he said we couldn't live in the past. Then recently he gave quite a large contribution to our cause. He called it guilt money."

"And Louisa?"

"I don't think Louisa ever thought about such things. She was usually out for a good time and didn't care with whom, as long as they were willing to foot the bill."

"Did that distress Johnnie?"

"At first, but lately he said he didn't care. When he moved into our guest flat, he seemed completely disgusted with Louisa. Marly and I wondered why it had taken so long. About the time he began divorce proceedings against her."

"Did you see any other changes in Johnnie?" Elspeth asked.

Marly smiled. "He seemed to care about things again, for the first time since Helen left him."

"How well did you know Helen, Marly?"

"We were quite good friends until about six months before she left. Inexplicably she suddenly stopped coming round to see me or inviting me to their home. Of course, we now know that she had met someone other than Johnnie. It crushed him you know. It was more than mere male ego; it was that she was everything to him, particularly as they were childless. When she left, it was as if he had died a little."

"Did Helen ever let you know whether this was a conscious choice on their part, the childlessness I mean?"

"No. She told me that they had tried in vitro fertilisation but that the embryo would not attach itself to her uterus. Strange that we all talk about these private things that would have been unspoken in our grandmothers' or even our mothers' day. Then one day Helen left a note for Johnnie that said she was going abroad and told Johnnie he could have a divorce without her contesting it. We all felt terribly sad for him. Afterwards he could have had his pick of several quite suitable women, which made his marriage to Louisa so unfathomable, at least to us."

"Do you have any idea why he married Louisa?"

"He started drinking heavily after Helen left him and probably was on a binge when he married her," Roger said. "He's too much of a gentleman to admit he made a mistake. All that changed when he left Louisa," Marly said. "It was as if the old Johnnie were back. We took him in, and one could tell that meant a lot to him."

"Did you try to find a suitable woman for him?" Elspeth asked with a half grin.

Roger laughed. "Johnnie said he was finished with women."

"Did you believe him?"

"No," Marly said. "I think there was someone else, but Johnnie was very tight lipped about it. We presumed that he was waiting until his divorce from Louisa was finalised, so she would have no counter grounds to use against him."

"Did you ever see any woman come to the flat to see Johnnie?"

Marly and Roger shook their heads in unison, rather like Tweedle Dum and Tweedle Dee. "He was very discreet," Marly said.

"Tell me about the night of the murder."

Roger began, "We had been at a dinner party with friends and had several rousing games of Scrabble afterwards. We must have got home about midnight, as it was finally getting dark."

"Marly, you said you saw Johnnie's car at the entrance to the flat and a light inside."

"I saw it when I let the cat in. Did you see it, Roger?" she asked her husband.

He bit his lip. "Didn't notice," he said. "Johnnie came and went as he pleased. And paid his rent on time, which is more than I can say for some of our tenants."

Marly stopped with her coffee cup in mid-air. "Do you think we might have to testify?"

"Johnnie's lawyer hasn't built his case yet, but, yes, you might, if he feels it's important. He needs to have all the information he can find about Johnnie's whereabouts on the night of the murder," Elspeth said. "Did Johnnie leave his car here when he went to San Francisco?"

Marly shook her head. "No, he must have taken it to the airport, and when he returned, brought it back here."

Biddy and Johnnie had returned on the same flight from San Francisco, but Richard had only been able get seats on a later one because they had changed their booking at the last minute. Elspeth did not know what arrangements Johnnie and Biddy had made to return to Perthshire.

"Was there a Land Rover here when he was gone?"

Marly shook her head. "We had a supper party when Johnnie was gone and were grateful to have the extra spaces for our guests."

"Do you recall if the morning after the murder, the car was still at Johnnie's flat?"

Again both shook their heads. "Haven't a clue," Roger said. "One needs to walk round the back to know for sure. Marly and I left the next morning for Edinburgh to see our daughter and her new baby. I'd left our car in the front. We didn't want to interfere in Johnnie's life."

"I see," Elspeth said, although she wished in this instance they had. "You have both been so helpful."

Before their leaving, Marly once again expressed concern about their testifying, and Elspeth assured her it would only be as a last resort.

*

As they drove back towards Charlotte Street, Richard noticed that Elspeth was unusually silent.

"Your thoughts?" he finally said.

"That Max will have a hard time making a case in Johnnie's defence. Johnnie had every reason in the world to want Louisa dead. The police said two eyewitnesses have come forward seeing him at the scene of the crime. Even his friends say his car was in Perth at about midnight on the night of the murder, and they can't confirm whether it was gone or not the next morning. Madeline says he didn't arrive at her flat until two in the morning. According to the witnesses they saw Johnnie leaving Louisa's Perth house around half past twelve. If you were one of the fifteen members of the jury, what would you conclude?"

Richard could hear the constriction in his wife's voice and did not know how to reply. They drove on in silence.

Finally she said, "I only hope Max and I can come up with a way to beat this. I just don't see how yet. There must be something."

21

Madeline sat in her two-seater at the dge of the pay-and-display car park and debated with herself. If she went through with it, she could not look back. She had considered every alternative. If she did not appear, did her running away reflect the reality of her feelings for Johnnie? What could a safe distance give her? She would save her family from notoriety, she would save her job, and she would save any hope of getting an equitable divorce settlement, but she probably would lose Johnnie and all the hope of the happiness they had imagined for the last year. The risk was enormous, but she loved Johnnie and wanted to spend her life with him.

"Are you parking, miss?" a pedestrian asked. "If not, please don't block the pavement."

This simple request set her resolve. She pulled into the car park and paid for an hour. She did not know that this hour would change her life irrevocably.

Madeline put on a large pair of sunglasses, adjusted the brim of her large and floppy hat, climbed the stairs to Maxwell Forbes-Douglas's law offices and was shown into his chambers. Relief spread through her when she saw Elspeth with Max. Taking off her sunglasses and hat, she swallowed hard and introduced herself to Max.

"I'm Madeline MacNaughton," she said clearly but rather

215

more highly pitched than her usual voice. "I don't know what I can do to save Johnnie, but he and I have been having an affair for the last year and I love him deeply."

Max smiled at her with gratitude in his eyes. "Ms MacNaughton, thank you for your directness. It makes my job easier. You know Ms Duff, I presume."

Madeline glanced over at Elspeth and nodded. "Thanks for being here, Elspeth. I need all the support I can get."

Max motioned Madeline to a chair in front of his desk opposite Elspeth and rang for his receptionist to bring some tea.

Madeline could feel the tears coming to her eyes, but she choked them back and hoped that neither Max nor Elspeth saw them. She had not thought coming to see Johnnie's lawyer would prove to be so difficult.

"What can I do to help?" She was not able to control her voice, which broke as she spoke.

Max frowned. "I can think of two things immediately, but there may be more. First tell me where you were on the night of Louisa Tay's murder. Start about dinnertime. Try to be as accurate as you can."

Madeline had expected this. "Johnnie rang me when he got back from San Francisco on Monday and told me he was staying with his sister at Tay Farm until Saturday, when he would return to Perth, but he wanted to get together as soon as possible. Normally we met at an abandoned cottage near where my parents live on Loch Tummel, but I couldn't get away on Tuesday, as I had an important meeting with clients in Aberdeen and did not expect to return until well into the evening. On Wednesday I had a presentation to complete that would keep me late at my office, so Johnnie and I decided to meet at my flat near Dundee on Thursday evening, or really early Friday. The housekeeper there is a terrible snoop, and I feared that she could have been employed by my husband's divorce lawyer, so I urged him to come well after dark. We arranged to meet at two in the morning."

"Did he arrive on time?"

"Actually he was a bit early."

"When did he leave?" Max asked.

"At about half past three. It was just getting light."

"Did he mention Louisa to you?"

"Mr Douglas-Forbes, we had other matters to attend to, as lovers do when they have not seen each other for over a week." She set her jaw, but strangely felt no embarrassment.

"Will you tell me how Johnnie seemed? Was he agitated or distracted or nervous?"

"No, he seemed just as he always was when we are together."

"How is that?"

"Warm, caring, tender."

Max held her eyes. "Are you willing to swear to this in court, when it's possible the Crown will try to undermine your testimony?"

Madeline looked over at Elspeth, who looked grave. Elspeth nodded, affirming Max's words. Madeline put her hands over her face and was glad when a light knock came at the door.

"Is it all right if my receptionist brings in tea?" Max asked.

She straightened herself in her chair, uncovered her face and assented. Elspeth rose and served them.

Madeline sipped her tea and was grateful for its warmth.

Then she said, "It won't be easy, and Elspeth has warned me of the consequences, but, yes, I will testify, if necessary."

"Will you tell the truth, even though it may seem harmful to Lord Tay?"

"Harmful?" she said, panic spreading through her. "How?"

Elspeth rose, came round to where Madeline was sitting and put a hand on her shoulder.

"Let me tell her, Max," Elspeth said. "Madeline, there are two eyewitnesses that saw Johnnie at Louisa's house in Perth just after midnight on the night she was murdered, which is well before he arrived at your flat. Your testimony will not clear him."

"He couldn't have murdered her! That isn't the Johnnie I know! Who are these people and why do they want to hurt Johnnie?" Madeline cried out.

"We don't know yet," Max said, "but I intend to find out. Now, Ms MacNaughton, there's another thing I must ask you. Did Lord Tay ever talk to you about Tay Farm?"

"Biddy's farm?"

"Is that what he called it?"

"It's hers, isn't it?"

"Not technically, although for all intents and purposes it is. The farm belongs to the current titleholder of the Tay earldom, and therefore as long as Lord Tay holds the title, it's his. After that, it belongs to the heir to the title, who at present is Lady Elisabeth's son, Charles Baillie Shaw. Did Lord Tay ever talk to you about his business?"

"Yes, often. He said I had a good mind for it and would ask my advice when he was thinking things out. I usually suspected he had already made up his mind and only wanted confirmation."

"How long ago did you and Lord Tay become intimate?" Max asked.

"On the fourth of July, American Independence Day, of last year. It was a bit of a joke between us." Madeline smiled at the memory.

"Did he mention Biddy becoming involved in his business?"

"He did mention that she had recently helped him financially but that she preferred her sheep and hens to the details of the running of his affairs. Could he have meant that she had financed him at some point?" Madeline asked. "Johnnie is very close to his sister. She would probably give him whatever he asked for and never regret it for a moment."

Elspeth chuckled, "Just about anything, except the running of the farm. Have you met Biddy?"

"I have known her at least to say hello to on the street all my life," said Madeline.

"Did you know that she was aware of your and Johnnie's relationship?"

"He said he hadn't told her."

"Madeline," Elspeth said, "Biddy and Johnnie have never needed to tell each other everything. You just mentioned their closeness, which is very real. Biddy was a pretty but foolish girl, but she has grown into a singularly wise woman. She probably saw the change in Johnnie after he met you and didn't need to stretch her imagination to guess why. Probably finding out that the woman was you was more difficult, but Johnnie may not have been as discreet as he thought he was being. I hope one day you will get to know Biddy as more than as a passing acquaintance. She's a remarkable person and a good ally to have if your relationship with Johnnie continues."

"I have every intention of continuing my relationship with him," Madeline cried. "I wouldn't be here now if I didn't. You warned me about the cost, Elspeth, and I'm willing to pay it."

Max rose from his desk and came over to when Madeline was sitting. He took her hand and shook it. "Thank you," he said with great sincerity. "Lord Tay will need friends like you in the coming weeks."

"Can I see him?" Madeline asked.

"I'll try to arrange it. He is being released from jail but is required to remain at the farm with the proviso that he can't see anyone involved in the case. Call me in the morning and I'll let you know."

Madeline left Max's offices, retrieved her two-seater, and turned it towards Dundee and up the coast road along the Firth of Tay. How many hours was it until tomorrow? Oh, Johnnie, I do love you and I will see you soon. The press and public be damned."

*

After Madeline left, Max asked Elspeth to stay on.

"I've made final arrangements for Earl Tay's bail and have conveyed the information to the procurator fiscal. He is now allowed to leave jail. I called Biddy, and she said she would come to Perth to fetch him immediately after she finishes the chores at the farm."

Elspeth breathed a sigh of relief. "He will be happier there than in prison," she said.

Elspeth's mobile rang, interrupting them.

Elspeth dug in her shoulder bag for her it. Robbie MacPherson came on the line, his voice breathless.

"Miss Elspeth!" he cried.

"What's wrong, Robbie?"

"Lady Biddy's been shot!"

22

Biddy Baillie Shaw looked down at Toby and with a pat acknowledged the look of satisfaction on his face as he finished driving the shorn sheep from the shearing pen.

"Well, done, Toby," she said and turned back to Robbie MacPherson. "Have the men make out their timecards and bring them to me. I'll draw the cheques tonight, when Johnnie and I get back from Perth." She did not mention the conditions of Johnnie's release and he did not ask. Suddenly a crack from nowhere hit Biddy, and she swung round, grabbing her shoulder. She looked down in horror as she withdrew her hand and saw it covered with blood. "I've been shot, Robbie," she said, as if she could not believe it. Then she slid to the ground.

Robbie was a slender man but a strong one. He had seen too many farm accidents to be daunted by the sight of blood, but to see Lady Biddy collapse filled him with horror. He knelt down, hoping she was alive. Mercifully she opened her eyes. "Help me to the barn," she said and then fainted away again. He picked her up as he would have a wounded animal and with gentleness and strength carried her to the barn, where he laid her on the clean hay outside the office. She groaned. Debating whether to call 9-9-9 or staunch the wound, he chose the latter, going into the bathroom behind the office and bringing out all the towels there. He pressed them as well as he could to Biddy's shoulder. She opened her eyes and looked

222

at him without focusing. Then Robbie dialled 9-9-9 on his mobile and was assured help was on the way, but he knew it would be at least twenty minutes before they got there. He drew off his outer shirt, ripped it into long shreds and tied up the oozing towels as tightly as he could. He found a bottle of whisky in the office and made Biddy drink. Most of it dribbled down her chin, but it seemed to revive her for a moment. Taking her wrist, he felt her pulse, which was erratic. Then he prayed. Nothing could happen to Lady Biddy; nothing like this. She was the soul of the farm.

He thought of the years when he was young, when the farm was a decrepit shell of a once prosperous country home, visited by the well-to-do friends of the Tays, it being the epitome of a well-run gentleman's working farm. His grandfather had told him of the banner years, when the MacPhersons had served the Tays and benefited from their bounty. Robbie also remembered the disdain of the old countess's face when Lady Biddy had announced she was going to marry Ivor Baillie Shaw, the son of an industrialist, and that they wanted to make their home at the farm. The countess had bigger ideas for her daughter, but had not enough money to present her to society even in Perth. Lady Biddy seemed not to mind; in fact she appeared blissfully happy from the very first and very much in love with Mr Ivor. His stewardship, and his ability to make all of those around him become excited at every detail in running the farm no matter how small, made the farm a going concern again. When Mr Ivor came into his father's money, his immediate action was to sell his parents' home in Edinburgh and pour his money into the farm. He embraced animal husbandry, learned about the most advanced methods of farming and the latest equipment, was an early advocate of organic methods of raising vegetables and soon had his neighbours as eager as he was to adapt to the new ways. The house was modernised, and soon was a centre for the farmers and landowners nearby who wanted to be included in the agricultural revolution of the late twentieth century. Lady Biddy was there with Ivor at every step and made the farm as much her labour of love as he made it his. Charlie, Alex, and Mary Baillie Shaw were born on the farm and grew up there, but none of the three of them wanted to stay. This saddened Robbie, who was now the farm manager. No one imagined that Mr Ivor would die; the disease was swift and painful, and it was all over in ten days. No one could fathom what would happen to Lady Biddy and the farm, but she had surprised them all. At Mr Ivor's funeral at the kirk in Kenmore, Biddy took Robbie aside and said, "Do you think you can help me run the farm?" Their partnership had begun that day, because, as Lady Biddy was so fond of reminding him, farms don't wait for people.

Sometimes, when night came early in the late autumn, however, he would see Lady Biddy sitting alone in the kitchen, her face in her hands, and he could almost feel her loneliness. She never mentioned it and he respected her silence, but he wondered what she must be feeling inside. The next morning, when she came out for the farm chores, her cheerfulness in caring for the farm and animals would be back.

He thought of these things as he tended to her, lying on the hay, eyes closed, simpering occasionally. Once she opened her eyes and through gritted teeth said, "I'm all right," but he knew she wasn't. Her pulse began to weaken, and he saw the bleeding had not abated. It seemed an endless time had elapsed before the ambulance arrived. Only then did he think to contact Lady Biddy's family. With Lord Johnnie in jail, he could only think of James Duff. There was no answer at Loch Rannoch, so Robbie rang through to James Duff's office in Pitlochry. They gave him Elspeth's mobile number.

*

Elspeth listened to Robbie, who in his excitement had reverted to a heavy burr, which she was having trouble following. Biddy was right; she must return to Scotland more often and not forget her roots.

"Where are they taking her? The Perth Royal Infirmary? Richard and I are in Perth right now. We'll go right round. Robbie, I'm certain you saved her life. How can we thank you?"

"There's no thanking, Miss Elspeth. Lady Biddy is precious to us all. Will you call me when you know how she is? Don't worry about things here. Jean and I can manage."

"Of course, Robbie. I'll call you as soon as I can. Give me your mobile number."

He did so and then said, "Why would anyone want to shoot Lady Biddy?"

"We'll have to find out, and I have every intention of doing so!"

Elspeth rang off and walked to the window. Max was right behind her. She told him the details.

"When you said "we" will find out, who is the "we"?"

Elspeth looked at him directly and said, "Me and you, Max."

Elspeth and Richard were waiting in the Accident and Emergency Department of Perth Royal Infirmary when the ambulance arrived from Loch Tay. A quarter of an hour passed before Elspeth was allowed to see Biddy, who lay on a hospital bed and was attached to numerous tubes. Her shoulder was wrapped in bandages, but blood had seeped out through them.

Biddy opened her eyes. "'Peth?" she said, and then closed them again. Elspeth sat by Biddy's bed in the cubicle and waited for the doctor. Biddy was only partly conscious. Her eyes had fallen into dark shadows of pain, and her face was white from loss of blood. Elspeth took her cousin's hand and held it without speaking.

Time seemed to pass slowly until she sensed Biddy was in one of her more lucid moments, when Elspeth spoke quietly to her. "Max wanted to come, but I told him not to yet."

Biddy half smiled. "Dear Max," she said and then grimaced with pain.

"I'll let Johnnie know as soon as I can."

"Dear Johnnie," Biddy said, this time rather drunkenly from the drugs they must have given her. "I was to fetch him. I don't think I can now."

A nursing sister came through the curtains and asked Elspeth to leave the cubicle, as the doctor would be in shortly see Biddy. The sister escorted Elspeth out of the room and led her to where Richard was waiting.

*

Richard was in the reception area, looking through some heavily fingered magazines with disinterest and disgust. When Elspeth entered the room, he stood up. She went to him and put her arms around him. "Damn, Dickie, who would want to shoot Biddy of all people?"

Disregarding others in the waiting room, he held her for a long moment and felt some of her tension flow away as he

226

stroked her hair.

"How is she?" he whispered in her ear.

"She's lost a great deal of blood, and they think the bullet is still in her shoulder. She'll be in a great deal of pain once the drugs wear off, but thankfully no one believes the shot will prove fatal. They'll have to remove the bullet as soon as possible, probably tonight, so that there is less risk of infection."

"And, how are you?" he asked.

Elspeth's eyes filled with tears, but she choked them back. "Awful," she said. "Why is all this happening to my family?" The question was rhetorical and for the moment unanswerable.

"What will Max feel about all this?" Richard asked, thinking of the legal implications, and was surprised by Elspeth's answer.

Elspeth smiled briefly. "More than he wants to for Biddy."

"Are you certain?"

"As someone who for a long time fought my own feelings towards the man I was in love with, yes, I think I have a right to presume that he does."

Richard closed his eyes in remembrance of Elspeth's long resistance of him and the joy of her final capitulation.

They sat in a corner as far from the others as they could manage and spoke little after Elspeth told the details she knew to Richard. He took her hand and found it cold. She put her other hand over his and held it there, saying she needed his strength and calmness, her own stores now depleted.

He thought she had dozed off, but all of a sudden, she sat up.

"Dickie, Johnnie will have to be told. He must be feeling frantic that Biddy didn't come to get him."

"Perhaps Max will have," Richard suggested.

"He won't know anything except the bare facts. I don't think he would tell Johnnie anything until he knew of Biddy's condition."

"Elspeth, is it absurd of me to think that Biddy's being shot has something to do with Louisa's murder?"

"Not at all," she replied.

Over an hour passed before the nursing sister came to get Elspeth, and told her Biddy was about to go into surgery to have the bullet removed.

"The doctor would like to see you, Ms Duff. There's another important matter."

*

She left Richard in the reception room and was shown to a small office. A doctor, as young as her son, came in shortly after her.

"Ms Duff," he asked, "Are you Lady Elisabeth's next of kin?"

Elspeth shook her head. "No, I'm her first cousin, but I'm here as representative of the family, her son being in the States and her brother otherwise disposed." She did not elaborate.

"Then I'll speak frankly," the doctor said. "If this shooting was not accidental, and it doesn't appear to be, we have to bring in the police. I'm sorry, but it's hospital procedure."

Elspeth froze.

"I've already called the police," the doctor continued. "They asked us to ring them as soon as we remove the bullet so that they can determine what sort of gun was used. I suggest that if she has a solicitor, he or she might want to be here if the police come."

"Yes, of course, I'll contact him directly" Elspeth said tonelessly. "Is there a place where my husband and I can wait close to the operating room?"

*

Max had been expecting Elspeth's call and was there beside them in less than twenty minutes. He found Elspeth, her head propped on Richard's shoulder and despair filling her face. She greeted Max with a smile that had no happiness behind it. Max shook Richard's hand and then laid his hand over Elspeth's.

"Let me handle the police," Max said, "and I'll collect Johnnie and take him to the farm."

He watched Elspeth straighten herself up, as if she were in physical pain, her body movements conveying the anguish she must be feeling. Max wished he could offer words that would comfort her, but there were none.

"Do you think this is connected to Johnnie?" she asked in a whisper, echoing Richard's earlier thoughts.

Max nodded almost imperceptibly. "Probably."

His lawyer's brain had been looking for a motive ever since Elspeth had told him the news about Biddy. Who was the intended victim, Johnnie or Biddy herself? Did someone really want to kill Biddy? Why? Did Biddy know something that made it necessary to scare her or silence her? Who could that possibly be? Max simply did not know. Thinking the evening would be a long one, Max suggested Elspeth and Richard take a break from their vigil and find some coffee. He would stay and watch and would tend to Johnnie later.

Their departure and promise of an early return with the

best coffee they could find left Max time to think, not about the motive but about the victim. He was too intelligent to ignore his own feelings and no longer wanted to, knowing that he cared deeply and personally that Biddy get well again and suffer no permanent damage from her attack. Suddenly he felt fully committed to Elspeth's earlier 'we' in finding who had perpetrated this crime.

He sat there alone for half an hour before Elspeth and Richard returned with some decent coffee, not the pallid offering in the canteen below. They also had brought some sandwiches that looked edible.

Just past five a doctor with a grave face emerged from the operating room.

"She is resting now," he said. "Fortunately the bullet was lodged in her non-vital tissues and, although she'll need a long time to recover the full use of her shoulder and left arm. I expect a substantial recovery in several months. Your cousin, Ms Duff, is extremely lucky. Three inches lower and the bullet would have entered her heart."

Elspeth's eyes grew wide. Richard put his arm around her shoulders to steady her. Max clenched his jaw. "Do you have the bullet?" he asked.

"Yes," the doctor said. "An unusual one. I had to look it up. It's a .62 calibre bullet, most probably fired probably from a high-powered Ingram sporting rifle, popular with gentlemen in Victorian times. The rifle is quite rare now. Do you know of anyone who would want to shoot your cousin? I would imply that this was more than an accident."

Elspeth did not reply other than to say, "May we see her, doctor?"

"She is too drugged right now to recognise you. I suggest

you return in the morning. You need have no fears tonight. She is sufficiently medicated that she won't be ready for guests until tomorrow. I'll make arrangements for you to be admitted when you arrive.

"And the police?" Max broached. "I'm Lady Elisabeth's lawyer. Have them contact me and not the family. I'll leave my card."

Elspeth reached out to him and put her hand on his arm. Max saw that she was stretched very thin and the usual challenge in eyes had died away.

"Thanks," she said hoarsely to him. "Take care of her and Johnnie, Max."

He knew he wanted to more than anything else in the world.

*

When leaving the hospital, Elspeth and Richard debated whether to return to Tay Farm or Loch Rannoch, and finally decided to stop by Tay Farm before returning to the Duff home. The house was dark, meaning Johnnie had not yet arrived. They went into the kitchen, and the emptiness of the room was profound without Biddy or Johnnie's presence. They walked out to a point above the loch. The land around it had never seemed sinister before but somewhere out there earlier in the day a sniper had hidden and almost taken Biddy's life. Elspeth could see the farm from where she stood and tried to imagine where the gunman could have hidden, the land used mainly for sheep grazing, but there were small copses of trees up beyond the road. Perhaps the gunman had stood in one of these. Elspeth could see the sheep pen from where she stood, its fencing standing out against the sky. Had the sniper stood where she was now and raised his gun when he saw Biddy, and if so to what intent?

She did a quick survey of the road to see if any of the media had heard of the shot but mercifully the landscape was empty. She then made her way back to the house. Biddy's sign that warned passers-by not to disturb the tenants still hung from the gate, but now dangled on a single wire and was gyrating in the breeze. Richard bent down, reattached the second wire and opened the gate.

When they returned to the kitchen, Elspeth saw the FedEx envelope addressed to Johnnie. Not constrained by the dictate that letters should only be read by the addressee, Elspeth tore open the packet and inside found a single sheet of paper, on which was computer generated the text "NEXT TIME I WILL AIM AT HER HEART". Elspeth let out a small choke of disbelief. She turned over the stiff container that held the paper and read the return address. It was labelled "A. Rifleman" and the address was scrawled "Earltay Court, Perth" with a postal code that matched the house where Louisa had been killed. The implication could not be missed.

"What horrible joke is this?" she cried, showing the message to Richard. "It sounds like a vendetta. I've no idea at all what this means but can only think the shooting was some sort of warning."

"I think we need to show this to Max soon," Richard said, "and we should return to Loch Rannoch now. I don't know what else we can do here."

Elspeth scribbled a brief note to Robbie and Jean MacPherson, letting them know that Max and Johnnie would be at the farm soon, and she and Richard had been there and would return as soon as they could. She followed Richard out the door, locking it behind her.

Elspeth's father was waiting for Elspeth and Richard by the gate as they arrived at the Duff home. Richard parked Biddy's cumbersome vehicle and received a vociferous greeting from Bounce in a homecoming that seemed less than joyful. They shed their coats, and James Duff led them in by the fire.

As they settled in, Elspeth said with despair in her voice, "I feel like such a failure in defending Johnnie, and now I have to go off to Canada and pretend all is well in my life. If only I could get a grasp on what's happening here and why, I'd have some way to help Max with the case. I feel so helpless. Johnnie and now Biddy are being targetted by some devious person, and I haven't a clue whom. I always go back to Louisa. What had she done that someone would murder her? Strangulation is a violent act and yet, thinking about it, was it premeditated? Who might come to her house in Perth other than Johnnie last Thursday night and hate her enough to silence her? It also bothers me that two witnesses so conveniently appear. Who are they, are they telling the truth or were they paid to lie? If the last, why? Now we have to leave day after tomorrow and have no way to find out. Damn! I feel so inadequate," she said violently.

Bounce, wagging her tail sympathetically, came to comfort Elspeth, but she only acknowledged the gesture with a distracted pat. The dog lay down with a grunt. "What else can I do? Biddy's in hospital and now Johnnie has to remain at the farm and not see anyone involved in the case."

Elspeth's uncharacteristic sense of gloom dismayed her, but she could not pull herself out of it. She appealed to her father and husband.

233

Her father came up to her and put a hand on her shoulder. She turned to him and threw her arms around his chest. He held her as he had done when she was a child.

"My dear daughter," he said with the same tones he had used so many years back, "Biddy and Johnnie both must take responsibility for where they are now in their lives, and your trying to take it on is highly commendable, but you can't be blamed for it. Let them have your counsel but don't berate yourself for not being able to rescue them. Help them, if you can, of course, but don't become their saviour."

Elspeth pulled back from her father. At first she did not want to hear his words, but, from long admiration and love for him, she knew they were true.

He continued, "Please try to distance yourself from this, Elspeth, and get back to your own life. You have contracted the services of one of the best criminal solicitor advocates in Scotland. Trust him, and, if you can help him, do so. But ultimately, Elspeth, Johnnie and Biddy have to find their own way out of this morass."

After her father had retired to bed, Elspeth went over to where her husband was sitting, and he embraced her.

"Your father's a wise man," Richard said.

"Yes, I know," she said. "I should listen to him more often."

"And," Richard said, "I expect you won't.

23

Maxwell Douglas-Forbes woke early with an acute sense of dissatisfaction. As much as he wanted it to, the Tay case was not going well, and he was wise enough to ascribe this to his own emotions. Ever since his wife's fiery death in a car crash with her lover, who also had been his law clerk, Max had wanted to marry again, but no opportunity had presented itself. His tastes were particular and not just any woman would do, despite the many who made themselves available to him. Being single and respectable was a dangerous state for a middle-aged man. He was continually asked to social events sometimes given by his friends and frequently by his clients, but he never had followed up with a return invitation. He was not dropped, he was too good a prospect, but hearts were bruised along the way.

He rolled out of bed and went to his kitchen. His housekeeper had left the coffee machine ready for his use, even setting out a tray for him. Like a mystical spirit, she came in daily for several hours to keep his household running and then disappeared to goodness knows where, the only whiff of her existence being the preparations she had made for him in his absence. Max liked it this way, doubted if he would recognise her in the street and paid her well enough so that he did not have to do so.

He pressed the button on the coffee machine and went to his exercise room, not from commitment to fitness but rather

235

from his need to keep his weight in check. He chose the stair climber and began his morning routine. Half an hour later, sweating and flushed with an endorphin high, he showered and considered the day to come. What he wanted to do most in the world was to see Biddy Baillie Shaw. She had made no advances towards him, which he appreciated, but the smile that came to her face each time she saw him lingered in his memory and lightened his heart. Now with Biddy in hospital, and with Elspeth's plea that he take care of her, he felt redoubled in his need to help Johnnie.

His interactions with Johnnie bothered him. Johnnie's aversion to answering Max's questions was thinly veiled and left Max feeling disquieted. Elspeth Duff warned him that Johnnie might be distrustful of him, but why? Was Johnnie hiding something? The thought had come to him before. Perhaps Biddy would know. Max looked at his watch and saw it was only seven. As Biddy's lawyer he probably could see her at any time, but he expected that the morning routine at the hospital would necessitate his delaying returning there at least until later in the morning. In any case, he needed to talk to the procurator fiscal about the shooting at the farm and also wanted to see Johnnie, now sequestered at the farm where Max had left him the evening before. Seven was too early to ring Elspeth, so he looked in the fridge to find something edible and found some dreary looking tinned peaches his housekeeper had left in a bowl for him, with a note that there was cereal in the larder. He gathered the newspapers from his doorstep and took them to where his coffee and makeshift breakfast were waiting. The story of Louisa Tay's murder had migrated to the inner pages even in the tabloids, the story's freshness having faded due to both lack of new evidence and more pressing news. There was no mention of the shooting the afternoon before.

At ten o'clock, Max was standing at the window of his chambers looking out over the River Tay with a feeling of acute anticipation regarding Elspeth's forthcoming visit. Only six days had passed since he first met her, but his whole life had in that short space of time taken on a new perspective and had become filled with people who fascinated him much more than his usual clients. Seen on the street any one of these people would appear to be ordinary Scottish gentry, not people caught in the web of a murder charge that may have its roots in a grant of peerage well over two centuries before, and a mysterious sniper attack on a respectable lady, who ran a farm.

Elspeth walked into the office with the same self-assured air she had when he first had met her, but he could see an emotion, perhaps anger, on her face that had not been there before. He bade her sit down, but she chose to stand. She drew a Federal Express envelope from her large handbag and dropped it on his desk. He took the envelope and pulled out the single sheet of paper. Her response after he had read it was not what he expected.

"Max, they're hiding something from us, the two of them, and we have to find out what it is. I only have today and tomorrow morning, and I want to help you as much as possible."

"I suspected there was something after Biddy refused to answer me when we went down to the edge of the loch, and I won't be surprised if we find a link between what they are hiding, the shooting, and this." He pointed to the FedEx message. "Have I become too cynical?"

"No more than I. I want to confront Johnnie today. Do you think he will be responsive? I'm going to the farm now to find out."

*

Finishing his lunch, Johnnie allowed Jean to take his plate, and he wandered into the main part of the house, a rambling affair built by the fifth Earl of Tay, who was the only earl to make a fortune, and who had built on to the old farm with a zest of Victorian zeal. Johnnie remembered his grandfather, the seventh earl, who had despaired at his ill fortune, mostly self-inflicted, and moved from the larger house outside Perth to the farm out of pure poverty. The house had decayed along with the Tay family fortunes. Johnnie's father, the eighth earl, was a jolly sort, who cared little for the farm although he and his wife were forced to live there with their children, and he spent his days fishing, romping round the countryside with a rifle and his dogs, and playing cards with his friends. Ignoring the deterioration of the farm's infrastructure surrounding her, the eighth countess had taught her children, Johnnie and Biddy, to the manner born, but their eventual choices in life had disappointed her. She had also tried to reign in her niece, Elspeth, to little avail. Elspeth's high spirits distressed her, and the countess frequently chastised Fiona Duff on that score. Fiona listened patiently to her sister-in-law and allowed Elspeth to do as she pleased.

As Johnnie rambled through the house, he remembered all this. Until today, he had not realised how much the farm meant to him nor did he appreciate all that Ivor and Biddy had done to restore it, perhaps not to its splendour during the days of the fifth earl, but at least to structural stability. Ivor had seen to the installation of new plumbing and central heating, upgraded the electrical services, and finally added a connection to the Internet and the world of computers. Both Biddy and Ivor had become stewards to the land, renovating the barns, upgrading the farm equipment, restocking the flocks of sheep and fowl and restoring the farm gardens so that the farm became self-sustaining without any continued need for Ivor's personal income. Why had Johnnie not told Ivor, when he was alive, how important all this was? Had he even understood what large amounts of time, effort, and love the two of them had poured into the farm? He must tell Biddy as soon as she came back from the hospital, and he must tell Madeline when he saw her. Had Madeline ever been to the farm? He didn't know. Now he wanted to show Madeline everything, the house, the barns, the pastures and clumps of forest growth, the loch's edge, the rushing burn alongside the house, and the long views of the Highlands, places that were so much a part of him that he had never before considered them as anything out of the ordinary. Now they were everything, and he needed to save them, for Biddy, for Madeline, but most of all for himself.

*

Johnnie answered the door after Elspeth knocked on it. He looked defeated.

"At least they let me come home, but I'm stuck here with a clamp on my leg," He pointed to his electronic monitoring device on his ankle. "Have you seen Biddy? How is she feeling? Can she come home soon? This house is so empty without her," he said

"As soon as the doctors release her," she said. Then she

drew out a copy of the letter in the FedEx packet and handed it to Johnnie. "There's another matter, however, and it concerns Biddy. What do you know about this, Johnnie?"

After reading the note, Johnnie looked puzzled.

"Why are you and Biddy lying?" Elspeth said, not mincing her words.

"Lying, 'Peth? I don't understand."

Elspeth raised her eyebrows, set her jaw and glared at him. "Johnnie, I know when you're not being honest. You haven't changed."

He laughed defensively. "Always the challenging bratty Elspeth, ay, cousin?"

"I may have been bratty when I was fifteen, but I'm not bratty now."

"You are," he said glumly.

"I need to know what you and Biddy are hiding."

"What makes you think we are hiding anything?"

"Don't be daft, Johnnie, and don't suppose I am. Whatever it is, it may have bearing on your case. If you like, don't tell me anything, but do tell Max."

"If there were something, why wouldn't I tell you but tell him instead?"

"He's your lawyer. You can invoke privilege. But tell him! Why are you so pig-headed?"

"Perhaps it runs in the family," he said jauntily. "I've often sensed the same tendency in you."

Elspeth would not be deterred. "In San Francisco you asked for my help to save the farm. Am I anathema now? I don't understand you and Biddy. Can't you trust me? Damn you, Johnnie, don't you know I would do anything to save you? Have you ever considered what prison for life might be like?"

"Ever since they arrested me," he said. "I'm not a fool."

Elspeth twisted inside at her cousin's flippancy. Was it his defence against fear? He had erected a barricade between them, so she changed her approach.

"Madeline has agreed to work with Max."

Johnnie's face filled with delight. "You've seen her?" he asked.

"Yesterday. She came to Max's office."

"Please, 'Peth, tell me, how is she bearing up?"

"Bravely and without doubts."

"Meaning?"

Elspeth looked directly into her cousin's eyes without flinching. "She'll come to your defence, but if you lose, she too will lose everything. I'm certain you're aware of that. You're asking a very great deal of her."

"You have a cruel side."

"Cruel?" Elspeth cried, knowing she was on the edge of anger. "Cruel? Johnnie, is your ego so big as to deny what you are asking Madeline to do?"

Johnnie glared at her. "I know exactly what I want her to do. Stay out of this."

"She won't!"

"Then talk sense into her."

"I can try, but I think she's committed otherwise. She wants to see you, and I think I have a way to arrange that without alerting the procurator fiscal or the press, but I need your concurrence to do so. Would you consent to Madeline acting in your behalf in managing your business while we are trying to clear you? It would give her good reason to come to see you, and I understand you have already shared a great deal of the business with her. Think about it, Johnnie. At this point there's nothing linking her directly to Louisa's murder, and she'll not be deterred."

"I can't ask her to do that."

"Is she capable of doing it, particularly if she came to consult you here?"

Johnnie sputtered and finally said, "Yes, I think so."

"Then give her a chance," Elspeth said, her voice harsh. "Now, tell me what you and Biddy are concealing. We can't help unless we know. Tell me, Johnnie! It could save your life and Biddy's as well."

Johnnie took a long breath.

"Two years ago Biddy gave me money to cover a loan I had made using the farm as collateral."

"That's not only impossible but also illegal," Elspeth cried.

Johnnie said. "I hold the deed."

"No, Johnnie, you don't. The Earl of Tay does."

"The last time I looked I was the Earl of Tay," he smirked.

Elspeth shook her head. "You may be the ninth Earl of Tay, but you only are a place holder. Have your read the grant of peerage?"

Johnnie laughed. "Your father waved it at me when I assumed the title but who can read it with all those s's that look like f's."

"You should try, since it affects your title and lands," Elspeth said. "Somehow I suspect you knew that."

"Meaning I lied?"

"I spent a long time on Monday morning pouring through the s's and f's. I'm not conversant with eighteenth century law, but from what I could make out, you have no right to mortgage, sell, or in any way encumber the farm. I've often wondered why Grandfather Tay never sold the farm when he was financially ruined but did sell the house in Perth. He couldn't sell the farm according to the grant of peerage, nor did you have the right to use it as collateral for a loan."

Johnnie looked chagrined. "It was a business deal. I didn't think it would backfire," he said.

"How long ago was this?"

"Two years ago."

"I won't be put off. Tell me the terms."

"I needed cash quickly to buy a competing business. I thought I had sixty days to come up with the cash and knew no reason why I shouldn't be able to. I signed a note, but even my business solicitor didn't read the fine print after we had all agreed on the draft. The final agreement, which I signed, said if I defaulted after six days, which we thought it was sixty, and if I did not immediately pay in full I would forfeit the farm. I couldn't meet that demand for the money and knew I'd been devious about my title to the farm."

"And Biddy came up with the full payment?"

"From Ivor's life insurance settlement," he said.

"To save you from admitting you had committed fraud? Who was the person you borrowed the money from?"

"The Perthshire Land Development Consortium."

"Who was its legal representative who pressed you?"

"Paul Hodges, their solicitor in Perth."

Elspeth drew back in surprise. "Paul Hodges? Louisa's divorce lawyer? Then it must have been this Paul Hodges who put the idea of taking the farm from you into Louisa's head. There has to be a connection." Elspeth's anger drained away in realisation of the truth. "You're in deep trouble," she said, her jaw set and fire in her eyes, "and I won't let that rest!"

"You sound like you are on the warpath," Johnnie said.

"You can be assured that I am," said Elspeth. "Beware, Perthshire Land Development Land Consortium and Paul Hodges. Now that we know the enemy, we shall engage."

"Where did you get that from?" Johnnie asked, screwing up his face.

"I'd like it to be Sun Tzu on *The Art of War*, but I just made it up," said Elspeth with a mischievous grin that broke the tension of moment.

"God, 'Peth, are you related to the Gorgons?" Johnnie said.

"Don't tell Dickie," she said.

"I expect he already knows," Johnnie said.

*

Elspeth walked from the farmhouse, looking both vexed and concerned. Richard was waiting for her near the barn beside Biddy's Land Rover, and soon they headed back towards Perth and the Royal Infirmary. Richard reached over for his wife's hand. "Let it go, Elspeth."

Elspeth bit her lip and cried out, "How can I?"

"Didn't you listen to your father last night?"

"I did, but I feel I'm betraying Johnnie and Biddy by returning to London and going off to Canada to be cossetted by the Kennington Victoria hotel staff despite the fact I shall be on non-stop duty for over a week."

Richard seldom spoke censoriously to his wife the way he had often done to the young Elspeth many years before, but he did so now. "You can't be here and in Canada at the same time. Let Max handle it."

Elspeth broke out laughing, in remembrance of her childhood relationship with Richard. "Yes, Uncle Dickie," she said in a mocking tone she had used when she was fifteen. Then she brushed his cheek with the slightest touch that conveyed the multiple layers of feeling he knew she had for him now.

"Oh, damn," she said. "I feel so inadequate! I can't let this rest."

Richard loved his wife so well that he was reluctant to reprove her further, but he was deeply concerned by the conflict she seemed to be experiencing and her inability to resolve it. He had learned that Elspeth committed herself slowly but once her heart was given, she did not waver. He carefully formulated what best to say, not only to allow for her feelings but also to save her from her own ambivalence between duty to her family and to her employer. Lord Kennington expected her to deal competently and unemotionally with the high-powered guests at the Kennington hotels and see to their ultimate security when they were under her charge. As a consequence Richard fumbled with his words, which was uncharacteristic.

He cleared his throat. "Will you stay in touch with Max and leave the rest to him?"

She said sadly, "I'm going to have to, aren't I?"

"Yes, my dearest," he said. "When are you back from Canada?"

"A week on Sunday," she said.

"I'd hoped you would come to Malta then, or perhaps I can arrange to be in London instead."

Her face brightened. "Would you mind coming to Scotland rather than London?"

"My dear Lady MacDuff," he said smiling. "I never can resist your command."

As much as she had dragged him through her life, the very act of being with her fulfilled him more completely than any other thing in his existence, and he did not mind if coming to Scotland meant he could be with her. She always seemed to relish and honour every moment with him, despite the unanticipated paths she led him down. He had never regretted their marriage agreement that acknowledged their independence but commitment in each other. He smiled inwardly and negotiated the hill up to the Perth Royal Infirmary!"

24

Biddy was lying in her hospital bed in her private room and was conscious but obviously still groggy from the effects of her surgery the night before. All colour was gone from her face from loss of blood, and her shoulder was bound in multiple white layers of fresh gauze. The nursing sister had propped her up, and she appeared to be attempting to read a magazine, although when Elspeth and Richard entered, she was dozing. Numerous tubes extended from her arm and monitors recorded her various systems, all of which seemed to be stable. A large bouquet of flowers, roses, freesias, a blue flower Elspeth did not know, and ferns, sat on the sideboard with a card that Elspeth assumed must be from Max, although the signature was hidden. The scent of the flowers helped overcome the antiseptic smell of the room.

Elspeth and Richard's entry woke Biddy. Pleasure filled her unfocused eyes, and she seemed to recognise them. She was wrapped in a hospital gown but seemed unaware that it did not flatter her. Elspeth had spent enough time in her life in hospital to know that one's own nightclothes had a subliminal effect in the recovery process and consequently had thought to bring something for Biddy from the farm. Since she had seen the dreadful state of Biddy's nightwear, Elspeth had also included one of her own dressing gowns, which was smartly cut from a fine wool fabric of intense cobalt blue that she had once found in Hong Kong and had made up for her. The colour matched both their eyes. Biddy held out her good hand in thanks for Elspeth's caring gesture.

After appropriate words of sympathy, however, Elspeth confronted her cousin.

"Biddy, tell me what happened at the farm yesterday."

Biddy turned to look at Elspeth, but the attempt caused her to draw back in pain. Elspeth moved round and sat at the end of the bed where she was in Biddy's direct line of vision. Only then did she see Biddy's confusion.

"I saw someone standing above the farm on the knoll near the MacPherson farm," she said. "He had a rifle, I think, although he was a bit far off and it could possibly have been a walking stick. It's a common sight, particularly in summer when people come out to hunt rabbits, so I didn't pay particular attention. Suddenly something struck me so hard that it spun me around." Her face skewed at the memory. "You can't imagine the pain. It was so sudden, and then it spread all over me. After that, I remember Robbie laying me on the hay in the barn. He told me he had helped me walk in, but I have no recollection of it. I do recall that he staunched my wound with the same caring hands he has for the animals. Then the ambulance came, although it's all quite fuzzy. I vaguely remember you, 'Peth. Were you here at the hospital?"

"Biddy, why would anyone want to do this to you? Does it have to do with Johnnie?" she asked. She did not mention the Federal Express packet.

Biddy looked away from Elspeth.

"Please tell me, Biddy. I just saw Johnnie and he told me about you covering the loan."

"I see," she said her voice cracking, and then added

almost inaudibly. "Do you suppose there's a connection?"

"Do you think someone is threatening him and using you to do so?"

"I don't know, 'Peth."

Elspeth sensed Biddy's despair. "Does this have anything to do with Louisa's death?" Elspeth asked.

Biddy did not answer at first. "Please," she finally said, but Elspeth could not understand the reason for her request. Was it to stop her questioning, or was Biddy in too much pain to answer, or was she protecting Johnnie? Filled with a sense of frustration but also of empathy, Elspeth rose from the bed and went round to plant a dry kiss on her cousin's forehead, which brought relief to Biddy's eyes.

Before departing, Elspeth made the same plea she had made to Johnnie just an hour before. "Trust Max," she said. "You have a very powerful ally."

As Richard and Elspeth left, Biddy smiled weakly and closed her eyes without promising anything. Elspeth was not certain Biddy had heard her.

*

Despite Biddy's evasion of Elspeth's questions, she did not dismiss them and wished she had a way to talk to her brother. Besides Max had stirred in her feelings she had not had since Ivor had died, but she was distrustful of them and wanted to put them out of her mind. Yet they would not go away. She was wise enough to know that romantic feelings in a woman in her late fifties were common when any available man came within range, and, knowing the illusion of false hope, she hated what was happening to her when she was with Max. She tried to focus her attention on Johnnie and on Louisa's murder, but with the combination of pain and the

249

medications they had prescribed for her, her brain flitted in and out of reality. She kept seeing Max's face when she did not want to. Trying to avoid admiring the robe Elspeth had laid on her bed but unable to even in her diminished state, she pressed the button by her pillow and summoned the nursing sister.

The nurse bustled in after an interminable lapse of time. "Lady Elisabeth," she said. "How charming your cousin is and her husband! Quite dishy!"

Biddy had never heard Richard Munro described as "dishy" before and was amused. Had Elspeth really changed him so much that a provincial Scottish nurse would find something so appealing in him? But, then again, Richard's demeanour had altered since he had married Elspeth. Biddy had seen the change in him at Elspeth's wedding in Malta and then again at Peter's ceremony in San Francisco. It challenged Biddy's notion that unattached middle-aged people were doomed to loneliness and the thought unsettled her. She carefully brought her mind back to the moment.

"Sister, I need to make some telephone calls. Is there any way I can do that and have some privacy?" she asked.

"Unfortunately patients aren't allowed mobiles here because it interferes with our equipment. You could ring out on a public phone in the corridor, but everything goes through our central system and your call won't be private. My lady, you did have a call from a Mr Douglas-Forbes. He asked when he might come to see you and I suggested some time after lunch. Would you like me to ring him back?"

Biddy lay back, filled with emotion. "I would appreciate that," she said with all her dignity, but inside as she felt she was a girl. "Tell him two o'clock will be fine. And, sister,

I'm a bit chilly. Please you help me put on my robe as best you can and help me comb out my hair."

The nurse left wondering who Mr Douglas-Forbes might be and why Lady Elisabeth had made her requests, since until now she had seemed quite unaware of her appearance. The nurse always passed her quiet moments speculating on the lives of the patients under her care and enjoyed her fantasies although they seldom proved true.

*

After the hospital confirmed that he could go at two to see Biddy, Max put down his phone and turned to a message he had received from the procurator fiscal regarding the shot fired at Lady Elisabeth the day before. He consulted his contact list and dialled Adair Gordon's number.

"Max, you'll have to find a way to convince me to that there's no connection between the attack on Lady Elisabeth and the arrest of Lord Tay," Adair Gordon said.

"I'm certain the attack on Lady Elisabeth wasn't coincidental," Max responded. "It seems to me that the evidence shows Lord Tay's innocence, so it's obvious that something else is happening here."

"Tell me your theory on this, Max? Make it plausible, and I'll see if it will change my thinking in Lord Tay's case."

Max and the procurator fiscal went a long way back. They had played desultory cricket at Edinburgh University where they read the law together and an occasional round of golf afterwards. Neither was good at these sports, but they had a history reaching mutually satisfactory arrangements for the early release of Max's clients, when their guilt was in doubt.

Max had considered little else other than the attack on Biddy since hearing of it. His law practice had been limited to the more affluent families of Scotland, so he had therefore not come across a case before where a murder investigation led to the harm of someone associated with the crime, but he had heard such things happened particularly when illegal crime organisations were involved. Neither Johnnie nor Biddy Baillie Shaw seemed the sort to know such people, and organised crime was less prevalent north of the border. He must ask Elspeth Duff if she knew of any suspicious connections in Lord Tay's past life, although he found it unlikely.

"I don't have a theory yet," Max admitted to the procurator fiscal, "but the only thing that makes sense is that someone is trying to intimidate Lord Tay and using his sister as some kind of reminder."

"How serious was the injury?"

"The bullet entered the soft tissue in her shoulder, and therefore they were able to remove it cleanly. She should be out of hospital before the end of the week and recover in the next few months with only a bad scar, but the doctors said she will have limited motor function until then. I expect she'll return home by the weekend. The police took the bullet from the hospital last night. I suppose you're investigating, but my expectation is that the gun will be untraceable. Still I have real reasons for my suspicions," Max said.

"It is unlike you, Max, to take such a personal interest in a case," the procurator fiscal said. "I thought you disdained such things."

Over the years, Max had carefully cultivated a range of ways to respond to questions he did not want to answer straightforwardly: haughtiness, sneering, jocularity, or simple evasion being among them. He cast about to choose one of these methods, but he decided on the truth, or at least a part of it.

"Adair, this case intrigues me," Max said honestly. "I've dealt with the gentry and aristocracy for many years, but I have never before met any of them who have absolutely no pretensions. Lord Tay is a semi-successful businessman who happens to have an inherited title and his sister is, praise be, a farmer. I like them."

"More to the point, are you stretching your professional propriety?"

"I don't think so. I've never had an innocent relative of a client attacked by what seems to be a professional assassin. What's Scotland coming to?"

"Do you seriously consider the attack on Lady Elisabeth a professional job or merely a misguided shot by an overenthusiastic hunter?"

Max remembered the message that had come in the FedEx packet, but he did not yet want to reveal its contents to the procurator fiscal.

"I'm not certain. The burden of proof is on me then, I suppose."

"Yes, Max. Good luck to you."

Max entered Biddy's hospital room with a mass of mixed feelings. He did not know how much Elspeth might have told Biddy about her meeting with Johnnie that morning, although Elspeth had rung him afterwards. He was loath to confront Biddy about her covering Johnnie's fraudulent claims to his business lenders two years before, but he felt he must. He sensed Biddy's generous heart sometimes overcame her good judgment, a commendable quality even if deceit had not been involved in Johnnie's actions. He was resolved to confront her, but his heart bumped when he saw her, wrapped in a robe that set off her fine blue eyes and a smile that he felt could only have been meant for him.

"Thank you for the beautiful flowers, Max," she said. "The nurse brought them in this morning when I was asleep and set the card on my table. It was the first thing I saw when I woke up. Do you do this in all your cases?"

Max laughed. The arch of Biddy's eyebrow reminded him of Elspeth's, but there was graciousness, pleasure, and appreciation in the gesture, not challenge.

"Only to clients who are particularly charming," he said. "I'm glad they're to your liking. Biddy, as much as I had hoped to avoid it, I'm going to have to ask you questions that may be uncomfortable."

Biddy closed her eyes and turned from him. "Now?" she asked.

"Unfortunately, yes."

"Is it about what Johnnie told Elspeth?"

"About you covering his loan two years ago."

Biddy raised her chin. "I see. The money was mine to give. There was nothing illegal in that. Johnnie had been deceived."

Max inwardly winced at what he had to say next. "Johnnie had falsely pledged the farm to people who, it seems, wanted to develop it. How much did you know about these transactions? Enough for someone to silence you?"

"Silence me?" Biddy asked. "Do you think that's why I was shot? That's ridiculous. Johnnie paid his note on time with my help. That put an end to it."

"What do you know about the Perthshire Land

Development Consortium?"

Biddy looked confused. "I vaguely remember Johnnie mentioning them."

"As the holders of the note?"

"Max, for all your good intentions, I have had little to do with Johnnie's business transactions other than to give him the money when he asked me for it."

"Was it a loan?"

"No, it was a gift."

"With no return?"

Biddy's eyes flared. "We're brother and sister, Max. I didn't demand a promissory note from him, just as he doesn't demand rent from me because I live at the farm. What we have belongs to us both."

"I find that unusual," Max said.

"How sad. Now, Max, my shoulder is pounding. Forgive me."

Max was not certain whether Biddy's statement was evasive or true, but he not chose to judge her. Her dismissal was kindly said but conclusive. "May I come see you tomorrow?"

"Yes, please. I'll look forward to it."

He touched her hand lightly and took his departure.

25

Max was not surprised when Elspeth rang him on Wednesday afternoon and asked to come and see him the following morning before she and Richard departed for London. They set the time for eleven o'clock, which would allow them ample time to see Biddy beforehand and reach Edinburgh airport in time for their afternoon flight to London.

They arrived slightly before the appointed hour, and Max showed them into his chambers. He saw both in their dress and manner that they were on their way to their own lives beyond Perthshire, and Max felt he was losing an important lifeline to the Tay/Robertson family.

"Max," Elspeth said, extending her hand in what was a handshake but also a gesture of appeal, "it pains me to abandon you. We have a short time before we must be at the airport, but I couldn't leave without seeing you once more. Please tell Biddy that we've made arrangements to get her Land Rover back to Tay Farm. We told her so this morning when we saw her in hospital, but she still seems a bit muddled, so please pass the information on again to her. With Johnnie not being allowed to leave the farm, we'll have to rely on you to help her, which may be terribly presumptuous. Your time and expenses, of course, will be covered. My friend Pamela Crumm will guarantee that you be paid when my retainer runs out."

256

Max smiled. Elspeth seemed uncomfortable asking him to help, but he wanted nothing more in the world than to have an excuse to be with Biddy again.

"You set great store in Ms Crumm," he said, hoping that Elspeth would not detect his feelings. "She has already guaranteed Lord Tay's bail."

"If you knew her, Max, you would see how generous she is."

Max grinned. "I hope I shall someday, but rest assured I'll do all I can for Biddy. Her situation is a difficult one."

"Max, you may always call on my father as well. Despite his years, he misses very little. It's best to call him at his offices in Pitlochry. He and Mother had an answerphone once, but I don't think it's connected."

Max assured Elspeth he would do as she asked, but he could feel her tension, and presumed it was because she wanted to stay involved in Johnnie's case but had other obligations she could not ignore. Richard had retreated to the window and seemed extraordinarily interested in the River Tay beyond. Max suspected Richard preferred to leave the Tay case to his wife.

"We only have a short time," Elspeth said, beginning to pace back and forth despite Max's invitation to have her take a chair, "so I must be direct. What do you know of the Perthshire Land Development Corporation?"

"Not a lot, except what had been in the papers and on the court dockets. They have a reputation for acquiring land by unscrupulous means and then developing housing that looks flashy from the outside, but judging by the claims brought against them, are built to very low standards. Many of the new homebuyers, who were offered low interest mortgages through the consortium, have regretted their impulse to buy after only seeing the highly appointed kitchens and lavish master baths in the sales unit. Various suits have been filed against the consortium, but they have a barrage of lawyers attempting to keep them out of court."

"Do you know any of them?"

Max felt confused. "Any of the people suing?"

"The lawyers."

Max was startled at Elspeth's assertion. "I don't think so."

"Paul Hodges?"

"Louisa's divorce lawyer?"

Elspeth nodded. "Last night when Richard and I went back to Tay Farm before returning to my parents' home on Loch Rannoch, I had the opportunity to search the Perthshire Land Development Consortium on the web, since my parents have dodgy access to the internet at home and I did not take my laptop with me when we went to San Francisco. How long ago that seems. So I logged on to Biddy's computer at the farm and Googled the consortium. Not only does it have land interests, but it also has its fingers in banking, not just as a financing arm for homebuyers. It also it offers loans to businesses. That must be how Johnnie got involved with them. I expect he needed more cash than his bank would loan him, and he willingly offered the farm as collateral, as he told us yesterday. Probably rubbing their greedy hands together, the Consortium's lawyers never thought to check the grant of peerage, since Johnnie assured them the farm was his. Suddenly the consortium's lawyer, Paul Hodges, took over Louisa's divorce case, and she demanded the farm. Does all this make sense?"

Max listened to Elspeth's argument, which certainly

sounded feasible.

"Do you have proof?" he asked.

"None at all," she said.

He admired her honesty.

She stopped pacing across the room and took the chair he had originally offered. "Max, I can't stay in Perthshire to find the truth." He could feel the frustration in her voice. "I have to rely on you. Can I?" she asked. "If you are to establish Johnnie's innocence or at least have the jury find the case 'not proven', you must find an alternative reason for someone to kill Louisa."

"Do you seriously believe someone in the consortium would have Louisa killed? To what purpose? Once dead, she would have no claim."

"Your point is well taken," she said and blew out her breath. "How can we be sure if the consortium knew who would inherit the earldom after Johnnie? Passing through the female line, Biddy's son, Charlie will, but he isn't the least interested in Tay Farm. Could he be coerced into selling it? But, if the consortium finally realised that the farm could not be sold, I couldn't find any stipulation in the grant of peerage that the earl—whether it be Johnnie or Charlie—couldn't give them a long-term lease."

"Ouch," said Max, admiring Elspeth's reasoning. Would Biddy allow that?"

Elspeth's face went pale. "Biddy," she said with a moan. "The case somehow revolves around Biddy's strong will to keep the farm."

Max's heart turned inside him, but he could not suppress his thought. "Would she, and not Johnnie, murder Louisa for it? To stop the coercion?"

Elspeth visible gulped. "Max, I don't want us to even think about that."

"Nor do I."

"I must go to Canada tomorrow, but modern communication is good enough that we don't need to lose contact. Keep me in the loop and let me help. I think we need to deal with Madeline. Madeline is a force, Max, and I predict she may be the next Lady Tay, if Johnnie is acquitted. Will you approach her about taking over Johnnie's business until the trial?"

"Yes, of course. Your solution seems one that will please not only Lord Tay but also Ms MacNaughton because it will give them a valid excuse to be in touch daily. Since there is no indication that she was involved in the crime, there should be no legal problem preventing her from doing so. I'll ring her once we've finished here."

Max watched Elspeth straighten her back. She looked directly into his eyes.

"I spent last night drawing up a list of questions," she said. "I didn't have reliable access to a computer or a printer, so you'll have to put up with my scrawl. You probably have thought of all these things already, but my investigative soul could not rest. Take it or leave it. Some of the questions may be fishing in the dark, but if you do find any one of the answers relevant, pursuing them would not be a waste of time. I've tried to organise them using the evidence we already know to prioritise their order of importance."

Max read down through the list and was astonished with its perceptiveness and thought that the Scottish legal profession had missed a good advocate. "I'm impressed," he said.

She did not respond to his compliment. "Who's your best detective?" she asked. "I'm sure Pamela Crumm won't balk at the expense."

"You would be surprised," he countered. "She is young and audacious. Sometimes she even amazes me."

Looking down at her watch, Elspeth said, "I look forward to her reports. Please if you can, e-mail me what you learn. I've set up a private e-mail box through the Kennington Organisation that can only be opened using my password. You needn't worry about security."

Elspeth and Richard took their leave shortly afterwards. Max picked up his phone and rang Kaitlin Logan, not because she was the most experienced private detective on his roster, but because her tough spirit reminded him of Elspeth Duff. He knew Kaitlin was challenging, intelligent, fiery, and passionate about her work. She had been raised by two university professors in Edinburgh who seemed delighted but somewhat bewildered when their daughter had been born to them late in life, but who, after nurturing her curiosity and independence from an early age, were surprised when their child opted for police training rather than university. In the end Kaitlin's independent disposition could not cope with the strictures and male-dominated traditions of the Scottish police force, and since she was not beholden to make her own living, she had branched out on her own, brashly arriving in Max's chambers one day to announce that with her family background and police training she would be a suitable candidate for consideration in his cases with the educated and well-to-do, particularly if she would be required to operate under cover. Max liked her and expected Elspeth would too.

Kaitlin agreed to be in Max's chambers at one, and Max asked his clerk to enter into the computer Elspeth's suggestions on ferreting out new information on the now deceased Countess of Tay and why she might have been murdered by someone else other than Johnnie Tay. Max did not understand all of Elspeth's thinking, but felt instinctively that she would not have asked for an investigation that had no bearing on the case.

He ordered lunch at his desk and ate what the packet described as a Black Forest ham and Muenster panini with Italian herbed mayonnaise on saffron infused multi-grain bread. It was only a sandwich and a rather dry one at that. As he ate, he updated his schedule, adding his one o'clock appointment with Kaitlin Logan and noting he had to be in court at half past two for the final speeches in a case he knew he had already won.

Max greeted Kaitlin as she entered his chambers. He was surprised every time he saw her because she never looked the same. Max was not certain how old she was. At one time she appeared in her twenties, another time in her forties, although she probably was somewhere in between. Her face was anybody's face, neither pretty nor unattractive, and was easily forgettable. Her eyes were brown and lively when engaged in conversation, but when she wanted them to be, lifeless. Kaitlin's hair colour varied so constantly that Max would bet against himself as to its colour of the day. Today black won out over red. Her height depended on her shoes and her accent and clothing on the role she was playing. He wondered who she was when she was at home alone, but these varied qualities made her a crack private investigator.

Without divulging its source he handed Kaitlin the first few questions that Elspeth had left him. Kaitlin skimmed down the list and then read it more slowly.

"This should be easy and, if I'm lucky, will take me a morning at New Register House in Edinburgh. Any follow up will depend on what I find there. How long do I have?" she asked.

"The sooner the better," he said. "Tomorrow afternoon at two?"

"Do you want me to ring or e-mail you as I go along?"

"No, telling me tomorrow will do. I prefer that we do this in person rather than over the phone or by e-mail."

"Consider it done, the first ones anyway," she said. "I'll go to Edinburgh this afternoon and hopefully be back by two tomorrow. If I haven't found anything by then, I'll call you."

He wrote her appointment down in his diary, and then he looked up and saw she was gone. Max grinned to himself at her assurance and efficiency. She had not failed him in the past.

26

Johnnie was restless. He looked out the windows of the farmhouse and then down at the device around his ankles. He knew he couldn't escape and go see Madeline. The phone rang and Max was at the other end of the line.

"May I come out to Tay Farm and see you this evening?" Max asked Johnnie.

After agreeing, Johnnie began crafting the version of the truth he thought Max would need to know to exonerate him, but at the same time he needed to protect Biddy, whose regard for Max had not escaped him, even at a distance.

"I need to know about Louisa," Max said.

Johnnie had not expected this. "What about her?" He felt his throat constrict because he knew he did not want to admit his many human frailties, particularly in regard to Louisa.

"She was pregnant. Elspeth said she didn't believe the child was yours, but that Louisa had accused you of this. The postmortem showed the foetus was well over four months along. I need your permission to have a more comprehensive DNA test beyond the cursory one the pathologist did on the foetal material and the one for you as well. It will be costly, but I advise you to agree to pay for it."

"The foetus wasn't mine, Max. Yes, I slept with her but that was only about two months ago, and she tricked me into it, probably because she knew of her condition. I beg you not

264

to tell Madeline about this, not yet anyway."

"It will come out at the trial, and therefore I suggest you let Madeline know in your own way," Max said circumspectly.

"Will the DNA tests prove who the real father is?" Johnnie asked.

"It will give only the baby's DNA profile. We would have to have a sample of the father's DNA to prove paternity."

"How can we get that?"

"By knowing who he was."

"Which we don't?"

"No," said Max, "we don't."

"Do you have any ideas how we might find out?"

"It's early yet."

"Doesn't my brainy cousin have any suggestions?"

Max laughed. "She does as a matter of fact, but I think it's still not time to implement them, as we do not yet have a suspect. I've hired an extremely adept detective to help us, and will have more for you later, but in the meantime, Johnnie, I want you to think about Louisa both in terms of your relationship with her over the years and why someone else might want to murder her. You may not know the answers, but you might pose the right questions."

"May we talk over a brandy after dinner by the warmth of the hearth?" Johnnie asked sardonically.

"I'll be there probably a bit after seven as I have an appointment at five," Max replied.

When they had eaten an acceptable pasta dish that Johnnie had found in the fridge and shared a good bottle of burgundy that Max had brought, they finally settled in the morning room by the hearth.

"Louisa and I," Johnnie began, "met at a party at one of my employees' flats. Things had not been going well in my life since my wife had left me and quite frankly the lure of the malt was greater than the lure of the bedroom, but Louisa broke that spell. I wanted to go to bed with her from the very beginning, and she obliged me on the first night. She had that power, and I'll always owe her a debt in bringing back to me something my wife Helen's leaving had wrenched from me. I only regret that it was Louisa and not someone a bit more respectable. Perhaps you can't understand that."

Max smiled enigmatically. Johnnie wondered if he was thinking of Biddy. "I can understand completely. You see, my wife and I . . . well, that is neither here nor there."

Johnnie did not miss Max's grimace of pain and knew there was something in Max's background that mirrored his. This gave him the courage to go on.

"I went back to Louisa night after night because she was able to ease a pain that had festered in me for a long time. Louisa became an opiate. She knew how to please a man. I knew there were other men as well, but when I was with her, everything about me seemed right again. I'm not exactly sure why I married her. I vaguely remember the wedding that took place after we had been drinking all day. Louisa said she knew someone who would marry us. I never questioned it. Maybe it was because I thought she would be faithful to me if I married her, or at least not embarrass me. You asked earlier if I were guilty of anything. Yes, hubris in regard to Louisa, in that I thought I was capable of giving her all the sex she needed, so she wouldn't need the others. It didn't take me long before I knew I was wrong and, when I confronted her, she simply laughed and said she was good enough for me when I knew about her other men so why had things changed? Besides she liked being a countess, and her lovers found it scintillating to sleep with one. I'm not proud now, Max."

Max poured them the last of the wine and sat without comment or judgement.

Johnnie slumped down into his chair and continued. "She moved into my house in Perth, and the men came and went. I felt I had some obligation to her as I had married her, but soon even that wore thin. My family shunned her, as they should have. I hated her in the end, and then I found Madeline."

"Giving you a very strong motive to murder Louisa," Max said dryly.

"I didn't do it, Max," Johnnie pleaded.

"Tell me about the farm." Max said quietly. "Why did she want it?"

"I don't know. It wasn't part of the initial stipulations of the divorce settlement."

"So I understand. Do you have any idea of why she changed her mind?"

Johnnie set his jaw and did not answer.

Max lifted the snifter of brandy Johnnie had just given him. "Here's to truth, Johnnie. It can be avoided but it can't be changed."

"You sound a bit like Dickie," Johnnie said.

"Elspeth's husband Richard?"

"He always hoped I would reform." Johnnie rolled his brandy around the crystal glass and watched it cling to the sides and then slide back into its place. Finally he said, "All right, I'll tell you, although Biddy won't like it. I gambled with the farm when I knew it was illegal for me to do so because I knew the farm is not mine to dispose of, just as I cannot dispose of my title, although Elspeth is always chiding me to do so. Elspeth may have told you something about this, but I lied to her about knowing the farm was not mine to give. Only Biddy knew the truth."

Max said simply, "Tell me how you gambled with the farm." There was no judgement in his voice, only kindness.

"I had a chance to buy out a competitor, but it meant I needed cash immediately, five hundred thousand pounds. My bank said no, as the risk was too high. In hindsight, I should have listened, but the lure of my competitor's software secrets was too strong for me not to try elsewhere. Louisa had friends who are involved in financing development in Perthshire, so I thought of them. They had been drinking my wine, eating my food, and, I expect, sharing my wife long enough, and I thought they might do me a favour. I approached them, and they offered terms that were steep but which I thought I could offset with the release of a new version of my software that was due out within the month. The one thing they asked for was collateral beyond my business assets, most specifically the farm."

Johnnie stopped speaking, and Max held the silence. Johnnie took a deep swallow of his brandy before resuming his narrative. "I knew that pledging the farm was promising something that belonged to the earldom of Tay but not to me. If they called in the loan and I defaulted, they would find this out. I was guilty in that I signed the papers knowing I was posting as collateral something that was not mine to give, but I was so sure my software would pay off quickly, I thought there was no chance it would come to foreclosure."

"Did it?" Max asked.

"Very nearly, but partly because of some devious dealings on their part. I had the solicitor who handles my business affairs read over the draft loan agreement, as had I, and one of the terms was that they could call the loan and if I didn't pay in sixty days, I forfeit the farm. In that time, based on the amount of orders I had for the new software, I could easily cover the loan in two months, or if not, I was sure the banks would see how successful the new product was and advance me money on more reasonable terms. I signed the final agreement without reading the fine print once again. I didn't see that they had changed the sixty to six in writing and six in figures. As a result they could call the loan in six days."

"Who are 'they'?

"The Perthshire Land Development Consortium."

"Did the consortium call the loan?"

Johnnie slid further down in the chair. Max barely heard his assent. "Yes. I had no choice but to tell Biddy the truth and ask for her help. She gave me everything she had from the life insurance money she received after Ivor, her husband, died."

"Thus saving you from charges of fraud."

Johnnie winced.

"Thank you for telling me."

"Please don't tell Biddy what I just told you, Max. Can I invoke lawyer client privilege here?"

Johnnie rose and poured more brandy for Max because it gave him a way to avoid his eyes. Johnnie replenished his own glass but did not resume his seat. Instead he walked to the window and drew the curtains against the darkened sky and heavy rain that was now falling.

"Does anyone other than you have a copy of your loan agreement?"

"Yes, the lawyer for the consortium."

"Who is?" Max asked, although he knew the answer.

"A man by the name of Paul Hodges."

"Elspeth told me he was Louisa's divorce lawyer. Is that correct?"

"He wasn't the first one. I didn't know Louisa had hired him until just before leaving for San Francisco to go to Elspeth's son's wedding two weeks ago. That was when Louisa began asking for the farm."

Max bit his lip. "Why do you think the consortium or Mr Paul Hodges is so interested in the Tay Farm that they used subterfuge to get it?"

Johnnie responded truthfully. "I have no idea."

"Do you know if Paul Hodges was one of Louisa's lovers?" he asked.

"He isn't one that I knew about, but he may have been."

"Can you give me a list of the ones you did know about?"

"Is it important?"

"Tomorrow I'll be in court all day, and I'm afraid you are confined here. I want you, as far as possible, to write down for me every man you know that Louisa had sex with, or that you even suspected she had sex with. Give me times, dates, places, anything you can think of."

Johnnie groaned. "Are you purposely trying to rub salt in my wounds, Max?"

"No, not at all. I'm trying to save you from life in prison. The accuracy of your list is critical. We need to find someone in Louisa's life who had more reason to kill her than you did, and I want to know who might have been the father of the child she was carrying."

27

On their return to their flat in London, Elspeth found the post neatly stacked on the dining table, left there by their housekeeper, and began to sort through it as Richard took their cases upstairs to the loft. She threw most of the envelopes into the dustbin and ended up with a letter from her mother saying she was returning to Scotland and a postcard from Peter and Lucy from Maui dated six days after the wedding. She read the latter out as Richard came down the stairs.

> *Dear Mom,*
>
> *It's great just to have time for us to enjoy each other's company with nothing else to do. I hope we left everything in the house in Marin to your satisfaction, and you had a relaxing few days there. Thanks for the party and the new furniture.*
>
> *Love to you and Richard from Peter and Lucy.*

The first signature was large and untidy, the second small and neat.

Elspeth leaned her head into her husband's shoulder and said, "I'm so glad they don't know about Johnnie. I suppose I'll have to tell them when they get back to San Francisco. I hope Lucy and her family will be able to handle this. It's not the usual thing one wants to hear about one's husband's

271

family."

Elspeth and Richard ate the dinner the housekeeper had left for them, indulging in comfortable small talk about the days ahead of them; neither one mentioning the events in Scotland until they had washed up and retreated to one of the sofas near the fireplace. Elspeth lay stretched out with her head on Richard's lap as she had done so many times before. She reached out, took his hand in hers and examined his long fingers as if she had never seen them before. Richard knew she did this when she wanted to say something to him but was struggling to find a way to do so.

"It's about Johnnie, isn't it?"

She looked up at him with a half-smile. "Am I so obvious?"

He touched her cheek. "Blatantly."

"Who do you think killed Louisa? I can't make sense of it. Murder is such a violent thing and even the little I knew of Louisa doesn't lead me to believe anyone would feel so strongly about her. I may be being unkind, but she seemed too insignificant to provoke such a crime."

"Perhaps she knew something that threatened someone, a bit of pillow talk that he later regretted."

Elspeth looked up at Richard, puzzlement crossing her face. "Do you mean she might have been blackmailing someone? I wonder if she was clever enough to think of that and then carry it out. It's possible but I don't think plausible. I keep coming back to her pregnancy and the demand for the farm. There has to be something there, but I can't make the link. DNA testing so easily establishes paternity these days that even someone as dim as Louisa would know that she couldn't disguise that the child wasn't Johnnie's. Why would she even try? It just doesn't make sense. I also wasn't aware that people hunt round Loch Tay any more. It's become too civilized, unlike the days when my uncle was about and carried a rifle everywhere. He would shoot at anything, which is why I think Johnnie hates killing so much."

She sat up, stretching herself out, and sighed.

"Perhaps, my dear, if you let it rest for a while . . ." he said, but did not finish his thought.

"You mean stew in my brain. Perhaps you're right. Let's go to bed. It's been a long ten days. I'm sorry we missed our holiday, Dickie. We'll find a time again soon," she said.

Elspeth smiled at Richard as he lay waiting for her in their bed, and they consoled each other knowing they would not see each other for a long time, disappearing into their own special world that blocked out all else, even the troubles in Perthshire. In the morning Richard woke alone in their bed, and soon made his way downstairs where he found waiting for him toast in the toast rack and a bowl of yogurt with fresh strawberries that they had brought from the farm. Elspeth was dressed for travel and was on the phone in the kitchen.

He came and put his arms around her as she was finishing her call. "Yes, and have them sent overnight to Lady Elisabeth Baillie Shaw at the Royal infirmary in Perth, Scotland. She spelled out Biddy's name and gave the address of the hospital.

"A card? Yes, with a message saying, '*Use these as you choose*', and sign it with the letter *E.*"

"What was that all about?" Richard asked.

"I ordered three pair of silk pyjamas for Biddy, in colours that will show off her eyes, and a very fashionable fleece dressing gown."

Richard laughed out loud. "Elspeth, are you suggesting anything?"

"Me? No. Biddy is the one who needs to do that."

"With Max?"

"I'll leave that to them," Elspeth said.

"Elspeth, you're completely incorrigible."

She smiled a wicked cockeyed grin and pecked her husband's freshly shaven cheek. "My dearest, that's not the first time you have said so. Now let's have breakfast. What time is your plane? Mine's at half past one."

Elspeth reported to the offices of the Kennington Organisation in the City of London at nine as scheduled and was told by security that Ms Crumm had requested that she come to the twentieth floor as soon as she arrived at the building. Pamela was waiting by the doors of the lift as they opened and showed Elspeth into her office.

"How's he taking all this?" Elspeth asked, nodding towards Lord Kennington's closed office door.

"He's in Barbados, blessedly," Pamela said. "Now, ducks, I think you need to fill me in. I have quite a bit resting on this, as you know."

"Pamela, you didn't need to do what you did."

"Of course not. I did what I did because it pleased me to be able to do so. How is Lord Tay?"

"Irritated at being in confined to the farmhouse and worried about Biddy."

"Worried about Biddy? What for?" Pamela's eyes challenged Elspeth from behind large round spectacles.

Elspeth suddenly realised that the press had never reported what happened to Biddy. Could the police have suppressed the information while they investigated the shooting? Elspeth had been so concerned for both her cousins' welfare that she had not until this moment considered the lack of media coverage. Did Max have something to do with it? She must ask him.

"She was shot in the shoulder by a crack rifleman, who sent a warning afterwards saying he had purposely missed her heart."

"Your family, Elspeth, certainly seems to attract trouble. Now tell me all. I have cleared my appointments until twelve and ordered an early lunch to be brought here so we may speak without others hearing. I want you to be straight with me. You know I don't like to gossip, nor will I tell Eric. He doesn't need to know. He also doesn't know who is paying Johnnie's legal fees, and I prefer to keep it that way."

Before Elspeth left Pamela's office, her friend and also employer spoke to her with some seriousness. "I know you well enough, Elspeth, to suspect you are not going to let the case in Perth to be turned over completely to Mr Douglas-Forbes. Your assignment in British Columbia is more important than we have made it seem, and the Governor General has asked that you not be informed of the real purpose of her visit until you arrive in Victoria. As distracting as Lord Tay's arrest may be, please don't neglect giving your full attention to what you find in Canada. I don't need tell you that, but Eric instructed me to do so. He's pretending not to follow the case in Scotland, but every day he's in London he grumbles, saying he's sure I'll bother him with the news and then he listens eagerly. He cares, but he is more concerned about what will happen at the Kennington Victoria and the safety of the Governor General and any visitors she might have while she's there."

Pamela's warning did not escape Elspeth, and she left torn between loyalty to her job and to her family. She would have to walk a careful line, balancing between the two.

28

Max emerged from the Sheriff Court in Perth just after half past four o'clock on Friday and was surrounded by the family of the formerly accused, now exonerated from all charges against her. They insisted that he join them in a celebratory dinner, and he did not return to his home until well after ten. Regretting he had not been able to visit Biddy in hospital, although he sent fresh flowers late in the evening at great expense, and which he had not billed to Pamela Crumm. With a promise of a visit early Saturday, he arrived at his home in a sour mood.

Max went into his study and poured himself a brandy from a bottle that had sat on his sideboard since the Christmas before. How strange it was that this time a week ago he had never heard of Lord Tay, had not met the formidable force named Elspeth Duff and had not become smitten by an unlikely farmer named Lady Elisabeth Baillie Shaw. He toasted the still-light mid-summer sky through the window and drank the brandy more quickly than its quality deserved. Then he went to his bedroom, drew the curtains without thinking of the late countess of Tay and put himself to sleep anticipating the pleasure of his visit to Biddy the next morning.

His immediate attention, however, concerned Johnnie. So

277

much about Lord Tay disturbed him, most of all that he sensed Johnnie's aversion to him. Max wanted to break this animosity not only because it would not serve his defence of Lord Tay, but also because he wanted Biddy to think well of him.

He rang Johnnie at the farm the next morning and found his mood was prickly.

"Max, I hate being cooped up here. Have you heard from Elspeth? She's a woman of much force and conviction, but I have often found her impulsive and too fast when making judgements. I admire her for this, and it certainly has made her successful in her chosen field, but I'm a bit simpler by nature and habit. I love Elspeth's spark, but I don't want to be burnt in the fire. I want you to tell me what the two of you are plotting. I don't always agree with her."

Max knew that the moment had come when he could not mince words. "Johnnie, you must, of course, deal with Elspeth in the way you find most comfortable. She's expressed her deepest concern for your well-being and desire that this case conclude with your release." Max took in a long breath. "However, she has also told me that she has only limited knowledge of your life since she left Perthshire for Cambridge in 1968, almost forty years ago. We all change over time, but we expect our family members to stay the same. Elspeth has told me that she doesn't think you capable of murder but then admitted she hardly knows you today. Johnnie, I'm your lawyer and your best hope. Elspeth has put a great deal of faith in you, and her friend and employer at the Kennington Organisation, Pamela Crumm, has put up a great deal of money based on that, as she has agreed to finance your defence. Now let me know the whole truth."

Johnnie said, "I have done a good number of things in my

life I now regret, but I wouldn't knowingly kill another creature."

"Then you are innocent?" Max asked.

"Innocent? Of killing Louisa, yes. Of other things? It depends on what you have in mind."

Max did not like Johnnie Tay's tone. "You must realise you could spend over thirty years in prison if I can't get the jury to find you innocent or at least 'not proven'. Are you willing to have that happen? I understand there is another person who might not want that."

"Damn Elspeth for telling you about Madeline. Leave Madeline out of it." Anger suffused Johnnie's voice.

"I think Ms MacNaughton has her own ideas, and I'll let the two of you settle that. I've made arrangements for her to visit you at the farm, under the guise of her helping you with your business while you are awaiting trial. It's a fine line, as she may be a witness in your behalf at the trial, and I hope the procurator fiscal finds her visits to you acceptable. In the meantime, it's my responsibility to build a case in your defence."

"What is this about Pamela Crumm?" he asked, as if he had not heard Max correctly earlier.

"She has agreed to pay your legal expenses and posted bail as well."

"Why? I've only met her once."

"I think, Johnnie, because she has a great deal of respect and admiration for your cousin and because Ms Crumm is a wealthy woman who can spend what she wants on any whim that may take her fancy. I also suspect she does not want Elspeth to be distracted from her job at the Kennington Organisation. Your expenses will be high, particularly as

Elspeth has recommended an aggressive course to find out who actually killed Louisa. You have much to credit Elspeth with. She's your strongest ally."

Max wanted to like Johnnie, for Biddy's sake if for no other, but he was finding Johnnie's hostility tedious. This type of mental barricade was not unusual when a client had something to hide, so Max set out to find what was needling Johnnie. He knew from long experience that the direct approach often did not work. Where was Johnnie Tay vulnerable? Elspeth? Probably not at all. Biddy? Maybe. Madeline MacNaughton? Almost certainly. Max, however, did not want to draw any conclusions as of yet.

When Max went into his chambers at half past eleven, his clerk told him that Ms Logan had rung and said she had information for him that was so important that she hoped their appointment could be moved up. As he had no other scheduled plans for the day, Max conceded, and his clerk told him that Ms Logan was already waiting in the conference room.

"Mr Douglas-Forbes," she said breathlessly, "I've discovered a great deal about Lord Tay but not as much as you asked for about Louisa, but I think you might be surprised."

"Go on," he said.

"I can find no record that Lord Tay actually divorced his second wife, Helen, and there's no official certificate for Lord Tay's marrying Louisa."

Max at first did not take in what Kaitlin was saying. He stalled. "Are you sure?"

"I spent all of yesterday afternoon in Edinburgh researching the questions you gave me because I didn't want to make a mistake, I double checked all the records. Lord Tay was married to Helen Trenton. I found the record of that. He was listed as a widower and she as a spinster. So I went back and found the record of his first wife's death, which was also listed, but going forward there was nothing else."

Max said again, "Are you sure?"

Kaitlin said, "Absolutely. There's definitely no record of Lord Tay's divorce from Helen Tay née Trenton. You must remember that was one of your questions on your list. Was the divorce between them ever recorded? I searched very carefully, using both their names and all possible variations of them."

Max now wished he had read Elspeth's first question more carefully before giving it to Kaitlin, but how did Elspeth know to ask the question? Max needed time to process what Kaitlin had just said but did not say so. Instead he said, "What did you find out about Louisa?"

Kaitlin took out her notes, ran quickly down them with her index finger and said, "Louisa Jolene Boyd, was born in Perth on January 7th, 1970, to Jolene Boyd, age 16, and no father listed. There was no record of Louisa's mother's marriage. Louisa married a Timothy McNeal in June 1986, divorcing him in May 2000. There were no children, stillborn or otherwise. That was one of your questions."

"Yes, of course," Max said, floundering, because he sensed in her questions Elspeth had looked outside the box. "You're sure you found no certificate of Lord Tay's marriage to Louisa Jolene Boyd?"

"None."

"Kaitlin, as usual, you have surpassed my expectations. I'll have more questions for you shortly. Please come back after lunch. At half past one? I need to go on to my computer and get them."

When Katlin had left, he pulled up Elspeth's list. The first category asked for information that was readily available in the public record, including births, marriages, divorces and deaths. The second group of Elspeth's questions involved the grant of peerage, which could easily be accessed. The third asked for the background of the two eyewitnesses. The fourth wanted information on the land dealings of the Perth Land Development Consortium, particularly in regard to their banking activities and any designs for development in the Loch Tay area. The fifth concerned Paul Hodges, Louisa's solicitor, his background, his law practice, his connection to the Perthshire Land Development Consortium, any convictions against him, and any ethical complaints about him to the bar. The final one said, "Investigation into the names to be supplied by Johnnie particularly in their relationship with Louisa." Max's esteem of Elspeth rose as he progressed down the list. At the end of the list he read something he had not expected. It read, "Any chance of getting these men's DNA profiles?"

He should have been paid more attention to the list. He would the next time. He began to see how Johnnie Tay could feel trumped by his cousin, but Max knew Elspeth's intent was to be a thorough as possible in the short time she had, but at the same time not to diminish his own abilities. His esteem for her grew and he forgave her boldness.

When Kaitlin returned, he said, "I've changed my mind about your priorities," he said. "I want you first to find out what you can about the eyewitnesses. Let me give you their names."

"Right on," Kaitlin said, and almost as an afterthought, "A curious thing about my searching for Lord Tay's divorce from his second wife was that the clerk said someone else had asked to see the same papers about three weeks ago. She didn't say who, other than that it was a man who needed a hair wash, which reminded her that she needed to buy shampoo, which she hadn't put it on her shopping list."

After Kaitlin left, Max rang through to Elspeth's secure number and only got her voice mail. "Call me," he said. "I have rather startling news, although from your questions I guess you may already suspect what it is." He chuckled as he rang off, imagining an ah-ha gesture raising of Elspeth's beautifully shaped eyebrows and the seriousness of her face turning into grin.

When Elspeth rang him back several hours later, she explained her reasoning behind the first set of questions. "I didn't draw my assumption that there was something irregular about Johnnie's marriage to Louisa from thin air," she said. "My father meticulously keeps the family records in his office file room. When I examined Johnnie's, I noticed that there was an unsigned copy of the petition for divorce from Helen but that there was no official copy. That was unlike my father, who keeps all the family matters current. He had a copy of the so-called marriage certificate between Louisa and Johnnie which looked very unofficial and rather as if it had been filled out in a haze of alcohol. I needed to know if it ever had been recorded, and it seems not. So you see, Max, I'm not clairvoyant, only observant."

Max laughed out loud.

"Elspeth, what did you mean by your last comment on the

DNA?"

"DNA samples are harder to get than you might think. I'm sure you already know that, but when you get a list from Johnnie of possible suspects for the paternity of Louisa's baby, I think pursuing this line of investigation makes sense. By the way, have the police tried to verify positively Johnnie's DNA with the baby's?"

"Not yet," Max said, "but I suspect they will soon."

"Keep me posted, Max. I'll always get back to you as soon as I can, but I must put my job first."

29

Biddy Baillie Shaw was not an idle person and lying in bed in hospital rankled her. She worried about the farm, despite her trust of Robbie MacPherson, she worried about her ewe, and she worried most of all about Johnnie. She missed Elspeth's counsel and insight, and she was also bothered by her inability to control her affairs from her hospital bed. During the long hours she lay there, she kept coming back to the agonising question of why someone would shoot her. Instinctively she knew it was intentional. She had told Elspeth that she thought it had to do with Louisa, but she was not certain, fearing Johnnie's business activities might have something to do with it. Biddy had gambled almost all the money she had to save Johnnie. She could not have done otherwise, but she was not certain that her gamble would work, now that Johnnie was facing the possibility of life in prison. She could lose everything she had given him if he were convicted, leaving her to rely solely on the income from the farm, which was only barely adequate after all the expenses were paid each month. What if something happened to her or to one of her children? What then? The life insurance money had been her security, and now she could lose that as well as her brother. She knew she was not capable of running Johnnie's business, and she did not know to whom to turn. The dalliance she was carrying on with Maxwell Douglas-

Forbes only exacerbated her feeling of despair and ultimately of her own foolishness. She needed to get back to the farm and her daily routine, be among the people and animals she cared for and forget any notions of a future relationship with Max. She was in this brooding mood when Max himself knocked discreetly at her door, and, as he entered, all thoughts of giving him up fled from her. She was glad the nurse had helped her put on the dressing gown that Elspeth had sent her. Max's eyes told her he was too. Or, was she just imagining it? Bah, you're a silly woman, she told herself, and she wished Elspeth had not tempted her with her gift.

Max turned grave as he sat down next to her. "There have been some new developments," he said straight away. "Perhaps you can help me understand them."

Biddy bit her lip. "Are they serious?" she asked.

"I'm not sure," Max said. "Elspeth asked me to find out the answer to a number of questions arising from your brother's past, and I came up with some unexpected answers."

"Which are?"

"Johnnie's divorce from Helen was never finalised."

"Not finalised?" Biddy repeated. "Then how could he marry Louisa?"

"He couldn't, at least not legally."

"Then their relationship was. . . bigamous?" Biddy choked on the word.

"That, yes, but perhaps not because his marriage to Louisa was never filed with New Register House and therefore was never made official."

"How can that have happened?"

"Johnnie said he was in a sorry state during those days. Was he?"

Biddy thought back to the time. "Most certainly. After Helen left, he fell apart emotionally, and started drinking too much. Ivor, my husband, and I tried to help, but finally Johnnie stopped coming to the farm. We heard reports that he had begun seeing a rather rowdy crowd in Perth, which must have been where he met Louisa. I'm sure 'Peth has told you that Johnnie and I've always been very close, but during that time in his life we were not. It tortured me that he wouldn't confide in me, but I think he saw how happy I was with Ivor and could not face our happiness in his sorrow and hurt. I'd no way I could find to reach him, so I just left the door open and waited for him to return. He eventually did, but that hiatus was a very sad time for me because I care so profoundly for him. He came back when Ivor died because he must have thought I was in as much pain as he was. Is it wrong for me to say that?"

Biddy had told Max more than she might have done in different circumstances. She had spoken from somewhere in the depths of her heart and without regard for her own needs or future hopes.

Max reached for her hand and said, "No, it's not wrong." He sounded as if he wanted to tell her about some sadness from his own past, but he did not, and left Biddy to wonder what it could have been.

Instead he held out a piece of paper, and Biddy saw it was a handwritten list. She did not recognise the handwriting, but presumed Max had written it out. She took it with her good hand and saw that it contained seven names.

"Do you recognise any of these?" Max asked.

She read through them carefully and slowly, as Max's handwriting at times was difficult to decipher, but she did not know any of the names written there. Finally she shook her head. "Who are they?"

"Louisa's other men. Johnnie phoned me with the list before I left my chambers," he said as if it saddened and embarrassed him.

Biddy suppressed a smile, as she found Max's reaction protective of her. "Max," she said, "I live in the country and see all facets of life in a microcosm. I'm sorry for Johnnie but not shocked. I might have been if I had liked Louisa, but I didn't. In fact the only thing that surprises me is that Johnnie knew about so many of them. Louisa was certainly not discreet, and after all he was suing her for divorce on grounds of adultery, not that it's relevant anymore."

"Do you know if your brother had business dealings with any of them?"

"No. I invested in Johnnie's business to save him from accusation of fraud. I don't know any of the details, but I'd do it again, even though I could lose everything. My family is very important to me. But, no, none of these names are familiar."

Max nodded. "I thought they might not be. Please tell me, Biddy, when are they letting you out of here?"

"Blessedly, they say tomorrow."

"Will you be going back to the farm?"

"Yes, please," she said with a wail and a grin. "I've been away too long. Robbie can manage the farm for a few days and Tobias, the collie, thinks he runs it all the time in spite of me and Robbie, but I worry they may have forgotten something or that I may not have fully spelled out all the tasks for them because I was preoccupied with everything going on with Johnnie."

"Will you be well enough to manage on your own?"

Max's concern seemed real.

"The MacPhersons and the Robertsons have been taking care of each other for over two and a half centuries, and I expect Jean and Robbie MacPherson will take care of me equally well when I get home. I know Johnnie's there, but he knows nothing about the financial management of the farm. How is Johnnie?"

"I think I would have said hostile, but moody is perhaps more appropriate. You have a talent, Biddy, of using the right word and making things seem softer than I do. I think I've been a lawyer for too long. I've much to learn from you."

Biddy flushed at the compliment. "Let me ring you when I am back at the farm."

"Better yet," he said, "let me drive you home."

Relief flooded over her, and she relished the feeling that an attachment was forming between them that transcended his legal status in her family's lives. Biddy was suddenly glad of Elspeth's insistence that she have a flattering dressing gown.

"Are you up for a makeshift dinner from what is in the fridge prepared by a one-armed cook?"

"Do you promise fresh vegetables from the farm?"

"Since I'll have no opportunity to shop, you'll have no choice, although I might ask Robbie to pluck us a chicken," she said. "They're releasing me at noon tomorrow. Can you be here by then?"

"I will be waiting impatiently outside," he said, and grinned.

*

The many women who had pursued Max since his wife's death had never once offered a make-shift dinner of vegetables from their own gardens and an apology for a freshly plucked chicken prepared by a wounded cook. Max had suffered through countless so-called gourmet meals, too many bottles of expensive but unpalatable wines, and too many propositions of amorous activity after the meal. Biddy's gentle simplicity and shy beauty intrigued him. She made no pretence of being more than she was, but she seemed unaware of the allure of that. Max wanted Biddy to see him as a man, not just her brother's lawyer, but he was not sure she did. He heard the procurator fiscal's admonition to him. Was he overstepping the prescripts the bar expected of him? What might the procurator fiscal think of Max's infatuation with Lord Tay's sister? Max felt he must keep himself in check, at least until after the trial. Then Biddy smiled at him and all resolution faded away.

"Tomorrow at noon, then," he said as he departed. He would count the hours.

*

Once she arrived in Canada, Elspeth's preparations fell quickly into place and on Saturday morning allowed her time to step out on the street along the harbour by the hotel before the arrival of the Governor General an hour later. Elspeth mentally went over the arrangements for her visit once again and could find no fault in them. As Elspeth stepped out under the blanket of the mild summer air, cooled by the wind off the ocean, she thought of Johnnie for the first time since leaving London. On arrival in Victoria, she had immediately assumed her long-practiced professional role, which gave her little time to speculate on the fate of her family or the progress of the investigation.

She reached into the pocket of her smart linen tunic and dug out her mobile. Hearing Max's message, she dialled his number. As she waited for him to answer, she stared out over the harbour, imagining herself as a guest at the hotel without responsibility or family worries and paying eight hundred pounds a day or more to be cosseted in impeccable Kennington style.

Max finally answered, taking Elspeth's mind back to Perthshire and the dark reality there, the truth of which neither her attention to her professional duty nor the beauty of her surroundings could erase.

"I wish I had more to report beyond what I told you earlier," Max said. "Did I tell you Johnnie has given me a list of what he called 'Louisa's men', seven of them? I showed it to Biddy, and she doesn't recognise any of the names. Did I say she is being released from hospital tomorrow and I'm taking her back to the farm? I continue to find Lord Tay to be only grudgingly cooperative. Do you have any suggestions as to how I might break down his hostility towards me?"

"I know Johnnie well enough," she finally said, "to know that he resents advice. I'm sure he has already made disparaging remarks about my interference. It's an age-old ritual between us that dates back to our teenage years."

Max chuckled in confirmation. "He calls you either his brainy or bratty cousin."

It was Elspeth's turn to laugh, before becoming serious once again. "If he seems to push you away, it's possibly because of his needing to face the mistakes he has made, and having to admit them to you."

"I haven't passed judgement on any of them. I know all too well human error and weakness, my own included. Do you think your cousin finds me critical?"

"No, but he may find you more probing than he's

291

comfortable with."

"I can't stand back and see him convicted, Elspeth. There was a long time when I thought he could be guilty. Surely there's enough in his past for the Crown to build a case against him, citing all his mistakes, but I now believe he's innocent. I hope the detective I've hired will turn up some sort of proof."

"Of his innocence or of someone else's guilt? The latter would be best. What has your detective discovered regarding points two and three?"

"Her father's an historian, and she has asked him to research the grants of peerage while she investigates the eyewitnesses. What had you hoped to achieve with your latter question?"

"I think they were hired by the murderer to say they had seen Johnnie."

"Why?"

"They went to the police too quickly."

"Meaning?"

"Max, if you were coming home from a party slightly tipsy, and saw a man come out of a side gate after midnight, what would you think?"

"A secret assignation."

"Possibly, but would you think he had murdered someone? What gave the eyewitnesses the idea? I want to know exactly what was in their testimony to the police. Can you send me the police report and any pictures of the crime scene? I can get the images on my computer here."

With Max's positive answer, Elspeth disconnected the call, leaned back along the railing by the marina and tried to think how she could best help Max, and consequently Johnnie. She checked her watch and saw that she must go and prepare for the Governor General's imminent arrival and would not be able to return to the knotty problem in Scotland until much later in the day.

*

As it was late on Saturday afternoon, Max rang the procurator fiscal at his home as he had done on occasion before, hoping he had not gone away for the weekend. It was a risky thing to do, but Max drew on their long association with each other.

"Adair," Max said, "I need to know more about the eyewitnesses who saw Lord Tay leave Louisa's home the night of the murder. Can you let me see the eyewitnesses' statements?" The procurator fiscal assented. "And," Max continued, "can I get copies of the police photographs when they first went to the crime scene and found Louisa's body?" Max carefully did not give Louisa her former title.

"I'll see you get them. When will Lady Elisabeth be out of hospital?"

"Tomorrow," Max said.

The procurator fiscal said he would make arrangements to have the police reports sent to Max's office. Max thanked him and was relieved that he would be able to get the information to Elspeth. He realised how much he had come to rely on Elspeth's insights and penetrating questions and was sorry she was so far way and otherwise employed.

*

Detective Inspector Simon Kennedy was on weekend duty, and his wife had yet again made clear her wish that he might find a desk job with more regular hours, as their son had a lead in a play at school that once again only one of his parents would attend. He would have preferred his son to be in a football match, but his wife said it was best for the lad to have wider interests than sports. DI Kennedy was not pleased that he received a call from the procurator fiscal, asking him to assist the bloody lawyer representing Lord Bloody Tay. The Tay case was more complicated than DI Kennedy wished. He preferred his murder cases to be more straightforward, with the motives clear and the relationship between the victim and the accused obvious. The Tay case involved bloody aristocrats, and they always demanded things that they considered their privilege, despite the fact, that in DI Kennedy's opinion, it was a clear case of wife murder. Without any pretence of courtesy, DI Kennedy arrived at the lawyer's office on Charlotte Street and handed Mr Bloody Douglas-Forbes the documents.

Max came straight to the point. "We understand that two eyewitnesses have come forward to identify Lord Tay as being at the scene of the murder. Mr Gordon said you could tell me about their statement to you, as well as provide a written copy of that interview to me.

Damned cheek, DI Kennedy thought, but he answered Max's question as the fiscal had ordered him to do.

"On the afternoon of July 20th, two lads came into the station to report that they had seen a man leave Lady Tay's home just after midnight. Normally we would have taken their statement and let them go. The station has had numerous complaints against her from neighbours because of the loud parties she held, and men leaving her home at all hours of the night were hardly an unusual occurrence, but the week before Lady Tay had rung the police station and said she thought she was being stalked by someone and was afraid for her life. We had noted that, so when the lads came by, we took them seriously."

Max said. "Did Louisa indicate who might be stalking her? Did she mention Lord Tay?"

The inspector turned down his mouth, but replied, "She said her husband because they were in the middle of a divorce."

"Is that why you were so quick to arrest Lord Tay? It was the eyewitnesses' word against his."

"At the crime scene we found a mackintosh with a letter to him dated the fifth of July in the pocket. The coat had been flung in the back of a cupboard in the room where the victim was found. Then the two lads described a man who met Lord Tay's description almost exactly: tall, light brown hair parted on the left side, clean shaven, well-dressed in a tweed jacket belted in the back and dark trousers, dark blue eyes, handkerchief folded in his breast pocket."

"Did the lads, as you call them, say they had seen anything through the windows before they saw the man come out of the gate?"

"They said they could see the man through the windows of the drawing room confronting a woman with his hands raised."

"Why were they in the street?" Max asked.

"The lads? They said they had just left a party further up the hill and were on their way to find their car, which was down by the river."

"Are they local?"

"No, each gave his address. One was from Dundee and the other from Edinburgh."

"Will you give their addresses to me?" Max asked.

"They're in the police report. The fiscal said I should give that to you, as well as the photographs taken when the police arrived at Lady Tay's home."

"I have one more question. How did you know where to find Lord Tay when you came to inform him of Louisa's death?"

"We traced his driving licence. It listed Tay Farm near Kenmore on Loch Tay."

30

Max had devoted his life to his work and his love of the law, and in the years since his wife had left him, he had subsumed himself in his cases and the people they involved. Max considered the Tay case. He needed to get the information on the eyewitnesses to Kaitlin and hoped she would be receptive to a Sunday morning call. He wanted her to track them, rather than confront them. Kaitlin's instincts, at least as Max had experienced them in the past, were trustworthy, and he now regretted telling her to convey her information to him only in person and at his chambers. If she were able to find the eyewitnesses over the weekend, he would have to wait until Monday to get her report.

Elspeth's fourth request had been about the Perthshire Land Development Corporation. Max had heard of them, usually regarding cases against them in the local courts, homeowners suing over items like faulty plumbing or leaks in the roof. He tried to reason out why Elspeth thought they were so important. Remembering Johnnie's tale about his loan and Biddy's sacrifice to save him from what appeared to be the unscrupulous practice of changing legal papers after the draft had been approved, Max could not decide how much this actually had to do with Louisa's murder and if bringing up the matter in court would only tarnish Johnnie's character in the eyes of the jurors. Yet Elspeth had considered the Perthshire Land Development Consortium important.

He felt compelled to call her in Victoria and ask, but she had warned him that British Columbia was eight hours behind Scotland and so her availability would depend on that and the demands of her current assignment. It was ten in the morning in Perth, two o'clock in the morning in Victoria. He expected that Elspeth's work did not allow for weekends off but was frustrated that he would have to wait at least six hours to talk to her directly.

*

Max had no way of knowing that Elspeth lay wide awake, listening to the breeze off the ocean, feeling the fineness of the sheets on her bed, but not finding any comfort in either of them. The Governor General was charming, confided that she had met Sir Richard several times in the course of her journalistic and government career, and wished Elspeth every happiness in her marriage. Elspeth acknowledged silently and with admiration the thoroughness of the Governor General's advance staff, who had undoubtedly checked the names of the people who would be in charge of the Governor General's security.

Arrangements had been made for the Governor General to hold a private dinner at the Kennington Victoria for the other representatives of the heads of state from the Pacific Rim, whom she was meeting quietly to set up preparations for talks to discuss fishing rights, although the occasion was billed as a social event. To Elspeth's relief the other heads of state had chosen different accommodation. The Governor General, however, had made a request of Elspeth that only the most trustworthy staff serve at dinner. Elspeth consulted the manager, found out that some of the staff had come from other hotels, and she vetted the waiters to assure their discretion and dependability. It was neither the dinner nor the Governor General that was keeping Elspeth awake, however. Such activities had become common enough in Elspeth's professional life that she seldom worried about them, even when they involved world leaders at the highest levels. Elspeth, like Max, was fretting about the Perthshire Land Development Consortium, and she wanted to talk to Max about it. She looked at the large LCD numbers on the clock at her bedtime and decided two o'clock was too early on Sunday morning in Perth to call Max.

She had meant to ask him if any of the seven names on the list of Louisa's men were connected with the consortium, although she expected at least one or two might be. Was there any way to associate Louisa's pregnancy or murder with these men? Elspeth went back over what Johnnie had said about his involvement with them. The men at the consortium had asked specifically that the farm be placed in collateral for the loan they were making to him. She wondered why. A housing estate on Loch Tay would be an abomination but the consortium might want to build a hotel, much as the old and venerable Loch Rannoch Hotel that had been upgraded and expanded in recent years. Elspeth could not imagine either a housing estate or a hotel on the Tay Farm land. She finally drifted off in an uneasy sleep after deciding to ring Max on Sunday at three o'clock in the afternoon his time, seven in the morning hers.

*

Before leaving for the hospital, Max called Johnnie at the farm and came right to the point. "Elspeth suggested that I look into your divorce from the second Lady Tay."

"Elspeth again?" Johnnie said, but this time there was less

anger and more amusement in his voice.

"I've hired a detective who is brilliant at finding out about things and people. She did the research at New Register House and found out information on both Helen and Louisa," he said. Max then told Johnnie what Kaitlin Logan had discovered the day before.

"Elspeth also has suggested that there might be a link between Louisa's men, the Perthshire Land Development Consortium, and Louisa's sudden shift to wanting the farm as part of the divorce settlement. Do you have any idea why the farm would attract them? Housing would be the logical answer, but Loch Tay is sufficiently far from Perth, or even Pitlochry and a railway connection, to make one suspect the consortium might want to find property closer to town. I've thought of other reasons and need to appeal to you as to their validity. Do you have any knowledge of mineral deposits in the area, or oil, or any public development that could involve a long-term lease of the farm? Or, is there the possibility that a developer could see advantages to a tourist resort there, and the consortium wants to jump in, secure the ownership of the land or a lease, and then sell it for a large profit?"

"I have heard nothing of the sort," Johnnie said.

"Can you tell me the names of anyone on your list of Louisa's men who might know?"

Johnnie paused before saying, "Miles Markham and George Hiller."

"Who are they?"

"Miles is director of development and George one of the financial vice presidents of the Perthshire Land Development Consortium."

"What are they like?"

"I don't know them very well. Miles seems tame enough, except for his almost casual attitude towards his liaison with Louisa. He's a bit of fun, Louisa used to say, but harmless. George is, how should I say it, more devious. He would probably deny his relationship with Louisa although I saw them come out of the bedroom, both in disarray. I never liked either of the men."

"Would either make Louisa pregnant as a way to get the farm?"

"You mean deliberately?"

"Yes, particularly if they could convince Louisa into seducing you and claiming the baby was yours?"

"Max, I'm bright enough to know that paternity is easily established these days. They might try, but I'm not so naïve."

"Why would they try?"

"If they did, they could have thought there was a great deal of money to be made," Johnnie said.

Max approached his next subject and hoped he did so sensitively. "You and Helen never had children, did you?"

"We tried every way possible. She couldn't hold on to the foetus," he said.

Max was not sure what emotions were hidden behind Johnnie's suddenly expressionless voice.

"Why didn't you and Louisa have children? Obviously, she was capable."

"She said she didn't want children. They would have disrupted her lifestyle."

"Did you know that when you thought you had married her?"

"Max, I remember so little of that time. I wanted a child, God knows. I'd lost one once with my first wife, Kathleen.

301

Helen wanted children too."

"Louisa must have known you well enough to know this. Could she have said something about it to anyone on your list, particularly those in the consortium who seemed to want so desperately to get their hands on your land? It sounds as if Louisa was an easily manipulated person."

"Louisa's brain focused on pleasure, sex, and men." Johnnie sounded bitter as he said this. "I felt a certain sense of relief when you said I wasn't legally married to her. Do you plan to bring this out in court, Max, the fact that we were not married?"

"Only if it is to our advantage. You've just admitted not knowing the divorce from Helen wasn't finalised, but the Crown can easily dismiss this or even accuse you of bigamy. If it is brought up, I want to make the jury feel you were taken back by the news when you learned of it, but I think you should tell Madeline, about the lack of the divorce from Helen and about Louisa's pregnancy, I mean. You're of course aware that Louisa's pregnancy will be a large factor in the trial. You must tell Madeline the truth before she hears it in court or from the press. Madeline is no blushing virgin. She knows you were supposedly married three times before, and yet is still willing to take you on. A thirty-three-year-old woman does not fall in love with an almost sixty-year-old man without knowing he has a past. I think Madeline is more concerned with the future and isn't balking at what happened before. My impression is that she is a strong woman and not frightened of the truth."

"How can I tell her about my encounter with Louisa two months ago?"

Max considered his answer carefully. "With as much

honesty and love as you possibly can. I don't think it will be lost on Madeline."

*

Biddy was wheeled down in a chair to the entrance of the hospital by the same nursing sister who had been so curious about her relationship with Maxwell Douglas-Forbes. The nurse, who had become aware of Lady Elisabeth's relationship to Earl Tay, was eager to know if there was any news about his guilt.

Biddy brought all her good breeding to bear and answered that she knew nothing, the implication being that the nurse had spoken out of turn, but Biddy was too polite to say so directly.

"I am sorry, my lady," the nurse said. "I've poked my nose in where I shouldn't have. We read too many newspapers to pass the quiet times. Good luck to you."

"Thank you, sister," Biddy said in an excessively polite but dismissive way and gave a grateful smile to Max, who came to help her to the car.

"It's just as well we're going back to the farm," she said, as Max took her arm. "I can't bear gossip or innuendo. I suppose the life of a nursing sister lacks much sensationalism aside from patient care."

They spoke little as they made their way back to Loch Tay, as if the nurse's words had cast a pall on them. Not for the first time Max considered what he was doing, playing chauffeur and protective hen to his client's sister. His legal responsibility to Johnnie went only so far, and Max was well aware he was skirting the boundaries by becoming too personally involved. Once again, he wished Elspeth were in Perthshire to help bridge the gap between what was professionally correct and his growing personal relationship with her family. He missed Elspeth's directness and dispassionate approach to the problem of the charge of murder against a family member and then remembered James Duff's admonishment that Elspeth had always been able to push her intellect above her feelings. He had always been able to do the same thing in the past but suddenly found it difficult.

They arrived at the farm to find Jean MacPherson in the kitchen and lunch waiting for them on the table. Tobias greeted them with great enthusiasm, and Robbie came forward to welcome Lady Biddy home and assure her that all was well at the farm and that the ewe's eye was now on the way to being saved. Johnnie joined them, and they ate Jean's simple meal, consisting mainly of salad from the garden and a warmed piece of ham, which Max suspected Robbie had provided for them. Biddy's gratefulness at the kind ministering of the MacPhersons was reflected in her eyes, which Max noticed looked fatigued after the drive from Perth. Seeing this Max rose to make his excuses of an early return to Perth. Johnnie sulked off to the interior of the house.

"Stay a little longer, Max," she said, rising and touching his arm. "Let's go and see how the ewe is doing."

At that moment Max wanted nothing more in the world to see the wounded ewe at Biddy's side.

"Biddy," he said after they had admired how well the ewe was healing, "do you know either Miles Markham or George Hiller?"

"No, who are they?"

Max thought how best to put it discretely. "Two men on Johnnie's list of Louisa's liaisons, both of whom worked for the Perthshire Land Development Consortium."

Biddy turned around and looked straight at Max. "So one of them might be the father of Louisa's child? She was, as my son would say, quite a piece of work, wasn't she? I'm glad the marriage wasn't legal. Poor Johnnie."

"Did you ever hear from Helen after she left?"

"No. I liked Helen, but, after she ran off with a man named Ross MacCombe, she broke all ties with us, as you might expect," Biddy said.

"Did you know Ross MacCombe?"

"Yes, we all did. He was one of Johnnie's friends, until he ran off with Helen."

"Do you know his family?" Max asked.

"No, but they were from Perth. I think they may still live there."

"They might know where Helen is."

"Perhaps. I suppose you could try contacting them. They're probably in the directory."

They walked out of the barn together.

"Is this where you were standing when you were shot?" Max asked. "Tell me about it."

"Robbie and I were going up to see if the vestiges of the shearing had been cleared away. We were here talking when I was hit."

"Did you see anything beforehand?"

"Yes, there was a man standing up on the hill above the pasture with what might have been a gun or perhaps a walking stick, I didn't pay much attention, as all the time in the summer there're both rabbit hunters and walkers along the areas above the road."

"Can you recall anything about him, the person who shot you?"

Biddy frowned. "He was wearing a deerstalker's cap. That doesn't help much, does it? He was too far away to see much else."

"Not enough to identify him in court?"

"No. I didn't even see him raise his gun."

"Did Robbie?"

"You could ask him, but I think if he had, he'd have tried to protect me."

"Robbie MacPherson is very special to you, isn't he?"

"Yes, his family is both special and loyal to us. We're inseparable, particularly when it comes to the farm."

Max smiled at this and tried to imagine what a bond such as the one Biddy described could be like. His own family had mainly been urbanites, where relationships are fleeting and seldom lasted beyond a generation. He envied the length of the Tay-MacPherson alliance, without thinking of the social inequality attached to it.

The rain began and they withdrew into the barn.

"I must go," he said, noting once again the fatigue in her face.

Biddy simply smiled, and then came over to him and put the fingers of her good hand to his cheek. "Thank you," she said.

Later, as she walked him to his car, she flushed. "I've often been accused by both my brother and my cousin of being too spontaneous and unthinking. Please forgive me for my reaction in the barn."

"There's nothing for me to forgive," he said with a broad grin. "I've been wanting to do the same thing for a long time but thought it might be, how shall I put it, a bit early."

*

Biddy watched him pull from the drive and lingered afterwards before making her way back to the farmhouse. She did not notice that it was now raining quite hard and her fatigue seemed to have dissipated.

31

Kaitlin Logan did not get back to Max until late on Monday afternoon, but because he was busy with another case, he did not worry. He had fifteen minutes before having to leave to meet his client when Kaitlin was announced.

She gushed out her news. "They're nothing to speak of," she said. "Riffraff."

Max, whose mind was on the other case said, "Who?"

"The two eyewitnesses. I found them in a pub in Edinburgh on Saturday night and they cadged several drinks off of me. Can you imagine?"

Max could, knowing how easily Kaitlin morphed from one personality to another.

"Tell me about them?"

"They used to work for Billy Bong, you know the so-called Australian chap who everyone thinks is the biggest crook in Scotland. What a fake name! He sacked them about two months ago and they're on the dole."

"Sacked the eyewitnesses?"

"Yeah. They didn't have a lot to say about him that you might call good."

"Did they mention being in Perth on the night of the murder?"

"I tried to push them on that, but perhaps I was being too devious when I asked. Then one of them, Ron Dawes, pulled out a fifty quid note and implied it might be mine if I had a mind to do 'some things'—with the two of them. Fifty quid, when he was on the dole."

"I hope you left at that point, Kaitlin. I don't want you endangered."

"Mr Douglas-Forbes, I learned many years ago to take care of myself. I excused myself, saying I needed to 'go to the toilet', and left them laughing at the possibility of my return. I escaped through the back door. I was a bit angry, so I was more thorough than I might have been about checking their backgrounds. On Sunday I went to see if I could discover where they lived. Here are the photographs. Josh had said he lived here in Dundee." Kaitlin pulled out a photograph of a Costa coffee shop. "Ron 'lived' in a vacant lot in Edinburgh. I'm amazed the Tayside police didn't check."

"Did you find out anything else?"

Kaitlin nodded. "Actually they live together in a small room above a garage in Leith. Here's the address, but I'd prefer you to find someone else to question them the second time."

"I agree. Perhaps I could ask the police, but I may not. I might want to wait and discredit them at the trial."

"They could be telling the truth—about the murder I mean."

"I think not, but I don't want the Crown prosecutor at the trial to see where I'm going when I challenge these witnesses. Find out anything more you can about them, but don't try to contact either of them again. I want you to discover if there's any hard and fast evidence they were in Perth on the night of the murder. There's something else I want you to check, and I assure you this time it will be quite mundane. I need anything and everything you can find in the public records or people

309

you can talk to who might be relevant to the following topics."

He went to his desk and scribbled some questions, handed them to her, and she smiled. None of the items were on Elspeth's list, although her thinking had stimulated them. "There's no rush. Take a fortnight if you need to, but be thorough."

She grinned and took her departure, promising to get back to him if anything pertinent turned up.

After Kaitlin Logan left, Max rang to have his car brought around to the front of his office, as he was due in Scone to meet other clients. The ringing of the phone on his desk interrupted his departure.

"Douglas-Forbes," he said impatiently."

"Adair here, Max," the procurator fiscal said. "There's something I need to tell you that I think will have a major impact on the Tay case, although I expect his lordship already knows and has perhaps not told you."

"What is that, Adair?"

"Further and more complete DNA tests prove that Lord Tay was the father of the countess's baby."

"What? Are you certain?"

"There can be no doubt. The DNA match is one in a million."

"Well, well," said Max without knowing how to react to the news. "This is rather unexpected. Thank you for telling me."

When the procurator fiscal rang off, Max stood dumbfounded. This news completely destroyed one of the major points in his case and added a dimension to Johnnie's past. Why had Johnnie lied to both Elspeth and to him? Johnnie's mood swings distressed Max, and now he had to contend with Johnnie's prevarications. Except for meeting Biddy, he began to regret he had been convinced by Elspeth to take on the case at all.

He checked his watch and saw he had a few minutes to spare before departing for Scone. On the off chance he might be able to reach her; he dialled the number of Elspeth's secure line. On the second ring he got her recorded message. 'Blast!' he thought, took up his mackintosh and tried to contemplate what he would say to Johnnie the next time he contacted him.

When Max confronted Johnnie that evening, he did not anticipate Johnnie's reaction.

"It's a damn lie!" Johnnie said. "Don't believe it!"

"The scientific evidence is there. I'll have a hard time at the trial refuting it."

"I wasn't with Louisa four and a half months ago. That was the age of the foetus, wasn't it?"

Max confirmed this.

"Can you tell me where you were at the time?"

"Probably in Perth. I can't prove otherwise."

"Is there any way you can prove that you didn't see Louisa then? As a lawyer, I can anticipate that the Crown prosecutor will tell the jury about your continuing relationship with Louisa long after the two of you separated. You've admitted your main attraction to her was sex."

"That's an injustice!" Johnnie cried.

"You admit to sleeping with her once after your separation. Will the jury believe that you weren't tempted another time? I always have to think in terms of the jury's reactions. You can't be acquitted, nor the case 'not proven', if the jury has any strong suspicion that you got rid of Louisa

311

after you had formed a new alliance with Madeline as an attractive alternative."

"Do you always think about juries, Max?"

"In criminal cases, always. That's why I often get my clients off. Juries are made up of fifteen people, only eight of whom need to be convinced of your innocence."

"And you manipulate them."

"Of course. That's my job."

"Whether I am innocent or not?"

"Yes, but it is easier if I am convinced you are innocent. I thought you were, but now I am no longer sure."

"Are you deserting me?"

"Absolutely not, but I'm having a harder time believing you."

"Is there any way I can convince you that I didn't kill Louisa?"

"I thought you had told me the truth. Normally I can sense if someone isn't, but you fooled me."

"I *did* tell you the truth. I wasn't anywhere near Louisa four and a half months ago."

"You have no proof other than your word, and a gentleman's word isn't accepted as his bond in a court of law, especially these days. Juries prefer scientific evidence, and the DNA test results will hold more credence with them than your outrage."

"There has to be an explanation for the results of the test," Johnnie cried out in desperation. Can't you and Elspeth find a reason for all this?"

"I thought you didn't want your cousin involved."

"I didn't but right now I think I need her—and you. Can't the two of you . . .?"

Max was growing impatient with his client. "Do what? Controvert the evidence? DNA tests are all the rage these days with juries, and the prosecution will use the results as one of the main pieces of evidence against you. Wife, or supposed wife if we want to use that fact, becomes pregnant after separation from husband, and husband, or supposed husband, kills her to be with his current lover. The media will love it as well as the jury. I can't make this plainer."

"This can't be happening! What am I going to do?" Johnnie said.

"I expect the date for the trial will be set shortly. We may have a month or two. I only hope in that time I can construct a case that will save you."

"Only hope?"

"Yes, realistically, only hope," Max said, although he was feeling little hope at all.

*

Elspeth did not take the news lightly when she spoke to Max later. He just told her that Johnnie was due to stand trial at the High Court when it sat in Perth in late September, a fact he had just learned.

"Which gives us just two months to find out who murdered Louisa," Elspeth said.

"Do you still presume Johnnie is innocent?"

"I must, Max. If I suddenly think he committed the crime, I can't work with you in good faith. Unlike a lawyer, my job is always to discover the truth, where yours may be simply to get your client off."

Elspeth hoped she was not sounding defiant, but she was afraid she was. It hid her feeling of discomfort, with Johnnie, with Biddy, and now with Max. Elspeth's father's advice

313

came back to her. Stay out of this. She could not, and she needed to make all of them aware of this.

Having time before the Governor General was due to come down for breakfast, she walked out along the harbour. She stood at the rail by the pavement, deep in thought. She was grateful for Richard's love, and her father's, but she knew Max was different, as he had no personal connection with her. Was she so self-confident that she could solve Johnnie's dilemma from five thousand miles and eight time zones away? She looked up as she heard the raucous call of a gull above her, and it seemed to be mocking her. She clenched and unclenched her hands.

Two months! What could she find out in that time? She returned to her room and took a long bath, but it did not calm her. She wanted to talk to Richard, not to get his advice but rather his comfort, but she knew he was at a diplomatic reception in Valletta. Her bargain with him that they pursue separate careers had its moments of loneliness, which she seldom wanted to admit to, and this was one of them.

32

Perth/Tay Farm/London, Early September

By the first week in September, Biddy Baillie Shaw's gunshot wound was healing without complications, her last physiotherapy session had come and gone, and her mobility was almost completely restored. An unforeseen benefit of her twice weekly visits to Perth to the physio's office had been that she saw Max frequently, which cheered her. Once she no longer needed to rely on one of the farm hands or Jean MacPherson to drive her into Perth and could manage the Land Rover herself, she extended her stays for as long as she wished and often dined with Max. Sometimes she would chastise herself for so pleasantly indulging herself, but she made the silent excuse that she was consulting Max on Johnnie's defence, a topic they discussed for only a short part of their time together.

*

Max made similar excuses, that he was keeping Biddy aware of the salient points he planned to use at Johnnie's trial. Max seldom indulged in self-doubt, but when he was with Biddy his confidence sometimes failed him. Was it her expectation that he would be able to free Johnnie? Did some of her attraction to him rest on the assumption that he would be Johnnie's saviour? Such thoughts made him cautious, although she never had indicated that she expected that much of him. He tried several times to broach this with her, but always at the last moment drew back because he feared she

315

might admit that Johnnie was the reason for her continued willingness to meet him. His heart and mind had become divergent, and he wanted to follow both. He had not touched her other than in politeness since the day she had brushed his cheek, but his imagination ran wild at night, wondering where that tiny moment of intimacy might have led had he not been Johnnie's lawyer. She never pressed him beyond companionship, so he held back, despite his desires.

He continued to consult Elspeth by phone or e-mail at least weekly, updating her on Kaitlin's investigations and seeking her advice where it might be helpful. Together they were building a case that at least could cast doubt on Johnnie's guilt in the minds of the majority of the jurors, the eight that were required in Scotland to get him freed, but as yet they had made only superficial inroads into finding another possible candidate for Louisa's murderer. Elspeth kept coming back to the gun that was used to shoot Biddy and the note in the FedEx packet, but they had made little headway in finding the rifle or the author of the threat. Elspeth kept insisting it was central to the case, but Max did not agree.

Max had chosen one of his favourite restaurants that evening, a six-table French bistro run by a tyrant of a French chef who had taken a fancy to Max. He had been a frequent patron over the years, but until now usually unaccompanied. He and Biddy had dined there before and the chef, standing behind Biddy, each time raised a suggestive eyebrow when he took their order. Max always scowled and the chef always looked as if he were disdainful of Max's Scottish prudery. Max suspected Biddy was aware of their exchanges, but with her customary good manners she never alluded to them.

The trial was now less than three weeks away and neither

he nor Biddy could ignore that fact as they sipped their aperitif, a wine that came with the compliments of the chef. Max knew it was time for him to speak.

He reached out for her hand, and she gently closed her fingers over his.

"Max," she said, pre-empting his words. "I sense there are multiple levels in our relationship. I don't mind if we speak of them."

The depth of Biddy's blue eyes disconcerted him, just as Elspeth's did, but for a different reason. Elspeth's eyes demanded intelligent discourse; Biddy's asked for honesty. He knew he was powerless to deny either one of these intense women, despite their differences. He admired Elspeth but he loved Biddy. How could he tell her? He was saved from this dilemma by the arrival of dinner, but he felt cowardly because he did not respond to her request.

At the end of the meal, he could see fatigue in her eyes, and she pleaded the need to get back to the farm because she always rose early to do the farm chores. She had left her Land Rover outside his house and declined an invitation to join him for a coffee before she left for Loch Tay. She once again brushed his cheek with her fingertips; he was not certain if only in thanks or something more. Then she was gone. He went up the stairs to his front door, unlatched it, and entered the empty space he called home.

*

Biddy, of course, was not oblivious to Max's attentions and was wise enough to be aware of the conflict within him. He had not divulged his feelings about his wife's death, but she felt its tragedy was too painful for him to tell her. She was walking a narrow path. She needed Max to defend Johnnie,

317

and she had every confidence he would do so brilliantly. She trusted that Max would argue Johnnie's innocence to the fullest extent of the law. Would he perceive that she was manipulating him if she told him that her feelings were split, that she considered him Johnnie's best hope, but that her personal feelings towards him had little to do with that? Or was she just a lonely widow of a certain age who had found an attractive man on whom to set her cap? Ivor would have laughed at her, but she also knew he would have encouraged her because he had known her passionate nature. As she drove back to the farm, Biddy blew out her breath at the deepening twilight and chastised herself for her silly fantasies, but she went to bed that night and dreamed of being with Max as she had been with Ivor. Her sensual dreams, however, did not suppress the thought that came in to her the middle of the night. She suddenly remembered that she and Richard had discovered her father's most valued hunting rifle was missing from the gun cabinet on the night they had sent the men to chase off the media foxes, and she had no idea for how long it had been gone. She knew little of guns but could still see her father cleaning that particular rifle, saying that for accuracy there had never been a better one made. No one had used the rifle since her father's death over forty years before, and she was sure the original ammunition was still in the rifle case in the gunroom. She must let Max know. What did it mean if the bullets matched the one they took out of her shoulder?

She could not get back to sleep. The gunroom was always kept locked and only she and Robbie MacPherson knew the combination to the gunroom lock. She tried to remember when she had last opened the gun cabinet before they had seen the empty slot in the rack. She was positive the rifle had been there two years ago when Johnnie brought around some men from Perth, who seemed interested in knowing all about the farm and its history. Johnnie had mentioned his father's gun collection and asked Biddy to let them into the gunroom. She had dialled the combination on the lock on the door and unlocked the rifle case using the key that was in the barn office, but she had not stayed to watch Johnnie show his guests the guns. Surely one of the guests could not have taken the rifle. It was not something one slipped in one's pocket. After that she could not remember going into the gunroom except on the few occasions when one of the farm hands needed a shotgun to scare off foxes from the henhouse or crows who hovered around a wounded lamb. The shotguns were kept in the locked gunroom but on an open rack, separate from the locked case that housed her father's rifle collection.

Biddy waited until after the morning farm chores were complete and she had met a butcher from Pitlochry who wanted to buy lambs from her. She negotiated what she considered a fair price and the bargain was struck. It was just after ten when she returned to the kitchen, set the kettle on the Aga to boil and brewed herself a pot of tea. Sipping the hot liquid, she came back to the problem of the rifle. What if the bullet that had struck her shoulder did match those shot from her father's rifle? Who would that condemn? Certainly it would not implicate Johnnie, as he was in jail when Biddy was shot, but Biddy kept coming back to the note that came by FedEx. It was clearly meant as a threat. Did it also mean that the rifleman was unaware Johnnie had not yet returned to the farm? Yet how would the rifleman have obtained her father's rifle? Biddy wished she could talk to Elspeth. Her only other alternative was to talk to Max, and she was torn between revealing the carelessness with which she had guarded the rifles and his need to know the rifle was gone. If only Max had answered her question at dinner the night before about the different levels of their relationship, she would have felt more comfortable admitting her lack of oversight. She put down her cup and put her head in her hands. Max was making her life more complex than she wished, especially since she should be concentrating on helping Johnnie as much as possible to deal psychologically with his trial, and not her own fantasies. He had been broody ever since he had been confined to the farmhouse and often retreated to his bedroom.

As Biddy went to find Elspeth's mobile number, which she had scribbled into her diary, she smiled wryly, considering the role reversal that was about to occur if she could reach Elspeth, who might at that moment be anywhere in the world. In recent years Biddy had been the advice giver and Elspeth the advice seeker. Now Biddy needed that to change.

*

Elspeth was in fact in London, having just returned from three days in Malta with Richard, with whom she had discussed the case and its many ramifications. He had listened attentively, offered support where he could, and then when she began to repeat herself tried to divert her on to more pleasant subjects. He was only partly successful.

*

In London, Pamela Crumm was almost as anxious about the forthcoming trial as Elspeth was. When Elspeth had returned from Valletta, Pamela had arranged for her to handle a problem at the Kennington Mayfair that might have just as easily been handled by someone of much less ability or experience in the Kennington Organisation. Pamela wanted to keep in close contact with Elspeth because the time for Lord Tay's trial before the High Court in Perth was approaching quickly, and she had begun insisting on daily updates from Max.

*

Elspeth had been kept late at work the night before. It was well past two o'clock in the morning when she finally got to bed, and the next morning Biddy's phone call woke her. Elspeth had trained herself over time to come from sleep to full awareness when needed, and Biddy's revelation about the rifle required this talent.

"I don't know how to tell Max," Biddy said to her cousin. "He'll think me an awful fool for allowing the gun to be taken."

Elspeth wiped her eyes to clear them from the night's brume and shook her head to bring herself fully awake.

"Let me help," Elspeth said. "I've just come from Malta and, if you like, I'll call Dickie, mention you not seeing the rifle in the gunroom, and then get back to Max. I'll see if Dickie remembered the gun was gone."

"Bless you, Elspeth," Biddy said with real relief in her voice.

"And now, how are things going with Max?" Elspeth asked.

"I find him quite, eh, quite, . . ." she blustered and then stopped. Elspeth wondered if their connection had been broken, until she heard Biddy's almost whispered cry. "Oh damn, 'Peth, I think I have fallen in love with him."

"And he with you?"

"I don't know."

"Have you asked him?"

"As best I could. We were interrupted."

Elspeth chuckled, which perhaps was unkind. "As I remember, you had no trouble telling Ivor."

"I was nineteen then, not middle-aged, and . . ."

"And what, Biddy? I sense Max feels more for you than perhaps he can admit right now, but he also has the responsibility of getting Johnnie free. That must colour everything he feels when he is with you. I suspect he thinks you will judge him in the light of his success at the trial."

"I don't care, 'Peth. Yes, of course I do care, but for Johnnie. How can I get Max to know his success at the trial has nothing to do with how I feel for him?"

"Tell him."

"How?"

"Invite him to the farm for the night. I don't suggest that you lure him to the hayloft the way you did with Ivor. There are more comfortable venues there. I'll leave the mechanics to you but advise you to wear the silk pyjamas I sent you. I can send some very fine wine from London by express post if need be as well."

"You are horrible and devious, 'Peth. I couldn't. Besides Johnnie's here."

"Are you certain? Biddy, I have faith you can make the arrangements."

*

In the end it was Max who invited himself to the farm after he heard from Elspeth that the rifle used to shoot Biddy could be one from the eighth Earl of Tay's collection. It was Friday afternoon, and he had spent the day instructing a witness for a trial coming up the following Tuesday. It was a task he seldom enjoyed but one of the witnesses was vital to his defence and required special handling. As the witness finally seemed to grasp the importance of delivering her evidence without emotion, he let her go and went to check his messages. Elspeth's was brief. He picked up his phone and reached her immediately. He listened carefully, but also suspected that there was more than Elspeth was telling him. She ended her information about the rifle with the suggestion that Biddy might be a better source than Richard regarding the missing gun. Max was suddenly glad to have an excuse to call Biddy, and was even happier when she suggested he come to the farm for dinner and gave him the option to stay the night if he did not want to drive back to Perth after dark over the narrow roads leading from the farm to the motorway. This time he would bring his own things and not try to make do with Charlie's pyjamas and one of the disposable razors Biddy kept for guests.

Biddy had left the gate open for him. She was waiting for him by the kitchen door and was dressed as his mother often did, in well-cut tweeds, but she had added a scarf in a colour that heightened the blueness of her eyes and simple gold jewellery which became her. He noted she had taken some care with her hair and make-up and was delighted at the result. Biddy caught his look, and he thought she flushed.

She led him directly to the barn and showed him the gunroom behind the office.

"My father was an avid hunter," she said, "and often had shooting parties here when he could afford it. I think the only positive words my mother had for their impoverished state were that these parties were few and far between, as she disliked killing as much as Johnnie does now. My father had inherited some of his guns from my grandfather, but he also,

323

when he had won at cards, would contact a gun dealer in Edinburgh and buy another rifle to add to his collection."

"Which rifle is missing?" Max asked.

"One of Daddy's favourites. He said the bore, I think that is the right term, was absolutely true and said he never missed a shot when using it. I don't think it has been out of its rack since my father died in the early sixties. Johnnie is not a hunter and here at the farm we only use the shotguns when needed. Those are kept here in the gunroom but not locked away in the gun cabinet."

"Who has access to the room?"

"Only me and Robbie MacPherson. We have a combination lock on the door."

Biddy showed Max the lock. It was of the type where one rotated though a string of numbers and when the right combination was reached, the lock sprung open. He read off the numbers as Biddy twisted the dial. "Is that the combination?" he asked after watching her.

"It's not terribly secure, is it?" she said. "If anyone saw the lock opened, I suppose they could memorise the combination, but no one came in here, Max, when the door was opened unless Robbie or I were with them." Then her face clouded.

"What is it?" Max asked.

"Johnnie did have some people from Perth to see the farm. One of the men expressed an interest in the rifles, and I opened the gunroom for them and left them with Johnnie. I suppose one of them could remember the combination afterwards, but why?"

"Do you know who these men were?"

Biddy shook her head.

"How long ago was this? Could it possibly have coincided with Johnnie's signing the note for the loan?"

Biddy thought. "It was possibly about two years ago. I was busy seeing that the fields were mown, and the hay put in for the winter. I didn't pay much attention, but it might have been about that time."

"Hmm," Max said equivocally. "Elspeth keeps coming back to the Perthshire Land Development Consortium. I wonder if her assumptions are proving well-founded."

Biddy locked the gunroom, and they walked from the barn to the kitchen. Something was roasting in the Aga that smelled suspiciously like lamb with garlic and rosemary. Biddy offered Max a drink; he poured one for them both as she busied herself at the cooker.

"I promise this is the last I will speak of the trial tonight," he said, "but I may need you to testify at the trial. I'd hoped to spare you, but the shot fired at you may help us to find the real murderer. I may bring it up in court, if Elspeth and I can make a link between the gun and the real killer. Would you mind?"

"To help Johnnie? Of course not," she said, determination and love filling her eyes.

She turned back to preparing the dinner. He came up to where she was standing.

"You asked the other night if we could clarify the various levels of our relationship, but I never replied. I hope we can."

"Thank you, Max," she whispered.

Max noted that Johnnie did not appear at dinner. Had this been Biddy's doing?

It was fully dark when they finished their meal, and Max went to his car to get his things. She led him up the stairs.

"Am I staying in Charlie's room again?" he asked.

She turned and looked at him and with only the slightest hint of shyness responded, "I'd rather hoped you would stay in mine."

He grinned, his eyes dancing. "I'd rather hoped so too," he said.

When he woke in the morning, Biddy was gone, but the freshness of the scent of her body and hair lingered together in the room, leading him in and out of a pleasurable early morning awakening. He finally rose, dressed, shaved, and made his way to the kitchen, where the kettle was simmering on the Aga, and the breakfast table had been laid. He found a note by the place where he had sat at dinner the night before. *I am in the barn tending to the animals. B.*

He found her with the hens. She came to him but did not touch him.

"About last night . . ." she started. "Max, you are under no obligation to . . ." Then she stopped, as if not knowing how to complete her thought. "It just happened," she finally finished.

He rose to his full height. "Are you saying you did not purposely seduce me?" he asked most haughtily. Then he began to laugh. "Biddy Baillie Shaw, your cousin tells me you are a very wise woman. Has it ever dawned on you that I'm very much in love with you?"

"In love with me?"

"In love with you."

She started to laugh too. "Oh, Max, I'm so glad because I'm in love with you too."

*

Robbie MacPherson had just come out of the barn when he heard the laughter, a loud crash of what sounded like a bucket hitting the ground and a mad cacophony of clucking made by the startled hens. As he rounded the corner, he saw Lady Biddy and Lord Johnnie's lawyer entwined in each other's arms and their lips engaged in what he later described to his wife as a 'fair and bonny kiss'. The bucket of feed that Biddy usually carried out to the hens in the morning had fallen to the ground at her feet, and the hens, now recovered from the initial surprise that their food had not been cast to them, were pecking at the disgorged contents of the bucket at Biddy's feet. Above them Biddy and Max were completely oblivious to anything that was happening except between the two of them.

33

The flat had been unoccupied for five rainy and damp days. Elspeth flung open the windows to let the stale air out, despite the pollution that might come in from the streets of Kensington below. Gibraltar, from where she had just returned, had been hot, crowded with tourists, and cloudless. The opening of Lord Kennington's new hotel, including a royal visit, had been accomplished without incident, and Elspeth was soundly congratulated by her employer for the quiet way the security force at the hotel had kept watch under her skilful tutelage. Back in London Elspeth welcomed the heavy clouds that obscured the late afternoon sunlight and breathed in the cool air. The constant but familiar far-off roaring of the traffic, the branch with dead leaves on the tree outside that still needed to be pruned, and the acrid smells of car exhaust filled her with a sense of coming home. Elspeth seldom tired of her job, even the more routine assignments, but recently, after her experience with her family in Perthshire, she had begun speculating what another sort of life might be like. Did others find the excitement in their life that matched what Elspeth felt when overseeing the visits of heads of state, prime ministers, royalty, and the powers-that-be of the corporate world? Did other people's lives provide the adrenaline rush that the crimes, and even murders, with which she had to deal gave her? Where did others find satisfaction in their lives, if at all, or had they merely settled for their lot?

Elspeth's life was hardly settled, knowing that Johnnie's trial was only a few weeks away. She always let her unconscious mind work on solutions, but only shadowy inklings had come to her. Now she had a few days free between assignments and was determined to use it to Johnnie's advantage.

Considering she now needed to take direct action, she picked up her mobile and dialled Richard's private line at the British High Commission in Malta.

"Dickie," she said to her husband, "I've just arrived back in London and am going up to Scotland for the rest of the week, leaving tomorrow. Is there any chance you can join me? I'll be staying at the hotel in Edinburgh, as I need to explore one or two things there which I don't want Johnnie or Biddy to know about. If what I think may have happened actually did happen, I'll let Max know, but right now I'm following a hunch that may prove foolhardy."

"I may be able to join you on Friday evening. I'll see if Margaret can book me a direct flight from Luqa to Edinburgh, if they exist. I'll let you know. Will you have a car?"

Elspeth grinned. "Pamela promised me a car and driver. She said she had a lot riding on it."

Elspeth heard Richard chuckle. "Yes, I expect so. Max and his crew cannot be inexpensive. Any more news from Perth or the farm?"

Omitting Biddy's private news, she said, "None that I haven't told you, but I've rung Max and asked that we get together when I'm in Edinburgh. Only so much can be conveyed by phone or e-mail, and I think a face to face meeting will help."

"So you still haven't given up?"

"No, Dickie, and I won't."

"I thought not," he said.

She was not sure if his tone was conciliatory or congratulatory, but it was reassuring to hear his voice and know she at least had his tacit support.

As she rang off, Elspeth picked up the card her son and new daughter-in-law had sent from Maui on their wedding trip, which she had left next to the phone after reading it to Richard. She smiled and then frowned.

"Of course, that's it," she said out loud, but no one was there to hear. She took the card and tucked it in her handbag.

Lord Kennington made sure that each of his hotels offered the amenities his guests expected, but he also tried to make each one unique. The Kennington Edinburgh had been a challenge. The greyness that overlaid the Scottish capital did not appeal to the primness of his Englishness, but he felt the presence of one of his hotels was essential there and had found a Georgian mansion that caught his fancy and decided to make the hotel small and exclusive, brightening the granite exterior with constant power washing to combat the grime that descended like the night during the long, dark days that enveloped Scotland during the late autumn and winter months. He had expanded the building with great respect to its original character and had been recognised by the local government planners for his success. Elspeth still did not like the hotel, and entered it remembering that her last visit here had been with the full intention of deceiving Louisa. That was over two months ago, and the life of her family had changed irrevocably. How strange that someone as insignificant as Louisa could have done so, and probably without guile.

The concierge greeted Elspeth by name as she entered the hotel and called the manager, whom Elspeth knew from his previous post as assistant manager at the Kennington Mayfair. She made her arrangements for the next few days and mentioned that her husband might be joining her on Friday but that their plans were not certain. Now she needed to set up her meetings and try out her hypothesis. She picked up the room phone and confirmed her Thursday morning meeting.

*

On Friday at lunchtime Max Douglas-Forbes entered the Kennington Edinburgh. She was waiting across the lobby for him and crossed the space with such unstudied grace and dignified bearing that he drew back to admire her. He had not seen her in her own milieu before and, although he was not expecting to be impressed, he was. Elspeth in country clothing suitable for Perth and the lochs was one thing; Elspeth dressed as she would have in the most sophisticated places in London, Paris, or Milan was quite another. Max had often dealt with clients who considered themselves to be in the height of fashion, but they did not have Elspeth's impeccable sense of classic style. Her clothing was business-like but beautifully cut even to the untrained eye. Max had a glimmer of the world that Elspeth normally inhabited, a world completely apart from Tay Farm, from Perth, and from the Scottish Highlands. As she approached, she smiled genuinely at him, as if none of this mattered.

Max had been to the Kennington Edinburgh before but only for an occasional meal with clients, but he had never seen the upper rooms. Elspeth took his arm with a touch that fell between familiarity and guidance and led him to the lift.

"I hope you have no compunctions accompanying me to

331

my room. After I had worked for five years for Lord Kennington, I insisted that he provide me with a suite whenever I stayed in the hotels, and that one room be arranged as a meeting room, so that I could see people away from the back offices of the hotel. Although I'm here on personal business, somehow the orders have stood, and they have provided me with a suite where we can meet and have lunch without being disturbed. I hope this doesn't disconcert you, being taken by a woman of a certain age to her hotel room."

"Not at all," Max said laughing. "I'm sure my reputation as well as yours will stand the test."

When they arrived at Elspeth's suite, she went to the phone and notified room service that they were ready for lunch. As she did so, Max looked around the room and began to get the sense of why people paid such outrageous fees to stay at a Kennington hotel. Every appointment in the room was clearly thought out and coordinated. Elspeth had drawn back the curtains, and he looked out over the city from a new vantage point to him, the view of the very wealthy. Edinburgh Castle jutted into the sky as if framed there solely for the purpose of delighting Lord Kennington's guests. A small, round table had been set for lunch, with colourful linens, fine china, shining silver cutlery, and cut glass. Bouquets of flowers were placed around the room, complementing the dominant colours of the decor, and the flowers on the lunch table that matched the linens. Elspeth was as at home in this atmosphere as Biddy was at the farm, and Max wondered how the two cousins, so alike in appearance, had taken such diverse courses in their lives, each seeming comfortable in her choice.

Elspeth had ordered lunch without consulting him on his preference, but the food was delectable, and he told her that.

Elspeth sat back and laughed, a twinkle appearing in her eye. "The spicy fish here is exceptionally good, but I thought you might prefer something else."

"Are you thinking of Louisa?" he asked with a twisted smile.

"In the back of my mind I've thought of little else since the murder," she said. "Max, I have an idea and yesterday I had it partially confirmed. I want you to promise to tell no one, not Biddy or Johnnie, or even your detective. I think we need to consider the element of surprise at the trial. What I learned yesterday may catch the murderer out, and, if so, we can prove Johnnie's innocence."

"Then you still believe in Johnnie's innocence?"

"Yes, and now I'm sure of it, but I still haven't worked out all the finer details. I'll need some help from you, and that's why I need your discretion and pledge of secrecy."

"Do you think the murderer will be at the trial?"

"Oh, yes," she said, "because you are going to subpoena him."

"It sounds as if he, you're sure it's a he, will be a hostile witness."

"I want you to find a way to make him think he's not a suspect."

As they finished their main course, Elspeth offered Max a slice of chocolate torte with nuts and fresh strawberries, kiwis and a drizzle of bitter chocolate on top that the waiter had left on the sideboard, and a coffee.

"Now you must tell me what you have in mind," he said, with a sigh of pleasure. The taste of the coffee matched its tantalising smell and far surpassed his normal morning quaff extracted from his coffee machine. The cake was even better.

She leaned forward on her elbows and told him where she had been the day before. Then she laid out her plan. "There're a few more things you and your detective will have to find out. Here's a list. You may have more ideas, but I think you can build your case on this," she said.

Max spent a moment looking at Elspeth, who sat watching him with only the slightest hint of a smug smile and the mere arch of an eyebrow, and then slowly he nodded his head up and down. "Yes, for the first time I'm beginning to believe I can get Johnnie freed."

"Max," Elspeth said as they were finishing their coffee, "my biggest concern is finding who really did kill Louisa. I think discrediting the eyewitnesses will be a simple matter after all that Kaitlin discovered about them, but they must have been paid by someone who wanted to see Johnnie convicted. If we could only find out who gave them the fifty-pound note. Is this something Kaitlin could investigate?"

"It probably was given in cash, which makes it harder to trace, but I have some ideas," Max said. "I already have Kaitlin on it."

"Do you think you can break the eyewitnesses down at the trial?"

"I can try, but it will be a gamble. I may be able to split the two of them and make one think the other has confessed where the money came from, but I'd rather have something more definite. What are your thoughts?"

"That somehow the Perthshire Land Development Consortium is involved in Johnnie's arrest and in Biddy's being shot. Are you going to introduce Biddy's injury at the trial?"

"I hope not to, unless it will help Johnnie."

"What about the gun?"

"Gun?"

"The one that was used to shoot Biddy. Have the police traced it through the ballistics?"

"I can find out."

"Also find out if any of the men in Louisa's life, either her lovers or people she knew from the Consortium have a background that might include the military, hunting, target shooting, or anything that would associate them with precise marksmanship. I keep coming back to her men. Is that narrow-minded of me?"

"Probably not. I'll get Kaitlin on that too."

"Oh, I almost forgot. I wanted to give you this," Elspeth said. She drew her son's postcard from her handbag. "Did I ever tell you that I have a British daughter and an American son? Lizzie wanted to come back to the UK from Hollywood when she was ten, and Alistair and I let her, but Peter was always glad to be a Californian, and could think of no other place to live. I think the note in the pocket of Johnnie's Macintosh was from Peter. See if you can get a photocopy of the note, read it over again carefully and see if the writing and the style match this postcard. I think it will help prove that Johnnie was not at Louisa's home shortly before Peter's wedding in San Francisco."

Max looked puzzled, but Elspeth only grinned like the Cheshire cat.

Later in their discussions, Elspeth asked Max if he had traced Helen, Johnnie's second wife or the man she had run off with, Ross MacCombe.

Max assented. "At Biddy's suggestion, I contacted his parents. They still live in Perth and were able to confirm his address in Italy. I gather it's somewhere near Rome."

"Do you have the address?"

"Yes, do you want it?"

"Yes. Let me see if I can find Helen. I've given you such a long list of things to consider; it's the least I can do to repay you. Call me if you think there is anything else I can do."

*

When Max left, Elspeth made an impromptu decision, and once again rang Richard in Malta. "I'm coming to Malta on Saturday," she said, "by way of Rome. I hope Margaret hasn't yet booked your ticket here."

There remained one thing left for her to do in Scotland before leaving for the Mediterranean, and she sought out her father, wanting his guidance. Luckily her mother was at home and answered Elspeth's call, as although the Duffs had finally conceded to buying an answerphone, they often forgot to turn it on. Elspeth did not identify her whereabouts to her mother but did to her father, who came on the line once Fiona Duff had finished making sufficient clucking noises over her daughter.

"Do you have a car?" he asked.

"Access to one."

"It will take you as much as two hours to get to Pitlochry at this time of day from Edinburgh."

"No matter, Daddy, Pamela Crumm has hired a car and driver for me."

"Then meet me at the office at four, or as soon afterwards as your driver can make it here. Will you come home for dinner?"

"No, I have an early flight in the morning, but I promise next time. Indulge me, Daddy. I want to tell you how I think

Louisa was murdered, and I want you to tell me if I'm completely going down the wrong track."

Taking Pamela's example, Elspeth hired a car and driver when she got to Rome, aware of her time constraints before her evening flight to Malta and not wanting to get lost. The driver professed to know the location of the address Elspeth gave him and swept out of the airport, talking non-stop in broken English, while simultaneously seeming to flow sublimely in and out of the morass of traffic as if endowed with some protective force. Elspeth hung on to the strap by her seat and let him ramble on, her thoughts on the piece of paper her father had given her as he departed from his office the afternoon before and her forthcoming visit with Helen, Countess of Tay. The driver found the house in the suburbs after several attempts. The house was surrounded by plastered walls that had suffered damage over time and sported a cracked blue and white house number plate.

Helen Tay opened the door to Elspeth and, frowning, stood trying to place her. Finally she said, "Elspeth?"

Elspeth nodded, knowing she would not have recognised Helen if she had been in any other place. Elspeth and Helen were the same age, but Helen had not aged well. Her once robust frame had shrunken into itself, she had a stringy neck, and she had tied back her greying hair with a black ribbon without any apparent consultation with a mirror. She was wearing old overalls and a tee shirt covered by a loose-fitting apron with secateurs and cotton gloves in the broad pocket in the front. She carried a basket filled with clippings, and from the tell-tale signs of the mud at her knees she had been gardening. The large pots of prospering red geraniums testified to her care.

She invited Elspeth in, after motioning to Elspeth's driver to move his car from the narrow street. She led Elspeth through the garden and into the cool interior of the house, and, although it was still morning, she offered Elspeth wine, which she declined.

"Pellegrino, then," Helen asked." Come into the kitchen. I'll find some."

The kitchen showed its age as did the appliances. Helen was either a poor housekeeper or didn't care. She found two tumblers, poured the Pellegrino and did not offer ice, although the day was baking hot, and Elspeth was still dressed in the clothes she had put on that morning in Scotland.

Helen toasted Elspeth and said, "You are looking well, and I see you still spend a great deal of money on your dressmaker. I read about your marriage in *The Times*. Who would have thought of you and Dickie together? Not quite what one could have imagined. I hope you two have found happiness together." The words somehow lacked real warmth.

"We're very happy," Elspeth said, knowing her voice edged on defensiveness. She had not remembered that Helen could be unkind.

Helen rose and said, "I knew when I read of the trial that someone might come to find me. Come into the other room. I have the paper you are looking for."

"How did you know?"

"Because it will undoubtedly come out at the trial that Johnnie's and my divorce was not finalised, and that Johnnie may have killed the woman, but she was not legally his wife."

"I brought a copy of the divorce papers. Would you be willing to sign them now?" Elspeth asked.

"There is no need. I signed them several years ago, but they still need his signature. I've kept them, assuming Johnnie would ask for them back. He never did. Here, you may take them. I've no need for them. Let me know when they are final, although at this point it makes little difference."

Elspeth left Helen standing by the old, badly painted gate and retreated into the air-conditioned car that would take her back to Rome. She did not ask about Ross MacCombe.

"Dickie," Elspeth said to her husband after they arrived at the house which he had set up for them in Malta, "do you think we are a mismatched couple?"

He frowned. "Who said so?"

"Several people."

"Well, then," he said with a grin, "let me show you differently."

The next morning Elspeth sat with Richard, sipping her coffee, he his tea.

"Well, if Johnnie is acquitted, which I hope Max can accomplish, I suppose we will have two more family weddings shortly,"

"Two?" he asked puzzled. "Johnnie and Madeline, certainly, but two?

"Biddy and Max. It may take longer but there's no doubt at all that it will happen."

"And how, my precious sleuth, did you come to that conclusion?"

"Biddy asked me if she could come to London and have me help her buy some new clothes and perhaps advise her on a new haircut."

"Is that enough for you to predict a second wedding?" Richard asked.

Elspeth nodded. "So I plan first to take Biddy to my hair stylist, then to my dressmaker, and treat her to some rather fine things. She deserves that after all I put her through at the hotel in Stresa.

"With all this finery, why do you predict a delay? Are all the women in your family as reluctant to acknowledge a man's proposal as Biddy's cousin was?"

"You know I took so long because I didn't think I could make things work out between us. I was wrong. Still I think Biddy may take time because her marriage to Ivor was so idyllic. She will want to make sure Max will give her the same amount of happiness. She will find he will if she lets herself give in to him."

"Why do you think that?"

Elspeth kept a straight face, but her eyes were twinkling. "I would trust the power of silk pyjamas I sent her in hospital any time. Didn't I use silk pyjamas to seduce you?"

Richard burst out laughing and took his wife in his arms. "No, I was seduced by your incorrigible personality. You haven't changed a bit since you were fifteen," he said.

Part 2

The Trial

34

The media had let the news of the Tay trial lay dormant over the late summer, but the day before the trial the papers and television crews were actively working outside the Perth Sheriff Court building, where Johnnie's trial would soon take place. The pundits were speculating on the forthcoming trial and promising up to the minute coverage once the proceedings began. Even the BBC and *The Times* had sent minor reporters to cover the story.

Maxwell Douglas-Forbes was ready. He had asked Elspeth to come to Scotland a day early to discuss their trial strategy once more. After several sessions with her, he decided not to call her to the stand. He preferred that she stay in the courtroom, seated near him in the visitor's section, in case he needed to consult her. She had no direct knowledge of the evidence that was not corroborated by other witnesses, and was more useful as an observer. She was well aware of where Max planned to take the case and could advise him whether or not his approach with the jurors seemed to be effective. He had thought of having her assist him at his table but decided against it at the last moment. Her anonymity, he thought, was preferable.

The trial was to commence at nine by which time the visitor's section was filled. Max and the advocate depute, who was pleading for the Crown, shook hands as they entered the courtroom and assumed their places on either side of the

342

advocate's table beneath the judge's bench. The clerk of the court who was dressed sombrely in black, but sporting a bit of cleavage, busied herself, assuring that the computers for both advocates were linked up and that the technicians had all the electronics working. The chatter of the crowd did not seem to faze her. Adair Gordon, the procurator fiscal, came in shortly after Max and took the advocate depute aside, whispering some last-minute information, to which the advocate depute nodded in response. Max took his chair and checked his computer. The crowd waited impatiently as the nine o'clock hour passed, and the judge had not yet appeared.

Shortly after nine Lord Tay was escorted in by a policeman. The courtroom buzzed as Lord Tay was led to the prisoner's table. Johnnie was dressed conservatively in a dark suit, white shirt and grey tie, which matched the deep shadows under his eyes and the pallor of his face. He was not handcuffed and took his seat on the stiff wooden chair with his hands gripping the table in front of him. He occasionally stretched his arms out, as if to relieve tension. Elspeth wanted to catch Johnnie's eye, perhaps even to send a small signal of support, but he was sitting slightly in front of her. He studiously averted his gaze from everyone in the room and stared up into space, not seemingly interested in anything but the ornate clerestory windows and filigreed vaulted ceiling above.

The visitors' section being packed full, no one except Elspeth noted that a small, bent woman, handsomely dressed, and heavily bespectacled with large round glasses, was sitting almost unnoticed at the end of one of the front rows. Richard was beside her. Pamela Crumm told Elspeth that she had not asked but informed Lord Kennington that she had personal business in Scotland and only planned to return to London when it was finished. Lord Kennington was not a fool and let her go. He could catch snippets of the trial on the television and demand the details later. Shortly before the court was called to order, Elspeth saw Richard touch Pamela gently on the arm. Elspeth was not able to see Pamela's reaction, except for a brief smile that crossed her lips, at which Richard leaned over and said something in her ear. Pamela looked up, saw Elspeth and winked.

The judge, taking his own time, arrived, robed and wigged and called the trial to order. The advocate depute, whom Max knew slightly, presented the case to the jury once they were empowered, and the charges read. He made the case seem very simple. John Edward Charles Robertson, ninth Earl of Tay, had on the night of Thursday, the 19th of July or possibly the early morning of Friday, the 20th of July, entered the house where his estranged wife lived and strangled her with the cord from the curtains in the drawing room. The advocate depute said he would show that the act had been premeditated by Lord Tay, as he was in the process of divorcing his wife, and had been provoked when she had made demands to which he did not wish to accede. Eyewitnesses had seen a man strangle Louisa through the windows that faced the street and could identify Lord Tay as he left the house a short time afterwards. There was further evidence to show Lord Tay had motive to murder his wife.

Elspeth admired the advocate depute's skilful way of laying out the facts, which suggested the case was an open and shut one, with Johnnie's conviction all but assured. The advocate depute, named Hamish MacDonnell, was a man of medium stature, which became diminished under his dark robes and sheepskin wig, but his voice belied his stature as he asserted his authority. The fifteen-member jury took notice of him.

In contrast, Max played down his size, his luxuriant head of hair which was showing under his wig, and the stentorian quality of his voice, by speaking gently to the jury, saying that the defence would present evidence to refute the Crown and would rely on the jury to make its own considered decision as to Lord Tay's innocence or guilt. Max returned to his seat and smiled at the jury. He then leaned back to Elspeth and whispered, "Note their reactions."

"I already have. They seem only mildly curious, but I think right now they would convict Johnnie."

She was certain they had no idea of what Max had in store for them. Elspeth knew he was saving himself, and the jury, for the careful construction of his case to prove Johnnie's innocence and the possible guilt of another person.

"Good," Max said. "Let me know when the Crown loses them. Hamish is a good advocate depute, but I think he looks a bit smug. The jury will pick that up."

The morning wore on. The police gave evidence on their findings when they entered Louisa's home. Max raised no objections and stated that he wished to delay his cross-examination of the police until a later time. The judge noted the request. The pathologist described in anatomical and medical detail the condition of the body and the probable time of death, which he surmised occurred between half past eleven in the evening and two o'clock in the morning, probably closer to midnight. The jury settled in comfortably. Eight men and seven women, all good Scots and dedicated to deciding the fate of John, Lord Tay, let the proceedings wash over them, although perhaps hoping the trial's duration would allow them to go back to their everyday lives as quickly as possible.

After the pathologist's tedious medical language was dispensed with, Hamish MacDonnell rose from his table, hitched his thumbs around the edges of his robe and addressed the pathologist.

"Can you describe the overall health of the victim before her death?" he asked so quietly that several jury members had to lean forward to hear.

"She was in excellent health and was expecting a child."

Hush came over the courtroom. Three of the jurors gasped, and most sat up in surprise. Elspeth surveyed their faces and made note of their individual expressions.

"And how far along was the victim's pregnancy at the time of her death?" Hamish MacDonnell asked.

"About four and a half months, give or take a week," the pathologist replied, after referring to his notes. Elspeth suspected this was a ploy he frequently used to stress the veracity of his information.

Hamish MacDonnell smiled and looked from one juror to the next. Several looked down, but one woman scowled at Lord Tay. An older man grunted. Most scribbled notes on their clipboards provided by the court.

The examination of the pathologist continued.

"During your postmortem, did you take DNA samples of the foetus?"

"Yes."

"Has paternity been established?"

The pathologist again referred to his file. "Yes. The DNA of the foetus matched that of the victim and also the DNA sample the police took from Lord Tay when he was arrested."

There was another gasp, this time more from the visitors than the jury.

"You are saying that the match was positive. Can there be any doubt?"

"No, sir. The match was indisputable." The pathologist, as if to emphasize his point, took off his metal frame glasses and laid them on his file.

Several members of the press box took out their Blackberries and began to type in this information, to be immediately conveyed to the outside world. All turned to Maxwell Douglas-Forbes, and he sat, arms crossed over his broad chest, and showed no reaction other than the brief and enigmatic raising of his eyebrows.

The judge asked, "Mr Douglas-Forbes, do you have any questions for the pathologist?"

Max rose with a flourish and adjusted his black robes over his large frame. Elspeth suspected he often used this to his full advantage.

Max looked at the pathologist. "Will you describe the contents of the victim's stomach and intestinal tract to us, please."

"She had eaten a meal four or five hours earlier."

"Did the victim have any drugs or medicines in her system?"

"No, none that we found."

"Which would be consistent with her condition, assuming it was a normal pregnancy," Max said to the air. "And alcohol?"

The pathologist looked over at the advocate depute, who looked back and gave a slight nod.

"Yes, there was evidence of alcohol."

"Was the victim inebriated?" Max asked.

The pathologist gave the blood alcohol level, which rested just below the level of legal drunkenness.

"Does that imply the victim was not completely sober at the time of her death?"

"I would say she was on the edge of intoxication." The pathologist did not look at his notes to confirm this.

Max spoke to the air again. "Do you find that unusual for a woman four and a half months pregnant? I understand that women in her condition these days are advised to forgo drink."

The judge brought him to task. "Mr Douglas-Forbes, please refrain from expressing your opinions at this point in the trial. You may do that at the time of the speeches."

Max did not look chagrined and simply said. "That is all I have for you now. However, I ask that I be allowed to question this witness again, if necessary."

During the pathologist's testimony, Elspeth kept looking across at Johnnie at the defendant's table. He sat without moving. Elspeth knew Johnnie was aware of all the facts the pathologist was making, but she hoped Johnnie's reaction to the actual giving of the testimony would be neutral. She was well aware that Johnnie's fair skin sometimes flushed, not hiding the rush of his inner feelings. Luckily Johnnie's face stayed bland, for which Elspeth was thankful.

"I may have further questions. You may call the next witness," Max said and returned with dignity to his chair.

The Crown next called Rosa Browne to the witness box. She was a wiry woman with a strong burr and was obviously dressed in her Sunday finery, carefully starched and old-fashioned. Standing stiffly, she swore by Almighty God to tell the truth, the whole truth and nothing but the truth with the vehemence of Presbyterian vengeance. Mrs Browne testified that she had been the char for the earl and countess for over three years, ever since their marriage, and had continued to serve the countess after the earl left the house.

After establishing this initial information, Hamish MacDonnell began his examination of her, "Did you ever see the earl after he stopped living with the countess?"

"No, sir," she said, standing up more rigidly than she had before.

"Did the countess ever mention him to you after that time?"

"Yes, sir, now and then. The countess was a chatty one."

Elspeth expected Louisa enjoyed what little social advantage she had over Mrs Browne and found discussing her plight with someone closer to her class more comforting than with Johnnie's family and friends, or with her male admirers.

"Did she mention he had visited her two and a half months before her death, which would have been in May of this year?"

"Now that you say so, aye, the countess did say so. The countess said she hoped for a reconsil . . . " she stumbled over the word, "that they might get together again, but I would have known that without her saying. I found things of his lying around."

"Such as?"

"A scarf he was fond of, a cardigan, that sort of thing."

"Are you sure?"

"Yes, sir. She said she had bought the jumper for him as a Christmas present."

The Crown prosecutor turned Mrs Browne over to Max.

He rose and looked her straight in the eye before

beginning his cross-examination. Finally she broke his gaze and looked down uncomfortably.

"Mrs Browne, I applaud you for your faithful service to the victim." He avoided Louisa's title. "When did you last find evidence of Lord Tay's presence in the house?"

Mrs Browne straightened up. "About weeks days before the murder I should say. I found one of his handkerchiefs with JT stitched on it clear as day."

"And where did you find it?"

"In the hallway just inside the main door on the table there for the post."

"Did the victim call attention to it?'

"Now that you say so, yes, she did. She said she had found it just outside the night before and was afraid he was stalking her. She said she was going to the police this time."

Max walked from behind his table and over to near the witness box. "Were those her exact words?"

Mrs Browne stiffened. "As close as I can remember," she said defensively. "It was a Friday, because I asked her if she was all right or if I should check back over the weekend. She said she would be safe after going to the police, and not to worry, but I could tell she was worrying."

"Did you know she was pregnant?" Max asked blandly.

"Hard to miss," the char snorted. "I've got four of me own."

"Did the victim tell you who the father of the child was?"

"No, sir, but it must have been Lord Tay. Who else?"

Max did not reply but instead asked, "Did she entertain other gentlemen at her home after Lord Tay left?"

Mrs Browne twisted her shoulders. "She had one or two men friends."

Max went back to his table, drew an envelope from his stack of documents and took out several photographs. "Do you recognise any of these men?" he asked. He handed them to her. She went through them one by one. Finally she handed him two back. "I've seen these two," she said, "just on and off, nothing special," she said.

"Thank you, Mrs Browne. I would like to enter these photographs as evidence to be used at a later time." Several jurors looked concerned at this new turn of events, particularly the woman who had frowned before.

"I have two more questions, Mrs Browne. First, did you usually find the curtains drawn when you came in the morning to clean for the victim?

"Yes, she liked to sleep in and dinna like the light, even in the lounge."

"When you found the victim's body the morning after her death, were the curtains drawn?"

"I think they were, but I canna swear for sure."

"Thank you, Mrs Browne. You have been most helpful," Max said. "I have no further questions for this witness."

Hamish MacDonnell did not redirect any questions to Mrs Browne, but looked over at Max with curiosity after reviewing the photographs of the men. He leaned over to the procurator fiscal who whispered something in his ear. Max suspected Adair Gordon could not fail to recognise warning signals about what was to come. He had faced Max several times in the High Court before and only once won his case.

Next the Crown called Joshua MacCallum, Louisa's neighbour next door to the Tays in Perth. He assured the jury that he had lived at his current residence for twelve years and remembered both Lord Tay's second wife and his third. He asserted without being prompted that the second countess was a kind and friendly woman who had left about five years before. The victim, he acknowledged, had little time for her neighbours and seemed to prefer outside company.

"Where were you on the night of the murder?" the advocate depute asked.

"At home. I always find it hard to sleep when the sun stays out for so long. I don't sleep well, anyway, not since my wife died." Joshua MacCallum was of an age that made this statement believable.

The testimony that followed was straightforward and crisp, and Max did not raise any objections.

"Did you hear anything next door at about midnight, or thereabouts on the night of the murder?" Hamish MacDonnell asked.

"I had the window open to catch the night air. Yes, there was a bit of a row going on next door."

"Can you tell us the time?"

"I should say about half past eleven. It was still twilight and I heard the half hour bell from the kirk nearby. I heard the midnight bells later."

"Could you hear the voices well enough to identify them?"

"I knew Louisa's voice. It was always a bit shrill."

"And any others?"

"There was just the one."

"A man?"

"Yes, for what it's worth."

"Did you recognise the voice?"

"It could have been Lord Tay's," the witness said, "but it was a bit muffled."

"Were they quarrelling?'

"Definitely."

"Did you hear any of the words?"

"A few."

"Can you tell us what they were?"

"I heard the man say 'baby' and 'you betrayed me' and then 'you can't pin this on me'.

"Did she reply?"

"I heard her laugh. She didn't have a pleasant laugh."

"And then?"

"She cried out. I didn't hear anything after that."

"Did you see Lord Tay at any time during the evening?"

"No, but I wouldn't have. I can't see the drawing room windows directly from my window as my house sits slightly forward from theirs."

Max did not question the witness other than to ask if he could see if the curtains in the drawing room windows were closed, if they were fully open or only partially. Joshua MacCallum said he was not able to see because of the location of the houses, as he just had explained previously.

The advocate depute called two more witnesses before lunch. The first was the dustman who picked up the bins outside the Tays' house. He testified that he had picked up the bin at Lady Tay's house the morning after the murder was announced in the press and had taken it to the police station without going through it. He had been watching a crime investigation series on the television and thought he might help. The Crown then summoned a forensic technician, who testified that two of the bottles found in the dustbin had Lord Tay's fingerprints on them.

The Crown then asked that since it was now half past twelve whether the forensic technician could continue testifying after lunch.

The judge agreed and called a two-hour lunch recess.

Johnnie was led out of the courtroom before any of the others left. The media was a fast second, rushing to file the latest news. Max, his attending clerk, and Elspeth lingered behind. Elspeth looked over to the corner where Pamela Crumm and Richard had been sitting, but they were gone.

They adjourned to Max's chambers and found lunch waiting for them. Elspeth was grateful it did not include sandwiches, far too many of which she had eaten in Scotland recently, but rather a hot meal of curried chicken, rice pilaf, a fresh green salad and hot, freshly brewed coffee of recognisable quality.

As they settled into their meal, Max turned to Elspeth. "Tell me where we are in your view," he said.

Elspeth swallowed a crisp bite of rocket, sharply dressed, and enjoyed the tartness. "The Crown is, of course, showing every possible way that Johnnie could have been on the scene, but all the evidence could just as easily be planted, which I think you can show, don't you, Max?"

"I hope so. Hamish has been very clever in using witnesses who are unsophisticated, and therefore the jury won't suspect them of lying. I've no way of discrediting them, and therefore I didn't cross-examine them with any thoroughness, as you saw. Elspeth, tell me your take on the jury."

"So far, I find the women are mainly sympathetic to Louisa. Several have glared at Johnnie, and others, particularly the older ones, looked in their laps when the pregnancy was mentioned."

"Prudish?"

"Yes, perhaps. I don't know whether they don't like sex openly talked about or if they consider Johnnie reprehensible for his treatment of Louisa."

"And the young woman on the end?"

"She is thinking about something else, probably her boyfriend. Johnnie must seem a relic to her."

"And the men?"

"The one at the other end, the older man with the large moustache, seems sympathetic to Johnnie; the others probably haven't decided. Two are taking copious notes, including the one in the smart business suit with the trendy wire frame glasses. He seems the most intelligent of the lot."

"You might talk to him when you address the jury," Max's clerk suggested.

Elspeth said, "Try the woman in the back row in the middle, the one with the curly hair. She's the only one of the women who looked more thoughtful and serious than shocked."

Max leaned back in his chair. "So far our odds are not good. Are you two ready for some fireworks this afternoon? Let's let Hamish MacDonnell finish his case and then we will change the minds of the jurors." Max absolutely beamed as he said this.

Elspeth sensed Max was in his strongest element.

35

Perth, Outside the Courtroom, the previous evening and Day 1 of the Trial

Richard Munro had, out of love for his wife and loyalty to Johnnie, accompanied Elspeth to Perth for the trial, but he felt superfluous. Elspeth had spent most of the evening before with Maxwell Douglas-Forbes. Richard had invited Biddy to dine with him, but despite their efforts in making polite conversation, their minds were both occupied with the forthcoming trial and not on social niceties. Finally they resorted to a companionable silence. When Elspeth returned to the hotel well after ten, Biddy had retired to her room in the suite where they were staying. Although Elspeth normally exuded complete self-confidence, Richard had learned that she was often taken by doubt, and when in this emotional state she became quiet. She hardly spoke as she sipped the decaf coffee she had ordered, and he could feel her tension. He sat quietly and respected her silence. In his past experience, she eventually spoke what was on her mind, particularly if she was not pressed by him.

She set her cup on the table, rose and came over beside him. Still not speaking, she took his hand and put it to her cheek.

Then she said, "Max and I think we know who killed Louisa, but the only way we will ever prove it is if the murderer confesses. That's the devilish thing about this case. Curtain cords do not leave blood on a murder's hand nor do

356

they retain fingerprints. Max and I are purposely leaving you, Johnnie and Biddy in the dark. You must feel slighted, but if we are successful in the possible coup we are planning, you'll all be delighted, and Johnnie will walk free. If not, we don't want to raise your hopes."

She slept restlessly beside him, seeking no solace. She left early for Max's chambers, and he knew her mind was there and not with him, but he regretted her absence.

He entered the courtroom soon after it was first open to the public.

Richard immediately spied Pamela Crumm, who had seated herself in one corner of the visitor's section where she could best see the jury's benches. It became obvious to Richard that she was trying to look inconspicuous. She might have succeeded because of her small size, but the obvious richness of her clothing and uniqueness of her black round spectacles had turned several heads as they entered the courtroom. Richard crossed the room and sat down beside her. She looked up, smiled, and put her hand in his.

"Richard, my dear," she whispered, "do you think Elspeth can pull this one off?"

Richard as always amused at Pamela's use of language. "Pull this one off?" he said with a twinkle in his eye.

She laughed. "I never know whether to trust Elspeth completely. She has a way of turning things about when one least expects it. Surely you have noticed that?"

Richard chortled. "Far too frequently. Sometimes it exasperates me, but more often amuses me now that I have learned there's no malice in it."

"Then stay sitting by me, Richard. Let's see what your wife and the renowned Mr Maxwell Douglas-Forbes, QC, can

357

do to make my investment worthwhile."

They watched the morning proceedings with all its technicalities. Neither could avoid the close consultations between Max and Elspeth when there was a break in the testimony. Elspeth had taken a seat in the first row of the visitor's section in close proximity to Max's position at the advocates' table. Richard knew Elspeth's doubts about success were greater than she was showing. He watched her frowns and saw her rub her temple as she often did when perturbed. Max's demeanour carried more gravitas and less open emotion. Max exuded competence, and Richard did not know him well enough to know it this was only a pretence.

Just before the lunch break came, Pamela asked Richard to take her out of the courtroom and to lunch at The Royal James Hotel, which, like the Perth Sheriff Court building, lay along the banks of the River Tay. Pamela had booked a table beforehand in a secluded corner, the waiter offered suggestions for their luncheon but no menu, and no bill was presented at the end. Richard suspected Pamela had paid generously to have the table held until the moment of her arrival, no matter how late the court might adjourn that morning. Pamela was charming throughout the meal, they shared superficial chatter about many mutual acquaintances, and neither mentioned the trial, although their minds were never far from it. As they strolled back along the River Tay, Pamela broke their self-imposed silence.

"Was I rash, Richard, to have wagered so much money on Lord Tay's innocence? You have known him a long time. Do you think Mr Douglas-Forbes will get him off? Elspeth has put great store in Johnnie's innocence, and I've learned to trust her judgement, but I can't read the dour faces of your countrymen well enough to know if they will be adversely influenced by his title or the fact that Louisa was having his child when she was murdered. It's all too lurid, even for someone who enjoys tittle-tattle as much as I do."

Richard honoured Pamela's great friendship with Elspeth when he replied. "She told me that she and Max think they know who committed the murder, but that proving it will be difficult."

"Isn't it true that in Scottish law that a case can be 'not proven' and the accused will be let free and not have to face another trial? I've read several novels where that happened."

"Yes, but the stigma always remains. I'm sure Elspeth doesn't want that for Johnnie, nor do any of us close to him."

They walked on a way in silence, Pamela's arm in Richard's. "Then," she said, "we will have to put our trust in both Elspeth and Maxwell Douglas-Forbes. I like him, you know. Let's get back before the courtroom becomes crowded, and reclaim our seats."

*

When Madeline MacNaughton first received the subpoena, she thought it must be from Maxwell Douglas-Forbes, and therefore was disconcerted to find she had been called by the Crown and not by the defence. She rang Max immediately.

"How did they know about me and Johnnie?" she wailed. "I thought you said I wouldn't need to testify. Did you tell them about us, Max?"

Max had expected this reaction when the procurator fiscal had approached him about the subpoena earlier. During the intervening months between the murder and the trial, Max had only superficially approved of Elspeth's idea that Madeline contact Johnnie at the farm to discuss his business, but Max had softened to the love affair between his client and this intense but vulnerable younger woman, and finally conceded with grace to the arrangement Elspeth had suggested. After Johnnie's meetings and phone conversations with her, he was always more cooperative, and his spirits perked up enormously. Max could not hide from Madeline, however, that her visits had come to the attention of the procurator fiscal. Adair had called Max and wanted to know who the femme fatale was who visited Lord Tay on a regular basis. Max made excuses that Madeline was a business associate, but rather gave the game away when he had requested that Madeline only be called if her testimony proved essential to the Crown's case. Adair chuckled at the request, stating that Madeline might only be a business associate but the interaction between Johnnie and Madeline suggested more. Max had to concede but asked that Madeline be treated with the courtesy of an honest but perhaps hostile witness.

*

Madeline was called to testify on the first day of the trial and sat in the small, airless witness room off the courtroom. She sank into her own thoughts. The first time she visited Max's office, she committed herself to Johnnie's defence. The hours she had spent with Johnnie discussing his business, but fearing to speak about their future, had cemented her resolve, but now that the moment of the trial was here, now that her public testimony was about to become part of the stop press of the day, and now that her parents and husband would hear the truth, Madeline knew she could not turn back, even had she wanted to.

She let her eyes roam around the witness room and tried to remove her feelings from the place. Her own testimony, sworn before Almighty God, would establish that Johnnie was not with her at midnight, and had only arrived at her flat at two o'clock. When he had arrived, she would testify that he was in no way agitated, but the jury might consider that was Madeline's own impression, not the true one. Was there a way to convince them otherwise? Max had instructed her to tell only the minimum of facts, to answer the advocate depute directly but never to expand on the question. 'Yes' or 'no' was best; a short phrase or sentence directly answering the question but no more was acceptable. Max had assured Madeline that he would object to any questions that allowed the prosecution to badger her. She leaned back against the wall and steeled herself. The worst had been telling her parents, but they were surprisingly understanding. Her father had even chuckled, saying he thought it odd that for the last year Madeline took so many walks up above the loch, a place that never had attracted her before. Her mother tittered a bit, and then came over and hugged her, saying she was old enough to make her own decisions and she hoped this was the right one. Now Madeline had to admit to the entire population of Britain that she and Johnnie were lovers, not just business associates. Perhaps the advocate depute's use of language would make this admission easier, not 'lovers' but perhaps 'intimates. Bah, Madeline thought, this is the twenty-first century. Women do have lovers, but she still was not sure she wanted to have herself bandied about in the media as the paramour of the 'murderous earl'.

At half past twelve, a policewoman came in with a plate of sandwiches and a mug of tea. Madeline sipped the tea, which had too much sugar, and nibbled at a sandwich, but she had no appetite to finish. How much longer did she need to be here? How much longer before she committed herself irrevocably to Johnnie, whether he was convicted or not? How much longer now? The tea left a saccharine taste, and the sandwich became putty in her mouth.

By two o'clock Madeline's energy level slumped, and she asked the woman police constable if she could use the ladies' room, anything to get out of the stifling room.

At half past two Madeline was called. She rose, squared her shoulders, and walked, as if to the gallows, to face the jury and possibly condemn Johnnie to life imprisonment.

36

Max always relished the moment when he could go on the attack. The proceedings were going quite as expected. Adair Gordon's case against Johnnie was mundane, despite the brilliant deliveries of the advocate depute, and the police investigation stopped at the obvious. The Crown called its last two witnesses, the two young men who testified they had seen Lord Tay leaving Louisa's house just past midnight. Their testimony was straightforward, and Max asked if he could call them back rather than cross examining them at that moment. They were led back to their individual witness rooms.

The advocate depute then summoned one of his two last witnesses, the first being Madeline MacNaughton. She entered the courtroom, head held high and face expressionless. She tried to avoid looking at Johnnie, but her eyes met his and she smiled sadly. He looked at her pleadingly.

Hamish MacDonnell approached Madeline standing in the witness box.

"Ms MacNaughton, are you acquainted with the defendant?"

"Yes," Madeline said, following Max's advice regarding brevity.

"Did you see him on the night of the murder, or rather early the morning of the July 20th?"

"Yes."

"At what time, where, and how long?"

"At my flat outside Dundee. He arrived at two in the morning and left at half past three."

Max took a deep breath and waited for the next question.

Hamish MacDonnell was discreet.

"I won't ask the nature of your business together. Have you accurately stated the time?"

Max watched a slow flush come over Madeline's face. She looked up again at Johnnie. He frowned, then bit his lip. Max saw the jury take notice. Max hoped Madeline would answer as he had prompted her.

"I have an old clock that rings the hour," she said, her head slightly raised. "I heard Lord Tay's car as the clock was striking two."

"Were you expecting him at that hour?"

Madeline turned her head toward Max, and he gave a brief nod.

"Yes," she said and did not elaborate. Good girl, thought Max.

"How long have you known Lord Tay, Ms. Naughton?"

"A little over a year."

"When he arrived at your flat, did he seem agitated or in any way different from his normal manner when he was with you?"

"No, he seemed quite the same."

"Again, what time did he leave your flat?"

"Half past three."

The Crown rested and Max rose.

"Ms MacNaughton, can you tell us how Lord Tay was dressed when he arrived at your flat that night?"

Madeline seemed to relax under Max's questioning and smiled as if the memory were a fond one. It was raining terribly hard," she said, shedding brevity. "I took his mackintosh, which was soaking wet and hung it in the hall."

"Did he have an umbrella?"

"No, he doesn't like them."

Max wished that she had not expressed such intimate knowledge of his lordship's preferences, but he saw it as an opportunity.

"Do you remember what sort of car he was driving?"

"I'm not certain. Probably his own, an old Sterling saloon car, but I didn't take particular notice. It was raining too hard, and I just wanted to make sure he was in safely from the weather."

Max said, "Yes, I understand. Thank you, that is all."

The Crown's last witness was Marly Beaufort. Unlike Madeline, she strode in, jaw set.

Hamish MacDonnell established her friendship with Lord Tay and the fact that he rented a flat at the back of the Beaufort's home, where he had been a tenant since leaving Louisa.

"Mrs Beaufort, did you see Lord Tay on the night of the murder, July 19th, or early on the morning of July 20th?"

"I did not," Marly said.

"Will you tell us what you saw that night, please."

Although at first telling Max she did not want to testify, Marly seemed to settle into her testimony with a certain relish at being in the spotlight. Unlike Madeline, she had not been coached to be brief.

"My husband and I were returning from a party. It was getting quite dark, so I am assuming it was close to midnight. I looked round the edge of the house and saw Johnnie's, Lord

Tay's, car in the parking space in beside the flat."

"Was that unusual? Wasn't he your tenant there?"

"Oh, yes, but he had been away, in San Francisco at a cousin's wedding. We hadn't expected him back so soon."

"But you didn't see Lord Tay in person."

"No, just his car and the lights in the flat."

"And can you tell us what sort of car?"

"It was a vintage silver Sterling saloon car."

"Which is quite unique and easily distinguishable these days," Hamish MacDonnell said. "That's all, thank you, Mrs Beaufort."

"Mr Douglas-Forbes, do you have any questions of this witness?" the judge asked.

When Max had seen Marly Beaufort's name on the Crown's witness list, he had thought a great deal about using her to his advantage, particularly in light of the strategy he and Elspeth had devised for Johnnie's defence.

He rose pompously.

"Mrs Beaufort, how long have you known Lord Tay?"

Marly Beaufort seemed surprised by the question and took a moment to think. "I should say about twelve years."

"I see," said Max. "Did you know his second wife, Helen?"

The advocate depute rose and objected. "I can't see how this has any relevance."

Max bowed to his colleague and addressed the judge. "I will connect it, m'lord, if you will allow me to proceed." The judge nodded for Max to go on.

"Can you tell me about the relationship between Lord Tay and the second Lady Tay that caused her to leave him, particularly in regard to her attempts to become pregnant."

The advocate depute rose again, but the judge waved him to sit down.

"Mr Douglas-Forbes," the judge said, "I've known for you a long time and know you undoubtedly have a point to make, but I urge you make it quickly and tie it to this murder investigation."

"Thank you. It is my intent to prove that Lord Tay's relationship with the second Lady Tay has significant ramifications in this trial, and I had hoped by questioning Mrs Beaufort about a matter important in my defence, so that I'll not have to recall her to the stand."

"Then you may proceed," the judge said.

"Mrs Beaufort, did Helen, Lord Tay's second wife, ever tell you about her attempts to become pregnant when she was married to Lord Tay?"

Marly Beaufort turned and looked directly at Elspeth, who raised her head without expression and looked directly back at her.

"Helen told me that she and Johnnie had tried to have a child by IVF but it didn't succeed. She blamed herself."

The advocate depute rose and said, "This is hearsay, m'lord."

"Objection sustained."

Max changed his tack. "When did you last see her?"

"About five years ago. She left Johnnie shortly afterwards."

"Thank you, Mrs Beaufort. I have no further questions," Max said.

Hamish MacDonnell then rested his case. The jury, all of whom nodded, contented with what they had heard from him, but they all had looks of bafflement regarding Max's latest round of questioning despite being told to disregard it.

From the advocates' table Max looked at them one by one, allowing about ten seconds for each face. None of them looked directly back at him, which was usual. Finally he rose.

"I would like to begin my case by cross examining several of the Crown's witnesses," he said. "First I would like to call Ron Dawes back from the witness room. If you remember Ron was the first of the two eyewitnesses."

Ron was brought in by a police constable and entered the witness box with the same smirk he had worn during his original testimony.

Max walked up to the witness box and stood at a distance that he calculated would make Ron uncomfortable.

He began, "When I read the original police report, I noted that you said the morning after the murder that your address was in Dundee. Is that correct?"

Ron squirmed," Yeah, but I've moved since then to Leith, so my new address is the one I gave today."

Max read off an address in Dundee. "Was that your lodging at the time you gave your report to the police in June?"

"Yeah," Ron said, his eyes shifting to the side.

"Thank you for confirming that," Max said, and walked back several steps. "Now, Mr Dawes, you said on the night of the murder you saw Lord Tay coming out of the side gate of a building on the street where the victim lived. Why were you on that street then?

Ron relaxed slightly, "Me and me mate were at a party a few streets up."

Max nodded and smiled. Had Ron been a better observer, at that point he should have become wary. "What street?" Max asked.

"I don't know. I went there with me mate to a party of some of his friends."

"At his friends' home," Max said, as if he were trying to understand correctly. It was a strategy he often used when attempting to plant a fact in the jurors' minds. "Was it a large party?"

"Large enough," Ron said without quantification.

"Ten people? Twenty?"

Ron wiped his hand across his chin. "Maybe twenty."

Max turned away from Ron and then back towards him. "Who held the party?"

"A friend of me mate. I don't know his name." Max could feel Ron's discomfort level grow.

"Did you drink a lot?"

"Not much. I was driving. A beer or two."

"Ah," said Max. "So when you were crossing the street where the murder took place, you saw quite clearly the man come out of the side gate of the house."

"Yeah." Ron seemed to be regaining some of his composure, and the cockiness came back. Max thought he was now reaching the part of Ron's story that had been rehearsed.

"Do you see the man you saw that night in the courtroom today?"

Ron's eyes became a trifle mean, and he pointed to Johnnie. "That's him."

Max said. "You sound quite sure. Will you describe him to the jury as you saw him on the night of the murder, please."

Ron repeated almost verbatim what was in the police report.

"Are you sure he was not wearing a mackintosh and was

not carrying an umbrella?"

"Yeah. Just like I said."

Max walked back to his table and picked up a piece of paper, which he pretended to read, although he knew the contents thoroughly. He returned his attention to Ron. "It was raining on and off that evening. He didn't have any protection against the rain?"

Ron moved in his chair. "I don't remember."

"You said he was wearing dark trousers. Do you remember the exact colour? Blue? Black? Brown?" Max asked casually.

"I don't remember. I couldn't quite tell. One of those."

"Why was that?"

"Colours is a bit hard to make out under a streetlight."

"Yes, I have always found that to be so," Max said in agreement. "And yet you are sure his eyes were dark blue and not brown, and his hair light brown and not auburn?"

Ron looked away from Max and the jury. "I told you."

Max came right up to the witness stand. "I think you are lying, Mr Dawes."

And then, knowing the judge might not approve of his last comment, Max said, "That will be all."

Max watched the jurors as Ron was led from the courtroom. Several looked baffled, and Max hoped they were recollecting their own experiences with colour under streetlights at night and Madeline's previous testimony.

Max's questioning of Jake Jones, the other eyewitness, took a different turn, but in doing so Max led the witness in a direction he planned to pursue later.

He moved around to the end of his table but stood back from the witness this time.

"Mr Jones, are you currently a resident of Edinburgh?"

Jake was more sophisticated than his companion and eyed Max suspiciously.

"Yeah."

"At this address?" Max read the address in the police report. Jake assented.

"How long have you lived there?" Max's tone was bland.

"Oh, I don't know, maybe a year, maybe more." Jake did not squirm like Ron, but he looked down at his closely bitten fingernails, as if wishing to pare them down them further.

"Are you employed?" Max asked.

"On and off."

"On the night you saw a man come out of the side gate of the house where the murder was committed were you employed?"

"Probably not. I don't quite remember." These remarks had not been rehearsed.

"Probably not? Please answer yes or no. You are under oath." Max's tone became severe.

Jake swallowed. "I was temporarily out of work," he said.

Max knew he had the witness on the defensive. "On the weekend after the murder you were seen splashing a lot of cash in several bars in Edinburgh. How do you account for that?" Kaitlin Logan had discovered this fact and was willing to testify, although Max hoped he could avoid her doing so, at least on this point.

"It was my birthday," he said.

Max rotated on the ball of his feet toward the jurors. "Did someone give the money to you to report you had seen Lord Tay coming out of the side gate when you were nowhere nearby?" Max roared.

The advocate depute rose and objected to Max leading the witness. The judge was upheld the challenge, but Max knew he had cemented his point in the jury's mind.

"No further questions for the moment, but I would like to call back both of these witnesses at a later date." Max returned to his table and began to thumb through his notes. He had planted his first seeds so as to discredit the Crown's case, but he knew that would not be good enough to prove Johnnie's innocence. In order to start building his own case, he called another witness, a forensic technician from the police, whose name was Norman Smith.

Max drew back from the aggressive stance he had taken with the eyewitnesses. He stood at the far side of the advocates' table, rather than approaching the witness box. He needed exact information from the technician and had no fear that he would lie.

"Mr Smith, did you make a thorough examination of the victim's house in the course of your gathering evidence after the crime?"

Norman Smith acknowledged he had. Since the Crown had already established the state of the drawing room, the condition of Louisa's body as it was found, and the clothes she was wearing at the time of the murder, Max moved further afield.

"Did you make a complete inventory of the contents of the victim's residence?"

"A photographic one."

"Did that include all her personal effects?"

"Yes, sir, we photographed all the rooms, including the clothes cupboards, and even the larder."

"Did you examine any of the spaces where the victim kept

medicines?'

"Yes, there were several bottles of tablets on the countess's dressing table."

"Did you make a list of them?"

"Yes."

Max went back to his files and drew out a piece of paper.

"Is this the complete list of the medicines?"

Max handled the paper to his clerk, who took it over to the witness.

Norman Smith read through it and looked up. "You can see my initials at the bottom of the page confirming that's correct."

Max then said, "The pathologist has testified that the victim had no medicines in her system at the time of death. That being the case, did you note when each of the medicines was dispensed and how many tablets of each had been taken?"

"The number of tablets remaining has been included in my report, also the name of the dispensary. I'm sure they'll have the records that will verify the prescriptions."

Max asked that the list of medicines be recorded. As the procurator fiscal had already seen the list and knew Max had put it in evidence, he nodded to the advocate depute to make no objection.

"There's one more thing of a more general nature. How long do fingerprints last generally?" Max asked.

Norman Smith knit his eyebrows. "There's no exact rule. It all depends on the surface the fingerprint is on and what oils or other materials might be on the fingers when they were laid on the surface. They can last for years."

"Exactly," said Max, without explaining himself further. "Thank you for your thoroughness. You're a credit to the

Tayside Police."

Norman Smith beamed and stepped down from the stand.

"I am adjourning the court until tomorrow afternoon," the judge said, and rose. All followed.

37

After she testified, on Max's advice, Madeline had asked for a police escort out of the courtroom, held up her large handbag up to avoid the many cameras and was whisked by a police car out beyond the courthouse. The police constable, a sympathetic young woman, drove Madeline back to the police station, where earlier she had parked in the visitor's car park. Not being able to face the possibility of being pursued, she asked to come into the station and wait to see if anyone had followed them from the court. One reporter had, but soon became bored when Madeline did not emerge. After half an hour he left his vigil, and Madeline assumed he had retreated back to his post at the courthouse. Where now? Having given her testimony, she was torn between fleeing and staying close to hear the minute-to-minute progression of the trial. She wanted someone to talk to, but no one came to mind other than Elspeth, who was otherwise engaged. Everything about her life had now been altered. She had left her job and all of its security when she had committed herself to keep Johnnie's business afloat as he lingered at the farm. If he were convicted, that link could be broken as well.

Her mind went back to the courtroom. While testifying, she felt the hostility of the jury as she stood across from them, her back aching with its rigidity, facing the advocate depute and later Max. Johnnie sat at the edge of her vision, but she

375

had looked around at him several times, briefly taking in his gaunt face and agonised expression. She did not see his love, only his anxiety and plea to her. Had she answered the questions sufficiently to help him, or had what she said only laid down the foundations for his conviction? She had no idea, and the loneliness of her thoughts overwhelmed her. She wanted time to fly to the end of the trial, but she recognised the moments would crawl and leave her depleted.

She left the police station an hour later, headed out of Perth and chose the road to Scone rather than the main route to Dundee. Her car spun out on a bend as she tried to overtake a slow-moving lorry, and hit a tree full force, smashing the windscreen and knocking Madeline into oblivion, a state she might have desired but not one she necessarily would have chosen. Her last thoughts were 'Wretched lorry!' The police did not find her for half an hour. The lorry driver had gone on to Scone and there reported the accident after expostulating on the driving habits of young women these days.

*

At the hotel where she, Richard, and Elspeth were staying, Biddy Baillie Shaw spent most of the day with her mind in distress, but by afternoon she could no longer tolerate the confinement of the suite and went for a walk along the River Tay. The broad promenade was normally the choice of the desultory population or lunchtime meanders, but today Biddy marched up it and down again as if on parade. She must have been mumbling to herself, as several passers-by turned their heads. Although her shoulder was now healed, on wet days, such as this one, it caused her pain, and the agony of not being at the trial exacerbated it. Yet Max had advised her that, if all did not work out as he and Elspeth had planned, he might have to call her as a witness, thus barring her from being in the courtroom beforehand. This exclusion seemed sensible enough when Max had proposed it, but it did not assuage her concern for Johnnie's fate.

Biddy had not only come to love Max over the last two months but also to see his skills as an advocate. When Elspeth had returned to the hotel the night before, after she had spent most of the afternoon and evening sequestered with Max in his chambers, she conveyed a sense of confidence that heartened Biddy, but Elspeth had been evasive as to what to expect the next day in court. While waiting for Elspeth, Richard and Biddy had made polite conversation for much of the evening, without listening to their own words much less those of each other. Biddy finally pleaded fatigue and retired to her room.

As she lay in bed, she thought of Max and the times they had been together. He had awakened in her all the passions that she had once shared with Ivor and all the tenderness that exists between a man and a woman when they love each other. Two nights ago, as she had lain beside him, he had told her the story of his wife's desertion and her death, his own sense of guilt over having neglected her in favour of his career, and the grief that still filled him when he thought of her. Biddy had listened closely and carefully, without comment, and then made love to him quietly rather than ardently, for which he seemed grateful. In the morning she thanked him for his trust in her and assured him that what he had told her was safe with her. He held her for a long time and then let her go.

Walking swiftly along the promenade, Biddy knew Max would now turn his attention to the trial. The time had come for her to put complete trust in his other self, the tough advocate, with a reputation of melting juries and ending trials with fireworks that exonerated his clients. Biddy had never seen this side of Max and was agonised by the fact that she was being held back from doing so now.

The wind blew off the river and a shower passed. She took refuge in a tobacconist's shop doorway off the main thoroughfare and saw the stop press. *Murdered Countess Pregnant* the scrawled handwritten news sheet read. Biddy ground her teeth and snarled to herself. She took out her umbrella, destroyed the poster and retreated to the hotel. It was now three o'clock, and she expected the court would not adjourn for another hour and a half. She went to the hotel tearoom and ordered a pot of tea, but let it cool without sipping it. The waitress came to ask if the tea was satisfactory, and she just shook her head. "It's quite all right," she said, but she did not know if things were 'quite all right' or not. She would have to have faith in Max, as well as Elspeth. Not knowing what was happening at court was agonising. She went back to the suite and took up a book she had been reading but did not remember anything about the plot or characters. She did not want to turn on the television and hear any news of the trial second hand. Instead she rose and stared out of the window at the river below. She did not know how long the trial was expected to last, but she had heard that Scottish trials were always expedited, unlike their American or English counterparts. A few days? A week? Perhaps two? How long could she go on staring at the river and fretting? She leaned against the wall of the deep-set window and wished it were over, for better or for worse.

*

Richard Munro and Pamela Crumm lingered after the courtroom emptied, waiting until only Max, his clerk, and

Elspeth remained in the room. The three were deep in hushed conversation, their faces serious, but when Pamela and Richard came close, they looked up. Elspeth's face lightened as she saw her husband and her close friend, and she introduced Max and his clerk to Pamela, remembering that Max had never met her in person. The clerk made excuses and left the four of them alone.

"I propose," Pamela said, making her words sound more like a finality than a proposal, "that we all adjourn for dinner. I'm staying at our hotel in Edinburgh and have a car waiting to take me back there after dinner, but in the meantime I have made arrangements for a private room at the Royal James, and I won't take no for an answer. Elspeth, you look as if you need some sustenance, and Mr Douglas-Forbes, I feel I need to get to know you better."

Max bowed most elegantly. "Ms Crumm, as you are so strongly invested in Johnnie's predicament, I can hardly refuse."

Elspeth frowned at Pamela. "I think this might not be an appropriate . . . ," Elspeth began.

"Nonsense," said Pamela.

The corner of Richard's mouth quivered with amusement. His wife had a strong will, but he suspected Pamela, after years of having been badgered by Lord Kennington, could hold her own against the best and most certainly against Elspeth's objection. Richard watched Elspeth and saw her raise her head in protest and then concede with a humorous smile.

Pamela turned to Max. "Can Biddy Baillie Shaw join us?"

Max shook his head. "I think it best Biddy stay at the hotel, as I may have to call her to the stand tomorrow, and, Ms

379

Crumm, you still have a great deal of money resting on the reliable testimony of the witnesses."

Pamela chuckled. "I'll take your good advice. As you have pointed out, I do have some interest in this."

Pamela's car and driver were waiting outside and took them directly to the restaurant. Elspeth rang the hotel and, when Biddy did not come to the phone, Elspeth left a message, saying she and Richard would return after dinner, but, after she admitted she regretted that Biddy was not included, she turned off her mobile phone during dinner and neglected to leave another message for Biddy saying she could not be reached.

*

After they finished their meal, Elspeth said, "I suppose, Pamela, since you have given us a most delightful meal, we should all allow you to have a good night's sleep and will see you tomorrow in court." They bid Pamela goodnight, and Max offered to drive Richard and Elspeth back to their hotel. As they drove out along the quiet streets, Elspeth searched in her shoulder bag and dug out her mobile. She tapped in the voice mail retrieval button and was horrified as she listened to the three frantic messages from Biddy.

"Oh, no!" Elspeth cried, her face contorting in disbelief. "Madeline! No!" She paused, looking at Richard and Max's faces.

"Biddy said Madeline has smashed her car into a tree. She's alive but unconscious. They took her to hospital in Dundee."

"Damn," said Max.

Richard thought for a moment and said, "Let me go to Madeline. You two stay with Biddy at the hotel."

"I'm coming with you, Dickie," Elspeth said. He knew too well the recalcitrance in her voice and did not argue. "Max, I think you can help Biddy most by being with her."

Richard retrieved their hired car from the car park at the back of the hotel and pulled it around to the front, where he found Elspeth waiting. He had spent most of his career in places where he had a driver at his disposal, and one of them had instructed him in the fine art of driving well beyond the posted limits and the precautions one needed to negotiate around slower traffic, come out of a skid, and, if necessary elude pesky traffic enforcers. As they sped down the motorway towards Dundee, Elspeth hung on to the strap by her seat and gulped more than once as he displayed these skills, which she confessed she did not know he possessed. Richard, by nature, was calm in emergencies, which had contributed greatly to his professional success, but inside he was delighting in at last having something to do other than sit on the side-lines.

"You must be well aware how much is resting on Madeline's recovery, for Johnnie's sake if not for her own," Elspeth gasped, as he sped past a car.

"Absolutely," he said. "We need to be back in the courtroom by ten in the morning, and we need to decide what to tell Johnnie."

"Dickie, why would Madeline do this?" He glanced over and saw the set of her jaw. "Do you really think it was an accident? Please, Dickie," she said with a gulp as he swerved in front of a lorry.

"Fear not, Lady MacDuff. I shall get thee to Dundee in no time, provided that thee unravelleth the mystery."

"If we get there at this pace without mishap and find Madeline conscious," she said. She closed her eyes as he skirted around another lorry and sped past a tradesman's van.

*

Max, perhaps more than Elspeth, realised what a profound effect Madeline's accident, if that were what it was, would have on Johnnie. He found Biddy in the suite, pacing up and down beside the table set out for her dinner which lay uneaten.

"Max," she cried, staring up at him, grief filling her eyes "Oh, Max!"

He took her in his arms, and she did not withdraw. He stroked her hair and then kissed her. He might lose Johnnie's case, but he had no intention of losing Biddy Baillie Shaw, after all they had shared together in the last few months. He hoped desperately that she would not regret her affair with him after the trial ended and that she might consider making their relationship permanent under the law.

Finally he took her over to the sofa and firmly set her down.

"What does all this mean?" she asked.

He sat down beside her and touched her now tousled hair.

"It means we must hope that no one," she said "but you, Elspeth, Richard, and I tell anyone what happened to Madeline tonight. Johnnie most of all cannot be told. It will destroy the little confidence he still has. The Crown may have been gentle on Madeline today, but the press tonight will not be."

Biddy's face saddened. "Alice MacNaughton would not have rung me if she was unaware of Madeline's relationship with Johnnie. She had to convince Uncle James that her business was serious enough to warrant him giving her my mobile number. Yes, you're right, they have a great deal to lose, both for their daughter and their own standing in the community. I never particularly liked Alice, even at school, but I admire her courage in letting me know about Madeline. I suppose if Johnnie is found innocent and marries Madeline, I'll have to get used to the MacNaughtons being part of the family."

Max knew by now that Biddy seldom spoke unkindly of others, but he could not help noticing that a small grimace crossed her face.

*

Biddy slept restively after Max left her, her emotions piling one on the other, for Johnnie, for Madeline, for the MacNaughtons, and also for Max. The numbers on the bedside digital clock turned over slowly, and it was well past three o'clock when she heard the key in the lock. She grabbed her dressing gown at the foot of the bed, wrestled it over her silk pyjamas and came into the sitting room, looking tired but relieved that Elspeth and Richard had returned.

"How is she?" Biddy asked.

"The doctors say she'll recover but will have some permanent scars. Her face was badly lacerated, but that can be repaired with reconstructive surgery. She has two enormous black eyes and has broken several ribs, both of which will heal quickly," Richard said.

"It was rather like old times. Here we are all here rescuing Johnnie once again," Richard said with a wry smile.

Biddy looked up at Richard and her cousin. Tears came to her eyes, and she knew this was enough thanks for their efforts.

38

Max always thought carefully about sequencing his witnesses. The element of surprise played an important part in breaking down the Crown's case, but the logical building of the defence was equally important. Although he normally made his own decisions in a trial, he had spoken to Elspeth at length about their strategy two evenings ago. He admired the way her mind worked, and she had been responsible for devising one of the main arguments in Johnnie's favour. They had decided to play her trump card first. He first called the chemist who dispensed the medicines. He confirmed that the tablets identified in Louisa's home had been brought to his dispensary seven months before the murder. He produced copies of the prescriptions, but Max did not at that point read them out to the jury. Before naming the medicines, he would call the next witness, who had been responsible for the writing of the prescriptions.

The jury turned as a smart, middle-aged woman entered the courtroom.

"Will you tell us your name and position, please," Max asked.

"I am Dr Joan Nicholson, director of the Edinburgh Assisted Conception Unit, which is a part of the Royal Infirmary there."

The woman instantly became a credible witness.

"How long have you held that position, Dr Nicholson?"

384

Max asked.

"Four years," she answered.

"Did the victim in this trial contact you six months ago?"

"Yes."

"How did she identify herself to you?"

"As the Countess of Tay."

"Did you have any record that the countess had been a client of your clinic before?'

"Yes. Six years ago the Earl and Countess of Tay began the procedure of in-vitro fertilization, IVF as we call it. At the time it wasn't successful."

"Did you store the earl's sperm at your clinic at the time?"

"Yes."

"And is that sperm still existing?'

"Yes, in frozen form."

"Ms Nicholson, you weren't at the clinic at the time. Did you check the records when the countess came to your clinic?"

"Yes, of course. We're always very thorough."

"Were you aware that the Countess of Tay who presented herself to you was not the same Countess of Tay who had been there six years before?"

"Most certainly." The director looked shocked that it might be otherwise. "Sperm donors who have a noble background are scrutinized particularly thoroughly these dyas. Our business is prey to women wishing a good paternity for their future child."

"How did you verify the victim's relationship to Lord Tay?"

"She had a copy of their marriage certificate. She was quite honest that she was not Helen Tay, but rather Louisa

Tay, but that she and Lord Tay had tried to conceive with no results. She asked if perhaps his frozen sperm were more as she put it 'virile', that she would have a better chance."

"Was Lord Tay with her?"

"No. There was another man, who said he was their legal counsel. He produced a paper signed by Lord Tay that matched our signatures in the files."

"I see," said Max. "What was the man's name?"

Dr Nicholson consulted her notes. "Paul Hodges."

"Ah," said Max, as if he had not already known the name. "Will you describe him to us?"

"Of course. I was rather amazed at his appearance. We, of course, deal with solicitors all the time, since often our treatment is highly confidential. Mr Hodges was not what I expected."

"Will you describe his physical appearance."

"I will. He was small and thin, badly dressed, particularly for a man of the legal profession, and had rather oily, badly cut, dark hair. I noticed he had long fingers, but the nails were not well manicured. Why that should make any difference, I don't know."

Max admired her attention to detail.

"Dr Nicholson, I have two photographs here which have been entered in evidence. Will you tell me if either one is Mr Hodges?"

Joan Nicholson took the photographs, examined them and handed one back to Max.

"This is Mr Hodges," she said, holding up one of the pictures.

"Are you certain?"

"Yes," she said. "I'm positive."

Max surveyed the jury briefly and saw their interest perk up.

"Now, will you tell us what treatment Louisa received at your clinic?" he asked.

"We were concerned that the pregnancy with Lord Tay's wife, Helen, had failed, and therefore were careful in prescribing a course of treatment for Lord Tay's new wife. We prescribed the usual drugs and were delighted when a month and a half later, after Louisa had come back for final implantation, they produced the intended results."

"Then Louisa became pregnant from the sperm Lord Tay had left frozen in the clinic eight years before?"

"Yes. As successful as we usually are, we are always delighted when we know the treatment brings the desired results."

"Did the victim visit the clinic again?"

"Yes, about two months after her pregnancy was confirmed. She seemed healthy at the time, but we requested that she come back periodically. She never did, which is highly unusual."

"Thank you, Dr Nicholson," Max said and, raising a quizzical eyebrow, turned to the advocate depute. Hamish MacDonnell looked as bewildered as the jury, but Max saw he was not pleased.

Max and Elspeth had talked at length about calling Kaitlin Logan as a witness, and Max's inclination to do so had prevailed. When Kaitlin was shown into the courtroom, she was dressed as conservatively as Max had ever seen her, in a trim, navy blue trouser suit, and white, polo-necked jumper, and she wore a gold chain necklace with a single pearl and pearl stud earrings. She had brown hair today, which suited her skin more than either the red or black she had sported before. Max suspected the colour was close to her original shade. As Kaitlin entered the witness box, she nodded to each juror, giving each a small smile, as she took up her stance. They seemed to warm to her.

Max came from behind his table and addressed her. "Ms Logan, you are in my employ, are you not?"

He had counselled Kaitlin to be brief.

"Yes," she said.

"Last July, did I ask you to explore the divorce and marriage records of Lord Tay?"

"Yes."

"Will you please tell the jury how you did this and what you discovered."

"I went to New Register House in Edinburgh, at your suggestion, and researched Lord Tay, Helen Tay and Louisa Boyd."

"Will you please explain to the jury who Louisa Boyd is, or rather was."

"The woman who called herself Louisa Tay, the victim in this trial."

"Tell the court what you found?"

"I will. In examining the files for Lord Tay, I found that there was no official record that he had divorced his second wife, Helen, and that his marriage certificate to Louisa Boyd had never been filed."

Max turned to the jury as he addressed Kaitlin. "Are you suggesting that Lord Tay and Louisa Boyd were not married?"

"I'm suggesting nothing. I'm only reporting what I found at New Register House in July. I'm afraid it's a lack of evidence rather than proof." Kaitlin delivered her last line convincingly, although Max insisted that she rehearse it several times before in his chambers until she got the right tone.

"Your lordship, I request that this witness step down, unless the Crown has further questions, but I want to call her later," Max said.

Next Max called Cecilia Clarke, a mousy woman who seemed rather agitated.

Max treated her gently. "Mrs Clarke, will you tell us what your current employment position is?"

Cecilia Clark shifted from one foot to the other and said with a squeak, "I work for the New Register House in Edinburgh helping people find family records."

"And on Wednesday, July 25th of this year did a woman approach you about the records of John Edward Charles Robertson, Lord Tay."

"Yes, sir. Lord Tay and also his wife, Helen Tay."

"Did you find record of their marriage and divorce?"

"The marriage was recorded. There was no record of the divorce."

Max raised his large head, smiled reassuringly toward Cecilia Clarke, and saw her face soften. He waited for a moment, trying to assess what his next question might raise in the minds of the jurors.

"Ms Clarke, had anyone else in the last three or four months asked the same questions?"

Cecilia Clarke straightened herself in the witness box. Max had warned her that he would ask this question, and he had prepared her for it. Her eye caught his as if in a small triumph.

"Yes, sir. At the beginning of July."

"Can you describe the man?"

"I'll try, sir. He was small, not terribly well dressed but in a suit, and his hair was longish and greasy. I remember, because I had not put shampoo on my shopping list that morning, although I needed it."

"Thank you, Ms Clarke. I want you to look at these photographs. Do you recognise the man who asked about Lord Tay?"

Cecilia Clarke identified the photograph of Paul Hodges, and the jury took note. Suddenly Paul Hodges had shifted from a peripheral figure to a central one.

Hamish MacDonnell had stopped raising objections or demanding cross-examination. Max suspected the advocate depute was conceding to the evidence just presented, and at that moment Max knew he was close to succeeding in his defence.

"My lord," Max said to the judge, "I have several witnesses that I wish to postpone until tomorrow, but I would like to call one last witness today. Is that agreeable to you?"

The judge leaned back in his chair and studied the clock at the end of the courtroom. "Mr Douglas-Forbes, we have at least an hour remaining before we need adjourn, and I don't like to hold witnesses' testimonies overnight. You may proceed with your next witness, but I also want you to bring back Jake Jones and Ron Dawes before the end of the session today, so that they do not have to return tomorrow.

Max had not planned to do this, but he had little choice but to obey the judge's order. The last information he needed from the two supposed eyewitnesses would undoubtedly be reported in the evening press and might even make national headlines. Max had hoped to delay this until the following morning. He turned to face Elspeth and saw her concern as well. He leaned over to her, and she whispered that she would try to think of something while he questioned the next witness.

Max next called Rodney Turnbull, a mild looking man who seemed shy over being the centre of attention. He identified himself as a neighbour of Louisa Tay in Perth. He surveyed the courtroom, and his eyes rested on Elspeth, as if he knew her but could not place her. Elspeth looked blandly uninvolved, and Max chuckled because she had found the witness. Rodney Turnbull's eyes did not stray to the corner of the room where Richard and Pamela Crumm were sitting, or he might have recalled where he had seen Elspeth before.

Max's questioning was benign.

"Mr Turnbull, did you on the night of July 19th at about midnight take your dog for a walk?" Max asked.

"Yes, sir."

"How did you find the street that night? Did you see any strangers cutting across the cul-de-sac?"

"No. It was unusually quiet. I remember thinking that. In fact, I remarked on it later to a couple who was visiting from Malta several days later. When there was noise on the street, it often came from Louisa Tay's house. She was fond of entertaining in the evening. I almost miss the noise now that the house is shut up."

"Did you see lights on in the Tay house?"

Rodney Turnbull thought for a moment.

"I don't honestly remember."

"Was there anyone else in the street?"

"No, as I said it was exceptionally quiet."

391

"And how long were you out with your dog?"

"Perhaps half an hour."

"From when to when?"

"From perhaps five minutes to midnight until perhaps just after half past. I heard the bells ring midnight and then the quarter-hour and half hour."

"Did you see Lord Tay at any time during your walk?"

"No."

"Did you see two lads who might have been coming from a party on one of the streets near you?"

"No. The dog and I walked both ways, down to the river and then back, and saw no one."

"Thank you, Mr Turnbull. That is all. If there is no cross examination, I would like a fifteen-minute recess."

The judge paused. "I'll give you ten minutes, and then I would like to meet both you and Mr MacDonnell in my chambers. I won't take long."

Max consulted Elspeth hurriedly before entering the judge's chambers. If Jake Jones and Ron Dawes had to come back, should Max play his trump card? Or should he prevail upon the judge to hold their testimony over for one more day? Elspeth opted for the latter and Max agreed, hoping he could convince the judge and the advocate depute. Max had known the judge for many years and was not sure his appeal would be honoured.

When he and Hamish MacDonnell entered the judge's chambers, the judge asked, "Where are you going with this new information, Max? I can understand you trying to discredit the eyewitnesses, but you have introduced a powerful motive for Lord Tay to murder Louisa, who, it now seems, was not his wife, and his guilt is possible, particularly in light of her pregnancy with his child, even if it was conceived by devious means. I'm sure the jury already has assumed Lord Tay and Ms MacNaughton were having an affair unless fifteen good and true Scots are completely deaf and blind, which I doubt."

"I'm trying to prove that Lord Tay was, as the Americans say, the victim of a set up. I believe Louisa's pregnancy was a way to coerce him into a business deal he did not want to pursue, but that it went wrong, and as a result Louisa was murdered by someone else."

"Do you have proof?"

Max raised his head and said, "All I have to do is raise the possibility in a majority of the jurors' minds that the case against John Tay is 'not proven'. I appeal to your lordship and you, Hamish, to let me fight my case."

"How do you propose to do that?" the judge asked.

"I plan to call a hostile witness, in the person of Mr Paul Hodges, who has been identified by several witnesses and whom I have subpoenaed. I think he may be someone who can give us some insight into Louisa's mind in the months before her murder and why she consented to go through IVF to have Johnnie's child. From what I understand from Lord Tay's family, she was a selfish person and not terribly bright, and wouldn't have agreed to the procedure unless there was sufficient compensation given to her of one sort or another. Paul Hodges was her divorce lawyer, at least towards the end, and he could have advised her on certain courses of action that later backfired and eventually led to her murder. I also believe that the reason she was killed has nothing to do with Lord Tay, and the truth will exonerate him."

The advocate depute shook his head. "I have no ill will

towards Lord Tay, my lord. If Max thinks he has something to vindicate Lord Tay, let him try. I'll offer no objection."

"Very well then," the judge said.

"Then let me begin by asking that you end today's session without my calling back Jones and Dawes. The defence will reimburse the sheriff for a hotel room for them and the police protection, as long they stay out of the clutches of the press. I want to know who paid them to lie in the first place, but I don't want the media to speculate tonight and spoil my arguments tomorrow," Max said."

When they returned to the courtroom, the judge dismissed the court for the day, and Ron Dawes and Jake Jones enjoyed an evening in the company of a police constable, who did not join them at drinks at the bar in an out-of-the-way hotel but allowed them to indulge in several quaffs.

The evening's headlines read: ***CONFLICTING EVIDENCE IN THE TAY CASE Was he really married to the victim? How did she become pregnant?***

39

Max entered the courtroom wishing that he had slept longer and better. He was less ready than he had hoped for the day's proceedings, and his mind kept drifting back to Biddy Baillie Shaw and their moments together, rather than her brother's defence. He slept beyond the protests of his alarm clock and did not have time for his morning workout, which left him sluggish, so he had drunk one more cup of coffee than usual, which made him jittery. He arrived at the courthouse, hoping to have a word with Elspeth before they entered, but she was not to be found, and only appeared a few moments before the judge appeared and the court rose. She looked as tired as he felt. Dark circles had settled under her eyes, which lacked their accustomed acuity. Yet she bore herself with assurance as she always did and only betrayed her thoughts when she glanced over to where Johnnie was sitting. He looked the worse for wear, his eyes downcast and worry traced across his face. Max now was glad he had not informed his client about Madeline's accident.

Once the jury had been seated, Max rose, straightened his large frame and began. "My lord and members of the jury, I wish to call Mr Thomas Lawton."

Thomas Lawton, a man of some self-importance who was dressed in a well-tailored business suit, was duly sworn in. Max started the day's defence by questioning Thomas Lawton's business and his standing within it. He identified himself as the senior vice president of the Perthshire Land Development Consortium in charge of land purchasing. The jury looked slightly bewildered by the reason for introducing this witness, and the judge quickly admonished Max to come to his point.

"Mr Lawton, did you at any time during the course of the last few years approach Lord Tay about purchasing the farm that he owns on Loch Tay?"

Lawton acknowledged that he had.

"And what was the reason for you wishing to acquire this land?"

"Our firm had decided we wanted to build a resort on one of the lochs, and we found Loch Tay to be one of the more beautiful ones. The Tay farm was eminently suitable as it had magnificent views of the highland peaks and a large enough area for us to build a world class golf course."

"And was your purchase successful?"

"No."

"Tell us why."

"Although Lord Tay had initially agreed to consider the offer, our legal department found that the land could not be sold."

Max nodded his head, urging Lawton to go on.

"In checking the deed to the land they found that it was part of the initial grant of peerage to the Earls of Tay and as a result could not be sold."

"And then did you give up hope of the resort on Loch Tay?"

"No. We were as eager as ever. One of our legal consultants suggested that we purchase a ninety-nine-year lease."

"Did Lord Tay agree to this?"

"No, unfortunately."

"Did you still pursue the idea?"

"Yes. The site was too good to give up on so easily. Our legal consultant did some further research and found that the reason Lord Tay had refused the offer of a lease was that he had no direct heirs and that his sister's son would inherit the peerage and farm on Lord Tay's death. His sister is the current occupant of the farm and urged Lord Tay to reconsider his idea of selling or leasing the land."

"How much do you pay your legal consultants, Mr Lawton?"

"In this case he would have received ten per cent of the purchase price. If he failed, he would get nothing."

"What price did you offer to Lord Tay for a long-term lease?"

"Ten million pounds."

"Therefore your legal consultant would have received one million pounds for his effort."

"That's correct."

"At that fee, did your legal counsel have other ideas on how you might persuade Lord Tay to accept the lease?"

"Yes."

"Will you tell us what he proposed?"

"That if Lord Tay had an heir other than his nephew, he or his legal guardian might consider the price we were offering him for the lease."

Several of the jurors looked up at the witness at the mention of the heir, and Max hoped they would begin to see the connection.

"Will you please tell us the name of your counsel?"

"His name is Paul Hodges." Max watched the jury's reaction. Only two of them gave signs that the name seemed familiar. Max would soon change this.

"Thank you, Mr Lawton."

Hamish MacDonnell had no questions for the witness.

Max walked back to his table and caught Elspeth's eye. She acknowledged the look with a slight inclination of her head.

Next Max called a Mrs Gloria MacNeil. Mrs MacNeil was obviously nervous and kept touching her hair to make sure the grips were firmly in place. It only heightened the untidiness of her appearance and the cheap cut of her clothes.

"Mrs MacNeil, will you please give us the name of your employer."

Her voice was high pitched, probably more so than usual, and she looked down at the edge of the witness box as she spoke. She had to repeat Paul Hodges name twice before it was audible.

"And in what capacity do you work for him?"

"I keep his accounts."

"And in that position, are you aware of the state of his accounts?"

Gloria MacNeil swallowed hard, exaggerating the prominent bones in her throat.

"I would rather not say."

Max drew up his impressive form. "Mrs MacNeil, may I remind you that are in a court of law and that you have sworn to tell the whole truth."

She swallowed again. "I promised not to tell anyone."

"To whom did you give that promise?"

"Mr Hodges. He threatened me that if I told anyone about

some of the accounts, I would regret it and so would my family." Her face, which with imagination did resemble that of a rabbit, became scared.

"Mrs MacNeil, you are entitled to full protection of the law. Here you must tell the truth or face prison. Tell us which accounts."

"The ones showing his debts to the man in Edinburgh."

"What was the amount of that debt?"

"About nine hundred thousand pounds."

"That's a lot of money," Max said gratuitously.

The judge brought down his gavel. "Mr Douglas-Forbes, please refrain from giving your opinion until your closing speech."

Max smiled back at the judge and turned once again to his witness, this time adjusting his demeanour to one of warmth. "I admire your courage, Mrs MacNeil. Please tell us the name of the person to whom Mr Hodges was in debt."

Gloria MacNeil seemed somewhat bolstered by Max's compliment and held her head up. "His name was Billy Bong. Odd sort of name, isn't it? I think he's from Australia."

"Thank you, Mrs MacNeil."

Hamish McDonnell approached the witness with more sympathy than Max had.

"Mrs MacNeil, do you have any copies of these accounts."

Gloria MacNeil's face sunk back into its frightened mode.

"Oh, no. I'd have been afraid to make copies." Her voice quivered.

"So we only have your word that they exist?"

"Mr Hodges knows they exist," she said. "He was forever fretting over them."

"Fretting? How?"

"He was worried Mr Bong might do something nasty."

The judge intervened. "Members of the jury, please disregard the last statement, which is hearsay and cannot be entered in the trial as fact."

"Thank you," the advocate depute said. "I have no further questions."

Max paused before calling the next witness. "My lord," he said, "a witness has come forth that I didn't expect to be able to be here. It was he who wrote the note found in Lord Tay's mackintosh at the scene of the crime. I realise I haven't prepared the prosecution for this witness. I ask his and your indulgence."

The judge called them up to his bench. After whispered consultation, the judge drew back and said, "I have agreed to allow this witness." The clerk of the court nodded to the police constable to bring in the witness.

"Do you swear by Almighty God . . .," the clerk of the court asked. The witness did. "Now please state your name and where you are from."

The young man, tall, sandy haired and with intense blue eyes, responded. "My name is Peter Duff Craig. I live in San Francisco, California." He gave his address.

"Mr Craig," Max asked, "will you state your relationship with the accused."

"My mother is his first cousin. I think that makes me his first cousin once removed."

Max glanced at Elspeth, whose smile showed how thankful and proud that he had agreed to fly across a continent and an ocean to bear witness at the trial.

"Mr Craig," Max continued, did you write this postcard to your mother when you were on your wedding trip to Hawaii in July?" Max produced the missive.

Peter looked at his mother, who cocked an eyebrow.

"Yes."

Max said to the jury, "I want to read this out to you in full, as it was written and not interpreted by the police. *7.18.07 Dear Mom, It's great just to have time to enjoy each other's company with nothing else to do.* He read out the rest of the message.

"What date did you write that, Mr Craig?"

"On July eighteenth, of course."

"Mr Craig, you are an American?"

"Yes."

"Although your mother and father are Scottish."

"I'm American by birth and consider California my home. I was raised in the Los Angeles area, and my wife and I now make our home in San Francisco."

"I have another question," Max said. "Did you write this note to Lord Tay?" Max produced the note that the Crown had introduced in evidence as being found in Johnnie Tay's mackintosh, proving he had been in Louisa's home after July fifth.

Peter looked at the copy of the note. "Yes, I wrote that."

"When?" Max asked.

"On May seventh, of course. I was delighted to hear that Johnnie, my cousin Lord Tay I mean, could come with the rest of the family to my wedding."

"Will you read your note in its entirety back to the jury, Mr Craig?"

Peter picked up the copy that had been recorded in evidence. *'5.7.07. Johnnie, it's great that you can join us all! We look forward to it, P.',* he read.

"In America the month comes before the day when you are writing the date in numerals?"

Peter smiled broadly. "You're absolutely right. We Americans seem to always do things differently."

Max next recalled Kaitlin Logan.

"Ms Logan, during the time you were making inquiries for me, did I ask you to research a person who goes by the name of Billy Bong, an Australian perhaps?"

"Yes." Max had instructed Kaitlin to smile at this point. She did so. "But you told me only to find what I could in public records."

"Did you know why?"

"Not at the time, but I did once I found the public records."

A smile crossed the lips of several jurors, who might recognise the name as it had been in the press. Max noticed and decided Kaitlin had produced just the effect he wanted.

"Will you tell us what you found?"

"Billy Bong's real name is Trevor Mackay. He was born in Glasgow in 1968, but his family moved to Sydney, Australia, when he was a boy. He got involved with the criminal underground there and has quite a police record for extortion, causing grievous bodily harm, and racketeering. After serving out his last prison term in Sydney, he came back to Scotland, and if the press is correct, began his own operations in Edinburgh about five years ago. So far, however, he has eluded the clutches of the Scottish police. I found several reports of his money lending activities. According to these, he charges high interest rates, just short of usury, and has been suspected of enforcing regular payments by the use of threats of physical violence."

Max picked up papers from his table and showed them to Kaitlin. "Are these your reports?"

She flipped through them and said, "Yes."

"I have no further questions for this witness at this time."

Hamish MacDonnell had no questions.

Then taking a deep breath Max said, "And now, my lord, I would like to call back Ron Dawes. I'm sure you will be pleased."

The judge eyed Max, the corner of his mouth twitching slightly at Max's jest.

"Please, Mr Douglas-Forbes. We don't like to keep a witness waiting this long."

"I'm aware of that, my lord, but I think now you will understand the delay."

Ron Dawes wore a smirk and yesterday's clothes, as he returned to the witness box.

Max approached him so closely that Ron drew back.

"Mr Dawes, I need the truth. I'm sure that if you tell it to me now, I can make probably arrangements with my associates in the police for leniency on perjury charges. I want you to tell us what happened early on Friday morning, July 20th, the day you said you had seen Lord Tay leave the house where the murder occurred."

The smirk disappeared and the witness's eyes grew wary.

Max roared. "Tell us!"

The judge stopped him. "Do not badger, Mr Douglas-Forbes."

Ron Dawes's face lost all its colour. He began to shake visibly.

"Do you want to go to prison, Mr Dawes?" Max asked in quieter voice.

Ron closed his eyes and gulped. "That might be safer than telling," he said.

Max drew back and lowered his tone.

"Who approached you on the morning of July 20th in Edinburgh? Was it this man?" Max had been holding a photograph in his hand and drew it out where both the witness and the jury could see. It was a photograph of Paul Hodges that had already been given in evidence.

A spittle of fear escaped Ron Dawes's lips, and he wiped it away with the back of his hand.

He mumbled something.

"Was it?" Max demanded again.

"Aye, that's him."

"Mr Dawes, I must advise you that your testimony here may free an innocent man. What did Mr Hodges ask you to do?"

Ronald Dawes ran his hand across his mouth again. "He asked me to say I had seen a bloke come out of a house in Perth the night before."

"Did the man who approached you say who he was?"

Ron rocked a bit on his feet, but then seemed to regain his voice.

"He said Billy sent him."

"Billy?"

"Billy Bong."

"How do you know Billy Bong? Did you work for him?"

"On and off. More off than on."

"How much money did the man give you to say you were in Perth the night before."

"A hundred quid, with fifty more if I got a friend to say so too."

"Your so-called birthday present?"

"Yeah."

"I see."

"Then what you said in court earlier was not true."

Ronald's composure broke. "You don't know the Bong, do you? If he asks, you say yes."

"I'm sure, Mr Dawson. I have no further questions."

Max considered requesting a recess before he called the next witness. It was only eleven and early for lunch. He longed for a brief nap to compose himself and get some of the cobwebs that had accumulated the night before out of his head. He knew he needed to be on top form and more cunning than he would have been with a less important witness. But juries after lunch were notoriously lethargic, and Max knew he had to seize their attention now. He directed his remarks to the judge.

"The next witness I would like called is a hostile one, my lord. I've had him subpoenaed, but I expect he won't be cooperative. I feel, however, in light of the recent testimony, I have no recourse but to call Mr Paul Hodges."

The judge gave the orders for Paul Hodges to be called from his witness room. The delay was so long that Max could feel the jury getting restless. Finally Paul Hodges entered. After hearing the several descriptions given by witnesses to this point, Max was surprised by Paul Hodges' appearance. He clearly had not made an effort to appear other than he had been described. His suit coat fit badly and was wrinkled, and Max got the impression that his hair had not recently been barbered or washed. Max, a fastidious man, wondered why Paul Hodges would make this personal statement to the jury. Did he want the jury to see him as slightly downtrodden in comparison to the impressive figure of his questioner or was he simply as seedy as his clothes would imply? Max was not sure. Paul Hodges was slightly below medium height, but his defensive stoop made him seem smaller. Max found it hard to imagine that this man would command a million-pound fee from the Perthshire Land Development Consortium.

As he stood in the box, Paul Hodges's face was filled with a snarl of contempt. Max had expected this and decided to do what he could to disarm the witness with politeness. He doubted the strategy would work, but it would emphasize Paul Hodge's surliness. Max had never spoken to Paul Hodges before, but he had checked with several of his colleagues and discovered that Paul Hodges was by nature devious when under attack. The jury could not help but notice.

Max stood up from his chair after Paul Hodges was sworn in but did not come away from his table. Max placed his hands as if in prayer and touched them to his lips.

"Mr Hodges, I believe that you're a solicitor well versed in the laws of land development in Perthshire and that you serve in the capacity of advising the Perthshire Land Development Consortium on their land purchases. Is that correct?"

Paul Hodge's face exuded hostility but he answered straightforwardly. "I am."

"Are you also well versed in family law, particularly divorce?" Max asked blandly.

"I've done some divorce work."

"Do these specialities ever coincide?"

"Sometimes."

"Did they in the case of Louisa Boyd?" This was the first time that Max had used Louisa's correct name.

Paul Hodges did not answer.

"The woman who called herself the Countess of Tay? The victim in this case," Max clarified. "You knew she was not legally married to Lord Tay, didn't you?"

"I found out."

"But not until you had agreed to serve as the solicitor in her divorce?"

"She thought she was married to him," Paul Hodges snapped.

"Did she think if she bore Lord Tay a son, he would be legal heir to Tay Farm? Did she truly believe that?"

"Why shouldn't she? He said she was his wife, and he was trying to divorce her. Would he do that if he wasn't married to her?"

"I can't say," Max said. "Now, Mr Hodges, when did you find out that the farm on Loch Tay was not Lord Tay's to sell?"

Paul Hodges looked away from Max's gaze and said nothing. The judge instructed the witness to answer.

"When Mr Lawton of the consortium asked me to look into other ways to obtain the land. The legal department at the consortium couldn't think of a way around the terms of the grant of peerage, so Mr Lawton asked me to come up with a plan." A hint of pride that crossed his face.

"Is it your job with the consortium to come up with alternative plans when normal legal considerations fail?"

Max's tone stayed benign.

"There're always alternatives," Paul Hodges said.

Max smiled and continued to walk Paul Hodges into his trap. "Is that why they pay you so well, to find these alternatives?"

"They wanted to build a resort on the farm site. They had invested a lot of money on a feasibility study and didn't want their efforts to go unrewarded. That's the kind of thing I specialise in."

"You must be quite successful, Mr Hodges. I compliment you, but do you ever fail? In these alternative schemes, I mean?"

"There's always risk. That's the chance I take in my business."

"You do not get paid if you fail. Is that correct?"

Paul Hodges moved uncomfortably. "Yes," he said.

Max came around from his table and stood mid-distant between it and the witness box. "A million pounds is a lot to lose. In your efforts to keep your commission, did you recruit the services of Louisa Boyd?" Max ceased being polite. "Did you convince her that if she produced Lord Tay's heir and demanded a lifetime interest in the farm as a part of her divorce, she would have the power to give you the lease?"

A loud murmur rose from the courtroom. The judge brought down his gavel and silence once again filled the room.

Max did not wait for an answer. Instead he pounced. "Didn't your finding out that Louisa was not married to Lord Tay ruin your scheme?"

Paul Hodges let out a sound that resembled the growl of a wounded dog. "You have no proof!"

"No, but I have strong suspicions!"

The judge's gavel was more emphatic this time. "Mr Douglas-Forbes, I don't want to find you in contempt of court, but if you insist on your personal opinions, I shall need to. Do not harass the witness."

Max smiled a non-committal smile and continued.

"You have within the last year had other schemes fail, I understand. Do you or do you not owe a great deal of money to a Mr Billy Bong of Edinburgh?"

"That has nothing to do with this," Paul Hodges cried in protest.

"Then it's true?" Max said. "That you do owe Mr Bong?"

Paul Hodges drew back. His face showed the horrible realisation that he had just incriminated himself.

"Why, Mr Hodges, did you ask a lad who once had been in the employ of Mr Bong to lie about seeing Lord Tay come from the victim's house the night she was murdered?"

"He lied."

"Yes, he did, and later he told the truth. Did you ask him to lie because it was you and not Lord Tay who was with Louisa that night? That you killed her when your alternate scheme went wrong, and you did not have the money to pay Mr Bong?"

Paul Hodges was cornered. "It wasn't like that," he croaked.

"What was it like?"

"I have a right to remain silent," Paul Hodges said.

Max looked up at the jury and knew he had won his case. Relief flooded through him because he did not need to call Biddy to the stand.

40

Edinburgh, After the Trial, Late September

"Elspeth, I don't understand," Pamela Crumm said. "How did you come up with the idea that Louisa had gone to a fertility clinic?"

They were all sitting around the dinner table in a private room at the Kennington Edinburgh hotel the day after the end of the trial. Johnnie had his arm draped around Madeline's shoulder and she was beaming. Both her eyes were black, and the right side of her face was crossed with heavy dressings. Johnnie was being careful moving so that he would not hurt her cracked ribs. Max and Biddy sat together; she was smiling shyly, and he was grinning. Richard sat next to Elspeth, and he looked excessively pleased with his wife. Peter Craig sat between his mother and Pamela, who had put her heavily ringed hands over his. She was enjoying the company's gratefulness for her largesse. The defence team had been brought together, and there was no doubt it was Pamela who held the reins.

Her eyes twinkling, Elspeth raised her head at Pamela's question and gave a smile that had disarmed many Kennington hotel patrons, although Pamela would only be satisfied with the whole truth and knew Elspeth well enough to know she had given her full effort to the case.

"It was a chance remark by Marly Beaufort and my implicit faith in Johnnie that started me thinking about how Louisa could possibly be pregnant with Johnnie's child

410

without Johnnie knowing. Marly mentioned that Helen had tried IVF. It wasn't hard to make the connection, not with Helen but with Louisa. I only had to trace where Helen had gone for the IVF. Louisa would have to have gone to the same centre."

"Brava," said Pamela, and she raised her wine glass to Elspeth. "But I'm still not clear why Paul Hodges wanted to kill Louisa. Although he didn't admit to it outright, there could be little doubt that he did."

Max intervened. "My guess is that he told Louisa that her claim to bearing the heir was invalid since she and Johnnie were not officially married. She may have threatened him with exposure, for making false statements to the fertility clinic, and perhaps for continuing to press her claim to the farm after she knew she was not Johnnie's wife. If she did expose him, at the very least he would be struck off for illegal conduct."

Pamela cocked her head to one side and quizzed Max further. "Do you think he murdered her to silence her?"

Max gave a lawyerly reply. "That's for the procurator fiscal to decide. We'll see when he decides on the murder charge."

Biddy had remained remarkably quiet during the whole lunch and then finally spoke. "Elspeth, or Max, why was I shot? Goodness knows, I had nothing to do with the horrible Mr Hodges and little to do with Louisa."

Max and Elspeth exchanged quick glances, and Max gave Elspeth the nod.

"Biddy, you were unfortunately cannon fodder. The infamous Billy Bong was pressuring Paul Hodges for the money he was owed. When Kaitlin checked Paul Hodges' records, she found that he was an avid hunter and a crack shot.

411

He undoubtedly remembered that you had been present when Johnnie showed him and the men from the Perthshire Land Development Consortium your father's gun collection. I expect he memorised the number on the combination lock, saw you take the key from the desk in the barn office, and then only had to wait until he knew no one was in the barn to come back and take the rifle. Whether the theft was for the intent of shooting you to warn you to remain silent, or merely his coveting such a fine gun, I have no idea, but I expect the police will find the rifle among his possessions. Max and I also suspected he didn't know Johnnie was still in jail when you were shot, and he could have hoped to pin the shooting on Johnnie. He couldn't have known about Johnnie's aversion to killing."

"Well," Biddy burst out, "I hope Mr Paul Hodges never tries to cross my path again."

They all laughed, but Biddy's stated lack of aversion to death did not escape them.

Johnnie, who had been a bit giddy since his release, burst out laughing. "You're a formidable enemy, Biddy."

"Sometimes, Johnnie, I wonder if you will ever be fit to be a farmer," Biddy replied.

"I'm not fit in the least. The farm as far as I am concerned is yours for as long as you like, Biddy. I prefer life in Perth, but I will no longer downplay your running of the farm or neglect my duties as the titular lord. You must keep me informed, and I promise to attend every event that requires my presence."

"Don't be cheeky, Johnnie; you're better than that, but I'll see you attend every single one." Those present did not quite know if Biddy's words were in anger or jest.

Pamela relished in the family banter. She remembered Richard's words to her some time ago that one did not get involved with the Duff/Tay/Robertson family without being sucked into a morass of love, competitiveness, and laughter. Great warmth spread over Pamela's small body, and she was not in the least sorry she had invested in Johnnie's defence, particularly now that Johnnie was free, but she was about to extract a price. Her ability to stand up to her business partner, the sometimes irascible Lord Kennington, was about to serve her well with Elspeth's family.

"You are all my beloved reprobates," she cried, embracing them all in her heart. "But you may no longer lead your lives without including me in them."

Elspeth raised an eyebrow and laughingly addressed her family. "She's right, you know. Richard and I were caught in her spider's web long ago. But, Pamela, be warned, you may not always find it an easy task."

Peter Craig rose. "I would like to salute you all," he said, "but I want to give particular thanks to Mr Douglas-Forbes for his brilliant defence. I understand he saved the family a great deal of discomfort by refocusing the trial on Paul Hodges and away from Johnnie, Madeline, and Biddy. To you, Mr Douglas-Forbes."

Biddy suddenly reddened and the entire company, looking toward Max at her side, could not miss her sudden change in complexion.

Biddy cleared he throat and said quietly, "Peter, I think you'll have to get used to calling him Max. He soon is to be your cousin."

Max rose from his chair, his face beaming. "This afternoon I posed the hardest question of all through our long

413

ordeal," he said to all assembled, "I asked Biddy to be my wife and graciously she has accepted me."

The family gave rounds of congratulations. Pamela sat watching them and her whole soul soared. Now it was she who had made possible a real-life romance. It was far more thrilling than one supposed after reading all the fashionable gossip columns in the best magazines and more trashy ones in the tabloids. She knew she had spent her money wisely and well and would never regret having done so.

Epilogue

Loch Tay, later

The briskness of the morning breezes off the loch and the merry tune of the church bells enveloped them and then let them go as they entered the kirk. None of them had expected Biddy and Max to marry so quickly, but they all had dropped the business of their daily lives to be there. Pamela Crumm had commandeered the Kennington jet and insisted that Elspeth, Richard, Elspeth's daughter Lizzie, and her husband Denis accompany her from the private airfield where the plane was kept to the airport in Perth. Johnnie was staying at the farm and had invited Madeline to stay as well. With the most exaggerated of bows, he had seated his sister in the backseat of the Sterling. He drove with great solemnity from the farm along the narrow road to Kenmore, where the square tower of the stone kirk looked out over the River Tay.

When they arrived, the guests had already taken their places. Biddy's three children sat on the left of the centre pew and Max's two sons on the right. The Duff family, including its new honorary member, sat in the second pew behind Biddy's daughter and sons. Biddy's friends occupied the pews round the Duffs, and Max's friends filtered in and found seats round his children. Jean and Robbie MacPherson, dressed in their finest, sat near the door, so that they might make their escape as soon as the wedding vows were said, and return to the farm to see to the final arrangements for the reception.

Biddy had insisted that the kirk be filled with flowers.

Elspeth whispered to Richard that she suspected this was to cover the mustiness that usually filled the church, but for whatever reason, the kirk radiated the fragrance of love and commitment that echoed the ceremony between two people who, in middle age, had never expected to find themselves here among friends and family declaring their troth.

Max waited in front of the pews and watched as Biddy came along the right side of the centre pews, as the kirk had not one but two aisles. He saw no one but Biddy and hardly remembered the words the vicar spoke. Biddy held his hand tightly, and her eyes never left his face.

Almost a hundred people filled the ballroom at the farmhouse. Biddy had insisted that it be opened and aired out, that the ornate decorations ordered by the third earl be dusted, and that paint be applied on the walls that had not seen use for over fifty years. Biddy had personally invited all the farmhands, and all had come with their wives, who would talk about the event well into the winter, the beauty of her ladyship, and the great dignity of the bridegroom.

When the guests had departed, Lady Elisabeth Douglas-Forbes took her husband in her arms and said quietly in his ear, "I do love you, today, tomorrow and for ever." He did not need to reply; his eyes told her everything.

Perth, much later

After both of their divorces were finalised, his to Helen and hers to Daryl, Madeline and Johnnie were married just after Christmas at a much larger wedding in Perth. In the following years, they produced three children, the heir, the spare and in Madeline's thirty-ninth year a daughter. When this third child appeared, Johnnie rang Elspeth. "We have decided to give her only one given name," he said.

Elspeth laughed. "After all the grandeur of your sons' multiple names? What is it, Victoria?"

"No," Madeline said from the other line. "We are calling her Elspeth—Lady Elspeth Robertson. We hope she will be as fearless as you. And, from the fierce look already in her eye, she will probably drop her title."

"Intelligent girl," said Elspeth the elder. "I shall look forward to it."

Author's Notes and Appreciation

This Elspeth Duff mystery is a departure from my earlier books, most of which centre around the Kennington hotels, and takes on a more traditional form of mystery writing involving the police and the courts. The idea arose when a reader asked for more of Elspeth's family background. Consequently I set the novel in Perthshire, where I spent eleven wonderful days in September 2007 researching the area where Elspeth grew up. Special thanks go to Jim and Maggie Tyrell, who hosted me at Wellwood House in Pitlochry during that time and made me feel completely at home, even providing a space where I could write uninterrupted. Also thanks to Police Constable Graham Lee of the Tayside Police, who gave me a tour of the Perth police station, including the jail, and explained to me the arrest procedure in Scotland. A retired procurator fiscal, who asked to remain anonymous, helped me as well.

Since this is a work of my imagination, I have taken some liberties with actuality. The relationship between Lady Elisabeth and Maxwell Douglas-Forbes would probably have been discouraged by the Law Society of Scotland, as the procurator fiscal noted.

My apologies go to the people of Perthshire, particularly those who might be living in homes that may in some ways resemble Tay Farm, the Duff home on Loch Rannoch, or Louisa and the Beaufort's homes in Perth. No disturbance of your peace is intended if any curious readers nose about. The residences mentioned in the book are a composite of several places and not meant to be any particular one.

Many of the places I mention do exist, and some do not, but they all exist between the covers of this book, and I hope at least for the time you spend with Elspeth Duff and her family when reading this, they will become real as they are to me. I spent most of my trip to Scotland trying to discover likely places for the story to take place and trying to imagine how people would live there. My characters went with me to Scotland, as any author will tell you they do. Any deviations from the truth are of my mind's own making, and not those of the people who assisted me in my research.

For anyone who is not familiar with the Scottish legal system, I highly recommend going online and logging on to www.scotcourts.gov.uk. That website helped me understand the difference between Scots law and that of England, Canada, and the United States. Most Scottish courts are open to the public, and I had the good luck to be in Perth on a day when a juried trial was being held at the Perth Sheriff Court. Anyone exploring the Scottish judicial system needs only to go to the courthouse building along Tay Street and ask at the reception desk.

As always, I want to thank my friends in Scotland whom I have made over the years since writing this book. They continually corrected my misconceptions. I could not have managed without my wonderful editor, Alice Roberts, and final proof-reader Beverly Mar. Nancy Largent did a brilliant job designing the cover and formatting the book. I am truly indebted to them all.

Special love as always goes to Ian Crew, who has been my chief supporter throughout the process of writing the Elspeth Duff mysteries.

Ann Crew is a former architect and now full-time mystery writer who travels the world with her iPad, camera, and sketchbook gathering material for the Elspeth Duff mysteries. She lives near Vancouver, British Columbia.

Visit *anncrew.com* for more.